Altar of Blood

Empire: Volume Nine

ANTHONY RICHES

HODDER

First published in Great Britain in 2016 by Hodder & Stoughton
An Hachette UK company

First published in paperback in 2016

1

Copyright © 2016 by Anthony Riches

A CIP catalogue record for this title is available from the British Library

ISBN 978 1 444 73205 4

Typeset in Plantin Light by Palimpsest Book Production Ltd, Falkirk, Stirlingshire

Printed and bound in Great Britain by Clays Ltd, St Ives plc

Hodder & Stoughton policy is to use papers that are natural, renewable and recyclable
products and made from wood grown in sustainable forests. The logging and
manufacturing processes are expected to conform to the environmental regulations of
the country of origin.

Hodder & Stoughton Ltd
Carmelite House
50 Victoria Embankment
London EC4Y 0DZ

www.hodder.co.uk

For Helen

ACKNOWLEDGEMENTS

As ever with any inventor of stories for the entertainment of others, there are those who suffer what might best be called collateral damage when the pressures of making stuff up become too much for one (admittedly only moderately sized) brain to cope with. So I'll keep the thank yous short and sweet for this one in order to say a proper thanks to the person who absorbs most of my emotional shrapnel.

Industry types are important: Carolyn as editor, for her immense patience and occasional despairing email exhortation to just deliver something; Robin as agent, selling books to enable the creative stuff to have some point and Kerry as publicity, putting me in front of unsuspecting audiences. Booksellers matter hugely too, and none more so than David Headley and Daniel Gedeon at Goldsboro Books, bucking the trend and showing some others the way to make it work, quite apart from being lovely blokes.

Friends in the business matter too: people like Ben Kane and Russ Whitfield for armoured charity walking idiocy, Harry Sidebottom and Giles Kristian for excellent socialising, Robyn Young for the same and for also coming up with great book names while under the influence and Simon Turney for a series of more than generous reviews on his website. And, for that matter, a whole load more bloggers like Robin Carter, Kate Atherton and Gareth Wilson for the time they put into showing their love for the genre and posting objective criticism of my and many others' work.

'My' beta readers get a big thanks too, Viv, John and David, for waiting a year for a book which I then expect them to read in ten minutes and provide me with insightful criticism (and catch my stupid mistakes, which they almost invariably do).

The biggest individual thank you has to go to the person who tolerates my inevitable mid-book paranoia, who tells me to go and write when the words aren't coming naturally and TV looks infinitely preferable, and who helps me to celebrate when the book comes home and a brief respite from constant making stuff up is allowed. Helen Riches, you're the sail, the rudder and sometimes the anchor too, on this boat of ours, and I couldn't have done it without you.

Which only leaves you, the people who continue to read the *Empire* series, and provide me with the motivation – and sometimes even the character inspiration – to continue chronicling the Roman empire's travails of the late second century as seen through the eyes of a small group of soldiers who find themselves used as (if you'll forgive me the 20th century military term) the emperor's 'fire brigade'. I sincerely hope that you enjoy this, the ninth in the *Empire* series. Marcus and the Tungrians (to abuse the Bondian cliché) will return, but the next three books will be a trilogy with the series title *The Centurions*, chronicling the Batavian Revolt of AD 69–70 from the perspective of both Romans and rebels. I hope you'll stay with me for this new story: it has all the ingredients to be properly gripping.

Thank you.

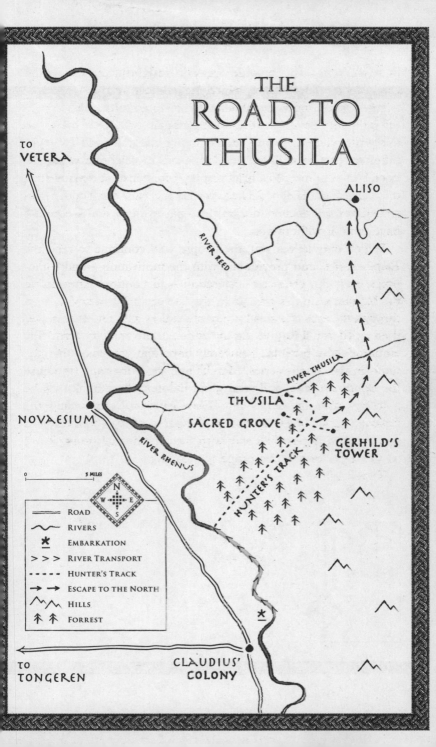

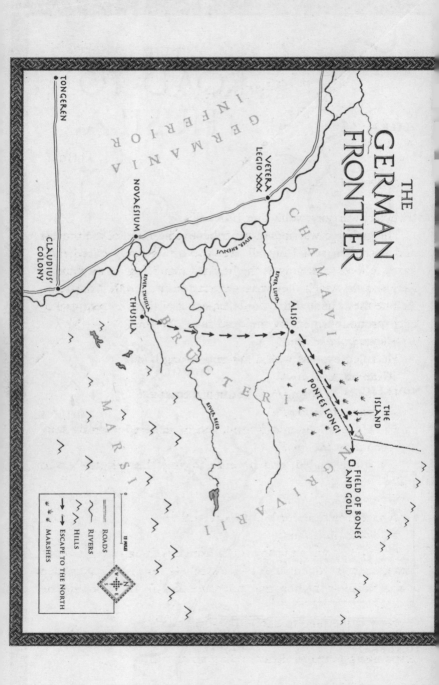

THE GERMAN FRONTIER

TONGEREN

GERMANIA INFERIOR

VETERA
LEGIO XXX

NOVAESIUM

CLAUDIUS'
COLONY

CHAMAVI

RIVER EMENUS

RIVER LUПА

THUSILA

RIVER THUSILA

BRUCTERI

ALISO

PONTES LONGI

THE
ISLAND

ANGRIVARII

FIELD OF BONES
AND GOLD

RIVER REED

MARSI

ROADS
RIVERS
HILLS
ESCAPE TO THE NORTH
MARSHES

15 MILES

N
W E
S

Prologue

December AD 184

'Bructeri warriors, your king is dead!'

The gathered warriors of the tribe, five hundred of the bravest and best men sent from all over the tribe's lands raised their gazes to look reverently at the bearded man lying on the funeral pyre around which they were gathered in the torch-lit darkness. As one they chanted the words expected of them in response to each pronouncement by the dead man's brother.

'Wodanaz, take him!'

'He ruled over us with a fair and strong hand!'

'Wodanaz, take him!'

'He made us stronger, to resist our enemies!'

'Wodanaz, take him!'

'His life was long and fruitful, and he fathered a strong son!'

'Wodanaz, take him!'

'His life is ended, and he goes to greet his ancestors with pride!'

'Wodanaz, take him!'

'Now is the time for him to leave us!'

'Wodanaz, take him!'

The noble took a blazing torch from a waiting priest and put it to the pyre's wooden base with a symbolic flourish, then handed it back to allow the holy man to ensure that the fire was properly lit.

'Now is the time to anoint his successor!'

The encircling warriors' chanting became more urgent, the responses pitched as if demanding an answer.

'*Wodanaz, name him!*'

The dead king's brother ushered forward a younger man dressed in the ceremonial armour of a prince of the Bructeri, his body clad in enough iron to equip a dozen men of the tribe for war.

'The king's son Amalric is his son and successor!'

'*Wodanaz, anoint him!*'

He swiftly smeared holy oil across the younger man's forehead, tracing an ancient rune of power over the pale skin.

'We his warriors declare him our king!'

'*Wodanaz, crown him!*'

Bowing solemnly to the prince, the noble held a simple gold crown, taken from the tribe's treasury for the occasion, over his head, then lowered it into place and stepped back.

'Will his warriors give their loyalty?'

A sudden hush fell, and the assembled men sank as one onto their knees, the iron helmets of the new king's household companions gleaming in the firelight.

'Swear the oath!'

The words were shouted proudly by every man present like an unstoppable force, a profession of their willingness to serve until death, at their king's command in all things, for his glory, for the glory of the Bructeri people and in the name of their god Wodanaz. When it was done they turned to the blazing pyre and bowed three times, each time roaring out their approval of the dead king's life, then repeated the homage for his son, their new ruler. The dead monarch's brother held up his hands to command their silence, and after a moment all was quiet once more.

'I, Gernot of the Bructeri, swear to serve this new king with all of the devotion that I gave to my brother, and to share what wisdom I have with him, to guide him on the path to equalling his father's glory and that of his father before him. I will strain every muscle in my body to help him outdo them both, and make our tribe's name echo in the halls of our neighbours, a name to inspire respect, and where needed, fear. In the halls of all our neighbours. In the halls of the Marsi!' The warriors cheered. 'The Chamavi!' They cheered again. 'The Angrivarii!' Again. 'And in the halls, my brothers . . .' They knew what was coming, and five hundred men drew breath to shout 'Of the *Romans*!'

When the tumult had died down he signalled to the priest, who nodded in turn to his acolytes. With great ceremony a wooden frame was carried into the gathering, a frame on which was suspended a man's naked body. Bound to the wood, his arms and legs spread wide, he was gagged to prevent any foul word sullying the ceremony, the rolling of his eyes his only means of communicating his terror at what was about to happen to him. He had been denied both food and water for three days to prevent any loss of bodily control casting a bad omen on the new king's succession. Gernot gestured to the prisoner, calling out to his warriors once more.

'See, I bring you a sacrifice to consecrate our new king's reign! A Roman soldier, the symbol of our tribe's oppression since the days of our forefathers! King Amalric, will you do us the honour as our chief priest of making the first cut?'

The younger man nodded graciously, taking the proffered knife from the priest the tribe called The Hand of Wodanaz, who would shortly be hard at work on the captive with his own tools – fierce, workmanlike knives, flenses for peeling away a man's skin from the flesh below, and the terrible saw with which he would liberate the greatest prize of all. He held up the knife, its blade liquid orange in the pyre's flickering light as the flames consumed his father's body, and the encircling warriors bayed for the helpless Roman's blood. Approaching the struggling captive, now writhing ineffectually against the ropes that held him tightly, he raised the blade theatrically before placing it against the sacrificial victim's right index finger, taking the digit in his other hand as was the accepted practice, pulling it tight for the first cut that had to remove the finger with one cut if the omens were to be favourable.

He dragged the knife backwards, severing the finger with a single pull of its ragged edge, staring into the Roman's eyes as they slitted with the pain, nodding slowly as the captive met his stare, then said two words in Latin that only the victim would ever hear.

'Forgive me.'

I

'Now then, here's a rarity, eh lads?'

The figure who had strutted out of the night's deeper shadows spoke with the confidence of a man who knew that he had the upper hand in whatever it was that was about to happen. Lean and hard muscled, he grinned in apparent amusement, the dagger in his right hand glinting in the glow of a crescent moon and countless stars. Insulae rose around them in rough-faced rows, lights extinguished and shutters firmly closed to keep out the sounds and smells of the Roman night, a time when robbers roamed the streets and the population's rubbish and faeces littered the cobbles. There would be no help forthcoming for any man foolish enough to find himself alone in such a place after dark.

'A man with money who chooses to walk through this part of the city at this time of night needs to have his wits about him, or better still a gladiator or two. He needs to have hired big men, friends, ugly men with scars and blades. Men he can depend on to scare bad people like us away, and bring him home safe.'

The robber strolled towards the lone pedestrian standing in the road before him with the easy gait of a man taking his leisure, grinning wolfishly at the tunic-clad man he and the men behind him had interrupted in his progress through the fetid streets of Rome's Subura district, stopping a few paces from the subject of his wry monologue. More men coalesced out of the night to either side of him, stepping forward to reveal their ragged clothes and hard faces.

'And yet here you are, unarmed and all on your own, without

so much as a well-built slave to steer you clear of trouble. It's not clever, not with you so clearly being a man with a lot to lose. Look at those shoes lads, that's proper workmanship. Worth a gold aureus to the right man, they are. And that tunic? What sort of man walks the streets of Rome after dark on his own in a tunic with a purple stripe on it? Your purse must be weighing you down like a bull's ball bag. And you'll have a house somewhere a good deal nicer than this shithole, probably with a pretty little wife waiting for you to get home and see to her needs . . .'

A more alert man would have seen the look that momentarily contorted his would-be victim's face, but the robber was too busy enjoying the opportunity for sport in front of his fellow gang members.

'She'll be expecting you home, once you're done with whatever it is you've been doing down here in the slums. So it's going to be quite a shock for her when *we* come through the door, isn't it?'

He smiled into his victim's flat expression.

'Of course, you're thinking that you won't tell us where your house is . . .'

He gestured with the dagger, raising it to allow the other man a clear view of the weapon.

'. . . but you will. Once we get to work on you you'll tell us everything, give us anything, just to stop.'

He tapped the blade.

'I favour the soft spot between the balls and the arsehole, personally. Half an inch of sharp iron inserted just so reduces most men to screaming agony in less time than it takes for a snuffed candle to stop smoking. You'll tell us where your home is, you'll shout for the doorman to let you in . . . you'll do whatever it takes to stop the pain.'

Leaning forward, he grinned at the man standing before him.

'So, friend, shall we be going? We've got a nice dark place where we can all get better acquainted. Some of the boys here, well, they like men like you, all clean and soft, and they've not had the sort of fun that I'm thinking about for so long that I think they'll be taking turns with you for half the night before we even get round to working out where you live.'

He waited for the inevitable reaction, for the lone aristocrat to make a break for freedom, knowing that more members of his band were waiting behind their victim, but his eyes widened slightly as the man stepped forward instead, close enough for the robber to see his face in the moonlight. The stranger's expression was set hard enough to send a shiver up the gang leader's spine, and when he spoke, his voice, though clearly cultured, grated out a single word with a chilling intensity that raised the hairs on his assailant's arms with a sudden jolt of fear.

'*Yes!*'

He struck, the move so fast that the footpad was nose to nose with his intended prey before he had time to react, finding his knife hand captured in an iron grip, while his assailant snatched a handful of hair and then snapped his head forward to deliver a head butt that took the life from the robber's legs. While he was still staggering at the unexpected attack's ferocity, his intended victim stripped the dagger from his unresisting grip and whipped the blade up into his throat, arteries and windpipe opened by a single wrenching thrust to release a sudden splatter of blood down both men's tunics. His assailant pushed the dying man at the nearest of his gang and turned away to confront the men closing in on him from all sides, raising the knife in a hand already slick with his victim's life blood. A heavyset thug rushed in with his arms spread to grapple the stranger, only to grasp at thin air as his intended victim danced sideways out of his reach, striking expertly to slit his tunic and the wall of his gut with the blade's viciously sharp edge. Staggering away from the fight with both hands clasping at the slippery coils of his intestines, the wounded thug obstructed the men behind him as they recoiled away from the stench and horror, and their would-be victim spun away from him in search of fresh blood. Two robbers ran at him, while a third loomed from behind their leader where he lay convulsing on the street's cobbles as his life ebbed away, advancing on the bloodied aristocrat with his fists bunched.

Hurling the dagger at the closer of the two runners to bury its blade deep in his chest, he turned without waiting to see the result, sidestepping the advancing pugilist's first punch and gripping his tunic, throwing his attacker off balance and counter-punching into the hapless thug's face, breaking his front teeth. While the man was staggering backwards, his assailant took another step forward, putting him down with a trip and following through with a half-fisted punch to his throat that left him straining fruitlessly for breath through a ruptured windpipe.

'*We've fucking got you now!*'

He straightened his body to find himself ringed by half a dozen more of the gang, eyes hard with hate as they closed around him with shuffling feet, eyes darting glances at each other as they readied themselves to attack, momentarily deterred by the stranger's blood-soaked rage and the bodies of their comrades littered around him.

'We're going to fuck you up, you *cunt*, and then we're going to open your guts and leave you to die here while we go and have our fun with wherever it is that you call home.'

'Tell me how it happened again.'

Annia tensed in her husband's arms in the bedroom's darkness, her body turned away from his and snuggled back against his chest. Her response was no louder than a whisper, but the distress in her voice was as evident as if she'd shouted at him.

'I've already—'

Julius's interruption was gentle but insistent.

'I know. You had to tell the Legatus the whole sorry story, and worse than that, you had to tell Marcus.'

Legatus Scaurus and his officers had been delayed in their arrival at Marcus's house on the Viminal hill until well after dark, caught up in the myriad tasks occasioned by getting two cohorts settled into the city's transit barracks after their long journey back from the empire's eastern frontier. Surprised to be greeted by the First Spear's wife rather than the lady of the house, their bemusement had turned to horror as Annia had haltingly related the story of what had happened while the Tungrians had been away from Rome. After the first initial stunning blow, literally staggering Marcus with its stark horror, his recovery had been as swift as it had seemed complete, on the surface. Taking a seat in the house's atrium he had composed himself, taken a deep breath and then looked up at his wife's friend, his face a stone-like mask, asking only one question.

'*How?*'

Julius clasped her tighter, stroking her tear-stained cheeks.

'I need to hear it again. I need to know every detail, because I need to know what he's going to do, once he's thinking straight again.'

Marcus had listened to Annia recount the events of the previous year in grim silence and, when her tale was done, had stood without speaking, walking out into the Roman night.

She was silent for a moment.

'And if I tell you? If I scoop all that . . . *shit* up and pour it over myself one more time?'

'We'll never speak of it again. Not that we'll need to.'

Annia sighed.

'No. The little one will remind us every time we look at him.'

'So . . . ?'

She sighed again, and then began to tell the story that had shattered their friend's life once again.

The circle of men tightened, the biggest of them spitting imprecations at their intended prey.

'I'm going to cut off your prick and stuff it into your fucking mouth!'

'No, you're not.'

All eyes turned towards a heavyset, bearded man walking up the street, his voice grating harshly in the night air despite the matter-of-fact tone of his roughly accented Latin.

'All you're going to cut are your losses. Now get out of my sight before this all gets much worse for those of you who are left alive.'

The big man turned to face him, reckoning the odds as the newcomer stopped six feet from him, flexing muscular arms and clenching his fists. In the background the choking sounds from the robber frantically struggling for breath through his ruined throat ran to their natural conclusion, and he fell silent. A series of sobs and groans from the darkness of an insula's deeper shadow, into which the gutted member of the gang had staggered after incurring his horrific wound, told their wordless story of his plight.

'Or what?'

'Or we take your ears.'

The robbers spun to face a new threat from behind them, a pair of men with daggers and the look of knowing how to use them. The older of the two grinned at them and waggled his knife at the nearest of the robbers with a smirk.

'My mate here's from Dacia, see, and everyone knows those barbarian bastards are cannibals. He's got a fondness for ears, see, and you've all got ears, which means he's got a hard-on like a donkey's meat stick at the thought of it.'

The gang's new leader shook his head in amazement.

'What the *fuck* . . . ?'

His incredulity was cut off by a third voice, so hoarse from a lifetime of shouting at soldiers that it was little better than a harsh whisper. Its owner stepped up alongside the bearded man, the moonlight revealing a spectacularly battered face, as he raised a massive, scarred fist and grinned happily at them.

'First we'll beat you dumb fuckers senseless, then we'll cut you up badly enough that none of you will ever get a woman to look at you again without showing her the weight of his coin first. Or you can fuck off. *Now.*'

He watched impassively as the robbers vanished into the street's shadows, stepping forward to look at the blood-spattered aristocrat with a slowly shaking head.

'Sorry to have spoilt the fun, little brother, but you looked to have bitten off more than you could get in your mouth. And now you've spilled some blood let's have you away home, shall we?'

Marcus nodded silently and turned away, looking down at the dead man whose throat he'd punched in before nodding and lifting a hand in recognition of the fact that his friends had saved him from the gang's violent revenge. The man with the battered face impassively watched him head back down the street the way he'd come, speaking to the bearded soldier next to him without taking his eyes off their friend.

'What are we to do with him, Dubnus? I know he's always been reckless, but this?'

His comrade nodded slowly.

'He's out of his mind with it, Otho. Your saw his eyes, not a flicker of emotion. Come on, and bring those idiot watch officers of yours with you. Knowing our luck he'll find another gang round the corner and we'll have to do the whole bloody thing again before we get him home.'

They followed the lone figure at a sufficiently close distance to deter any further attack, Dubnus watching his friend walking through the darkened streets with a troubled expression.

'Look at it through his eyes. His family murdered, him forced to run as far as the Wall and find his feet as an officer in the biggest tribal rebellion for decades while the emperor's men hunted him like a dog, fighting in Germania, Dacia, Parthia, and now . . .' He shook his head in evident disbelief. 'And now this. You have to wonder how much more he can take without losing his mind completely.'

Otho laughed mirthlessly.

'You think *this* looks like he's sane? You're his closest friend, but even you can't believe he's got a firm grip on himself.'

Dubnus grimaced.

'Since the first day I met him he's always been as taut as a loaded bolt thrower. I hoped he'd find some peace once we'd settled accounts with the men who slaughtered his family, but this . . .'

His comrade nodded.

'He'll keep on finding ways to provoke men to attack him, so he can put them down and take their lives to no good purpose.

And soon enough he'll go too far, and find himself in shit too deep for you and me to pull him out of. Are you willing to die alongside him?'

The big Briton shrugged.

'He may be blinded by his rage, but he's still my brother. And yours. Uncle Sextus may be a long time gone, but I still live by the rules he gave us. If one of us is threatened then it's a threat to all of us. So if my brother Marcus chooses to throw himself up the palace steps with a sword in his hand I'll be there to fight and die alongside him.'

Walking behind them, the older of the two soldiers leaned closer to his comrade, muttering in his ear.

'Well, I fucking won't.'

The Dacian Saratos looked at him with a raised eyebrow.

'Is cow's shit you talk. You make promise to soldier called Scarface, before he die. You promise to guard he life with you life.'

When Sanga remained silent he opened his mouth to renew the discussion, only to close it again as Otho growled at them over his shoulder.

'You two belong to me, you pricks. The Prince here,' he gestured to Dubnus, 'gave you both to me, which means I own the pair of you. And if I say we're going to take on every stinking guardsman in the city for the sake of that man, you'd better not be stupid enough to question my order. When he comes back to us from the dark place his mind has gone to, he's going to find me, and Dubnus, *and* you two, guarding his back. And that's all there is to it.'

'We made the mistake of thinking that because you'd been ordered to the east by the emperor's chamberlain, then we were under the throne's protection. And it all seemed safe enough, for a few weeks. There were always one or two of Cotta's men around the place, just keeping an eye out for us, and the local gang knew to keep their distance for fear of what he'd do to them if they didn't.'

Annia stopped speaking, and after a moment Julius prompted her.

'And then?'

'It was on the day of the Agonalia holiday to Janus, in Januarius. I was cutting up onions in the kitchen and looking out of the window when the gate banged opened and Cotta's man came staggering back through it as if he'd been thrown. For a moment I thought it was the gang that used to control this street, come for revenge after the way Morban and his men treated them last year, but then a Praetorian walked through the gate and I knew that it was something worse than that.'

She was silent again for a moment.

'I hurried out into the garden to find half a dozen of them, armed and armoured and led by a centurion. At first I couldn't work out why the Guard would have taken any interest in us, unless they'd come for revenge on Marcus for what he did to their prefect, but then I saw him.'

One of the guardsmen had nodded to the centurion, looking pointedly at the house, and the officer had promptly barked out an order, pointing at two of his men and telling them to search the building.

'He was dressed and armed like the other praetorians, but he wasn't one of them, that was obvious from the way that the men around him were careful not to get in his way, or even touch him. He might have been wearing their uniform, but he was clearly their master. He stepped forward and looked me up and down with those dead eyes, drinking in every detail of my body with a single long glance in a way I used to see occasionally in the brothel when a particularly depraved client came looking for enjoyment. He was like a racehorse trainer assessing a potential purchase in the sales ring, calculating whether the beast would repay his investment. I met his eye for a moment . . .'

She shivered in her husband's arms.

'I knew exactly what he was looking for. Something to spoil. Something pure and untouched, that he could ravish and leave soiled. It would have been better if he'd found what he was looking for with me, the gods know I've been used often enough for one more not to have made any difference, but perhaps something in my face put him off. I knew only too well the sort of man he was, and my disgust must have been obvious. And then he saw Felicia, and that was that.'

In her mind's eye Annia conjured up an image of her friend as the younger woman had emerged from the house with the ghost of a quizzical smile, clearly shaken by the soldiers' unexpected appearance.

'Can I help you . . . Centurion?'

The detachment's officer had deferred to the man in the midst of their armoured throng, instantly confirming Annia's suspicions as to his identity. Stepping forward with a grin, he'd pulled off his helmet to reveal his true identity, nodding to the mistress of the house as his gaze devoured her body in one long sweep from head to feet.

'Your forgiveness for this intrusion, madam. My chamberlain told me that a famous gladiator was recently buried here, and as Rome's most devoted follower of the sport, I was naturally drawn to pay homage to his memory.'

Felicia had bowed deeply.

'No apology is needed when so eminent a man honours my home with his presence. And you have me on the horns of a dilemma, Majesty. On the one hand your desire to pay your respects to a great man is not one that I can in conscience obstruct, even without consideration of your exalted status, but—'

The emperor had laughed in a conspiratorial manner, leaning closer to her.

'That nonsense about not burying the dead within the walls of the city?'

He'd waved a dismissive hand.

'He won't be the first great man to have been honoured with interment inside the city, and I see no reason why this shouldn't be an exception to the rule. The man buried in your garden was the champion gladiator when I was a younger man, and I took great inspiration from his exploits.'

A wistful tone had crept into his voice.

'Someday I hope to emulate his achievements . . .'

He'd turned away from the amazed women, pointing to the mound of earth under which the gladiator had been buried, after his last, climactic fight in the Flavian Arena.

'Is that his last resting place?'

Not waiting for the answer he'd walked across the garden to stand in silence before the grave, the Praetorians casting knowing glances at his back and eyeing up the two women while they waited in silence for him to rouse himself from his reverie. At length he'd turned back to face them, wiping a tear from his cheek.

'Truly inspiring. For such a master of his art to be buried here, so close to the palace, is quite inspiring. And so convenient.'

The emperor's gaze had returned to Felicia, and Annia's heart had sunk as she saw that same cold-eyed appraisal play across her friend's face and body once again as he stepped closer to her.

'So handy for me to come and pay my respects whenever I feel minded. And whenever I feel the need to honour you, my dear, with my presence in your bed.'

Felicia's eyes had widened in shock, but before she'd been able to speak, Commodus had continued in the same light, conversational tone.

'Oh I know, I've heard all the half-hearted objections so many times. You're a respectable married woman, but your husband is away doing my bidding, a very long way away, and here you are, with your own needs. And besides, what woman could fail to be honoured by the prospect of coupling with Rome's first citizen? And in case that fails to persuade you, consider this . . .'

He'd leaned closer, speaking quietly in her ear, though not so softly that Annia hadn't heard every word, just as she had little doubt he had fully intended.

'There is, of course, the inevitable consequence of rejection to be considered. Your emperor, it has to be said, is not a man for whom the word "no" is acceptable. Having been somewhat overindulged from an early age, it would be fair to say that my ill-temper can be quite prodigious upon being faced with a refusal.'

He'd turned to look at Annia as he spoke, his expression as empty as before although a bestial look had crept over his face, as if in reality he hoped for nothing more than to see through the threats he was muttering in her friend's ear.

'Your companion here looks a little . . . used . . . for my tastes, but I'm sure she would make an entertaining diversion for my bodyguard. If you provoke me to it, I'll have them fuck her until she bleeds, here, where her cries of protest and pain can be heard by your neighbours. And then there are your children to consider. It was a boy for you, my dear, and a girl for your friend here, if I'm correctly informed?'

Felicia had nodded, a look of horrified resignation starting to settle on her pale features.

'It would be a shame for their young lives to be snuffed out in the brutal manner that might be required to cool one of my rages. Now, what else did Cleander tell me . . . ?'

A pair of guardsmen had emerged from the house, one pushing the boy Lupus before him at the end of a stiffened arm, the other shepherding the German scout Arabus, left behind by Marcus to protect his wife and child, at the point of his sword.

'Ah yes, that's it. The German and the boy from Britannia. I'll prove just how serious I am, Madam, by the simple expedient of allowing you to choose which of these two shall live to see the sun set tonight.'

'Surely you can't be serious—'

He'd nodded solemnly, his blank-eyed certainty silencing her in mid-sentence.

'Serious? Oh but I can. *Deadly* serious. Long experience of these matters has proven to me that a practical demonstration is so much more effective than any number of threats, no matter how serious they might be in nature.'

He'd nodded to the centurion who, without any change in expression, had drawn his dagger and walked across to the pair of captives.

'So, Madam, choose which of these two should die and which should live.'

Felicia had looked over at Annia with an anguished expression, shaking her head slowly.

'I can't.'

'But you can. And you will. Because if you don't I'll just have them both put to the sword and then, just to reinforce the lesson, I'll make you choose between your own child and your friend's daughter in just the same way.'

Annia had looked across the garden at the pair of captives to find Arabus staring back at her with a weary, knowing look, nodding at her in acceptance of his fate. Knowing that a choice had to be made, before Commodus followed through with his threat to their children, she had spoken out loudly, staring hard at Felicia in an attempt to persuade her to see the only way out of the situation.

'Arabus.'

Felicia had started at the man's name, looking first at Annia and then turning her head to stare helplessly at the German.

'Yes.'

Commodus had grinned, nodding delightedly.

'Yes? Yes is no good to me. You have. To say. His *name*.'

Felicia's face had turned to face the emperor's with a sudden hardening of her expression, her voice soft in the silence.

'Arabus.'

While his face had been suddenly beatific, exultant in his breaking of her will to his own, the emperor's command to the waiting centurion had been issued in a matter-of-fact tone that told both women how accustomed he was to ordering the death of his subjects.

'Kill the German.'

She felt Julius shake his head behind her, his voice incredulous despite already knowing the story's outcome.

'They put an innocent man to the sword? Just like that? There was no hesitation? No sign of—'

'Remorse? None. It didn't feel like the first time the order had been given. The bastard cut poor Arabus's throat with his dagger and then wiped the blood off on Lupus's tunic.'

'Would you know any of them if you saw them again?'

'Only the centurion. He had a scar through one eyebrow and down his cheek.'

Julius thought for a moment.

'And then?'

'And then? They took Arabus's body and left, leaving a man on the gate to make sure we didn't try to escape. We heard nothing for two days, then on the third they came back. And that filthy bastard took Felicia to her bedroom, forced her to lie with him and left her sobbing on her bed with his seed in her belly. He came back three times in less than a week, before he tired of fucking an unresponsive victim and moved on to whoever it was that was next in line for his attentions.'

'And that was all?'

'If you can call something like that "all", yes. When he failed to come back the fourth time we thought that it was over, that she might be able to reclaim her old life, and never tell Marcus of the indignities that had been forced on her. Until she missed her monthly bleed.'

Her husband was silent, and Annia stared into the room's darkness for a moment before continuing.

'I know what you're thinking, Julius. You're wondering why she didn't get rid of the baby while it was still unformed.'

'I—'

'An abortion? How could she? She was a doctor, Julius, sworn to care for her fellows and never to knowingly do harm. She could never have murdered an innocent child, and that's all there was to it. She planned to have the baby and then have it adopted, find a family without children who longed for such a gift and pass the infant to them. We would never speak of it again, and Marcus would never be any the wiser.'

'She'd have kept it from him?'

Annia laughed softly at his incredulity.

'I'd have kept it from you, if the emperor had chosen to put his child in my womb. Look at what's resulted from him discovering the truth! What sane man takes to these streets at midnight dressed in no more than a tunic? If she'd lived it would have been better for him never to have known, never to have the scars of his family's destruction reopened.'

'If she'd lived?'

'We thought her delivery would be simple enough, after the ease with which she had the first one, but the baby was too big, and refused to turn, and when she called for help it was too long coming. The doctor who attended her was no better than a butcher. He got the baby out by cutting her open, but she lost too much blood. She died in my arms, her eyes wide with the pain, and as she slipped away she made me promise to care for the child. I swore an oath, Julius, an oath to raise the baby as my own.'

He wrapped his arms more tightly about her.

'And what else were you to do?'

Silence fell over them.

'What happened? Is he wounded?'

Dubnus shook his head at the question, shepherding Marcus into the walled garden with an arm around his back, physically supporting the Roman while the man who had been waiting for them closed the gate. The smell of herbs and fragrant blooms was strong in the warm air, a vivid counterpoint to the iron stink of spilled blood from his gore-streaked tunic.

'He took on a dozen street robbers with nothing more than his bare hands.'

The Briton raised a hand to forestall the veteran's anxiety as Cotta stared aghast at the gore caked across the Roman's tunic and body.

'It's all other men's blood, but he's pretty much burned himself out in the doing of it.'

Cotta sized up the man whose long-dead father had employed him to educate his son in the fighting skills of the legions from the age of ten, assessing his exhausted posture and blank, empty eyes. He snapped out a command at one of the retired soldiers who formed the tight-knit company of men he had brought to the Tungrians' close family on their arrival in Rome the year before.

'Fetch me the hot water from the kitchen, and all of the towels! Here, let's get him onto that bench.'

The younger man sank gratefully onto the seat, his body trembling with reaction to the mayhem he had visited on the street robbers. Cotta stood over him in silence, staring down at the man he had tutored in the use of blade and point as a boy, when Cotta himself had only recently retired from legion service.

'Get that tunic off.'

Taking the garment he passed it to Dubnus with a meaningful glance.

'Be better if this went onto the fire, I'd say. The less evidence of this night the better, if the Urban Watch come asking questions.'

His man returned with a pail of water warmed over the kitchen fire and took the bloody garment away for incineration, and the former centurion knelt in front of his friend, wetting a towel and working at the drying blood that coated Marcus's face and limbs.

'How many did he kill?'

'There were three corpses on the cobbles when we left, and another man trying to stop his guts from falling out without the wits to know that he was already dead.'

Cotta shook his head, putting a finger under the Roman's chin and lifting his head to stare into the half-closed eyes.

'And why? You've no idea, do you? If one of those street scum had got lucky and stuck you with a blade, *you* could be dead now, and for no better reason than you're filled with rage you can't turn on anyone who actually matters.'

He worked with water and towels until his friend's body was completely clean, then wrapped him in a military cloak and handed him a beaker.

'Wine and warm honey. Once you've got that down your neck you can eat this bread. And no arguments.'

Acquiescing to the commanding note in his former trainer's

voice, Marcus drank deeply, nodding slowly in response to Cotta's harangue.

'I know . . . it was pointless . . . stupid . . . but . . .'

'You couldn't help yourself.'

The Roman nodded, drinking deeply again, shivering with reaction to the night's events.

'No.'

The veteran looked down at his former pupil for a moment.

'And is that it? Or are you going to be *stupid* enough take it to the streets again tomorrow night?' Marcus looked back at him with an expression of pure misery. 'I'm serious, boy. Tonight was the easy one, with no one out there any the wiser to the fact that a lone aristo out after dark on his own could be anything other than easy meat. By tomorrow morning the word will be out there, and you'll not only get yourself killed but lead these men into the same trap. Is that what you think you owe them, a meaningless death in a city that's not even their home?'

The younger man shook his head slowly, and Cotta dropped into a squat to look into his eyes, grimacing at the pain in his knees.

'No. You owe them better, and you know it. Swear vengeance on the men who killed your wife by all means. I'll sacrifice alongside you, and make common cause with you, but you'll hold that vengeance for the right time, and not waste it in a meaningless slaughter of men who never had any part in Felicia's death.'

Marcus nodded wordlessly, leaning his head forward onto Cotta's shoulder. The veteran took a gentle grip of the hair at the back of his former pupil's head and pulled it away from him until he could stare into the younger man's eyes.

'And if that's not enough to keep you from throwing your life away, I'll remind you that there's something altogether more precious than any thought of revenge. Your son.'

The younger man stared back at him, tears welling in his eyes.

'Exactly. Do you want Appius growing to manhood without ever having known his father, even if your friends manage to spirit him away to safety with every praetorian, urban watchman and gang member hunting for them?'

'No. I owe him – them – better than that.'

The veteran soldier nodded.

'Yes you do. So when that bastard Cleander summons you and Rutilius Scaurus to the palace, and gloats over your agony like the animal he is, will you hold back your anger or will you buy his life at the cost of your own, and that of the Legatus?'

'I won't enjoy the rank of legion legatus for much longer, Centurion Cotta, any more than you'll be a centurion.'

Cotta leapt to his feet with as much dignity as his knees allowed, saluting crisply, but Gaius Rutilius Scaurus waved a dismissive hand.

'No formalities, please Cotta, not at this time of night and under these circumstances. How is he?'

Marcus stood, saluting his senior officer.

'I'm tired, sir. It's been a trying day.'

Scaurus nodded, his face an expressionless mask.

'Trying is one word I might have used. Devastating is another. Go to bed, Tribune, and sleep as long as you need to. And when you wake, come and see me to discuss the last of Centurion Cotta's questions. I expect we'll be called to the palace tomorrow, now that Cleander knows we're back and has allowed a day for your wife's death to sink in. He'll be wanting to see your face, I expect, and see what havoc his machinations have wrought on you.'

Marcus looked at him for a moment and then nodded, saluting again reflexively as he turned away and walked into the house.

'You think he'll be able to resist the temptation to smash the bastard's windpipe?'

Scaurus shrugged.

'For one thing it would be a brave man who'd give him the chance. I fully expect the chamberlain to conduct his interview with us, when the invitation comes, from behind a wall of Praetorian armour.'

'And if he doesn't?'

'In that eventuality, Centurion, I expect that both the chamberlain and I will have significant grounds for nervousness. Not that I intend to lose any sleep over it.' He turned away, stopping and turning back as something occurred to him. 'Oh, and I'll be needing an escort in the morning, I'm planning to visit a professional man and I'll need enough muscle to make sure we're not disturbed.'

'Will you not be taking that big German lump Arminius with you?'

Scaurus shook his head solemnly.

'He tells me that he has a more important task to perform. I'll take Lugos along with me, if only to get a professional medical opinion as to the state of his leg, but the presence of a few of your rougher-edged veterans would be useful, I suspect.'

'Arabus died instead of me, Arminius. He died like a slaughtered animal, choking on his own blood.'

The big German sat opposite the boy Lupus in the house's atrium, close enough to reach out and take the young man's hand had he felt it appropriate, but something deep within him instinctively recognised that the time for comforting the child that they had left behind on sailing east for Parthia was gone, along with the child himself. The sword-armed soldiers Scaurus had set to guarding the house stared stolidly out into the morning's sunshine, knowing better than to intrude in such a sensitive moment. Not only was the boy the orphaned grandchild of one of their own, considered a child of the cohort and welcome at any Tungrian campfire or barrack, but the German slave's disregard for his apparent position among them was well known, as was his implacable temper when he was gainsaid.

While Lupus struggled for self-control, Arminius looked for what was left of the boy he'd left behind the previous year, marvelling that so much could have changed in the still-familiar face in such a short amount of time. Harder lines in the jaw and cheeks spoke of the onset of manhood, something in which he would have quietly exulted under different circumstances. Swallowing his own sorrow for the teenager's distress, he forced a note of harshness into his voice.

'A lesson to be relearned, then.'

'A *lesson*?'

The German nodded into Lupus's hot stare.

'Arabus did what was right, offering his own life to protect yours, knowing how much more living you have left to do. Just like Antenoch.'

The boy pursed his lips and nodded.

'They both died because I was not strong enough to defend myself.'

'They both died because they loved you enough to give their lives to keep yours intact. They both died because they were honourable men who knew what they had to do. And they both died because their time had come to die. Have I not told you this before?'

Lupus nodded slowly.

'But Arabus—'

'Arabus knew what he had to do. There were wolves in the house, wolves who demanded a life, and he knew that his was the life they must take. He was man enough to offer it, and for that we should both hold his memory in high esteem for the rest of our days. And now you tell me this story with the wounded pride of a man who feels he should have done something to save his friend. Except, Lupus, you could have done nothing, because you are not yet a man.'

The boy looked at him with eyes suddenly hard, and Arminius smiled slowly back at him to draw the hurt from his words.

'Understand me, boy. You may be close to manhood but you cannot consider yourself as a man until I have finished helping you to become a man.'

The boy protested, his voice raised indignantly.

'Not a day has passed without my exercising with my sword and spear. My body is getting stronger—'

Arminius shook his head, raising a finger to his lips.

'Marcus is still asleep – do you want to wake him and have him discover that my master has gone to take some share of revenge for his wife's death without him? A *man* can make such a point without once raising his voice. What I speak of is more than your muscles, or how tall you've grown. You will possess great strength, given another few years, and perhaps even be tall enough to look me in the eyes, but true manhood comes from more than the body the gods have seen fit to gift you. True manhood is in here, Lupus . . .'

He tapped his forehead.

'*True* manhood is measured by whether the man is worthy of the term. I will train your body and make you strong, give you skills with spear and sword that will make you a great warrior.' He leaned forward to stare into his pupil's eyes. 'Becoming a man, however, will be a different matter.'

The half-dozen people waiting for a consultation with the doctor were suitably respectful when they saw the purple stripe that adorned the latest arrival's tunic, while the size of the party accompanying him spoke volumes as to his significance in the city's complicated social structure. While the man himself was clean-shaven and bore no obvious scars, the fact that he was a serving officer was obvious, not least from the size and demeanour of the men accompanying him.

The first member of his party to come through the door was a stocky figure dressed in a military tunic with cropped hair, scarred arms and an evident disdain for the waiting-room's occupants, but if his appearance gave the clients a momentary frisson of apprehension, the man following him was altogether more disquieting. Built to an entirely different scale, he was forced to duck through the door, and as he limped across the room to join the soldier, the waiting patients watched his progress with wide eyes, mesmerised by his slab-like muscles and long, plaited hair. Their master entered next, to general and evident relief at both his civilised appearance and the likelihood of him preventing any unpleasantness on the part of the hulking barbarian, but the three men who completed the party quickly reinforced the initial impression. Hard-bitten soldiers to judge from their short hair and beards, they clearly regarded the citizens present with a mixture of distrust and open curiosity. A tense silence fell upon the room as the new arrivals looked about them, with the sole exception of the equestrian who was evidently the head of this close-knit familia, apparently too deep in the scroll he was reading to pay much attention to the goings-on around him.

After a moment, the doctor's assistant appeared through the door that led to his consulting room, noting the new arrivals with a raised eyebrow. Upon his call for the next patient, concerted efforts were made by the waiting room's other occupants to encourage the aristocrat to take their turns with the physician, although whether this generosity was born of respect for his rank or fear of his companions was not entirely clear. In any case the efforts were to no avail, as he simply smiled and gestured for the next patient to accompany the doctor's assistant, happily reading his book while the room slowly emptied as each of its occupants saw the doctor and left until, an hour or so later, only his party was left. Pulling a face at the unexpected lack of any further custom, the doctor's assistant ushered him through the doorway, on the sensible assumption that he was likely to be the only one of the party with the wherewithal to pay for such expensive services, moving hastily aside as both the stocky soldier and the giant followed. The doctor looked up from his chair, gesturing to one on the other side of his desk.

'Good day to you, sir. Please do take a seat.'

The aristocrat sat down, inclining his head in thanks.

'And good day to you, Doctor.'

The medicus smiled approvingly at the reply, couched as it was in the same language that he had used for his greeting. It might have been hundreds of years since the first Greek doctors had abandoned their home country and claimed Rome for their own, but a gentleman still spoke to his physician in the language of the greatest civilisation the world had yet seen. Clearly this was an individual of some substance, despite the rather villainous appearance of the men who had accompanied him into the surgery. He drew breath to enquire as to what might be the malady on which his esteemed client sought counsel, only to find the man before him speaking somewhat out of turn.

'You'll have to forgive me, by the way, I've taken the liberty of posting a pair of my men on the street outside to deter any new clients from attending upon you for the time being. I will of course compensate you for the lost custom entailed, but I thought the precaution essential given that I'm here not with regard to matters of my health, but instead to clear up a rather sensitive matter.'

He fell silent and looked at the doctor with what might, under other circumstances, have been taken for a severe expression but which, the doctor was swift to decide, was understandable enough if the man was about to present him with the painful evidence of the pitfalls of a debauched lifestyle.

'Is it . . . ?'

He raised both eyebrows and inclined his head to indicate the man's crotch. To his surprise the patient laughed tersely and shook his head.

'Indeed no, although I can see how my previous comments might lead you to assume that I've dallied with the wrong sort of lady. No, Doctor, my visit is to do with something entirely different. A question of childbirth, as it happens. But before we speak of that matter, I'd appreciate your opinion as to the state of some wounds my companion here incurred in the course of our duties in the east, a few months ago.'

He gestured to the hulking giant waiting silently beside the ex-soldier who was apparently guarding the door in the absence of the doctor's assistant, who had failed to return to the room having summoned the patient and his associates.

'Come forward, Lugos, and show the doctor here your leg.'

The medicus studied the scars that pitted the massive thigh muscles before him, consulting a book from his shelves before voicing an opinion.

'I can't claim to be any sort of expert on the matter of wounds incurred on military service, but what I see here would appear to be a pair of arrow perforations to the upper leg that seem to have been expertly treated, presumably by a legion's doctor, and which, given the time required, seem to have healed as well as might be expected for such intrusive damage to the muscles involved.'

He switched from Greek to Latin.

'I noticed that you limped as you crossed the room – do you have any residual pain from the wounds?'

The giant looked at the man who was presumably his owner with a look of bafflement.

'Forgive me, Doctor, my colleague here is from Britannia, and still finds our language a little difficult to understand on occasion.'

The equestrian spoke slowly to the subject of their discussion. 'Does it still hurt?'

The big man shook his head, his voice a deep rumble.

'No. Only a little stiff.'

The doctor nodded sanguinely.

'To be expected. Letting blood from around the wounds will reduce the stiffness, I diagnose. I'll be happy to perform the procedure.'

He sat back with a smile.

'And the other matter? You mentioned childbirth? Perhaps we might start with your name, sir?'

The equestrian nodded equably.

'My name, Doctor, is Gaius Rutilius Scaurus. I was until recently the commander of the Third Gallic legion, but now I am little more than a private citizen awaiting his next imperial duty. I have been away in the east, with my colleagues here, fighting the Parthians and restoring the emperor's rule over those parts of the empire that were disputed by our enemies.'

The doctor inclined his head respectfully at his client's evident eminence.

'Then you are to be congratulated, sir. How might I be of service to so celebrated a client?'

The man before him fixed him with a stare of uncompromising directness, clearly intent on communicating the seriousness of whatever it was he wished to discuss.

'As I said, it is a matter of an unresolved debt, I'm afraid, a debt incurred to yourself during a matter of childbirth.'

The doctor nodded slowly, his expression becoming suitably grave.

'I think I know the matter in question, Rutilius Scaurus. A childbirth early last month?'

'Yes, not far from here on the Viminal hill.'

'Indeed. In truth I'd written the debt off, in the light of the lady's unfortunate demise.'

He paused, looking at Scaurus with the expression of a man intent on setting the right tone for their discussion.

'In which case, Doctor, I may bear the resolution you had given up hope of receiving. All you have to do is ask, and I will pay you out the sum owed, plus a consideration for your lost custom this morning.'

'Ah . . .'

The medicus thought for a moment, then smiled with evident gratitude.

'In which case I will be happy to accept twenty-five denarii for my services that fated evening and declare the slate to be wiped clean.'

'You're sure? A gold aureus will suffice?'

The doctor nodded magnanimously, and Scaurus reached into his purse, placing a single coin on the table before him.

'Then the account is paid.'

He stood, looking down at the doctor with that same serious expression that might have been mistaken for a glare under other circumstances.

'Paid from my side, that is. Having accepted my gold in return for services which, it seems, were never offered freely, there remains the question of the way in which you discharged your responsibility to your patient.'

He raised the scroll he'd been reading in the waiting room.

'A responsibility made very clear by the writings of the imperial physician Galen. There also remains the other question, as to what should be the reckoning for your evident shortcomings.

How, to be blunt, you are to make amends for your errors and failures that cost a dear friend of mine her life.'

The doctor started, sweat beading his forehead.

'You took money, Doctor, for attending the birth of a child to the wife of a good friend of mine. In the course of which my friend's wife died.'

The other man looked up at him, his face reddening.

'She died because she left it too long to call for me. It's not my fault if my clients hold off seeking help in order to save themselves money.'

Scaurus stood up and leaned forward, placing his bunched fists on the table and staring down intently into the doctor's face.

'Her companion sent a man to your house shortly after dark, by which time she'd been in labour for 12 hours, more or less. And you arrived when, exactly?'

'Soon enough!'

The hard-faced aristocrat shook his head slowly.

The runner deduced your location by talking to your slaves, then tracked you down to the house of a friend where you had just started dinner and delivered the suitably worded and urgent summons to your patient's bedside directly to you. He waited, at your instruction, and accompanied you to the lady's house three hours later. By which time you had consumed enough wine to have made you less than steady.'

His answer was a terse laugh.

'I'd like to see you prove that. And where's this runner, for a start—'

He fell silent as Scaurus gestured to Cotta, who opened the consulting-room door to admit a vaguely familiar man who had been waiting outside.

'Here. And the fact you don't recognise him seems like something of a giveaway. But let us consider the facts. You tried to turn the baby and then, when that was a failure, you cut the lady open in order to conduct a caesarean birth, performing the operation with sufficient butchery that she died shortly afterwards. You were drunk—'

'*No!*'

The doctor had surged out of his chair, but froze when he saw the expression on Scaurus's face, then sank back into a sitting position. When he resumed, the equestrian's voice was cold.

'You waited three hours to answer your patient's call for help, and by the time you arrived at her house you were too drunk to operate safely. You killed the lady, as surely as if you'd handed her a cup of hemlock. Had you been working for nothing, helping a patient in distress, I might have seen fit to let the realisation of your incompetence be your punishment.'

Silence fell over the room as the doctor stared down at the gold coin before him.

'But you weren't working for the public good, were you? You expected payment. You harassed the dead patient's friend for the money every day for a week, and when she wouldn't pay you, you gave coin to some aged crone to put a curse on her.'

He dropped a thin folded sheet of bronze onto the table in front of the doctor, shaking his head in disgust.

'My men found it pushed into a slot that had been gouged out of the mortar in the wall that surrounds her house, and after that it wasn't hard to find the witch who'd placed it there. She retracted the curse quickly enough, of course, when the alternative became clear to her. Indeed she very promptly replaced it with one directed to yourself.' He tossed a second bronze wafer onto the table before the doctor. 'I believe it suggests that you turn your instruments on your own body, which I found rather instructive. Funny how we take inspiration from the most unlikely of sources, isn't it?'

Turning away from the sweating physician, he walked to the other end of the room before turning back to face the object of his ire.

'My travels to the east took me to Nisibis, a city with a substantial population of Christians, and while I'm sworn to the service of Mithras, I'm not above talking to followers of other religions, if only to understand what motivates them. I soon enough realised that they're not all that different from we followers of the one true faith, especially in the area of their beliefs about retaliative justice. The one phrase they have that really struck me the first time I heard it was their idea of "an eye for an eye". If you wrong me, the same wrong should be visited back upon you. How do you find that concept, Doctor?'

The medicus looked up at him in disbelief.

'You can't—'

'No indeed, *I* can't. The obvious repercussions might well lead to an equally harsh penalty being visited upon me, were I to be implicated in your murder. But that's of no concern, because I don't intend killing you. I'm going to leave that to you. After all, you're the expert in the field of inflicting death.'

The doctor shook his head slowly.

'You expect me to . . . *kill myself?*'

Scaurus pursed his lips and shrugged.

'It may seem a little outlandish, I suppose. But let's consider the facts, leaving aside any debate as to whether you were responsible for your patient's death. Or rather one simple fact. You see, the good lady in question was married to a young man who has been blessed and cursed in life. Blessed with quite remarkable skills with a blade and having been born as Marcus Valerius Aquila, the son of a family wealthy enough to develop that talent, but equally cursed by the destruction of that family on false charges of treason. So now he's forced to live under an assumed name, as Marcus Tribulus Corvus, a wanted man, while the emperor who condemned his family to death uses their rather grand villa on the Appian Way as his country palace.'

The doctor shook his head with a horrified expression.

'Why . . . why are you telling me these things?! Stop it, I don't want to—'

'You don't want to know because it makes you party to a felony that could see you executed if you don't promptly inform on the man. Don't worry, it won't come to that.'

He stared at the doctor until he was sure the other man wasn't going to open his mouth again.

'So, to continue my story, my friend was just starting to find a place for himself in the sun again, with the love of a good woman, when you managed to undo all that by bringing about the death of his wife. I didn't bring him with me today because, to be frank, I'm not sure I could have kept him from killing you as soon as he laid eyes on you. Which would have been temporarily satisfying for all of us, but also a little self-defeating in terms of the consequences. So, as you can see, I'm actually doing you a favour in allowing you to choose the way you're going to leave this life, once you've written a note explaining why you're doing it in order to obviate any responsibility that might cling to myself and my colleagues. You can slit your wrists if you like, we've all the time needed to make sure you do the job right. Or perhaps a swift-acting poison would suit you better? I'm sure you've something suitable in your medicine pots. So, either you choose, or I will.'

He looked down at the doctor in silence for a moment.

'Making sure that you're dead before we leave isn't going to do the lady's husband much good, obviously, since it won't bring her back, but it will stop him brooding on yet another person he needs to bring to bloody justice. It's a long enough list without adding your name to it. And besides, nobody wants to spend the rest of their short span of days looking over their shoulder for the man who'll end it for them, do they? Were you to have avoided death today you'd only have spent the rest of what's left of your life dying small deaths a dozen times a day, every time someone caught your eye or jostled you in the street. This way really is so much kinder. So, what's it going to be, Doctor?'

Scaurus took a sideways look at his subordinate as the two men sat waiting for their summons into the imperial chamberlain's presence. Marcus kept his gaze fixed on the mural on the room's far side, the painted figures illuminated by the soft glow of the late afternoon sun through a window above their heads, his lips twitching into a humourless half smile.

'Don't worry, Legatus. I'm not going to tear Marcus Aurelius Cleander's throat out. Not today.'

The older man returned his own stare to the painting before them, grimacing at the artist's representation of two lines of men facing off across an open piece of ground with half a dozen bodies strewn between the two forces.

'I've often wondered just who advises these artists as to what happens in a battle. Anyone who's never served the empire could go away with the impression that it's a big game of push and shove, and that we all walk away afterwards.'

The two men stared at the bloodless scene in silence until Marcus turned his head to look at his superior.

'Cotta told me what you did to Felicia's doctor this morning . . .'

Scaurus shrugged, his smile bleak.

'Disappointed you weren't there to watch him die? We all take revenge in our own ways, and I knew that mine was likely to be a good deal more subtle than yours, and less likely to invite the attention of the city authorities. Whether we like it or not, our only outward reaction to this outrage has to be one of stoic acceptance of the fates that the gods visit upon us. And besides, your wife was a friend of mine too.'

A tunic-clad slave crossed the chamber and stopped before them with a bow.

'The Chamberlain will see you now, gentlemen. Please follow me.'

As he led them towards the door that led into Cleander's office, he spoke softly over his shoulder, a hint of caution in his voice.

'I gather you've been away for a year, Legatus, in which case I should advise you that the chamberlain has come to favour open shows of respect in his audiences with supplicants such as yourselves. A bow, perhaps, or—'

Scaurus nodded tersely.

'The power does it to them all, given enough time. And I do not consider myself to be that man's supplicant . . .'

Ignoring the slave's raised eyebrow, he led Marcus into the audience chamber past a pair of armed Praetorians who closed the doors behind them. Seated before them, on the far side of a desk large enough to have served as a bed for two people given a mattress, the imperial chamberlain was writing on a sheet of paper, intent on the words he was inking onto the smooth, pale surface. He spoke without looking up, the quill tracking across the silky smooth surface without interruption.

'One moment, gentlemen.'

Scaurus stared hard at him for a moment before snapping to attention, his example swiftly followed by Marcus, and waiting impassively while the man who effectively ran the empire completed his message, passing it to his letters slave for folding and sealing.

'For immediate dispatch to the governor of Germania Inferior.'

The slave bowed respectfully.

'And to be carried by a different messenger to the other letter, Chamberlain?'

Cleander smiled glacially, with very little humour evident.

'I think so. Best not to risk the two being mixed up.'

He looked up at Scaurus, sitting back in his chair in silence for a moment.

'It has become customary for the granting of an audience with the imperial chamberlain to be acknowledged by some small show of respect, Legatus.'

Scaurus nodded.

'Your appointments secretary was good enough to suggest it to us, Chamberlain.'

'And . . . ?'

'I chose to ignore his suggestion.'

Cleander grinned broadly, lounging back in his chair.

'And that's what I like about you, Rutilius Scaurus. No pretence, nothing but the most blunt of opinions stated in such a matter-of-fact way that only the most irascible of men could take offence. And trust me, a year of governing this empire on behalf of a man like Commodus has been *more* than enough to make me irascible.'

He opened his arms to highlight the fact that the three men were alone.

'Under which circumstances I would have at least expected some appreciation of the fact that you have my undivided attention? No bodyguards, no Praetorians to stand between us . . .'

'Nobody to overhear whatever it is that you want from us this time? Besides, we know you well enough. Were we to offer you violence your revenge would be spectacular in both reach and method.'

The chamberlain smiled again, shaking his head in an affectation of sadness.

'Cynical, Legatus. But true enough. So, to business.'

He reached for a waiting sheet of paper covered in script, dipping his quill into a small gold pot of ink and signing it.

'You are hereby discharged from the rank of legatus, with the heartfelt thanks of a grateful emperor for having managed to quell the threat from the Parthians and secured the status of our colony of Nisibis.'

Looking up from the paper for a moment, he nodded soberly.

'A job genuinely well done, by the way. I read your report of the battle you fought with the King of Kings' son and his allies, and it seems as if you provided the man with the most salutary of military lessons. I also noted that this young man's diplomatic efforts seem to have resulted in a fresh lease of life for the current holder of the Parthian throne, one way or another, which is very much to the liking of the men who advise me on these matters, given his age and disinclination towards war. All in all, an excellent result.'

Scaurus nodded tersely.

'*However . . . ?*'

Cleander nodded.

'Indeed . . . *however*. In the short time between your arrival in Antioch and your departure for the border with Parthia, you seem to have caused no small degree of upset among the men of the senatorial class with whom you interacted.'

He waited for Scaurus to comment, and when the soldier showed no signs of doing so a hint of irritation crept into his voice.

'You managed to completely alienate the outgoing governor, for a start. And a man like Gaius Domitius Dexter isn't going to take that sort of embarrassment sitting down. I spoke to him a week or so ago, and it's safe to say that you've made yet another enemy to add to your long list. An influential enemy.'

Scaurus shrugged.

'A venal man, Chamberlain. A man whose theft from the imperium was breathtaking not only in its monetary value but the degree to which it weakened a strategic frontier. He deserved every embarrassment I could heap on him.'

Cleander shrugged equably.

'Indeed he did. Just be warned, Rutilius Scaurus. And that's before we come to discussing the apparent murder, at least if Domitius Dexter is to be credited with having the truth of it, of a young broad stripe tribune by the name of . . .' He looked down at a tablet. 'Ah yes, Lucius Quinctius Flamininus. You'd be more than a little perturbed, Rutilius Scaurus, had you been present in any of the interviews I've been forced to endure with that young man's father, given the depth of his righteous anger towards yourself and your tribune here.'

Nodding to himself as if he'd just recalled an important detail, he turned his attention back to the paper before him.

'Which reminds me, Tribulus Corvus, or whatever it is that you're calling yourself these days, you too are discharged from your position as a military tribune, thanks from a grateful throne, etcetera, etcetera. I commend you for your role in the Parthian matter, and I recommend that you never allow Flamininus the elder's men to corner you on a dark street.'

Putting the quill down he looked at the two men before him with an expectant expression.

'Nothing to say, Rutilius Scaurus? No protest at having your rank stripped away after having done such a fine job in the east?'

Scaurus shook his head, his features impassive.

'It wasn't my rank, Chamberlain. It belonged to the empire.'

The chamberlain raised a sceptical eyebrow.

'Oh how *very* noble. And these Britons you've dragged halfway across the empire and back again? How sanguine will your reaction be if I reassign them to a new tribune? Some ambitious young man with a career to build and somewhat less concern with how he might do so than you when it comes to the preservation of his men? After all, there's always a war brewing somewhere, an opportunity for such a man to make his name at the expenses of a few thousand soldiers' lives . . .'

He looked at Scaurus for a moment.

'Does that prospect not concern you, Rutilius Scaurus?'

The subject of his scrutiny shook his head.

'Nothing lasts forever, Chamberlain. If you've chosen to retire me then I shall simply have to make the best of it. If . . .'

'*If* indeed. You're a perceptive man, Scaurus, I've never denied that, even whilst cursing your gift of causing upset among the richest and most influential men in Rome. I do have *something* in mind for you both, and for the men who follow you, although you might find yourself wishing I'd decided to let you idle away the rest of your life.'

2

'Germania? Again?'

Scaurus smiled at the most outspoken of his centurions in the transit barracks' lamplight. He'd decided to decamp from the house on the Viminal Hill in order to ensure that no hint of the Tungrians' latest mission, or even their immediate destination, could reach prying ears. A former prince of the Brigantes, the tribe through whose lands the Roman defence of northern Britannia ran from sea to sea, Dubnus had long since given up any pretence at moderating his forthright manner.

'Yes, Centurion, it's Germania Inferior. Again. But this isn't the Germania Inferior you know. What you saw was the civilised edge of the province where it abuts Gallia Belgica, farmland for the most part with the occasional vineyard. Whereas in reality Germania Inferior isn't really much more than a military buffer zone, a strip of land no more than thirty miles deep protected by legions and auxiliary cohorts camped along the length of the river between the sea in the north-west and Fortress Bonna two hundred miles to the south-east. The governor of the province has two simple tasks to perform, the most important of which is to ensure that the barbarian tribes who inhabit the land on the other side of the river don't get any ideas about crossing the Rhenus and settling in the Gaulish provinces to the west. And while the mission that the chamberlain has set out for us will initially take us to Germania Inferior, we won't be staying there for long.'

The men he'd gathered for the briefing seemed to collectively lean closer to their newly reinstated tribune. In addition to Dubnus, who had acted as the 1st Tungrian cohort's first spear while Julius had been temporarily ranked as the Third legion's senior centurion during their time in the east, he had summoned Qadir, a centurion who hailed from the city of Hama in Syria, a man he valued highly both for his imperturbable steadiness and his men's skill with their bows, and Cotta, simply for the veteran's experience and forthright opinions. His German slave Arminius stood behind him, having long since become more companion than bondsman, the first member of the small group of men Scaurus had come to consider as his familia. Ignoring Julius's disgust at being left behind, Scaurus had swiftly decided that since only a small portion of his two cohorts' strength would be marching north he would leave a strong leader to ensure that those men left behind were kept fit and ready to fight, and since Marcus already knew the detail of their mission he'd sent the younger man home with the first spear to spend a little time with his son before the time came to leave. Taking a sip of the wine that he traditionally served at such gatherings of his officers, he pointed to the map that lay unfurled on the desk before him.

'I'll be taking a small party of men north to the provincial capital, and leaving the rest of both cohorts here, a distance of a thousand miles that I expect will take twenty-five days or so on horseback. From there we'll cross the river by whatever means is deemed to be the most likely to get us onto the far bank without being discovered.'

Cotta looked up at him in surprise.

'We're going to *cross* the Rhenus?'

Scaurus's lips twitched into a wry smile.

'It'll be fairly difficult to carry out the task I've been handed by the emperor's chamberlain if we don't.'

The veteran centurion shook his head with a stubborn expression.

'But . . . everyone knows that barbarian Germania's just a mess of forests and bogs, Tribune. How are we going to make any progress through *that*?'

He fell silent as he realised that both Scaurus and Arminius were looking at him with expressions of amusement.

'You shouldn't believe everything that you're told, Centurion Cotta. The lands across the Rhenus are no better and no worse than those on the western bank, they just haven't been subjected to Roman influence. There's some fertile farmland, some deep forests and yes, even some mountains and bogs, but very little of it is completely impassable. The biggest challenge won't be the terrain, it'll be making sure that we're not detected by the tribesmen who inhabit the land we'll be crossing to reach our objective. Because if they find out what it is that we're hoping to take away from them then both cohorts wouldn't be enough to protect us. Not nearly enough.'

Dubnus stared at him in open disbelief.

'What is it that's so important to these tribesmen that we have to take it away? Gold?'

Scaurus shook his head.

'It isn't a what, Centurion, it's a who. We're ordered to effect an abduction, gentlemen, a kidnapping of the most dangerous person in the whole of Germania.'

'Since you're here you can hold this young man while I sort out their dinner.'

Marcus took his son from Annia, placing the squirming infant onto his knee and jigging the child up and down to both their delight, his misery forgotten momentarily at the sight of his son's innocent enjoyment.

'And you, infamous daughter-namer, can have this wriggling bundle of delight.'

Depositing her daughter Victoria into her husband's lap she turned on her heel and stalked into the kitchen, noisily rattling pots as she prepared the two children's evening meal. Julius and Marcus exchanged knowing glances, the heavily bearded first spear grimacing at his friend.

'Best not to say anything when she's in this mood. She only brings up the fact that I chose the girl's name without consulting her when she's raging about something or other.'

The retort from the kitchen was instant.

'I heard that. And you needn't pull that face either.'

Silence reigned for a while, broken only by the children's giggles, Julius's eyes narrowing as his daughter first found his beard and then discovered the fun to be had from pulling at it.

'So it's Germania?'

His question went unanswered for a moment, while the Roman watched his son's face beam with delight at their game.

'So it seems. A simple enough task, as long as we don't let the Bructeri get scent of us.'

'Bructeri?'

'A German tribe who live on the land across the river from the provincial capital.'

He moved the child to his other knee, repeating the jigging trick to provoke another giggling shout of delight, and Julius stared at him for a moment before speaking.

'Marcus . . .' The Roman looked up at him, eyebrows rising at the troubled look on his friend's face. 'Are you sure that you're ready for this?'

'Which means you're sure I'm not.'

Julius shrugged helplessly.

'You're your own man. But . . .'

'But I'm not myself. Withdrawn most of the time, distant, as if I'm not really interested in what's happening around me. Yes. I believe my wife would have diagnosed a severe reaction to a number of events that have happened over the last few years. The death of my family, several pitched battles, the killing of my enemies both for the empire and for my own purposes and now her rape and effective murder by the one man I can't take any revenge on. I lack focus on the events around me, my former speed with my swords has deserted me and when I go to my bed sleep eludes me. I can hardly see the point of it all any more, Julius, and there are times when all I want to do is curl up in a corner and cry.'

His friend stared at him in silence for a moment, then nodded.

'We've seen it before, in men who reached the limits of their courage and surrendered to their fears. And you and I both know that they swiftly become useless in a fighting unit, much less a detachment tasked with crossing the river Rhenus and taking on these . . .'

'Bructeri.'

'So why go, Marcus? Why put yourself at such risk when you're clearly not ready? Stay here with us, enjoy your son! The gods know you've seen little enough of him since he was born, and here you are threatening to go away and in all likelihood never come back.'

The younger man jigged his knee again, setting Appius giggling once more.

'I know. And I know I should stay. But I can't. What if my friends went across the Rhenus and were never seen again? How could I forgive myself? And what is there for me in Rome anyway, other than the ghosts of my family and my wife, and the grinning, fornicating bastard that murdered them all?'

Julius shook his head in disbelief.

'You're going with them. You're going to turn down the chance to rest, recover your wits and spend some time with the child, and go north as part of some idiotic scheme that's more than likely been dreamed up by that bastard Cleander simply as a way to have you disappear.'

'Yes. I should feel some emotion at the prospect of leaving Appius fatherless, but all I feel is . . . numb.'

'He'll never be fatherless, I promise you that.'

'Here, you can shovel this into the little monster.'

Annia had returned with a pair of bowls, placing one on the table in front of Marcus.

'Perhaps you'll have more luck than I normally do in avoiding him getting it all over himself *and* whoever's feeding him.'

Taking their daughter from Julius she sat the child on her knee and reached for the other bowl, only to freeze as an infant's wail came from the nursery on the floor above them. Giving her a knowing look Julius reached out and took Victoria, who looked up at him with the same slightly baffled expression with which she had regarded him since his return the previous day. Returning with the baby, Annia went into the kitchen and busied herself with a pan of milk whose contents, suitably warmed, went into a terracotta bottle which, once filled through a trio of slots in a dished section at the thicker end, had only a tiny hole at its pointed end from which the baby might drink. Marcus looked up as she walked back into the room with the infant, his face hardening at the sight of the child. The woman took her seat in silence, lying the child back in the crook of her arm and positioning the bottle to dribble a thin stream of warm milk into his mouth. Only when he was contentedly sucking away at the spout did she look up at Marcus with an expression he'd learned brooked no argument.

'I know what you're thinking. You look at this baby and all you can see is Commodus violating your wife and bringing about her death. And you're right. The emperor did rape her, and the blame for her death does lie with him. But it doesn't have *anything* to do with this innocent. I promised Felicia before she died that I'd raise him as my own, and that's exactly what I'm going to do.'

She tipped her head at her husband, who wisely concentrated on putting food into his daughter's mouth.

'Julius has already agreed, not that I gave him any choice, and you're going to promise me never to do anything to bring harm to the child. You'll keep the facts of his birth to yourself, no matter what provocation might come your way, and you're going to allow him to grow up to be the best man he can possibly be, with Julius and me to guide him. And do you know why?'

The Roman shook his head in silence.

'Then I'll tell you. You'll be gone again soon enough, away to perform whatever suicide mission it is that's been dreamed up for you and Rutilius Scaurus this time, leaving me here with these three. A pair of two-year-olds and a newborn to raise—'

'We can hire a nurse. More than one if need be.'

Her smile was thin enough for the meaning to be clear.

'Nurses feed children, bathe them and clean their backsides three times a day. But they don't often raise children, talk to them, entertain them, or give them love.'

'But the right nurse—'

'Will still only be a nurse and not a mother. I'll be mother to the three of them, and Julius, given he's not going with you, can play at being a father for a while. While you go and do your best to get yourself killed, no doubt.'

She looked at Julius again.

'He's told me the sort of thing you get up to.'

Julius shrugged apologetically, and Marcus found himself unable to resist a wan smile.

'I surrender. All I have to offer is abject apology . . .'

The woman stared at him for a moment in silence, her expression softening.

'The gods know you've been through enough, Marcus, your family destroyed, your name and honour trampled into the dirt, and now this latest horror. Doubtless you'll be happier killing barbarians in whatever part of the empire it is you're being sent to this time than moping here, with your fingers twitching for the emperor's throat. Perhaps you'll even be able to forget all this, for a while at least. Just don't forget, while you're out there killing Rome's enemies, that you've got a son here who'll need a father if he's to grow up whole.'

Marcus nodded gravely.

'I can't argue with you, Annia. And I thank you for your devotion to my wife, and to her memory. I promise by the name of Our Lord the Lightbearer never to harm the child through act or word. What name have you given him?'

Annia's face softened again as she looked down at the feeding baby.

'I decided upon Felix.'

Marcus smiled bleakly.

'Felix? He's certainly had his fair share of luck, I'd say, but—'

He looked down in dismay as Appius buried a food-streaked face in the wool of his tunic.

'Ah. I see what you mean.'

★

'Every man is to wear mail. No scale armour or crested helmets for the centurions, no bronze for the officers and no segmented armour to be worn by the men either. I want nothing to differentiate any of us from each other, or to indicate who might be a centurion or senior officer.'

Scaurus looked at the gathered centurions with an expression that told them he was deadly serious.

'Vine sticks will *not* be carried, and medal harnesses will *not* be worn. The glorious panoply of the legions is all very well if you're marching into enemy territory with four eagles and forty cohorts at your back, but not quite as well advised when your party numbers as few men as ours will. There will be no decorated equipment of any sort, just standard-issue items straight from the stores with nothing to make the user stand out. Shields, oval shields mind you, will be painted plain green and kept in their covers until such time as we're across the river, and their metal edging will be removed and replaced with rawhide. I want any casual observer to think at first glance that the men he's looking at are German, and I want as much uniformity between every man's armour and equipment as possible.'

'If I might be so presumptuous as to question this decision, Tribune, why is it that you wish all of us to appear identical?'

Scaurus turned to face Qadir.

'Because, Centurion, if any of us are captured the best we can hope for is a quick death, with as little further unpleasantness as possible.'

The Syrian raised an eyebrow.

'You imply, Tribune, that these Germans habitually use torture on their captives?'

Scaurus shook his head.

'Not always. It depends on the tribe, and how their interactions with Rome have left them feeling towards us. I myself heard enough screaming from enemy camps during the war with the Marcomanni and the Quadi to know that being taken prisoner is often by far a worse alternative than stopping an arrow or a spear. Of course a chieftain may order his men to spare captives, looking to sell them back to Rome or simply enslave them, or he may choose to punish their audacity in breaching his territory by making an example of them. The histories mention soldiers being caged and starved to death, or set alight to burn for the Germans' amusement, but when it comes to officers their ferocity is unbounded. The survivors of several defeats have returned with tales of men having their eyes pulled out and their tongues severed, but the most bestial treatment is sacrifice on an altar in one of their sacred groves. There are tales told by the very few men who survived German captivity of more than one senior officer having his ribcage cut open with a saw, then pulled apart with simple brute force, and his heart pulled still beating from his body.'

He looked around his mesmerised audience and shrugged.

'A fate that I'd be happy to avoid if the only price I have to pay is to be parted from my bronze for a while.'

He'd hoped the quip would lighten their mood, but Cotta shook his head in disbelief.

'They actually sacrifice men to their gods? I thought those were just—'

'Stories used by the veterans to keep the younger men in their place?'

All eyes turned to the tribune's slave Arminius, whose usual practice was to sit in silence and observe proceedings with a faint air of disdain.

'Not in the case of my people, the Quadi. We sacrifice men, and women, to our gods, Tiwaz the god of war, and Wodanaz who guides our souls to the underworld. Some sacrifices are entirely voluntary, such as a slave who wishes to be with his dead master . . .' He paused, nodding at Scaurus. 'Others, obviously, are not. But do not imagine that the tribes east of the Rhenus reserve this treatment especially for you Romans. Any captives in time of war are treated with just the same disregard for their lives. It is simply our way.'

'But that's—'

'Barbaric? It is harsh, certainly, to have your heart torn from your body and held up before your dying eyes. But is it really any worse than the way that you Romans treat your captives? When I was taken prisoner by my master there,' he pointed to Scaurus, 'every other man of my tribe who was made captive by the Romans was chained to several other men and marched away into slavery. Not the type of slavery I have lived over the last ten years, with a respectful master who values me for my abilities, but enslavement to the arena. They were taken to be gladiators, marched away to Rome in order to provide your people with entertainment in the Flavian arena. They're all dead now, of course, unless any of them survived long enough to win their freedom, but instead of a swift death they suffered an agony of waiting for their fate to come for them, and for Wodanaz to finally walk with them on their journey to greet their ancestors . . .'

He fell silent, and Scaurus looked at him for a moment longer before resuming his instructions.

'Every archer is to carry two quivers full of arrows. Once we're across the river we'll depend on them for protection against our being detected as we move towards our objective. The soldiers are to carry an oval shield, a dagger, a sword and a single spear, of a design which is currently being manufactured for me by the armourers who supply the gladiatorial schools. Of course the swords will undermine our disguise as tribal warriors the moment anyone gets close enough to see them, since that much iron is a rarity among them, and they usually make do with a spear. But not a throwing spear, gentlemen, it's something entirely more daunting, both to use and to face.'

'Not a throwing spear? If it's not made to be thrown then how much use can it be? Don't tell me we're going back to those ten-foot-long horse-poking sticks.'

Arminius spoke again, his face creased into a knowing smile.

'Oh it can be thrown, Dubnus, we just don't often choose to do so. The weapon my master has in mind is called a framea. And I will teach you soon enough just what it can do.'

*

'I think we're safely out of earshot, First Spear. So what is it that you wanted to discuss in private?'

Julius had suggested that he and Scaurus take a turn around the practice ground while their cohorts were exercising the next morning, and the tribune had simply extended a hand to indicate that he would follow his first spear's lead, waiting until there was no danger of their discussion being overheard. His subordinate's next words were every bit as blunt as he had expected them to be.

'I don't think that you should be planning to take Centurion Aquila with you, Tribune.'

Scaurus looked away across the ranks of sweating soldiers in silence for a moment before responding.

'I'm inclined to agree with you. Not only is he deep in the grief of his wife's unexpected death, but he's clearly unbalanced. First he went on the rampage through the night-time streets and now he's retreated into himself. All I can get out of him is mono-syllabic answers for the most part. Respectful, considered, but not meaningful responses.'

Julius stopped walking, pointing with his vine stick at the nearest century and raising his voice to a bellow.

'Rear rank, put some fucking effort into it or I'll come over there and take my fucking stick to the lot of you!'

Both men watched the soldiers in silence for a moment, Julius smiling grimly as the men's centurion, clearly smarting under the criticism, promptly laid about him with his own vine stick in a random but apparently highly effective display of his moti-vational skills.

'So we're agreed then, he's in no way ready for another one of this man Cleander's little suicide missions? You'll order him to remain behind?'

Scaurus shook his head.

'I'm afraid not. There's a third opinion that you're unaware of, but which carries a good deal more weight than mine. And it belongs to *that man* Cleander.'

Julius stared at him in disbelief.

'He ordered you to take Marcus with you?'

'Yes and very specifically.'

The chamberlain had called Scaurus back into the room as he and Marcus had made their exit at the end of his briefing as to their new task.

'One more thing, Tribune?'

Scaurus had exchanged glances with Marcus and gestured for him to take a seat in the anteroom, turning back to Cleander with a look of apprehension as the doors were closed again. The freedman who now exercised almost untrammelled power on behalf of his master the emperor had shaken his head knowingly in his place behind the desk.

'Don't worry, Tribune Scaurus, I'm not intending to do you any harm. Not for the present.'

The soldier had smiled thinly.

'Nor did I expect that you were, Chamberlain. My concern is for that man out there, not myself.'

'Perceptive of you, not that you're anyone's fool.' Cleander had leaned back in his chair. 'And this does concern young Aquila.'

'Yes?'

'Under no circumstances is he to remain in Rome when you leave for Germany.'

Julius stared at his superior in disbelief.

'Why? Why would he order you to take the man with you, unless . . .'

'Unless he wants to get him killed? I asked him the same question.'

'And . . . ?'

Cleander had regarded Scaurus with a calculating expression.

'What do you think he'll do, left here to brood? Given the violence of his initial reaction to the news of his wife's unfortunate death?'

Scaurus had mused on the question for a moment.

'I think he'll grieve for a month or so. And then, if he stays here, I think the constant reminders of his wife will harden his mind in ways that might not be that constructive.'

'Indeed.' The chamberlain's tone had been acerbic. 'He may very well take it into his mind to come looking for vengeance. And at that point, one of two things will happen. Either, by some fluke or stroke of fortune he will succeed in his attempt on the emperor's life, or entirely more likely, I'll simply be forced to make him disappear before he can try any such thing, never to be seen again. Either of which eventualities would be a shame, don't you think?'

Scaurus had bowed fractionally in acceptance of the point.

'I'll take him along for the ride, although I can't see him being of very much value in his current mental state.'

Julius grunted his agreement as the tribune replayed the end of the conversation.

'You have that point right. He'll either have his mind elsewhere when the time comes to face the locals or lead the detachment into a bloody-handed goat fuck that you can't win.'

'Which is why I plan to make Dubnus my senior centurion for the mission. Marcus will support the decision, he told me as much during our walk back from the Capitoline Hill when I'd informed him that I was going to have to drag him away from his son once more.'

Julius nodded in appreciation of the decision.

'Dubnus? He's a good enough choice. And it *might* stop him from going back to his role as the king of the axemen.'

'Only ten men, Tribune? Surely you'll be wanting the whole Tenth Century?'

Dubnus shook his head in amazement at his commanding officer, ignoring Marcus's raised eyebrow, but Scaurus simply raised a hand to silence him.

'I appreciate your zeal, Dubnus. Not to mention the fact that now you're back in command of the Tenth you've reverted to type and started swaggering round like a man with balls made of bronze . . .'

He paused, allowing the gentle jibe to strike home, but if the big Briton was discomfited by the barb that he was emulating the pride and bombast of the officer his men had simply called the 'Bear', he showed no sign of it.

'You can't intend marching into enemy territory with a handful of men, Tribune, it'll be no better than taking a knife to your own throat!'

Scaurus shrugged.

'Possibly. Or possibly there's strength in stealth and guile, rather than numbers. Either way you have my orders – select ten men from your century to accompany us across the Rhenus. And while you're choosing them please keep in mind that I'm not recruiting for a weightlifting contest, and neither do I want men who despise their fellow men for not being six feet in both height and breadth. Bring me your thinkers, Centurion, men who are as quick on their feet as they're good with an axe. If I see any of the usual sneering suspects from your front rank when we muster then I'll make my own choice of their replacements and leave you behind along with them.'

The big man nodded grimly.

'Understood, Tribune.'

Scaurus smiled tightly.

'I hope so. It would be a shame to have to abandon my senior centurion before we've even marched a step.' He smiled at the Briton's baffled expression. 'You heard me. Your plans to relax back into the role of big brother to my cohort's centurionate will have to wait. Responsibility calls, Centurion.'

'My ten best archers? The selection will be an easy matter, Tribune, but surely a stronger force would be advised?'

Scaurus shook his head at the Syrian.

'Ten men are all that we'll need, thank you Centurion. But as to your selection, it's not going to be as simple as lining them up in front of a row of targets and taking the men who can hit their mark with the greatest frequency.'

The Hamian inclined his head in respectful question.

'Rather than picking men who can hit the same spot ten times with ten arrows when the greatest pressure on them is nothing more dangerous than the approval of their peers, I need you to select those men who are your most prolific hunters.'

Qadir nodded his head slowly.

'You want me to choose those among my command with the ability to move through the forest without disturbing leaf or branch? Those with the ability to bring down a startled deer as it turns to flee, with sure aim and the nerve to use it in the moment of greatest advantage?'

Scaurus patted him on the shoulder.

'I think you discern my intentions clearly enough, Centurion.'

'I need ten men.'

'*Ten?*'

The chosen man's expression was a perfect match for the face Dubnus himself had pulled when Scaurus had made his requirements clear, and he found himself smiling wryly at the man despite his continued sense of disbelief.

'It's worse than that.'

'Worse? How can it be *worse*, Centurion? The tribune plans to ride north with only a handful of archers and ten of our lads to stand between him and an entire German tribe. The only way it could be worse would be if—'

'Enough, Angar.' Like Dubnus and most of the Tenth Century's men, his chosen man had declined the option to take a Roman name on joining the cohort. 'It's worse, because the Tribune's requirements of those ten men are very specific.'

'Specific, Centurion?'

'Specifically these . . .'

Dubnus looked across the transit barracks parade ground, taking stock of his century's men as they exercised as was their practice each afternoon once the morning's drill had been completed under Julius's watchful eye. Lifting improvised weights, performing press-ups with a comrade on each man's back, they were sweating in the sun without regard for the heat in pursuit of physical perfection.

'The tribune wants men who will back down from a fight if doing so will keep the detachment undetected.'

He waited in silence for his deputy to digest what he had said.

'He wants . . . *cowards?*'

'No, Angar, he wants *thinkers*. He wants men who have enough brains to know when it'd be better to crouch in the cover of the forest and allow a stronger enemy to pass by, rather than sell their own lives, and those of their brothers, for a brief moment of furious bloodletting.'

The chosen man looked at the ground, shaking his head slowly.

'It goes against everything we teach these men. We select the biggest and most capable—'

'Not to mention those with the hottest temper.'

Angar shot him a hard glance.

'– and we train them, make them stronger, harder, unbeatable in a fight – brothers until death. Ten of these men are worth fifty of any other century in the cohort when the blood's flying! We are the tribune's proudest and most dangerous men, and with that danger comes a sense of . . .'

He groped for a word, and Dubnus took his opportunity.

'Arrogance.' He spoke the word quietly, raising a hand to forestall any retort. 'Cocidius as my witness, I feel it too. I strut around in front of my fellow centurions like a muscle-bound prize fighter, and I've even taken to calling some of them "little brother" in just the same way the Bear used to.'

Both men fell silent for a moment, remembering the centurion that his men had idolised, and his assumption of the role as their warrior king, the only man capable of snapping them out of their misery and making them fight like madmen at a desperate time.

'We make them arrogant for a reason, Dubnus.'

The Briton smiled at his subordinate's use of his given name rather than his formal title, a relaxation of formality that was taken for granted by the Tenth Century's tightly-knit brotherhood.

'We make them—'

Angar shook his head impatiently.

'Hear me out, Centurion.'

He raised an eyebrow, but gestured with a hand for the other man to continue.

'We make them arrogant because they have to believe in themselves and each other over anyone else. So that when the tribune gives the word they will run at the enemy with their axes ready to kill, taking far greater risks than those delicate flowers in the other nine centuries. They hide behind their shields and kill with the first few inches of their swords, dainty little stabs and thrusts to open their opponent's arteries and let them bleed to death. Whereas we—'

'I know. We court death every time we raise our axes to strike, and invite the man facing us to stab in with their spears.'

'Exactly. We fight like tribesmen, smashing and hacking at the enemy. We leave the battle blasted with the blood of men we have cloven in two. We don't kill on the battlefield, we slaughter, we decapitate and we tear men apart. We are warriors, Dubnus, where the rest of them are only soldiers. Our men need that edge of arrogance, or why would they throw themselves into the fight without concern for their own lives?'

Dubnus slapped him on the shoulder.

'Well argued. You make me wish for a pack of tribesmen barking at our shields, and the command to take our axes to them. There is nothing finer in life . . .'

'But?'

'Exactly. But. In this case Tribune Scaurus has asked me – ordered me, to select ten men who have cooler heads. I know, there's not a warrior among us without that sense of being the equal to three men from any other century, and I won't back away from that pride, but I need you to find me the thinkers among us. You're the first, by the way.'

'Me? A *thinker*?'

Dubnus shook his head again in amusement.

'You. A thinker. How else did you get to be the Tenth Century's chosen man? And besides, if I'm going to prance around a German forest playing nursemaid to Qadir's archers while they pick flowers and pull each other's pricks like the eastern perverts they so clearly are, I'm not going to suffer the indignity on my own. So get thinking, Angar, and find me nine more thinkers to share my pain.'

Qadir smiled thinly as the two men before him snapped to attention, waving a hand at them and shaking his head in disgust, addressing them in the language of their mutual home-land.

'Save the punctilious displays of respect for parades, it would make a nice change from your usual slouching and coughing.'

The younger of the two men standing before him, his age roughly the same as his centurion with whom he had been enlisted on the same day, kept his face carefully impassive as was his usual rule. The older of them, a goatherd before his recruitment into the army six months before them both, and therefore by his own estimation a man of greater experience and cunning, grinned knowingly.

'We wouldn't want to set any higher expectation among your brother officers, would we, Centurion?'

Qadir smiled thinly, recognising his comrade's jibe for what it was intended to be, a reminder of the fact that they had all begun their military lives as simple archers, before their friend's rise to command them which, given his birth, had been something of an inevitability.

'Indeed, Husam. Why look professional when with just a little less effort you can remain a goatherd for the rest of your life?'

His friend bowed his head in recognition of the returned insult.

'How can we be of service, Centurion?'

Qadir dropped his helmet on the desk of his quarter and gestured to them both to sit.

'I have been selected to join the tribune and centurions Marcus and Dubnus in a delicate mission to the northern wastes. To Germania.'

'You are clearly under the blessings of the goddess. Once more you have the opportunity to accompany your betters to a distant part of the empire, where unfriendly men will do their very best—'

Husam fell silent as he realised that Qadir was smiling at him in a not entirely humorous manner.

'That is correct. But you are mistaken in one thing, old friend. She smiles upon all three of us.'

He turned away to place his vine stick on the office's table, muttering quietly to himself.

The younger of the two raised a tentative hand.

'If I might enquire?'

Qadir spread his hands wide, as if granting silent permission for the question.

'Husam is your chosen man. I am your watch officer.'

'And so you are asking me who is to lead the men while we are away from the city, Munir? Select someone. I very much doubt that there will be any call for our archers, here in Rome. They will be free to relax, and forget the horror of our recent battles against the Parthians. Whereas we will be reacquainting ourselves with the German forests.'

'Cold, damp, miserably dark even in summer. There is little with which I have the urge to reacquaint myself. And their language, all that growling and gritting of teeth. I had not thought to sully my mouth with it again in this lifetime.'

Qadir grinned at Husam.

'With luck you won't have to. The tribune hopes to be "in and out again" without ever being detected. But, just in case his fond wish for a boring and uneventful few days is denied, we are to take ten archers, including you two.'

'*Ten?*' The question was incredulous in tone. 'What use are ten bows against a tribe of screaming painted lunatics?'

His answer was an eloquent shrug.

'I do not know, and I fervently hope not to find out. But, just in case the opportunity for that learning comes to pass, you must select eight more men to join us on this journey into the green half-light. And trust me in this, my brothers, you must not simply choose those men who are the most precise shots with their bows.'

Husam nodded wearily.

'I know. You want the best hunters, the stealthiest, and the most deadly shots when it comes to dropping a man with a single arrow.'

Qadir nodded soberly.

'I do. But I want them all to have one more essential quality, something which cannot be learned, but which must have been part of the man's way of thinking when he fell out of his mother.' Chosen man and watch officer stared at him in questioning silence. 'Every man you select must have the ability to lose all fear of failure at the moment he releases the arrow, must be blessed with cold eyes that can measure the best point of impact for his last arrow even as the cataphract bears down on him in dust and thunder, knowing that if this last arrow fails him then he will surely die on the end of the horseman's lance, or trampled under the hoofs of his warhorse. And, in the instant of releasing the arrow that he knows will surely fly true and fell his opponent, not to care.'

The room was silent for a moment before he spoke again.

'I know you both possess this detachment from the fears of the battlefield, or neither of you would hold the positions to which you bring great honour. Now go and find me another eight like you. Men who are not shy of killing, but who more importantly are not afraid to die.'

The two men bowed to him briefly rather than saluting, and left him alone with his thoughts. On the steps outside the office the chosen man put a hand on his colleague's arm.

'Did you hear what he said in there, when he turned away and thought his words were private? That the goddess smiled on all three of us – *if she smiled at all?*'

Munir nodded his head soberly.

'It is not the first thing he has said in the months since the battle for Nisibis that has given me pause for thought. More than once his words have implied that he is a less fervent believer in the Deasura than was once the case. You have noticed too?'

Husam shrugged eloquently.

'I was hoping that it was more a question of my imagination

than his words, but it seems that our friend is losing his love for our goddess Atargatis. In any case our men must not discover his wavering belief, so keep this to yourself. I will speak with him, and encourage him to consider his position as our century's spiritual leader in this city of unbelievers. I am sure that he will understand my concerns.'

'Archers and axemen. The ability to kill at a distance or to hack an enemy to ribbons. We should have every eventuality covered . . .'

Julius looked across the table at Scaurus, tearing off a piece of the bread on the plate before him and popping it into his mouth, chewing vigorously as he responded to the Roman's musing. The tribune and his centurions had climbed the Viminal Hill with the sun's last light to join the senior centurion and his woman for dinner, and talk had inevitably turned to their preparations for the march north.

'You can kill anyone you see, hack anyone to ribbons that gets past the archers, and generally outfight anything short of a full tribal war band. So what's worrying you?'

His superior took a sip of wine before answering.

'The lack of . . . guile, I suppose?'

Julius snorted, shaking his head.

'Guile? Given some of the men you're taking, I'd say what you've got is more like villainy.'

Scaurus shook his head.

'You miss my meaning, that or perhaps my expression was poor. And you're right, we have as much power to kill or terrify we can muster in a group small enough to evade detection, but we still lack something . . .' He paused, spearing a piece of meat with his fork. 'Given that we're going to have to go in on foot, and cross the river into their territory at some point, I think it's a lack of intelligence that's the problem. We could make our way into the heart of Bructeri territory by the most subtle and devious of means and end up walking into something quite unexpected, simply because we'll have no idea as to the state of play where it matters the most.'

Julius nodded slowly.

'I take your point. You could always take Silus with you and send him ahead?'

Marcus shook his head, breaking the reverie that had descended on him upon entering the house's painfully familiar confines.

'Not Silus, and not any of our cavalrymen, I'd say. They're too obviously serving soldiers, which would make them targets for suspicion anywhere east of the Rhenus.'

The senior centurion thought for a moment, then his face lit up.

'If you're looking for someone who'll blend into the landscape, a man that no one would ever suspect of being a serving soldier, I've just the man for you. And he's right under your nose.'

He opened his mouth but before he could expand on his idea one of Cotta's men escorted a newcomer into the room. The officers watched as he saluted Scaurus.

'Rutilius Scaurus, a pleasure to see you again.'

Scaurus stood, returning the salute with grave solemnity.

'Gaius Vibius Varus. It's a pleasure to see you, even if somewhat unexpectedly. Will you join us for dinner, if the lady of the house can muster another seat?'

Varus smiled.

'I would be delighted, Tribune.'

Silence descended upon the room as another place was set at the table, and Varus took his seat with a bow of thanks to Annia.

'So, what brings a man of the senatorial class to this table? Shouldn't you be reclining gracefully on a padded couch and listening to poetry while the house slaves feed you delicacies and young ladies compete to catch your eye?'

The younger man took a piece of bread from the proffered basket.

'Thank you. As it happens I did have a dinner invitation tonight, an invitation issued by one of my father's closest friends. It seems I'm quite the social must-have at the moment, with a dinner to attend every night of the week and sometimes more than one.' He sighed. 'They all want to hear my war stories and have me tell them how I spilled blood for the emperor. As the only man of senatorial rank who took part in our mission to Syria, everyone makes the automatic assumption that I must have been in command. At first I insisted on telling the truth of it, but the collective incredulity that an equestrian such as yourself might have commanded a legion seems to be just a little too hard to believe for most of them. The ladies flutter their eyelashes at me and lick their lips, while their fathers and husbands slap me on the back and compliment me on my modesty. I could dine out for a year on the reflected glory of our victory, and probably share a bed with a different woman each night, and yet . . .'

'And yet what?' Julius stared at him uncomprehendingly. 'You did your part as well as any other man, and you've earned the opportunity to make the most of it. Eat, drink, suffer the bullshit and f—' He shot a guilty glance at his wife, whose eyebrow was raised in an unmistakable signal of disapproval. 'Er, enjoy as much female company as you can. The chance might not be along again for a while.'

Scaurus looked at the younger man for a moment before speaking.

'But that's not enough, is it, Vibius Varus? You're not content to play the hero and take the kudos, are you?'

Varus shook his head.

'I need something more. To be alive again, and see the world in vivid colours, to feel the blood sizzling in my veins . . .'

Marcus nodded knowingly.

'You've stepped over the threshold that divides us from those men who've never taken sharp iron to another human being, never spilled an enemy's blood to stop him spilling yours. And never laid awake in the middle of the night pondering those deaths.'

The younger man nodded.

'I want to march with your spears again. You're getting ready to go somewhere, perform some mission for the emperor.' He raised a hand to forestall the denial. 'Don't try to palm me off on this, Tribune, I quietly strolled down here this afternoon, with a couple of ugly slaves to make sure I wasn't interrupted, and I watched the most amusing thing I've seen in a long time. Archers and axemen learning to ride? Whatever next? And so I wondered to myself what the purpose of such an exercise, unless the men in question, a small number of men, I noted, are going to have to ride somewhere a long way away?'

Scaurus raised an eyebrow.

'And your conclusion?'

Varus leaned across the table, his eyes alight with speculation.

'You're only taking thirty or so men, from the look of it, which means it's something covert. If the job entailed fighting for whatever it is you've been tasked to win, or destroy, you'd be going in strength, whereas this, I'll wager, is something subtler. So I discussed the state of Rome's relations with her neighbours with my father. It seems that most of the frontiers are quiet now, especially since we put Parthia back in her place, but there are one or two spots on the map where the sparks of resentment still burn brightly. Places where, in some cases, there are Varus family members serving their emperor, hence my father's interest in the affairs both of those provinces and their neighbours as well.'

He leaned forward in his chair.

'Take me with you.'

Scaurus stared at him for a moment in silence.

'And your father? Where does he stand in all this? I'd be more than a little surprised if he were supportive of your disappearing from Rome just at the time when your exploits in the east have probably guaranteed you a favourable marriage, and made you the talk of the city?'

Varus shook his head.

'I've taken the precaution of not consulting him on the matter. He would most certainly say no.' His face hardened. 'And that wouldn't end well.'

Scaurus spread his hands wide.

'And as a tribune I have no suitable rank to offer you.' He saw a confident grin spread across the younger man's face. 'But you've already thought that through as well, haven't you?'

'Make me a centurion. You know I can carry it off.'

Julius closed his eyes and muttered something unintelligible. Scaurus stared at Varus for a moment and then nodded slowly.

'You might have something there, if you're idiot enough to lower yourself to such a thing. You know this will be looked upon askance by the influential men who have been so much in your favour though, don't you?'

Varus waved the thought away.

'Victory is a child with a thousand fathers, Tribune, you told me that some time ago. If I come back from wherever it is we're going in the company of men who've achieved a great success for the empire, then all will be well, perhaps even better than now. And if I don't come back? Well in that case you can be assured that no one's going to be all that worried about the rank I was carrying when I died.'

Scaurus looked at Marcus.

'No view on this, Centurion?'

His friend's haunted face turned to match gazes with him.

'We only have one life, and it's better to have lived it the way that feels right. Even if only for a short time. And doubtless one or two of our men will be honoured to keep an eye on our colleague and ensure that he comes to no more harm than the rest of us.'

Scaurus nodded decisively.

'Very well. Get yourself kitted out tomorrow morning – I'm sure Julius will be delighted to help you make sure you look the part. Just don't come complaining to me when there are hundreds of German tribesmen baying at the moon for your head.'

Varus smiled beatifically.

'Germania? I'd hoped as much. With a bit of luck you'll be able to make your acquaintance of my cousin. I think you'll find him a most entertaining and useful man to know.'

'Thugs, Tribune?'

Scaurus stared at Cotta for a moment before answering.

'Your hearing clearly hasn't deteriorated, Centurion Cotta,

although what I actually specified was the Briton Lugos *and* some thugs. We can't leave him here, he'll be lost without us.'

The veteran raised an eyebrow at the younger man.

'Far be it from me to contradict as fine a specimen of the equestrian class as yourself, Tribune, but my impression was that you were planning a swift raid on these Bructeri, an in and out with as little noise as possible, and with the Germans not even knowing that we're there until we're back on the right side of the river with the prize.'

The tribune nodded with an approving expression.

'That's exactly what I'm planning. My congratulations not only on the state of your hearing but your general cognitive powers as well.'

Cotta shook his head with a look of mystification.

'If it's all got to be done on tiptoes then why would you be asking me to recruit thugs to bring along, given that we both know that thugs usually operate in a manner that's the direct opposite of either subtle or restrained? Not that I would ever have thought to describe Lugos in those terms.'

Scaurus raised a knowing eyebrow.

'The why, Cotta, is something that I shall keep to myself for the time being, so I suggest you concentrate on what I've asked for, and who would be best selected to deliver it. Suffice to say that I need a few soldiers along for the ride who can pass for the sort of men one sees outside the rougher sort of brothel after dark. Men who can quite clearly handle themselves, and who, when the need arises, punch first, punch again and only then give even the most fleeting consideration to explaining to the man on the end of their knuckles exactly why it is that they're punching them.'

Cotta looked at him for a moment.

'And whatever it is that you think you're going to achieve by unleashing the ugliest men in the cohort, you want me to select them. Which also means that whatever it is you plan for them to do, I'll probably be right in the middle of it. Am I right?'

'Almost. Yes, I want you to be their leader in that part of the plan I have in mind for you. And you can thank Julius for that, this was his idea. But I didn't say I wanted the ugliest men in the cohort, but rather the most criminally minded and, if need be, the most violent. I want thinkers, Centurion, men who'll be working out the odds before they raise their fists and not after, when it's too late.'

'You're asking me to find the cleverest, most brutal bastards in the whole cohort and then keep them under control until the time comes to let them loose?'

Scaurus's smile deepened, and the veteran officer rubbed his face wearily with the palm of his hand, puffing out his lips in an exaggerated exhalation of breath.

'Whatever it was I did to deserve this, it wasn't worth the punishment.'

'Why us?'

Cotta stared back across the tavern table at the soldier called Sanga with an expression verging on disbelief.

'Why *you*? I tell you that I'm looking for a pair of men to do dangerous and dirty work, men who know which end of a dagger does the damage, men who can talk their way out of trouble but know when to stop talking and start fighting, and you ask me "why us"?'

Sanga stared at him, apparently uncomprehendingly, and the veteran centurion sighed wearily.

'If I must . . .' Without warning he lunged across the table, putting a finger in Sanga's face and smiling as the soldier visibly suppressed his urge to take the hand and break the wrist attached to it. 'There, *that's* why you. Your first spear tells me that you, Sanga, are without a doubt the most violent man in your century, possibly in the entire cohort. Not a pretty fighter like your mate there . . .' The Dacian Saratos grinned at the description. 'But nasty as a week-old latrine trench once you've decided to put a man down. Fists, elbows, feet, teeth . . .'

Saratos nodded his agreement.

'You'll use them all, without restraint and without mercy, until the other man's on his back and has stopped trying to get up again. Won't you?'

Sanga shrugged.

'A man has to look after himself.'

Cotta smirked.

'And you look after yourself so well you've been given to the hardest centurion in the cohort, eh? How's serving under Otho working out for you?'

'It's alright. He's hard, but he's fair – most of the time.'

'I'll bet. Sure you don't fancy a holiday from all that shouting and slapping he likes so much?'

The soldier shrugged again, a sly smile creeping onto his face despite his best efforts to keep it straight.

'Look at the alternative. On the one hand you're offering us the chance to ride a thousand miles, when I don't know one end of a horse from the other until it blows out some apples to give me a clue, to do who knows what in Germania, of all places! We done Germania before you poled up, Centurion, and it was without a doubt the biggest shithole I've ever served in! And I've served in some right horrible places.'

He looked round at Saratos, grinning at the muscular Dacian.

'Or, and here's the difficult choice, we could be stuck here in the centre of the empire, the place where there's whores *everywhere*, and they'll all do it for the price of a loaf of bread, even some of the pretty ones. Even a half-witted Dacian bum-fucker like my mate here can see the choice for what it is, can't you Saratos? Germania or Rome, eh?' He spread his hands wide, a pleading note creeping into his voice. 'Even you can see that choice for what it is, can't you?'

Saratos nodded, pretending to consider the question.

'Is easy.'

Sanga's smile widened.

'Is Germania.'

'Eh?'

'Is Germania, obvious. Is Germania because one week of whore enough for any man. Even you, Sanga. Is Germania because stay here while friends go fight is not—'

'Right?'

The Dacian nodded at Cotta, who was grinning at Sanga, enjoying his discomfiture.

'Yes, not *right*. And is Germania because Centurion Marcus go Germania, is true?'

Cotta nodded, his lips suddenly a tight line as he recalled Marcus's troubled state of mind.

'It's true. And that young man needs all the protection he can get, over the next few months.'

The three men fell silent, all replaying the bloody events of two nights before, and the horrific revelation of Felicia's death that had shocked every man in the cohort. Sanga put his head down until his forehead was touching the table, banging it against the wood and drawing a worried glance from the tavern owner. Cotta sat back in his chair with a smug smile.

'It's Germania then. But don't worry, Sanga, you're not the only man I've got my hooks into. Dubnus is breaking the bad news to a colleague of yours this very moment.'

'Let's face it comrades, we're getting left behind this time.' Morban smiled round at his usual circle of associates, half a dozen of the older sweats in the First Cohort, raising a cup of wine in salute. 'Wherever it is that the tribune's taking his picked men, I reckon they're going to be away for months. Perhaps a year or more . . .'

He looked about him with an expression bordering on delight, laughing at their confusion.

'Come on, the emperor's not going to be sending our boys out to buy him some eggs, it'll be another one of those dirty little jobs that means travelling to the far side of the empire . . .'

He drew breath, and one of his comrades interjected with the speed of a man who knew all too well just how much the standard bearer enjoyed hearing the sound of his own voice.

'But we've not been back from the east more than a day. Why bring us back, if—'

Morban cut him off with a dismissive wave.

'There's more to this empire than Britannia, Rome and Syria, mate! There's dozens of provinces with hostile tribes next door, plenty of things the emperor wants but doesn't actually own.'

He grinned round at them again.

'For all we know they're being sent south to bring back some nice dark-skinned girls for Commodus . . .' He nodded acknowledgement of another man's attempted interjection. 'Yes, or boys. And it doesn't matter what it is, just as long as they take their time finding it. We'll just have to sit here and make the best of it, eh? Wine, games and lots and lots of whores. I can't see any . . .'

He fell silent as the men around him transferred their attention from his beatific smile to a point behind him. Scrambling out of their chairs they snapped to attention, and Morban stood, turning on his heel and tightening his body into the brace position automatically.

'Well now, Morban, I was told I'd find you here.'

'Centurion.'

Dubnus looked around at the other men questioningly.

'Could you men perhaps grant me a moment alone with my old friend the standard bearer here? Leave your wine where it is, I'll be gone soon enough.'

Needing no second bidding in the face of the bearded officer's request, the Tungrians slid past him to either side with forehead-touching gestures of respect. When they were gone his expression softened.

'At ease, Morban.'

Morban relaxed slightly, putting his hands behind his back, staring intently at his former associate from the days when Dubnus had seemed stuck in the role of chosen man, before Marcus had found a way to have him promoted to centurion.

'Doubtless you're all speculating as to exactly where the tribune's picked men might be going. Knowing your long history of illegal gambling it wouldn't come as any surprise if you were already taking money on the outcome . . .' Morban opened his mouth to deny the accusation, but closed it again when he saw the look on his officer's face. 'Wise, Morban. Perhaps you're growing some wisdom in your old age. But I'm not here to warn you off. Far from it.'

He fell silent, watching the older man as Morban smiled hesitantly and then, as the full import of his words sank in, the expression slowly faded from his face.

'But . . .'

The centurion raised an eyebrow,

'But? But what, Morban?'

'You can't mean . . .'

Dubnus nodded slowly.

'You have skills, Standard Bearer, abilities that will make you essential for the success of our venture. You've been requested, you specifically, to accompany the detachment that's going north.'

The veteran frowned incomprehension.

'Skills?'

'Skills, Morban.'

Dubnus reached out a hand and tapped him on the forehead.

'This, Standard Bearer, contains more guile and calculation than is possessed by any other man in the cohort. And, whether you believe it or not, those traits will be vital where we're going. So pack your gear and report to the detachment's barracks.'

The veteran soldier saluted tiredly.

'Yes, Centurion.'

Dubnus turned away, then returned his attention to the older man.

'Look on the bright side, Morban. Doubtless you'll find a way to turn this to your advantage. Just as long as you don't use your inside knowledge to make money before we leave for Germania.'

'Germania? I thought—'

'As intended. Trust me, Standard Bearer, where we're going we really don't want the slightest anticipation of our arrival, because that could only end very badly indeed. So if you don't want to end up with a witch pawing through your innards you'll keep your mouth shut. Won't you?'

★

'I'm coming with you.'

Arminius stared back into the boy's eyes in the light of their solitary oil lamp, realising with a shock that the child whom he had looked down upon only a year before was suddenly a good deal closer to staring him in the face than before. He walked away to the barrack window, looking out across the dark parade ground on which the detachment would muster the next day before turning back to face the child, shaking his head, raising a hand to emphasise the point.

'Not a chance. You're too young.'

Lupus shook his head with a look that promised obduracy and a good deal more.

'You left me behind the last time, and I was stuck here for a year without anyone to talk to except the women and babies. And then . . .'

The German resisted the urge to put his arms around the boy by force of will, watching in impotent anguish as Lupus's eyes filled with tears.

'I know. And if I had my time again I'd have been there.'

The boy looked at him with eyes as hard as any he'd seen on a man, and once again Arminius wondered at the change in him.

'You would have died alongside Arabus. Nobody could have protected moth—' He swallowed painfully. 'Nobody could have protected Felicia from those men. But given enough time someone will make them pay.'

The stone-hard stare lingered on the German for a moment, and in that instant Arminius knew he was seeing the man to come, implacable in his hatred, his view of the world around him forever tilted towards hard words and deeds by his childhood experiences.

'Lupus . . . you shouldn't—'

The boy shook his head flatly.

'Not you, Arminius! The women can tell me that it's not good to hate, but not you! You helped the Centurion to take revenge for his parents, you told me he was an honourable man for doing so!'

The German regarded him levelly for a moment before speaking.

'So, ignoring the fact that you're sworn to kill the emperor and half the praetorian guard, what do you expect to contribute to this task that the tribune's been handed by the very man you're determined to see dead?'

Lupus stuck his chin out.

'My sword and shield. I've been practising with Centurion Cotta's men ever since you left, and I'm as good as any of them except when they use their strength to push me over, when they get bored with not being able to beat me.'

Arminius smiled despite himself, recalling Cotta's summary of the things the men he'd set to guard the two women while the cohort was in the east had told him about the boy's progress with his weapons.

'He's fast alright. Faster than any of my boys, and someone's taught him a halfway decent technique that I can probably get close to Marcus's standard, given enough time.' The veteran centurion had winked at the German's wry smile, knowing full well that Arminius's training had given the boy most of the sword skills he needed. 'Once he's grown another foot and filled out he's going to be a right monster, you can see it in him already. It just amazes me that a squat little waddler like Morban can have sired the man who put that into a woman.'

His smile faded as he recalled Cotta's other, less cheery comment.

'Given you're pretty much his father these days, there is something else for you to think about though. There's something changed in the boy since the day Arabus was killed by the praetorians. Before it happened he was still a boy most of the time, when he wasn't behind a shield and a sword, but from that day on my boys tell me they've not seen the child in him. He's been brutalised, Arminius, had his childhood ripped away from him in a way that's left him . . .'

'Scarred?'

Cotta had nodded unhappily.

'That's as good a term as any other. I expect Marcus's wife, the gods watch over her departed spirit, would have had a better term for it, but scarred covers it well enough. The boy's gone, and what's standing there is a man in a body that's not quite ready to fight alongside men. But he will be, soon enough. And he's going to need some help making the transition, if he's not going to get himself killed before his time.'

Man and boy stared at each other in mutual unease for a moment before Arminius spoke again.

'If you were to accompany us into Germania you'd be a boy among men. The tribune's taking ten axes and ten bows, plus officers and a few hangers-on for skulking and thieving, every man with a purpose. Having you with us would be a distraction. You haven't learned to fight with or against the spear yet, and that's the weapon the tribes use for the most part.'

To his surprise the boy just shook his head, where a year before there would have been tears of frustration in his eyes.

'So, you're all going away again, only days after you came back. You, Centurion Marcus, my grandfather, all the people who promised to look after me. And what happens to me if you all get killed? I'll be stuck here with no one to look out for me, other than Julius. Which means I'll be a soldier soon enough and taking just the same risks, just without anyone to look after me.' He stared the German in the eyes. 'I'd rather die in Germany with you.'

3

Scaurus's detachment paraded at dawn the next day ready to march, each man holding the reins of the horse he would ride north. The soldiers were wearing warm tunics and boots, their cloaks rolled up and strapped across saddlebags that contained everything they were likely to need during the march while a pair of doleful-looking mules were hitched to a cart containing their tents and cooking equipment. Every man had an oval shield strapped across his back and a long German-style spear in his hand, the Hamians' bows and the Tenth Century's axes carried in thick oiled leather cases attached to their mounts' saddles.

'Kit inspection! Open your packs and lay it all out!'

As Scaurus's appointed senior centurion for the detachment, Dubnus was taking his duties sufficiently seriously to have already become the focus of a deal of disgruntlement, as he chivvied Tungrians through their preparations to march.

'Packs on the ground and open! I want to see every item nice and clearly!'

Walking down the line of men with Cotta at his shoulder, the retired centurion relishing the spectacle of soldiers being inspected by a hard-eyed officer, he stopped in front of one of his own men, shooting the hulking pioneer a meaningful glance.

'So, what have we here? Bowl, spoon, sewing kit, spare hobnails, spare tunics, blanket . . .' Feeling something inside the blanket's folds he pulled away the rough material to reveal three spiky iron objects. 'What are these doing here? Why are you still carrying caltrops?'

The soldier stiffened his brace and shouted his answer in the time-approved manner.

'Centurion sir! Because you ordered us to carry them sir!'

'But that was . . .'

The Briton shook his head and turned to Cotta with a wry smile, picking up one of the caltrops and showing it to the veteran officer.

'They were told to carry these nasty little surprises almost a year ago when we marched on the Parthians, and ever since then they've been packing them away without a second thought. We'll be rid of those, I think, before some stupid bastard puts one through his hand and can't hold his spear.'

Cotta stared at the evil pointed device for a moment.

'Perhaps we should keep them. It's not as if they're any sort of burden, and who knows when they might come in handy.'

Dubnus shrugged.

'If you think so.' He turned back to the soldier. 'Very well, carry on.'

He walked on down the line, looking into every man's pack and pulling more than one of them up for the quality of his equipment. Picking up one man's wooden eating bowl he snapped it in two with a swift twist.

'It was cracked. If your bowl breaks in the field you've nothing to eat out of. Go and get another one. You, hold his horse for him. *Move!*'

At the end of the line he found Arminius and Lupus, the latter doing his best not to be cowed by actually parading with the Tungrians rather than watching them do so but still pale with nerves. Leaning closer and lowering his voice so as not to be heard by anyone other than the boy and his mentor, Dubnus stared Lupus straight in the face as he spoke.

'When the tribune told me he'd agreed to bring you along I told him I thought he was mad. And I still do. But if you're set on it, and the man who gives me the orders says you're coming along for the ride, then so be it. But if I don't see you practising with that spear every day, twice a day, then you and

I will be having a serious disagreement. If you want to be a soldier then you're going to have to become one. Quickly.' He stared at Lupus for a moment longer. 'If you ever need my help, if this German oaf isn't to be found, come and talk to me. I know what you're going to go through over the next few months.' Stepping back, he hardened his face and raised his voice to be heard along the detachment's line. 'Now, show me your equipment.'

He stared down at the display, shaking his head in disgust.

'Your bowl's dirty, your tunics are dirty and your blanket looks like a dog's had a shit on it. Do better. By tonight.'

Confused, Lupus looked up at Arminius, but found a broad finger prodding him in the chest, dimpling his mail shirt's ringed surface.

'And don't go looking at him, he's a slave with nothing to say on the subject. If you want to express an opinion on the matter, you talk to me. Well?'

'Nothing.'

Dubnus exchanged an amused glance with Arminius, but his voice was a whiplash whose crack the assembled soldiers knew only too well.

'Nothing, *Centurion*! You're a soldier now, not some wet-nosed brat who can sit around taking the piss out of us all day. Say it!'

'Yes Centurion!'

'Louder!'

'Yes Centurion!'

'Acceptable. See me tonight with clean kit.'

With a barely perceptible wink at Arminius he turned away and walked back out in front of the small detachment, looking across the line of men with a grim face, shaking his head as he watched one of Qadir's archers struggling to control his mount's restless urge to be away.

'We're taking a handful of archers, the meekest of my axemen and a selection of the most undependable characters in the cohort. Not to mention a retired centurion who's old enough to be my father and who, rumour has it, once killed an emperor with his bare hands, and a boy with less than fourteen summers behind him. If we're going to take part in some sort of mounted purse-cutting competition then we're well looked after . . .'

'Where we're going, Centurion, we're going to need every skill you see before you.'

The burly Briton turned and saluted his superior, clearly unabashed.

'Wouldn't we be better off taking every man we've got, sir, if it's going to be that risky?'

Scaurus shook his head with a grim smile.

'I've told you before that where we're going a couple of cohorts wouldn't do any more than get the attention of the locals, and given what we're going to do, I think that the ability to blend into the landscape is going to be our best defence.'

Dubnus nodded with pursed lips, looking along the line of men.

'I can't argue with that. If we have to fight our way out of any more trouble than a few underfed tribal hunters it's going to get ugly faster than Sanga went through his back pay when Cotta told him he was coming along with us.'

He turned to Scaurus.

'We will be travelling through the German forest, Tribune, and not going anywhere near the swamps and marshes that Cotta keeps going on about?'

The officer laughed.

'No matter how many times I tell that man he refuses to believe me. The land on the far bank of the Rhine is much like that to the west, farmland where the soil's good enough, forest on the hills and yes, along the rivers' courses, some boggy ground, which of course, without proper estate management, hasn't been dealt with the way it has to the south of the Rhenus. There's a good deal of it in the north of the tribe's territory, but we'll not be going anywhere near that.'

'Ah, but what about the mists, eh Tribune? Thick, impenetrable mists so murky a man can't see his own hand in front of his face.'

The three men turned to find Cotta behind them, dressed for the road and ready to march.

'The lands on the far side of the Rhenus are no more or less prone to mist and fog than the German provinces on the western bank. You need to put whatever nonsense you've been reading out of your head. Who was it again?'

'Tacitus.'

The tribune grinned at the veteran officer.

'Ah yes, Cornelius Tacitus. A great man of letters he may well have been, even if his understanding of military matters seems to have been sadly lacking, but I suspect that were we granted the ability to communicate with the good senator's spirit, we would discover that he never actually did any of his research first hand. Germania may well bristle with forests and reek with swamps, but don't expect the place to be some sort of sunless underworld, or the men we're going up against to be anything more than men, with the same strengths and weaknesses we all have.'

Cotta shrugged.

'I'll wait and see, Tribune. But one thing's fairly clear to me about the men who live on the other side of the Rhenus.'

Scaurus tipped his head to one side in silent question, and the older man turned to look at the men of the detachment.

'There's going to be more of them than us. A lot more.'

June AD 186

'Well, they're about as well trained as they're ever going to be. Although just how well these new tactics of yours are going to work is another question, Tribune.'

The detachment had ridden north at a rate of thirty to forty miles a day, twice the speed that could have been achieved on foot, but it wasn't the pains of adjusting to long days in the saddle that had troubled the Tungrians, nor, after a period of adjustment, the mismatched nature of their collective military

skills. The relationship between the archers and their counter-
parts from the pioneer century had soon settled down to the
predictable state of cordial enmity, albeit that the disparity in
their size and skills had not been allowed to get in the way of
the exercises that Scaurus had ordered Dubnus to put them
through each evening before dinner, in the time when digging
out a marching fort would normally have been the order of
the day. As a sign of things to come, the tribune made a point
of camping next to wooded land wherever possible, to make
the training that he was driving his men through all the more
real.

The routine that had quickly been dubbed 'the crescent'
saw each archer paired with an axeman, the former advancing
out into the trees from their starting point, spread out in an
arc covering slightly more than a half-circle with their bows
held ready as if to shoot, while their burly partners advanced
with somewhat less stealth close behind each of them. Ordered
to advance swiftly but without losing vigilance to their immediate front, their orders were to simulate a bow shot upon
spotting whichever one of the officers had vanished into the
undergrowth in the moments before, while their backs were
turned. Upon hearing the sonorous twang of the released string,
while the bowman in question was to go to ground, ready to
shoot again, the men on either side were ordered to close up,
tripling the number of arrows that could be put into the target
if it still remained a threat. While that little game had first
baffled the detachment's men, and then simply become a
tedious evening routine the point of which they found it hard
to define, the purpose of the other exercise that they were
drilled through late in every day's progress towards Germania,
was entirely evident. Spaced at five-pace intervals down whatever forest path could be found, the soldiers were ordered to
move forward at a speed that made the slow march look like
a headlong charge, while their officers dropped twigs and
pebbles in their path and listened intently to their progress.
Initial muffled curses and loud cracks as their feet encountered

the simulated and barely visible detritus that would be likely to litter a forest path soon gave way to utter silence and a renewed focus on avoiding the traps, as centurions pounced on each offender and informed them in vehement whispers that they had just been awarded the task of filling in the latrine trench next morning.

Scaurus finished his mouthful of stew before responding to Dubnus's comment.

'Well Centurion, whether all this practice will ever be of any value is indeed to be seen. At least we've got them accustomed to having a proper look at the ground beneath their feet before they put their boots down.'

Dubnus nodded as he chewed a mouthful of his dinner, conceding the point as Scaurus continued.

'And they seem remarkably well adjusted to each other's different abilities. Only today I heard one of your men refer to his archer companion in the crescent exercise as a "goat-punching faggot", in response to which Qadir's man was generous enough to bestow upon him the titles "oaf", "simpleton" and, for good measure and after a moment's thought, "arsehole". I would have mentioned it to you earlier if it weren't for the fact that they were actually both smiling at the time.'

Dubnus swallowed his last mouthful of stew and licked the spoon clean.

'Qadir's boys like having big men around, it reminds them of their husbands.'

The Hamian nodded from his side of the fire.

'This is true. And your men are appreciative of having an extra pair of hands for when the counting progresses past ten.'

'Excellent.' Scaurus stood, handing his bowl to Arminius. 'So we've all learned to get along, our practice exercises have made us all very good at walking through the forest without making much more sound then a charging boar, and we're very nearly at our destination. For once I feel a small degree of optimism with regard to our chances of actually surviving the next few days.'

He walked away, and Arminius found himself the object of

several pointed stares. Opening his hands with a frown he barked a question at the centurions.

'What?'

'This crescent thing . . .' Dubnus stood, stepping closer to the German. 'If anybody knows, you'll know. So tell me, just between you and me, eh? What the fuck is it supposed to be?'

The German laughed tersely.

'I discover information, Dubnus, when my master chooses to discuss that information in front of me, and at no other time. And on the subject of this particular exercise he has remained stubbornly silent. From which I deduce that he does not wish me, and therefore you, to know what it is he has in mind. And now, if you'll excuse me . . .'

He walked away to the stream close to which the detachment was camped, leaving Dubnus and Qadir looking at each other none the wiser. Cotta shifted his position, adjusting the lie of his back against the tree he was sitting against.

'Isn't it time you blew that blasted horn, Dubnus? How's anyone going to know they should be rolled up in their blanket without you waking up that half of the camp that's already asleep?'

The Briton nodded.

'A good reminder Cotta, thank you.' He walked away to the tent he shared with Marcus and Varus, ducking back out with a bull's horn in one hand. 'You'll thank me one day, when we're scattered in some gloomy German forest and this sound is all we have to bring us back together, blown by lungs that have been trained to the peak of perfection.'

He put the horn to his lips, dragged in a lungful of air and then blew with all his strength. A mournful note blared out across the landscape, eliciting the customary barrage of abuse from those of the detachment's men who had already been asleep or dozing, while those who had worked the centurion's night-time routine in with their own promptly turned over and closed their eyes. After a moment a plaintive voice shouted out into the night, disguised by the adoption of a higher pitch than the speaker usually spoke with.

'Centurion?'

Dubnus smiled to himself, putting his hands on his hips and calling out a reply.

'Yes?'

'Do you know who this is?'

Shaking his head in amusement the Briton nodded.

'Yes, Sanga, I know who it is.'

Silence fell for a moment, broken only by the titters of the men around Sanga and his own bitter profanity.

'In that case . . . well blown sir!'

'Fuck you too, Sanga. Now get some sleep. You'll need to be up bright and early if you're going to get that latrine filled in before breakfast.'

'There it is, the river Rhenus.'

The road had reached the top of a long, shallow climb, opening up a vista that the Tungrians had ridden a thousand miles to see. They stared down at the river's silver ribbon as it snaked through the countryside below them, Cotta nodding appreciatively as his gaze tracked the Rhenus from the southern horizon to the point at which it vanished from view to the north.

'Now *that's* a river.'

Lugos shook his head, his voice a bass growl.

'I sail Euphrates. *That* a river.'

Cotta grinned at him.

'That may be so, Lugos my friend, but I seem to recall that while you were sailing on that mighty river you got an arrow in your leg, and another soon after just to make sure you never forgot the first one! Seems to me like maybe rivers aren't your best means of travel!'

Scaurus pointed to a ship that was crawling slowly upstream to the south.

'It might not be as wide as the Euphrates, but it's certainly wide enough to act as a natural frontier for the empire in combination with the river fleet. That ship will almost certainly have sailed from the fleet base south of Claudius's Colony, which is where we're heading.' He spurred his beast to walk on. 'Come, gentlemen, I have no desire to approach a frontier city after dark, whether in times of peace or not. It would only take one jumpy centurion and a lucky bolt-thrower shot to ruin a man's entire day.'

The guard centurion commanding the city's southern gate snapped off a crisp salute to Scaurus as soon as the tribune had identified himself, calling for one of the twin doorways that controlled entrance to the legion's base to be opened. He was immaculately dressed, his mail and boots gleaming with the evident application of a great deal of polishing, his beard neatly trimmed, and those of his men who were in evidence were equally smartly turned out.

'You're expected, Tribune, you and your men. If you follow my chosen man he'll take you to the bridge fort, and show you where the stables are. Our prefect's allocated a spare barrack to you, not that space is hard to come by with half the cohort away in Britannia. Oh, and the governor asked to be informed as soon as you arrive sir, so I expect you'll be receiving an invitation to his residence once you've had time to bathe and put on your best uniform.'

Scaurus nodded with a faint smile.

'He's keen on appearances, the governor?'

The centurion nodded briskly.

'Exceptionally keen, Tribune.'

He looked as if there was more he might have ventured, but chose instead to indicate his second in command, waiting for the Tungrians by the twin gateways.

'Festus will take you to your barrack, and show you where to draw rations for yourselves and the horses.'

He watched as the Tungrians marched away, clicking his fingers to summon his runner.

'Give my regards to Decurion Dolfus, and tell him they're here. You'll find him at the cavalry barracks. Go!'

The detachment followed the chosen man down a long wide

street, turning right once they were past the open expanse of a large forum and exiting the city by another gate. A wooden bridge stretched out before them, crossing the river's wide expanse on a series of twenty or so stone pillars, and on the far bank the familiar shape of a cohort-sized fortress dominated the otherwise empty landscape, its walls surrounded by a three-sided moat filled with water from the Rhenus which itself provided the fourth side of its defence. Walking alongside the chosen man, Dubnus looked down the bridge's length at the forested land on the eastern side of the river, empty apart from the stoutly constructed fort.

'I expected the other bank to be built up, with a city of this size on our side, or at least farmed.'

The other man shook his head.

'That's the buffer zone. Tribes ain't allowed to build there, nor farm. Military land . . .'

He fell silent, and the centurion looked about himself in interest as they strode out onto the bridge, watching as a flat-bottomed warship approached the bridge from their left, its sail and oars driving it upstream against the river's flow.

'How the fuck are they going to get *that* under *this*?'

The chosen man grinned at Sanga's bemused question.

'Everyone asks that the first time they see a ship go under the bridge.'

The detachment's progress slowed to a dawdle as every man stared in unashamed amazement at the oncoming warship, its crew seemingly unconcerned with the impending disaster that loomed ever more likely with every foot the vessel progressed toward the bridge, the sail and mast looming over the heavy structure. Finally, when all hope of avoiding a collision between immovable stone and the warship's delicate mast seemed lost, the captain barked out a series of commands that saw the billowing sail swiftly furled. Then, less than twenty paces from the bridge, heavy wooden pins were struck from the mast's base, allowing it to pivot down on a massive metal hinge and lie flat against the deck, lowered into place by sailors straining at heavy ropes to prevent it crashing down.

'Fuck me . . .'

The chosen man grinned at Dubnus with the confidence of a man who had seen it all before.

'They do it all the time, going up and down the river, and as far as we can tell they all have some sort of obsession with lowering the mast at the last possible moment. Only a few months ago one of them got it wrong and waited just a moment too long. Took his mast clean off and tore a hole the size of a mule in the ship's deck. Our trumpeter was on duty, and the first spear told him to sound the retreat as loud as he could.'

Nodding in recognition of yet another scarcely believable feat, the Briton waved his men on.

'Get moving! Has none of you ever seen a warship with a collapsible mast before?'

Crossing the bridge they marched into the fort, finding themselves housed in a barrack of the usual design, a long run of rooms designed to house an eight-man tent party with an officer's room at one end of the building.

'I suggest we put five men into each room and the officers can share the last two.' The tribune turned to Arminius and pointed toward the block's far end.

'We'll take the centurion's room. I'll need you to unpack my bronze and get it polished, make sure my best tunic's clean and put a shine on my boots that would bring tears to a senior centurion's eyes. I'm going to sweat the dirt out of my skin, and I'm going to take my officers with me, since these two young gentlemen . . .' he indicated Marcus and Varus '. . . will doubtless be included in the governor's invitation if only to assuage his curiosity. And since we'll need Dubnus to act as a decoy for all the wretched thieves that breed in all frontier cities, Qadir and Cotta might as well come along too.'

The German nodded.

'Yes Tribune.' His eyes narrowed as he spotted Lupus easing back through the Tungrian ranks. 'No you don't, boy! Your centurion needs his boots polished, and I'm sure Centurion Varus would appreciate a similar service. Just because you're a soldier now you're not getting out of your duties that easily!'

Qadir hung his tunic on a wooden peg, placing his boots neatly beneath the garment and looking around the empty changing room with an expression that was almost fond.

'A proper military bathhouse. I've not seen one of these for a while.'

Dubnus shot him a dubious glance, eyeing the attendants with suspicion.

'I'll be happy if I never see one again. Every time I set foot in these bloody places I end up losing something to the light-fingered bastards that run them.'

'Which is why I suggested that we leave everything of value under the watchful eye of your men and walked here with nothing more than our tunics, belts and boots.'

The burly centurion shot Qadir another sour glance.

'And it's why I walked here in bare feet and with a length of twine for a belt. I've been robbed enough times to trust nobody in these places. And no, I don't want to start in the exercise room, given I've already ridden twenty miles today, and not forgetting the indisputable fact that it'll be full of weightlifters all oiling themselves up and gurning at each other.'

Grinning despite himself, Scaurus, who had gratefully but firmly resisted the suggestion that he might want to use the senior officers' baths adjacent to the governor's residence, led them into the warm room to get accustomed to the heat before braving the hot room. He flipped a coin to one of the boys waiting to provide the legion's bathers with their requirements and the child scurried away, returning a few moments later bearing a tray loaded with a flask of wine and cups, while two more followed him in with a plate of honey cakes and a bottle of oil.

Scaurus poured each of them a cup, raising his own in salute.

'Gentlemen, let's drink to the successful completion of this latest little jaunt over the empire's frontier.'

Seated across the room and feigning a dozing somnolence,

having hurried to the bathhouse in time to have taken his place, the decurion called Dolfus watched the Tungrians through slitted eyes. Looking at each man in turn he muttered his comments on each to the men on his either side, two of them carefully oiling their limbs in evident preparation for the hot room, the other pair apparently engaged in a close game of dice. His words were clearly that of a man from the highest ranks of Roman society, clipped and precise.

'Yes, they fit the descriptions perfectly. The tall one in the middle, hatchet face, black hair just starting to go grey, that's Scaurus. Mark him well gentlemen, because if I'm not mistaken the governor bears a serious grudge towards the man. There's bad blood there from something or other, and I don't think it's going to sort itself out without some kind of ugliness.'

He yawned and stretched luxuriously.

'The big one with the beard a bird could nest in, he's called Dubnus. He looks like a bit of a handful to me, and the men on the gate told me he carries an axe big enough to hack a man's thigh in half. Blasted barbarians . . .' He grinned at the man with the oil to highlight the intentional hypocrisy of his humour. 'You're all the same, aren't you, all sharp iron and mad eyes?'

The trooper stared at him uncomprehendingly, and after a moment Dolfus shook his head and resumed his commentary.

'Anyway, the Arab goes by the name of Qadir. Not worth much in a fight from the way he handles himself, but he's a Hamian, so he could probably put an arrow into you from two hundred paces, if you were silly enough to stand still for him.'

He paused for a moment, looking at Marcus with a slight feeling of bafflement.

'And the thin-faced, wiry-looking man is Corvus, although I'm told that's a false name. Apparently he was the son of Appius Valerius Aquila . . .' He looked at the uncomprehending face and tried again. 'The son of a renowned senator who was falsely accused of being a traitor and put to death, after which Corvus is supposed to have carved a bloody path all the way from Britannia to Rome, killed all the men involved and then vanished like a ghost. He's supposed to be sudden death with a sword, and better with two, although I'm damned if I can see it in him from the look on his face. But then I suppose we'll have plenty of chances to find out, given what we're being paid to do. As to quite who the other man is, I have no idea. There was no mention of him in any of the communications from Rome.'

He sat up, shaking off the torpor that was creeping over him in the warm room's comfortable atmosphere.

'And that's enough exposure of our faces, I'd say. Give me that oil and we'll go next door for a bit of a sweat while those gentlemen sit and drink their wine. They'll be earning this moment of peace and quiet with their blood, soon enough.'

Ushered into the governor's private office by a brow-beaten clerk, Scaurus and his two companions found themselves face-to-face with a big, bearded man dressed in the full panoply of his office, beautifully sculpted bronze armour over a perfectly tailored fine woollen tunic. His beard was worn full, in the imperial fashion that no senator would dare to ignore no matter how straggly his own facial hair might be, but trimmed so neatly that it was evidently the subject of daily barbering.

'Ah, Tribune! Thank you for responding to my invitation so quickly! It's good to see you after all this time!'

To his credit Scaurus didn't miss a beat, stepping forward and saluting, while Marcus and his colleague Varus came to attention with impeccable precision.

'Now gentlemen, please relax yourselves. Tribune, you, Centurion Corvus and I are old comrades in one of the most brutal wars of recent times, so we'll not stand on ceremony. Steward, wine for my comrades and their colleague!

The four men stood in silence as the wine was served, and when each of them held a cup the governor raised his in a toast.

'Gentlemen – we drink to comrades no longer with us.'

They raised their cups and drank, Scaurus eyeing the senior

officer over the rim of his cup. The governor smiled back at him wryly.

'I know, Rutilius Scaurus, harsh words were exchanged the last time we met. It would be fair for you to say that I've not behaved well towards you and your men of late, but I've had enough time to reflect on the matter to see that I was perhaps . . . hasty in my actions. I'm not too great a man to ask for your forgiveness, and a new start to our relationship, if you're willing to allow a man to atone for his errors?'

Scaurus nodded, his expression still composed.

'Of course, Governor Albinus. Neither myself nor Centurion Corvus have ever been men to carry a grudge any further than necessary.'

The patrician smiled broadly and held out a hand for Scaurus to clasp.

'I'm so pleased. The terms under which we parted in Rome have troubled me more than a little. My bad temper might have caused so much harm, and so I was desperately relieved to discover that no harm had come to your wife and child, Centurion Corvus. I trust they're in good health?'

Marcus stared at him for a moment before replying, unable to find any trace of guile in the senator's question.

'My son is well enough, thank you Senator, although my wife died in childbirth quite recently.'

Albinus's face fell in what seemed to be genuine distress.

'I'm sorry to hear that. The life of a soldier is hard enough without having to bear that sort of pain.'

He looked at Varus, essaying a tentative smile of welcome.

'And this gentleman is . . . ?'

'A colleague from our recent campaign in the east, Senator. May I present Gaius Vibius Varus?'

Varus stepped forward and bowed respectfully, then took the hand that the governor offered.

'Glad to meet you, Vibius Varus. Any relation to the Varus who commanded the emperor's cavalry in the campaign against the Quadi?'

'My uncle Julius, Senator.'

Albinus nodded approvingly.

'I was only a junior tribune at the time, but your uncle led his men from the front, and had achieved a considerable fame by the time the barbarians had been put back in their place. He was also, I'm told, somewhat instrumental in helping to ensure that certain of the tribes that face us across the river remained firmly allied to Rome, as much through his somewhat muscular style of diplomacy as the application of gold. If you're only half the soldier he was then you've an illustrious career in front of you!'

He sipped his wine again, turning his attention back to Scaurus.

'So, Tribune, you're clearly the emperor's current favourite when it comes to performing the impossible, with your remarkable ability to summon the goddess Victoria to your side when all hope seems lost. I read your dispatch from Syria with great interest! And now here you are, with me none the wiser as to exactly what it is that your orders might hold.'

He fell quiet, waiting for the other man to fill the silence, but Scaurus's tight smile of apology was no less of a rebuttal despite his reply being couched in the most diplomatic terms.

'I'd be happy to share that information with you, Senator, if it weren't for the fact that our mutual colleague the imperial chamberlain has absolutely forbidden me to do so. I am to procure whatever assistance I believe I need from you and then to proceed with my mission.'

The governor's face took on a rueful smile.

'And my instructions are to provide you with any help you request of me and, in the most diplomatic of wording possible given the nature of the message from Chamberlain Cleander, to mind my own business!' He laughed tersely. 'Which order I will of course follow to the letter, being both a good servant of Rome and quite fond of my current rank. After all, this may not be much of a province in terms of size or population, but it's a mark of trust that I'm granted the command of two legions and twice as many auxiliary soldiers, even if half my command is across the water in Britannia. And so, Tribune, perhaps you'd better tell me what it is that you're going to need from me. If it's within my power then it shall be yours.'

Scaurus shrugged.

'In truth, Governor, there's not much that I need beyond rations and a day or two to prepare my men for what we have to do.'

Albinus raised a sceptical eyebrow.

'Really, Rutilius Scaurus? There's nothing I can do to help you with this task that you've been ordered to perform? You don't perhaps need me to write to one of the tribunes commanding the bridges across the Rhenus, to prepare the way for you? Or perhaps a guide with a good knowledge of the territories of the tribes who live on the far side of the water?'

The tribune remained silent, and after a moment Albinus laughed heartily, clapping a broad hand on his shoulder.

'Well done, Tribune! You're not going to give me any clues and nor should you!'

He raised his cup in salute.

'I wish you good fortune in your endeavour, gentlemen! And I look forward to your safe and successful return!'

Draining the last of his wine he placed the cup back on the table next to him.

'And now, if you'll excuse me, I have a dinner to be attending in the town. That's the problem with this role, there's always someone wanting some favour or other, and only too willing to subject me to a night of average food, barely acceptable wine and their appalling poetry! I'll take my leave of you, gentlemen, but before you leave I suggest you finish the wine and listen to a briefing that I've asked my secretary to prepare for you. He collates all of the intelligence reports that we receive from the other side of the river, and some of it might be of relevance to your mission.'

'Attack me!'

Lupus was panting from the exertion of the exercises that Arminius was putting him through, the same routines that the

German enforced every evening regardless of the weather or conditions underfoot. Lunging once more with his spear, thrusting the point forward as if stabbing at an enemy, he gasped as his mentor stepped inside the weapon's reach, flicking out a foot and whipping it behind his leading leg to trip him, sending him sprawling headlong across the grassy riverside field that Arminius had selected for that evening's practice ground.

A month before the boy would have lain where he fell, the wind knocked out of him, but the German's continual imposition of trips and falls on him had wrought a change in his resilience, not just in terms of stamina but his ability to ride each tumble and come back fighting. Knowing what was expected of him the young Briton rolled, coming to his feet and springing forward with the spear's wood and leather protected head outstretched, forcing Arminius to dance away with a smile.

'Better! Now we'll practise the parry!'

Making the most of the momentary breather, while the slave fetched his own weapon, Lupus looked glumly down at the mud that sullied his tunic and which would need to be washed off if it were to pass muster at Dubnus's daily inspection of his kit.

'Arminius! We've been practising lunges, underhand stances, overhand stances, parries and falls for a month now! When am I going to do some fighting!'

The German shrugged, positioning himself ready to parry the boy's attacks.

'When your lunges, underhand stances, overhand stances, parries and falls are all second nature, that's when. Now lunge at me and I'll show you how it's done once more. And this time let's make it a bit more interesting, shall we? If you can get a thrust of your framea past my guard, and hit my body without taking more than one step forward, then I'll polish the tribune's boots tonight rather than making you do it!'

The three officers stepped out into the torchlit street outside the governor's residence an hour later, sentries on either side of the residence's main door snapping to attention. Scaurus looked back up at the building with a shake of his head, then turned to his companions with a smile.

'That must have been a little confusing for you, Vibius Varus, so you're to be congratulated on the fact that you managed to keep a straight face while the governor was seeking forgiveness so very fulsomely.'

The younger man shrugged.

'I have to admit that I'm used to that sort of thing, Tribune. My father used to take me with him when he greeted his clients, and to the senate on occasion, and I soon learned to differentiate between his friends and those people who just wanted something from him. It's in the eyes, I find.'

'Yes. And for all that his words sounded sincere, my experience with that man has taught me that he's dangerous when it comes to bearing a grudge. Although the intelligence he provided us with seemed straightforward enough.'

With Albinus's departure his secretary had entered the room, bowed to the officers and unrolled a map of the province, pointing first at the city's location on the river's western bank, and then at a point sixty miles or so to the north. A slight figure with receding hair, he had conducted the briefing with the diffident air of a man who was permanently on the verge of an apology for his own shortcomings, looking for the most part at the map rather than the men to whom he was talking.

'This is a map of the province, sirs, and the land to the east of the river Rhenus. We're here, in Claudius's Colony, and the fortress further downriver to the north is Vetera, which houses the Thirtieth Ulpian Victorious. Together with the First Minervia at Fortress Bonna to our south, the two legions constitute a primary military strength of twenty cohorts at their full establishment which, along with their auxiliary cohorts of which there are eighteen, and cavalry wings, of which there are seven, form the army of Germania Inferior with a combined military establishment of almost thirty thousand men. Although in truth it's a good deal less than that now, with a dozen cohorts having been detached to help deal with a rebellion in

Britannia that took place a few years ago. Most of a legion was lost, apparently.'

He'd looked up at the three officers with a tentative smile.

'But of course there's no threat from the tribes here these days, not really. Poor agricultural methods and the resulting lack of food keeps their population limited, and their relative poverty means that their weapons and armour will always be hugely inferior to ours, as is their military organisation. Their only tactics are the ambush and the massed charge, so we can usually outwit their tactical naivety, and they've never really managed to bond politically at any level above that of the tribe, which means that they find it impossible to band together and fight us as one people. It took a great leader like Arminius on one side and a lawyer like Varus on the other to put together the Varian disaster. Begging your pardon, Centurion.'

The younger man's smile had been reassuring, if a trifle frosty, wrapped around an answer he was clearly practised in delivering.

'Publius Quinctilius Varus was an extremely distant relation, and so far back in family history that I might as well claim descent from the Divine Julius. Please do continue.'

The secretary had bowed slightly with a look of relief.

'And so, unable to compete with Rome militarily, they're reduced to fighting the occasional war between themselves, usually with some form of encouragement from ourselves, as whatever weakens any one of them obviously makes us stronger. The local tribes have all got so used to trading with us that their brief and costly moment of glory in the days of the divine Augustus is long forgotten, and there's no pressure on them from the east, which means they've no pressing need to get across the river. Add to that the fact that a good deal of the farming labour in Gaul comes from the tribes through emigration, which keeps their numbers down and brings money back over the river, and you can see that the province is in no real danger of attack any time soon. Not unless some strange combination of their idiocy and our own stupidity sets off a local rebellion.'

He'd pointed to the land on the far side of the Rhine from the city, sketching a circle with his finger.

'Not that it's likely that such a thing could happen here, mind you. This land is occupied by the Marsi tribe. There's no problem there, they've been clients of the empire since long before I worked for my first governor fifteen years ago. To the north of them, however . . .'

His finger had moved to a section of the map bounded on the south by a range of hills that separated a river's plain from the Marsi's territory to the south.

'This land has been settled by the Bructeri tribe, on either side of the river Lupia, for a hundred years or so. They used to live on better land, further to the north, but after the revolt of the Batavians and their allies in the Year of the Four Emperors, and the loss of the best part of two legions to the rebel tribes whose strength included the Bructeri, it was only a matter of time before we found a way to take our revenge. In the event it seems that a particularly cunning governor called Titus Vestricius Spurinna managed to foment a dispute between them and two neighbouring tribes, the Chamavi and the Angrivarii. Given a quiet nod and a wink from Rome, they allied and made a swift and decisive war on the Bructeri, forcing them off their traditional lands and almost annihilating the tribe's people. They got the Bructeri's prime land and Vestricius Spurinna cemented his place in history with a triumphal statue at the suggestion of a grateful emperor, which meant that everyone was happy with the exception of the Bructeri themselves. And given that sixty thousand of their population were slaughtered, with Roman observers to ensure "fair play", it's no wonder that they still harbour a sense of grievance towards us. I wouldn't say they're on the verge of rebellion, but they're certainly no friends of ours, or the other tribes. And that works well, I'd say. The worst possible thing we could face would be a united German people.'

He had looked up from the map at his audience with a thoughtful expression.

'The situation is made more interesting by the presence among

the Bructeri of a priestess by the name of Gerhild, a healer with
the ability to foretell events which are yet to occur, apparently.'
He sniffed, his expression clearly sceptical. 'They seem to regard
her as the living embodiment of the "wise virgin" Veleda, a seer
whose every word was sacred to the tribe in the emperor Nero's
day. Veleda foretold that the Bructeri would go to war against
Rome alongside the Batavians, and would win mighty victories,
and so they set about proving her right . . . in the short term at
least. As I said, two legions were ripped to pieces and another
two turned to the rebel cause, although in the longer term Nero's
eventual successor Vespasian made them all regret the day they
set their standards against the empire by sending an army of
nine legions to rather forcibly point out the error of their ways.'

'And this Veleda, what happened to her?'

The secretary had looked up at Marcus with a steady gaze.

'The new emperor was a merciful man, Centurion, and more
to the point he was also politically astute. He allowed to her to
remain free until six years later, when she was offered asylum
from her own people who, it seems, were less than impressed by
her decision to espouse the cause of a king with distinct leanings
to Rome. As to where this woman Gerhild dwells now, I suspect
that the imperial intelligence service would part with a good-sized
sum in gold to know the answer to that very question.'

He had chuckled mirthlessly.

'Yes, I'd guess that they'd very much like to get their hands
on her. The men who govern this mighty empire may be many
things, but none of them are foolish enough to ignore the lessons
of the past.'

'Two more of these, eh?'

The tavern keeper nodded curtly, slopping more beer into the
beakers that Sanga had slapped down on the counter before him.
Shooting a glance at the soldier's younger companion he then
spoke to Sanga in the same rough Latin that the Tungrians, along
with almost every other legionary and auxiliary on the empire's
borders, spoke. The soldiers had been sent into the city with a

specific task that same evening, but their initial enthusiasm for the opportunity to consume the local brew had swiftly worn off in the light of its watery consistency and the lack of any other attractions to be found.

'Ain't seen you two in here before.'

Sanga nodded curtly at him.

'That's the truth.'

He dropped a coin into the barman's open hand and turned away with the beers, winking at his friend as the Dacian sank the first third of his beer in a single swallow.

'Don't you ever get tired of that stuff?'

Saratos shrugged.

'Is not wine. So I like.'

His friend took a swig of his own drink, grimacing at the taste.

'It's not really beer either. And I was just starting to get a taste for that red stuff.'

They both drank again, looking around the tavern with the jaundiced attitudes of men who had drunk in establishments both far better and much worse.

'And there's no women I'd touch with yours, never mind my own. See her?'

The Dacian looked across the room at one of the serving girls.

'She not bad.'

'Not bad?' His friend shook his head in amazement. 'You've been away from women too long. Her body's covered in all these red marks, see? And do you know why that is?'

Saratos raised a knowing eyebrow.

'Because she been fended off with spears by all men? Like Morban say, old ones still old ones.'

Sanga drained his mug, shooting his comrade a dirty look.

'Off you go then, your turn to get them. And ask him the question, eh?'

The muscular soldier shrugged, drank down the rest of his own mug and stood, stretching and winking to the serving girl. Walking across the tavern he ignored the stares of the establishment's other clients and put the empties in front of the landlord.

'Is two more.'

Filling the first of the mugs the taverner raised a speculative eyebrow at his new customer.

'Thracian?'

'I Dacian.'

His pronouncement was met with a blank-faced nod that spoke volumes for the other man's lack of interest in imperial geography.

'Where you in from then?'

'Is south of here.'

'Hah! Isn't everything!' The taverner grinned, displaying an array of untidy teeth. 'An' where you going?

'Is my business.' He smiled and spread his hands in a semblance of apology. 'No offence.'

The second mug filled, the barman held out his hand, wrapping his fingers around the proffered coin and looking back at Saratos with a faint smile.

'No skin off my dick, soldier, just making conversation. But I'll do you a favour, since you were civil. See those three by the door?'

Saratos nodded, keeping his attention fixed on the barman to avoid giving the men in question any clue that they were under discussion.

'Already seen. Purse boys?'

'You've got it. A soldier comes in here, sinks too many beakers of this stuff and finds his wits addled by the time he leaves. And then he finds himself face down in the gutter, with a sore head and his money stolen.'

He recoiled minutely at the Dacian's wolfish smile.

'We be careful. And I thank.' He turned back to where Sanga was sitting waiting, then shrugged and turned back. 'You help me, perhaps I help you. We looking for guide, man who knows lands across river. You know anyone, we got coin for you. We here tomorrow night.'

He walked steadily back across the tavern, depositing Sanga's beer in front of him and sitting, his lopsided grin enough to raise his friend's eyebrows.

'Is done.'

The Briton nodded.

'Good. Now perhaps we can stop drinking this watery piss and get our heads down.' Saratos smiled at him over the rim of his mug. 'What?'

'We got job to do on way back to barrack. Is service to people of city.'

The next morning was clear, if chilly, with a wind that ruffled the edges of the two centurions' cloaks. Varus eyed Marcus's double layered and hooded garment enviously, rubbing at the wool of his own with a disappointed expression as they trotted their horses south from the city.

'I can see that I'm going to have to make some adjustments to my equipment. What worked nicely enough in Syria seems somewhat inadequate here in the North, whereas your kit seems so much better suited . . .'

He paused for a moment, looking at the eagle-pommelled sword hanging at Marcus's side speculatively.

'Your weapons have always intrigued me too . . .'

He bit the end of the sentence off as if he already regretted the blurted statement. Marcus smiled knowingly.

'But you felt uncomfortable asking?'

The younger man looked down at his feet.

'One hears stories. Stories that a man hardly feels it's his place to query. After a while it just became a facet of our relationship, a question I was almost afraid to ask.'

Marcus shrugged, looking out across the river's iron-grey surface with a bleak expression.

'I try not to dwell on my past, Gaius. I've discovered the hard way that if a man spends too much time looking back, fate will find a way to trip him up when he's not concentrating on what's directly in front of him. And there are some parts of it that would be much better if they were never remembered again . . .'

He drew the gladius from its place on his right hip, reversing the weapon and handing it across the gap between their mounts.

Varus took the sword by the eagle's head pommel, nodding his approval at the blade's fine balance and viciously sharp edge.

'An old weapon?'

'A family heirloom, to the best of my knowledge. My father – my birth father, not the man who raised me – left it to me when he died on the battlefield in Britannia. I only discovered the truth of my birth after his death.' He smiled through the memory, patting the long sword on his left side. 'And this blade you know only too well . . .'

The sword had been given to him by a Parthian prince on their parting, a magnificent blade forged with the finest Indian steel by the painstaking patience of a master craftsman, its metal heated and folded until the result was almost supernaturally flexible and graced with an edge that would cut clean through armour and bone when wielded with deadly intent.

'I won another one like it in battle not far from here, but the blade felt . . .' Marcus shook his head at the memory . . . 'Wrong, somehow, in my hands. As if its metal had become tainted by the evil purposes to which it had been turned. I had it melted down and reforged as several of these.'

He pulled a long bladed hunting knife from its place alongside the Parthian weapon, holding it up for Varus's inspection. The weapon's surface rippled with the same irregular pattern that graced the long sword, and Varus returned the gladius, taking the knife from him as the sword hissed back into its scabbard.

'It feels . . . well, like a knife. Nothing more, nothing less.'

Marcus nodded.

'The reforging seems to have cleansed it of whatever it was that I was sensing. I asked Tribune Scaurus to pray over the hot metal and invoke Our Lord's protection and banish any lingering evil, just to be sure. My wife . . .'

He fell silent as the memory of her words pulled cruelly at his emotions.

'My wife told me that evil lives in the hearts of men, and not in inanimate objects, but that if it made me feel comfortable I should seek Mithras's blessing on the weapons that resulted from the blade's destruction.'

A long silence drew out between the two men, Varus handing the knife back to his friend and turning to look out over the river.

'She was right.' The younger man turned back to find Marcus staring away into the distance, his eyes focused on the horizon as he spoke. 'Evil does live in the hearts of men. And no matter how many of them I kill there are always more.' He shook his head as if dismissing the reverie. 'And this won't get our business done. Come on, let's give these horses a little exercise.'

He kicked his mount from its gentle trot to a canter, and Varus followed suit, neither of them giving any notice to a pair of cavalrymen who were exercising their own mounts on the road behind them.

Lupus looked up from his polishing in annoyance as someone stepped into the barrack's doorway, dimming the sunlight he was using to see what he was doing, then sprang to his feet as he recognised the man standing in the opening.

'Grandfather!'

Putting the boot to one side he stood up, suddenly awkward in the presence of his father's father in a way that would have been unthinkable a year before. Morban, having raised the boy's father on something of an absentee basis, recognised the signs and was having nothing of it with his last surviving blood relative.

'Never mind all that bashfulness!' He advanced into the room and put his arms around the boy, ignoring the potential for embarrassment that the child was now a good six inches taller than he was. 'Come here and give me a decent hug, you young idiot!'

Surrendering to the embrace Lupus wondered what had brought on such welcome but uncharacteristic behaviour from a man whose usual approach to his grandfatherly duties had been sporadic at best, perhaps in recognition that Arminius was in truth more of a father to the boy than he could ever be.

'I know, barely a word for a week and then the silly old bastard comes calling for a hug with his grandson.' Morban held the boy at arm's length, his eyes misty with sentiment. 'Forgive me Lupus, I know I've not been the best at looking after you, but you've never gone short when there's been money needed to buy you whatever was called for.'

A coughing laugh of disbelief from outside the barracks made him frown, and he turned to shout back through the door.

'That's enough of that, if you don't want your entry in the burial club to mysteriously lose a zero the next time I update the records. Give me the knife.' A soldier appeared in the doorway and passed him something wrapped in a military blanket. 'Now piss off and get back to polishing your sword, or whatever it is you do when the barrack's empty for five minutes!'

He turned back to Lupus with a forced smile.

'Your old grandfather's heading north in an hour or so, going to some place called Novaesium where there's a bridge, although why we couldn't just use this one's beyond me. I'll be safe enough, since I'm going with Cotta, Lugos and that pair of hard cases who used to serve in my century, and your beloved Arminius, but I thought I'd come and say goodbye, well, you know . . .' He shuffled his feet awkwardly. 'Just in case. And to give you this.'

He proffered the bundle.

'The blanket will help to keep you warm at night, and the knife . . .' He waited while Lupus unwrapped the blanket from its contents and stared, eyes wide, at what he'd revealed. 'It's German, see, made by a master smith, the shopkeeper said. What do you think?'

Lupus drew the hunting knife from its scabbard, looking at its shining foot-long blade with an expression of amazement.

'It's just . . . I wanted you to have something to remember me by, if we don't see each other again.'

The boy sheathed the knife, then put his hands on Morban's shoulders with an expression that combined affection with a hard edge of conviction.

'We'll see each other again, Grandfather, I know it! You'll have

Lugos to stop anyone from harming you, and I'll be safe with Arminius! And you've got to come back, you're all the family I have left.'

The standard bearer nodded dumbly, his eyes glistening as he wrapped the boy up in another embrace.

When Sanga and Saratos walked into the tavern that evening their appearance sparked a good deal more interest than had been the case the previous night. The three men who had been pointed out by the barman were sitting in the same places as before, but where their previous demeanour had been one of apparent ease, all three were clearly in discomfort, and their bruised faces told the story of what had happened after they had followed the Tungrians out into the city's streets as eloquently as any account of that brief and unexpectedly violent encounter. Nodding with a lopsided grin at their astonishment, Sanga led his friend across the room to the place where the barman was waiting for them with one beaker of beer already drawn and the second half full.

'I wasn't sure if you two'd be back, given the way that lot have been talking about what they'll do to you if they ever get the chance.'

The veteran snorted derisively, dropping a coin on the counter.

'Get them a beer and tell them to let yesterday be in the past. Did you have any luck with our guide?'

The barman tipped his head at a roughly dressed man sitting in the tavern's corner, his glowering expression keeping the bar girls at bay with effortless ease, and Saratos turned back to the barman.

'Him? He not look too happy about be here?'

'Hah! Gunda? Happy?'

The innkeeper threw his head back and laughed in genuine amusement.

'There may come a day when you see that miserable bastard look anything other than flat out pissed off, but it isn't coming any time soon. If you're looking for someone who knows every path and hunting trail on the other side of the river then Gunda's the best man for the job. Go and have a word with him, then if you want to hire him we can discuss my commission.'

The two soldiers picked up their beers and strolled across to stand in front of the guide, who glanced up at them without any change to his vaguely disgusted expression. Heavily bearded, his hair a shaggy, greying mane tied up in a long plait, and with a seamed and lined face that told its own story of a life spent under the elements, his forehead bore a small but distinctive tattoo, a single rune in a blue so dark that it was almost purple. Dressed in a rough woollen tunic and leggings that had clearly seen better days, his feet, stuck out before him and crossed, were clad in heavy military hobnailed boots, which were by contrast in excellent condition. A long hunting knife and purse hung from his ornately decorated belt, and a stout wooden staff as tall as a man rested against the wall behind him, both of its ends shod in polished iron. When he spoke his voice belied the sour glare that was apparently his habitual expression, the words and phrasing hinting at a lively mind.

'So you're the men that are looking for a guide. A man that knows the land on the other side of the water like the skin on his own knuckles?'

Sanga nodded.

'A month's employment guaranteed at legion pay rates, and probably no more than a week's actual work.'

The guide shook his head in astonishment.

'A month's pay for a week's work? Where the fuck is it you want taking, across the Styx and past the three-headed dog?' He raised a hand. 'No, I don't need to know and for that much money I doubt you'd tell me. I'm going to need half up front.'

Saratos laughed.

'You get half money, then you not seen until we gone!'

Gunda grimaced up at him.

'I want half money because if you're willing to pay that much, and given the look of you two, there's a decent chance you've got something really stupid in mind. So I want some money to spend before I leave, get some decent clothes and some nice new arrows for my bow.'

Sanga shook his head, and was about to speak when the guide's stare switched to a point over the soldier's shoulder. An angry voice behind them rasped threateningly, its owner clearly intent on the infliction of pain.

'Well now, just like you said, here they are. They must either be very brave or very fucking stupid.'

The Tungrians turned, exchanging significant glances. Sanga smiled broadly at the half-dozen men arrayed between them and the tavern's door. Three of them were the footpads who had attempted to rob them the previous evening, their faces dark with emergent bruises from the two soldiers' fists and boots, one of them sporting a vicious pattern of hobnail marks across his cheek and broken nose. The other three were ubiquitous gang muscle, the same type they'd met in cities across the empire, their leader a red-headed bruiser with a long scar down through one eye socket, which held a milky, discoloured orb. A knife dangled in his right hand, and the men on either side were similarly equipped.

'You two pricks are in deep shit. You hurt my friends here last night, it seems, friends who routinely pay me a share of their takings in return for which they've been promised my protection in the event that anything unpleasant should happen to them. And you two appear to have happened to them rather painfully, don't you?'

He looked the two soldiers up and down, shrugging to demonstrate his lack of concern.

'You're clearly nasty bastards, which is why my friends here called for me before attempting their revenge. So, got anything to say before we break your arms and legs and cut you up?'

Sanga took a slow step forward, deliberately closing the gap between them with a deceptively languid, almost sleepy demeanour.

'You're probably a legion brat, aren't you? Son of a retired soldier? Well you know those men that used to come round and drink with your daddy once they were all retired? Hard men who'd fought in the German War, with those dead eyes that scared you so much. Well, him and me . . .' he gestured to the Dacian without ever taking his eyes off the thug, 'we're like that. Only worse. So here's a promise, thimble dick. You raise a blade to me, I will make you eat it. If I were you I'd fuck off now, before this gets ugly, eh?' He stared at the gang leader for a long moment, watching the doubt slowly creep into his eyes. 'Except you can't back down, can you? 'Cause if you do all the other bully boys'll—'

And without warning he was in motion, pivoting on one leg to smash a hobnailed boot into his opponent's kneecap, the redhead staggering backwards with a shriek of agony, clutching the brutalised joint with one hand and pointing at Sanga with the other.

'*Kill him!*'

His fellow thugs came forward at the Tungrians with the eager, empty-eyed aggression of men freed of any restraint, the three men who had been beaten the previous evening crowding in behind them in search of revenge, knives raised and glinting in the tavern's lamplight. Sanga snatched up a stool and swung it low, the wooden legs tangling with those of one of the gang members who was slower than his mates in stepping out of their arc. He fell to the floor, and before he could regain his footing the Briton swung the stool back, stunning him with a smashing blow of the heavy wooden seat. He stepped back from the fallen man with the stool held ready to strike again, his eyes glinting with calculation.

'Still want to fight?'

For a moment it looked as if the remaining thugs would give up their cause, but then the biggest of the men who had come seeking revenge stepped forward, raising his own blade.

'They only got lucky! We do this! Two on one! Get them down and shiv the cunts!'

Bolstered by his aggression the remaining men came forward in silence with their knives held ready to fight, only the harsh sound of their breathing and the scrape of their boot soles across the stone floor breaking the silence. Sanga exchanged a swift glance with his comrade, both men knowing that their opponents' more cautious approach spelt potential disaster for them. Shooting a look back at Gunda he saw that the guide remained in his relaxed position, seated with his back against the wall, the iron-shod staff now lying across his knees ready for use if the fight threatened to spill over him but otherwise showing no sign of making a move. The German shrugged at him, eliciting a throaty chuckle from the thug closest to Sanga.

'He knows to keep his fucking nose well out of it. No barbarian's going to lift a finger to help you!'

He took a deep breath, clearly steeling himself to attack, and the Tungrians nodded to each other, stepping forward and taking the initiative. Saratos feinted at the man closest to him and then, as the thug danced back behind his knife blade, swivelled to intercept his comrade's attack, grasping his outstretched knife hand and dragging the man's arm down onto his sharply raised knee. The elbow broke with a sickening crunch of splintered bone, and with a howl of agony the crippled thief reeled out of the fight with his right arm flopping uselessly, leaving the Dacian one on one with the other man, whose ferocious grin had been replaced by a look of consternation.

Beside him Sanga simply stepped forward and shot a vicious straight punch into the closer of his assailants' faces grinning savagely as the other man's nose popped in a spray of blood, but as he stepped in again and pulled his fist back to smash deep into the thug's belly, he tripped over a misaligned flagstone and staggered forward into the reeling bruiser's arms. The last of the robbers saw his chance and slammed a vicious punch into his kidneys, his comrade wrapping brawny arms around Sanga's body and momentarily pinioning him, roaring a blood-flecked command at his mate.

'*Do him!*'

Casting about him, the other man grabbed a discarded knife from the floor, straightening up and stepping close to the helpless soldier with a snarl, raising the blade toward his throat. Sanga flexed his powerful shoulders, but the thug's grasp was vice-like. Frantically struggling as the knife-wielding thief stepped in behind him, he launched a crunching headbutt into his captor's damaged face, but the other man gritted his teeth against the pain and stood firm. His mate put the blade against the Tungrian's throat and pulled his head back with a handful of hair, snarling in Sanga's ear as his arm tensed to rip the sharp iron through windpipe and veins.

'Time for you to—'

Then, with a distinct thud of wood on bone, and a startled grunt of pain, his grip on the Briton's hair relaxed, and the knife clattered to the floor. Grinning ferociously at his would-be captor the soldier pulled his head back again and butted the thief once more, and again, further smashing his nose. Ramming his fists up across the staggering man's chest, he crossed his arms and then forced them inexorably apart to break the hold that had rendered him temporarily helpless. As the thief staggered backwards his would-be victim delivered a single kick to his groin that doubled him over, vomiting across the floor with the sudden shooting pain. He turned to deal with his other assailant, only to find him slumped face down on the stone floor, unconscious.

A grunt of pain announced Saratos's despatch of the last of the thugs, sending him sprawling across a table that promptly collapsed under his weight, his chin striking the bench behind it hard and snapping shut on his tongue. Those of the thugs who could still walk retreated haltingly toward the door clutching their injuries, their leader limping on his good leg and shaking a fist at Sanga.

'You've not seen the last of us, you bastards!'

The soldier bent and retrieved a knife from the floor, raising it in warning.

'You're still here when I've had a word with our new guide there then I'll make good on that threat to make you eat this. Your choice.'

He winked at Saratos and then turned back to the guide, who was sitting in the same place as if he'd never moved, nodding his appreciation.

'I reckon you and that staff just about saved my life.'

Gunda shrugged.

'No-one calls me barbarian and walks away clean. Now, half up front?'

The veteran grinned at him.

'Half up front.'

4

'I thought you might want to know, Governor . . .'

Albinus replied without looking up from the paperwork laid out before him, illuminated by the flickering light of half a dozen lamps.

'Yes?'

The single word was laced with acid, a state of affairs with which the governor's long-suffering secretary had become at first accustomed and then reluctantly resigned. He advanced into the office from his place in the doorway, adopting the slightly supplicatory stance that experience had taught him tended to defuse the cutting edge of his master's temper.

'I thought you might want to know that the Tungrians are on the move, Governor. From the look of their preparations I would expect them to march for Novaesium early tomorrow.'

Albinus looked up at him with a calculating expression.

'Novaesium? Why Novaesium? Why not just cross the river here?'

The other man inclined his head in agreement.

'Indeed sir, I find myself in total agreement with you, if . . .'

The governor's temper was as volatile as ever, his voice rising as he scowled at the hapless secretary.

'*If?* If bloody *what*, you half-wit? Stop talking in your damned riddles and get to the point!'

The secretary winced, bowing slightly once more.

'If your colleague Tribune Scaurus has been charged with a task that requires him to engage with the Marsi tribe, then your surmise would be entirely correct. If, however, his mission requires him to enter Bructeri territory, perhaps to perform some kind of abduction . . .'

Albinus nodded slowly.

'In that case he'd be far better off crossing further north.'

'Indeed, Governor.'

'At Novaesium, eh? Straight into Bructeri territory, more or less, and the minimum distance to be travelled to the tribal capital.'

He looked up knowingly.

'You think they've been ordered to bring this priestess woman back with them, don't you?'

The secretary allowed himself the merest hint of a shrug. Anything more expressive would probably have been deemed disrespectful.

'It was my suspicion, Governor, especially as most of the questions that Tribune Scaurus and his officers asked were about the Bructeri, but . . .'

'But what? Spit it out, man!'

'Well sir, it's just that most of their questions seemed to focus on the Bructeri capital. And the tribal treasury.'

Albinus sat back with a frown.

'The treasury? Why the bloody treasury? Surely Scaurus has all the gold he could ever . . .'

He fell silent, staring hard at the far wall, then slapped his hand down on the desk before him with a loud crack that made the other man flinch.

'Unless the young bastard has already spent his way through the gold he stole from me! Surely he couldn't be planning to raid the Bructeri king's personal fortune?'

His servant nodded slowly.

'A deduction of some perception, Governor.'

'Gods below, man!' Albinus was out of his chair, aghast at the thought. 'You think he intends to raid the treasury, and then make his escape with the Bructeri seer in the resulting chaos? It'd be enough to spark a full-scale war! The other tribes would be certain to rally to the Bructeri under that sort of provocation!'

The secretary shrugged again, more confidently this time.

'The idea you postulate would seem to be a credible modus operandi for such a venture. Perhaps this man Scaurus's instructions from Rome are simply to neutralise the potential for trouble that exists in the form of this Bructeri seer? An assassination, perhaps? And it could well be that he's come to the conclusion that he might as well turn some profit from the whole thing. After all, given your belief that he uses the gold that he appropriated—'

'Stole, more like!'

The secretary bowed his acquiescence with his master's prejudice against Scaurus and his men.

'Indeed, governor . . . if he uses the gold he *stole* to facilitate his clandestine activities against the throne, why wouldn't he look to replenish his purse, given the opportunity?'

Albinus sat back in his chair, nodding slowly as a hard smile spread over his face.

'In which case young Scaurus could fairly be deemed to have strayed just a little too far from his brief for me to ignore the likely results. After all, the Bructeri aren't going to have to look very far to find a culprit for the theft, are they? And the last thing I can afford to countenance is for some wild stunt carried out in the emperor's name to set the frontier alight again.' He looked up with a look that the secretary had come to recognise as intended to appear decisive. 'No, I can see that I'm going to have to take some action before this scheme of Scaurus's gets out of hand. Send for Decurion Dolfus.'

The secretary bowed and turned away to do his master's bidding.

'Immediately, Governor.'

'You want me to guide you into the land of the Bructeri?'

Scaurus nodded at the scout.

'My mission requires me to put boots on the tribe's soil, if only for a short time. I don't expect to be doing any actual fighting, this is purely an in and out, three days at most and all of those with my detachment hidden deep in the forest. Is that a problem, Gunda?'

The German pointed to the rune tattooed onto the flesh of his forehead.

'Do you see this, Roman? Do you imagine I wear it on my skin for decoration?'

The tribune sat back in his chair.

'I was wondering.'

'It is my tribe's symbol for a man who has been condemned to the status of *wargaz*. Or, in your language, outlaw. I am banished from my tribe's homeland under pain of death, to be administered by the priests of Wodanaz, if I am found anywhere within the borders.'

He stared at Scaurus for a long moment.

'Let me guess. Your tribe being the Bructeri, right?'

'Correct. So I'm hardly likely to want to go anywhere near their lands. I'm sorry, but the role of guide you're offering is not one—'

'How much?'

Gunda shook his head.

'You seem not to be listening. I cannot do this.'

Scaurus smiled.

'You clearly can. What you cannot afford is to be *caught* doing it. Or, from the sound of it, if you are caught, to remain alive for long enough that your estranged tribe's priests get the chance to practice their sacrificial arts upon you. We've established that you have exactly the knowledge that I will need to lead a successful foray into Bructeri territory, the only question now is how much money it will take to convince you that the risk of being caught is outweighed by the reward to be gained for what, with your assistance, will be a fairly minimal level of risk.'

The German looked at him for a moment.

'You're serious. Very well . . . three gold aureii.'

Scaurus smiled at him.

'Three? Let's make it four. A hundred denarii is a nice round number, isn't it?

Gunda looked up at the office's roof in evident disbelief, then back at the officer.

'Half now—'

'One coin now, to let you buy whatever you need, the rest payable the moment that our boots are on Bructeri soil. If you do end up having to take a knife to your own throat at least you'll have had the pleasure of possessing more gold than you've ever seen before in your life, eh?'

The Tungrians marched from the city shortly after dawn, Tribune Scaurus returning the gate sentries' salutes as his party exited the fortress and headed up the road to the north. The river's mist was still lying in patches across the countryside, thick curtains of vapour reducing visibility to almost nothing before another moment's march brought the column back into the morning's bright sunshine as they marched north towards Novaesium, thirty miles to the north.

After only half an hour's march, Gunda nodded to Scaurus, pointing to a paved track that ran away from the main road towards the river to their east.

'That's the way.'

Scaurus looked up and down the main road to north and south, confirming that they were unobserved before nodding his consent. The German led them down the narrow track, which ran east to the Rhenus and then turned north to follow the river's bank with heavy forest on the road's left-hand side, another hour's progress taking them to the spot he had decided would best suit Scaurus's plan. Turning off the track where it deviated away from the river to avoid a rocky outcrop, he took them through a belt of trees that would screen them from the path, and on down to the Rhenus. A narrow strip of shingle beach ran along the river's gently curving west bank, the river, like the track along which they had come, devoid of traffic.

'Perfect.'

Scaurus called his centurions to him.

'Get your men settled down. I don't want anyone visible from either the river or the far bank. And have them ready to move at short notice, no taking boots off or opening packs. We'll be away from here soon enough.'

Having trailed the Tungrians from the city at a distance, walking their horses on the road's grassy verge to prevent any sound from alerting their unsuspecting quarry, Dolfus and his men had shared mystified looks as the Tungrians had diverted onto the patrol road that paralleled the river's course.

Watching from the cover of the forest's edge, as the detachment disappeared into the shelter of the trees that separated road from river, the decurion shook his head in bemusement.

'Why stop there? And why in the name of all the gods are they on this road at all, it must be getting on for half the distance again, having to follow every bend in the river?' A thought struck him. 'Unless . . .'

He got to his feet, gesturing to his men to hold position.

'Stay here. If anyone comes along you're just getting a bit of sun while I go for a crap in the woods, right?'

He sprinted across the road and into the trees on the far side, instinctively following the slight rise of the ground until he judged that he'd reached the highest point possible. Gripping the lowest branch of a sturdy-looking oak he hauled himself up into the foliage, climbing nimbly upwards until he was high in the canopy. Judging that the higher branches were unlikely to take his weight he stopped climbing and inched out until he could see through the leaves, revealing a spectacular view across the river's valley, the Rhenus visible for miles to either side. Staring out over the trees he smiled, shaking his head slowly in appreciation of his quarry's audacity, as he realised what it was he was seeing moving slowly through the river's mist.

'You crafty bastards . . .'

Lowering himself carefully to the ground he ran back down the hill, hurdling fallen trees and kicking up leaves, stopping in front of his men breathing hard from the exertion.

'You said that the two young gentlemen rode down to the dockyard yesterday. Tell me what happened again.'

The man who had tailed Marcus and Varus south from the city the previous day shrugged.

'When they got there they just walked along the dockside like two men out for a stroll. One of the ship's captains hailed them and they had a few words, but that was all. After that they did a round of the ship shed like they were on an outing and then made their way back to the barrack. Like I said at the time, Decurion, nothing out of the ordinary.'

'And when they came back from the port?'

The trooper shrugged again.

'I watched their barrack all day from the empty one next to it. They stayed in it all afternoon, then went and joined their tribune for a couple of hours. Eventually a pair of soldiers delivered a message of some sort and the officers went back to their own barracks.'

Dolfus stared at him for a moment.

'These messengers. Were they about the same height and build as the young gentlemen in question?'

The man he'd set to watch Marcus and Varus frowned in concentration.

'Yes, I'd say they were.'

Dolfus sank to the ground and lay on his back looking up at the clouds towering up into the sky above him.

'So while they're down at the docks someone knocks a hole in the wall between the officers' quarters and the room next to it. Then when they get back from their outing they switch uniforms with a pair of soldiers who match them for size and while the decoys held your attention they were free to climb through the hole into the barrack next door and then go wherever they wanted as common soldiers. Clever. What better way to have a discussion that they didn't want witnessed?'

He got back onto his feet.

'You two, stay with the horses, you two come with me! Quietly now!'

The decurion eased into the cover of the trees, weaving through their thick trunks with his accomplices close behind. Something made him look over his shoulder, and he ducked into the cover of the nearest oak, gesticulating frantically to his comrades to do the same. The morning sunlight's mist-hazed brilliance dimmed a little as a wall of wood slid past their hiding place, close enough for the lapping of the river's water against the ship's tarred side to be audible. Raising his head the decurion watched as the vessel passed their hiding place barely twenty paces distant, making out the name painted on her stern.

'*Mars.*' He looked at the man crouching next to him. 'Was that . . . ?'

The trooper nodded, understanding dawning on him.

'The name of the ship whose captain had a good old chat with those two centurions? Looks like it.'

The decurion nodded to himself, his lips twisting in wry admiration.

'It seems that our master has somewhat underestimated the resourcefulness of these Tungrians. Come on, let's get a bit closer, and see if we can see or hear anything to reduce the sting of being left sitting here like fools while they sail away to who knows where.'

As Arminius stared in the direction that Scaurus was pointing he saw a shape resolve itself out of the mist. Rendered ghostly by the drifting vapour, a warship was sailing slowly down the river's western bank, her tiered oars furled up against her sides as the river's current pushed her gently downstream.

'This is what we're waiting for?'

Scaurus nodded without taking his eyes off the vessel.

'That's our ride. This, my friend, is where we simply vanish off the map. Centurion Varus!'

The young aristocrat rose from the cover of the trees and made his way down to the river's bank, waving a hand at the oncoming vessel, which was now close enough for her identity to be clear. Varus lowered his hand as the ship coasted towards him on the river's current, turning back to Scaurus with a broad grin.

'That's my cousin alright, see him in the bows? The man with the red hair?'

Standing on the vessel's prow, the officer in question clearly had a hands-on approach to the task of command, bellowing orders back to the men on the steering oars in a manner that left little doubt as to who was in control of the vessel. His voice reached them across the water as he shouted another command over his shoulder.

'Oars!'

The rowers responded with commendable speed and precision, dropping their wooden blades from their furled position to sit level with the river's glassy surface.

'Ready . . .'

The blades rotated, ready for the next order.

'Back! Water!'

With the perfect synchronisation of long practice the oarsmen dipped their blades into the river as one, executing a series of swift, efficient strokes that took the way off the vessel and left her drifting towards the bank at a slow walking pace.

The commander roared another order, reinforcing it with a swift pointing hand gesture.

'Stern anchor!'

The ship drifted a dozen paces and then stopped, held in place by her anchor. Her commander turned to the waiting Tungrians, shouting a greeting down to Varus.

'You see Gaius? I told you I wouldn't let you down! Have your men pull us in as close as possible and let's get you fellows aboard!'

The Tungrians' axemen nudged each other and guffawed in amusement at his patrician accent, but hurried to grab the ropes thrown ashore as their chosen man Angar bellowed orders and imprecations at them, swiftly dragging the ship in towards the bank until she touched bottom, close enough for boarding ladders to be lowered into the shallow water. The captain looked down at the detachment as they pondered the muddy water between ship and shore.

'Come on then you men, we haven't got all blasted day!'

Scaurus went first, wading into the river and climbing up the closest ladder, to be greeted by the ship's commander as he climbed over the side.

'Tribune Scaurus, it's good to meet you after what I heard about your exploits in the east from young Gaius here when I met him in the city last night!'

Scaurus stood bemused as his hand was shaken vigorously by the big man.

'The pleasure is mine, Prefect. And you have my thanks for entertaining this somewhat unorthodox diversion from your usual routine.'

The naval officer barked out a laugh.

'Any diversion is welcome, Tribune! There are only so many times a man can sail up and down this blasted river before ennui sets in, I can assure you of that! The most excitement we've had in the last month was sighting a deer on the far bank last week, and even that came to nothing when we missed the bloody thing with both bolt throwers! Ah, here's young Gaius now!'

He greeted his cousin over the ship's side with a bear hug, leaving Varus red-faced.

'Here he is! The black sheep of the family come good, and in no small part thanks to you, Tribune, giving him the chance to prove that he's worthy of the family name! Any friend of my cousin's is a friend of mine, eh? So let's get these men of yours off the bank and be about our business, shall we?'

With the detachment aboard the vessel he ordered the crew to pull up the anchor and cast off from the shore, turning back to Scaurus once the *Mars* was underway down the river.

'So tell me, Tribune, where exactly is it that you want putting ashore?'

Scaurus gestured to Gunda, who was standing by the ship's rail with an even more lugubrious expression than usual.

'I make a point of finding people who know the land intimately, wherever it is that my orders take me, and my native scout there says he knows the perfect place.'

He beckoned Gunda across to join them, the prefect calling for his pilot, and once the three men were in animated discussion as to the location the German had in mind, sidled away to join his officers at the vessel's stern rail.

'Well then, gentlemen?'

Dubnus shook his head, his expression rueful.

'I saw nothing, Tribune. My colleague here, on the other hand . . .'

Qadir turned away from the receding beach with his customary gentle smile.

'One man that I saw for certain, and enough movement besides to indicate another one or perhaps two with a little more skill at remaining concealed, if not sufficient.'

Scaurus raised an eyebrow at Dubnus.

'Which just goes to show that all those years squinting into beakers in dimly lit taverns weren't necessarily your best choice, eh Dubnus? Did you make out any detail, Centurion?'

Qadir shook his head.

'Almost nothing, Tribune. Perhaps a momentary glint of sun on armour, but my eyes might have deceived me. I could not swear an oath on the matter.'

Scaurus looked at Marcus, who was standing in silence alongside his colleagues.

'So it looks as if your suspicion that you were followed yesterday was well founded, and a good thing that you chose not to talk openly with your cousin about our needs but met him when you weren't under observation. It would also appear as if our old friend Decimus Clodius Albinus does indeed still secretly harbour ambitions of clipping our wings.'

The younger man raised an eyebrow.

'It's hardly surprising, given the humiliations that his previous attempts to put you down have heaped upon him. It seems that those events have only served to fan the flame of his urge to see us dead and disgraced, and while we have to fend off his attempts time after time, he only has to enjoy sufficient good fortune to put the blade in just once. Perhaps this should be the last time he makes such an attempt . . .'

Scaurus raised an eyebrow, surprised at the vehemence in the statement given the younger man's apparent loss of vigour of recent days.

'You feel that strongly that he needs to die?'

Marcus looked out over the ship's rail at the dark, forested hills to the east.

'I'm the wrong person to ask, I'm afraid. My urge for justice has run its course, leaving me with nothing more than a feeling of emptiness at having been cursed with being the cause of so many deaths. I have killed enough men in pursuit of my revenge to know with absolute clarity that not one of them ever gave me any genuine satisfaction.' He sighed. 'At least not beyond the brief surge of joy to be had from spilling the blood of men who had done my family wrong. The only man I would raise a finger to kill in cold blood now is too well protected for it to be anything other than suicide, and I have a child to raise. Leaving him fatherless would be the final insult to my wife's memory.'

Scaurus put a hand on his shoulder.

'I understand, and I would never ask you to do such a thing. But it occurs to me that the only way to stop Senator Albinus from continually plotting my early death is to arrange for his own premature voyage across the river, and it sounds to me as if you agree.'

Marcus turned to face him, his face set in tired lines.

'Tribune, if you're asking me to condone a decision to kill the man, I can only repeat what I said before. He only has to enlist the services of Fortuna once, whereas we call upon her every time we cross paths with him. I think you know the answer to that question well enough yourself not to need me to provide it for you.'

*

'The governor was right. That man Scaurus *is* slipperier than a bag full of eels.'

Dolfus shook his head in disgust, watching as the naval vessel pulled away from the river's western bank and got underway, the rowers working to an efficient rhythm that propelled the *Mars* out into the river's channel, and away to the north at the speed of a cantering horse.

'And there's no way we can keep up with—'

He reached up and pulled the trooper next to him down into the cover of the fallen tree behind which they were hidden.

'Keep down you idiot! They've got Hamians with them, and those easterners have got eyes like hawks. And if they can see you then they can also put an arrow in you.'

He leaned back against the tree's rotting trunk with a thoughtful look.

'We'll have to let the governor know about this, and then get after them as best we can. You . . .' he pointed at the nearest of his men, 'ride back to the city and with the following message. Tell him that we saw them board a warship, the *Mars*, under the command of that red-haired lunatic that commands the local squadron and who presumably has some sort of connection with one their officers given the party trick they pulled on us yesterday to get some time with him unobserved. They were last seen heading north, and likely to get off the ship on the other side of the river, and that's all we know. We'll pursue, but that bloody ship can sail downstream a good deal faster than the horses can manage for any length of time, so we've effectively been left for dead. We'll meet you at Novaesium with whatever orders he gives you. Go!'

The trooper slithered away across the forest floor, and Dolfus lifted himself to squint over the tree's bole, watching as the warship vanished around the river's next bend.

'They've fooled us alright, almost as if their tribune suspected that they might be followed.' He shook his head with a sour expression. 'Right, let's get after them. Nice and easy, mind you, there's no point exhausting the horses if we've no chance of catching them. They've got the jump on us for the time being, but if we play this right we can still find out what they're up to.'

'There.'

The prefect followed Gunda's pointing hand and nodded his agreement.

'Couldn't have picked it better myself. A nice little anchorage on the outside of the bend where the current keeps the water deep close in to the bank. Oars!'

He marched back down the ship's length barking orders, the rowers swiftly killing the vessel's way to leave it drifting slowly into the bank's leafy canopy. Scaurus glanced over at the western bank, looking for any sign that they were observed.

'Your guide has chosen well, Tribune. The road veers away from the river's western bank to avoid that outcrop of rock, and those cavalrymen who were following us will be miles behind us.'

The tribune nodded at Qadir's words, turning to Dubnus.

'Take them ashore, Centurion, and give me a perimeter for fifty paces in all directions, archers leading. The rules of engagement are to be as we agreed – if anything moves, we kill it.'

The Briton nodded and turned away, leading the detachment down the hastily lowered boarding ladders and splashing through the thigh-deep water to lead them away into the forest's gloom. Pausing a dozen paces from the bank he looked about him at their expectant faces.

'The Crescent, and just as we practised it. In pairs, keep your spacings and don't lose sight of the men to either side. Fifty paces and go to ground, watch and listen. Archers, if we're spotted and the man in question escapes we're most likely already dead, and our mission over before it begins. If you see a man outside bow range you wait for him to either come closer or go away. If there's more than one of them then you wait until they're so close that you can get them all. The rest of you are only there to protect the archers at this point in time, so go to ground, shut your mouths and keep them shut until you're relieved. Understood?'

The men gathered around him nodded confidently.

'Good. Don't fuck it up.'

He watched as they split into their predetermined groupings of archers and axemen, each pair heading away into the forest's shadows along their allocated bearings.

'All that practice seems to have borne fruit, I see? Perhaps now they can see the reason why you made them play that game so many times on the way north.'

He turned to find Marcus and Varus at his shoulder, the latter speaking softly as he watched the Tungrians disappear into the sun-dappled foliage. Dubnus nodded grimly.

'I think the game just turned serious, don't you? We looked at the map and said, "Yes, we can walk from the river into the heart of Bructeri territory," but it's not until you actually stand here on the ground that you realise just what a challenge we've set ourselves. We have no idea where we'll have to go to find this woman, but what we do know is that we'll have to walk all the way there through this. We'll just have to hope that the Bructeri king is keeping her close at hand and not in some remote hiding place fifty miles up the River Lupia.'

He waved a hand at the seemingly endless expanse of trees before them, directing a question to Varus.

'And when we've found her, and presuming that we can take her from her guards, we'll have to do it all over again to get back here, more than likely with tribesmen hard on our heels. Are you still pleased that you were so set on coming with us?'

Before he could answer, Scaurus climbed over the riverbank's crest and crouched next to his officers, watching in satisfaction as the detachment's men slowly moved out into the forest.

'Excellent. I see all that time spent drilling this little manoeuvre wasn't entirely wasted. Once we've got the perimeter cleared you can leave the Hamians on watch while turning your axes to a little bit of tree-felling for me before we head off into the unknown. Just a precaution, but I do like to make sure the ground's in my favour as much as possible.'

*

'Purpose of crossing?'

Cotta looked steadily at his interrogator with a slight smile. Having left the fortress without fanfare at dawn the previous day, it had taken his party the best part of two days to make the forty-mile journey to the bridge and its protective fortress at Novaesium.

'Trade.'

The legionary leaned forward, putting a hand on the hilt of his sword in a manner calculated to draw attention to the weapon.

'Trade, *sir.*'

Cotta's smile broadened.

'You're not a *sir* to me, sonny, I've already done my years. Left the army as a centurion, honourable discharge, handshake from the officers. You know, all that stuff you dream about when you've had a few.'

He turned his arm over to reveal the tattoo on his wrist, and the soldier's look of contempt switched to the men standing behind the veteran, the biggest of them holding the reins of a decidedly unhappy-looking mule.

'And this lot?'

The veteran waved an expressive arm at his immediate companions.

'This long-haired item is Arminius, my German slave and business partner. The big bastard holding the mule is his brother Lugos, born mute, the poor sod. The ugly fat one standing by the cart is my money man, and the two-nasty looking lumps behind him are Saratos, he's a Dacian, and a bit of a simpleton if the truth be told, and Sanga, who loves him like a son, which is why we tolerate his dim-witted ways and constant flatu—'

The soldier waved a hand to silence him.

'Enough! I asked you who they were, not for their fucking life stories! Stay here.'

The soldier turned away, beckoning his superior over.

'Traders, Chosen, asking for passage over to the far bank. Ex-army, or at least they say they are. This one says he was a centurion.'

The chosen man stalked across the road to stand face-to-face with Cotta, quickly summing up the veteran's confident stance and hard smile.

'So you're a trader, eh Centurion? You wouldn't be the first man to retire and reckon he can turn his local knowledge into profit. What are you trading then?'

The veteran shrugged.

'The usual rubbish. Coloured pottery, hunting knives, cheap jewellery, and wine, obviously. They can't get enough of that.'

The soldier nodded, familiar with the Germans' eagerness for Roman products.

'I've not seen you before. First time trading with the Bructeri?'

Cotta nodded equably.

'It is. Been dealing with the Marsi mostly 'til now, but I thought I'd broaden my horizons so to speak. After all, how hard can it be?'

The soldier leaned forward, tapping his nose significantly.

'I seen 'em come and go for years here, and most of them go out happy enough and come back a good deal less cheerful, or every now and then never come back at all. Drop the price of a few beers in my hand and I'll tell you why.'

Cotta nodded to Morban, and a coin appeared in the veteran standard bearer's hand with the dexterity of long practice. He dropped it onto the chosen man's open palm, and Cotta grinned encouragingly at the soldier.

'I was hoping you might be able to provide a fellow soldier with a tip or two.'

'Well . . .' The chosen man looked up at the sky for a moment, as if considering the words of what was undoubtedly a routine speech. 'Two things to remember. Firstly, they really don't like us, the Bructeri. Seems we fucked them over good and proper a hundred years ago or so, and they're not the types to forgive and forget. Not even a little bit, and not any of them. So any idea you've got about charming their women to buy pretty coloured cloth or tempting the young 'uns with a smart new knife is out the window. The more you try to get them on your side, the more they'll just tell you to fuck off and die. You need an angle to trade with these boys, and no mistake.'

'And . . . ?'

'And what?'

And what's the angle?'

The chosen man snorted derisively.

'How would I fucking know? You're the centurion!'

Morban nodded appreciatively at a fair point made well, while Cotta simply shrugged.

'So what's the other thing?'

'Try to avoid paying the bridge tax.'

Morban raised a disgusted eyebrow.

'The bridge tax.'

The chosen man nodded, clearly familiar with the hostile reaction of men asked to pay an unexpected tax simply for crossing a river.

'I'd have thought you'd be familiar with the idea, *if* you've been trading with the Marsi. By order of the Emperor, all trade between the province of Germania Inferior and the German tribes is to be taxed at a rate of one coin in twenty.' He leaned forward with a conspiratorial look to either side, as if to ensure that his next words were not overheard. 'We're not here to keep the long-haired bastards out, we're here to collect the Emperor's pocket money.'

'Five per cent?'

The soldier stuck out his chin pugnaciously.

'Ten per cent. Five going out and five coming back. We assess your goods going out, including the mule, the cart and those pretty swords you're all wearing, tax you five per cent of their value, then five per cent on the way back too. If you're lucky you can avoid paying on the cart and so on, since you clearly didn't buy them over there, but that only works if you don't get some bastard on duty. Someone like my officer. He'd tax the hole between your buttocks if he could work out its value.'

Morban's face went white.

'But that's . . .'

The chosen man turned to him with a smile.

'You must be the money man, given that face you're pulling. That's probably going to chew up a big piece of your profits? Seems that way to us too, what with all the unhappiness we get from the first-time traders we deal with when they get the good news.'

The standard bearer took a deep breath.

'So, you mentioned avoiding this . . . bridge tax?'

The soldier nodded.

'Two ways. Hire a boat . . .' He pointed to a rickety-looking vessel waiting by the river's bank. 'Mind you, they know just how much to charge, and given that you can't use the bridge to get back if you didn't pay to use it to cross over, they can get downright greedy when the time comes for the return trip.'

'Or?'

A slow smile spread across the chosen man's face.

'Seems your luck's in, what with you being one of the lads, and given my officer's away spending his salary on a spot of sausage hiding, you can pay the unofficial tax, rather than give ten per cent of everything you have to the emperor. We'll write you up as having an empty waggon and nothing more than a few silvers to your name, say you were off to buy some skins to trade back this side of the river, and you can provide us with a nice little drink for our trouble.'

Morban nodded slowly, shooting Cotta an encouraging glance.

'That would seem to be the most . . . pragmatic way to go.'

The chosen man smiled even more broadly.

'I thought you might say that. Shall we call it three per cent?'

Having made slow but stealthy progress into the forest, covering four miles by Gunda's estimate, the Tungrians camped in the shelter of a hollow, posting sentries around the rim of the depression and settling down for the night beneath the cover of their cloaks after a meal of bread and dried meat washed down with sips of water from their bottles. Scaurus had finally revealed the nature of their mission into Bructeri territory while the detachment sat around him eating the bread and dried meat they had carried with them from the fortress, looking about him as he talked, taking the measure of their collective resolve.

"So it's simple. We find this woman, we deal with whoever's been set to guard her and we take her back to the river. The *Mars* will be back here and ready to collect us from tomorrow morning, and they'll stay on station right where they dropped us off yesterday until we come back with her, or until three days have passed. I think it's reasonable for them to assume that if we're not back after that long on the ground we either won't be coming back or we've decided to march out overland.'

One of the pioneers raised a hand, and the tribune smiled, shaking his head at Angar as the man bristled at such temerity.

'No Chosen, we're all risking our lives to attempt this abduction, any man has the right to ask any question he pleases. We're brothers in arms alone in a dangerous place, so only the most robust honesty will see us through this.'

Abashed, but encouraged by his commander's gesture of solidarity, the man voiced the question that Scaurus already knew was on every man's lips.

'This priestess, Tribune. Is she really a witch? Can she . . . ?'

'Can she cast spells on us? Turn us into forest animals, or rip our bodies apart with a wave of her hands? I very much doubt it. I—'

'Tribune?'

All heads turned to Gunda, who had raised his own hand, tentatively but with a clear need to speak.

'Gunda?'

Aware that his presence in the detachment's small and tight-knit world was barely tolerated by some of Scaurus's men, and striving to ignore the fact that both Dubnus and Angar wore expressions which promised great tribulation if his words went astray, the guide spoke slowly and carefully, raising his open hands to demonstrate that he meant no harm.

'Being of the Bructeri, before I was banished from this land, I can tell you something of Gerhild, if you will allow me to do so.'

Scaurus gestured for him to continue, and even Angar leaned forward to hear his words.

'Gerhild is no witch. She is simply . . .' He shook his head as he searched for the right Latin word, then nodded to himself. 'Good. She is a good person, and her gifts should be considered with that in mind.' He looked around the silent hollow, painfully aware that every man was hanging on his words. 'She has three gifts given to her by the goddess Hertha at her moment of birth. She can heal the sick, on occasion, with her touch and her words, not simply those who are physically ill but also those who are troubled in mind. She can influence the minds of men, although she rarely chooses to do so. And she dreams what is yet to come. She—'

'She sees the future?' Gunda raised a hand as if to still the outburst from Dubnus, and to his own surprise the Briton froze just as he was in the act of rising to voice his disquiet.

'She sees a little of the future, and only very rarely for herself, nearly always for others. And the gift is fickle. She might foretell the birth of a girl child accurately, but fail to see that the child's mother will die in childbirth, which has made her wary of using it. Such a gift can be a curse, it seems.'

Scaurus pinned Dubnus in his place with a piercing stare, standing up and taking his man's attention back from the scout.

'So she cannot see us coming, and she has no witch powers for us to fear.'

'No, Tribune, she does not.' Gunda shook his head obdurately. 'And even if she did, she is a child of Hertha, the earth goddess. She could no more take a life, anyone's life, than fly to the moon.'

The tribune nodded decisively.

'Good. And that, gentlemen, concludes this briefing. Those of you who didn't draw guard duty would be well advised to get some sleep. Tomorrow will be another long day.' He caught the scout's eye and gestured for the German to accompany him to the other side of their small camp. 'You seem to know this woman Gerhild rather better than I would have expected, given your long exile from the tribe?'

Gunda nodded, holding the Roman's stare.

'Every man in our tribe knows of her, Tribune.'

'And had you known this was our mission, would you still have accompanied us?'

The German laughed softly, tapping the purse at his belt.

'Four gold aureii is a lot of money for a man with no tribe, and no one to care for him when times are hard. Yes, I would still have joined you. Although I might have been minded to demand more money, given the risks you run. If you manage to find Gerhild and capture her you will incur the fanatical enmity of every man in my tribe, and that would be a terrible threat for a hundred times your number.'

Scaurus nodded and turned away, then called back over his shoulder.

'Gunda? You wouldn't happen to have some clue as to her location you could share with me, would you?'

The guide laughed again.

'No, Tribune. I have been away from these lands for half my lifetime. I do not know where Gerhild is to be found.'

Varus drew the first spell as watch officer, slowly walking the roughly circular perimeter and stopping at each sentry's position to listen to the forest's night-time noises. After two hours Marcus, unable to sleep as was so often the case, rolled out of his cloak and climbed the slope to join him. He found his friend squatting down next to the slight figure of a Hamian, both men's heads tilted as they listened to something out in the darkness. Recognising the archer as Qadir's chosen man, he squatted down next to him with exaggerated care to avoid making any sudden noise.

'What is it, Husam?'

The easterner spoke quietly without taking his eyes off the almost invisible ranks of trees before him.

'A boar, Centurion. Sow and piglets. They would make good eating if there was light to shoot.'

The Roman nodded, and opened his mouth to speak again only to fall silent as another, more distant sound reached his ears.

'Can you hear . . . ?'

He frowned, trying to distinguish whatever it was he was hearing from the wind's gentle susurration through the branches above. Varus was silent for a moment, then leaned close to whisper in his ear.

'It sounds like . . . chanting?'

As they watched, a faint glow appeared in the depths of the forest before them, so distant and well shielded by the intervening trees as to be almost invisible, no more than a rumour of what had to be a sizeable fire.

'It sounds like some ritual or other. Who knows what gods these barbarians worship?'

Varus fell silent again as the chant's tempo stepped up, a man's voice now just audible over their incessant rhythm.

'And there is the priest.'

Marcus nodded his agreement with the Hamian's opinion.

'It certainly sounds like one. He's whipping them up into a frenzy.'

The priest shouted what sounded like a challenge to his followers, and the chanting started once more, louder than before. A scream reached their ears, its shrill, agonised note clearly audible over the chanting despite the distance, and Varus jumped at the unexpected sound.

'Mithras!'

Marcus shook his head slowly, closing his eyes.

'Mithras? I doubt it.'

The scream sounded again, more tormented than the first time, as if pain and outrage had suddenly been replaced by simple, agonised terror. They listened, the hair on their necks rising as the outraged voice rose to a horrified falsetto and then abruptly died away, as whatever was being done to the priest's victim apparently took his life and gifted him peace from his torment.

'What the fuck?!'

Dubnus was beside them with a hand on his dagger.

'Keep your voice down, Centurion, unless you fancy being the next man to enjoy the attentions of a priest of Wodanaz.'

Scaurus had climbed the slope behind him, and stood looking out at the flickering mote of torchlight.

'Wodanaz?'

'The locals' version of the god Mercury, as close as they can be matched. Like Mercury he is the god who acts as the spirit guide for the newly dead, leading them to the underworld. His priests tend sacred groves, clearings in the heart of the forest that are decorated with the bones and remnants of the tribe's enemies, rusted weapons and scraps of armour. Each grove is surrounded by the most hair-raising warnings to come no closer without the blessing of the god, which is to be dispensed, of course, only by the priest. And in that grove, when the time is deemed to be right, captives are sacrificed to Wodanaz, perhaps burned alive above the altar and pierced with spears as they burn, their blood channelled to spill across the stone, perhaps eviscerated and torn open to allow their hearts to be torn bodily from their bodies.' He stared out at the distant light for a moment. 'We're in no danger here, they'll all be away to get drunk and sleep wherever they fall soon enough, which ought to make tomorrow a good day for making progress through this green underworld.'

He fell silent, and the three centurions looked at each other.

'Have you ever seen a sacred grove, Tribune?'

The older man spoke without turning to face Varus, his voice suddenly bleak.

'Yes. At night, with my face black with ashes and a dagger in my hand. And trust me in this, young man, once was enough for one lifetime.'

After a night spent comfortably enough in the mansio situated close to the bridge's eastern end, Cotta and his companions made their way through the wooden walled fort that protected the crossing until they reached the gate through which they had to pass to enter Bructeri territory. Manned by a centurion and his command's full strength, the gateway was built on a scale that they hadn't seen before even on the northern frontier in Britannia. Massive timbers cut from mature trees were fixed in place by heavy iron nails driven in at different angles to ensure the gate's ability to resist attack, and reinforced with thick bars of iron designed to spread the load of any attack. The century's soldiers were arrayed along the thick wooden palisade on either side, their demeanour that of men equipped and ready for violence, given the opportunity. The centurion, by now well aware of Cotta's status as an ex-soldier, strolled down to the gate to meet them.

'Here we are, another group of lambs ready for the slaughter.'

His greeting was made without humour, or any hint of it being anything other than a blunt statement of his opinion.

'Really, Centurion?' Cotta put his hands on his hips and shook his head in apparent mystification. 'What's so bad about this particular set of long-haired lunatics? Me and my boys here have seen the same thing in every shithole from Britannia to Parthia, and it's almost always never as bad as everyone tells us.'

The officer looked down at him with something akin to sympathy.

'It's very simple, Centurion. This lot don't just resent our presence on their doorstep, they detest it. They hate us, they fucking loathe us, they want us all dead and preferably with our balls cut off and stitched into our mouths while we're still breathing. Of course they don't do anything to piss us off badly enough that the governor would sanction a punitive raid, and in any case my prefect says the man's shit scared of upsetting the Bructeri and having a war on his hands, the prick. No, they leave us well enough alone, apart from their younger men prowling around out there every now and then, barking at the moon to let us know they're there.' His eyes hardened again. 'But they must be getting Romans from somewhere, because every now and then we'll hear them sacrificing a man out there in the forest.'

He bent close to Cotta, lowering his voice.

'Do you know which word a man uses the most when there's a knife being taken to his balls?'

'No?'

'Exactly. "*No*". They shout it, they scream it, they roar their lungs out with it. Doesn't change a thing of course. Sometimes they scream for their mothers, or their loved ones, but always, *always* in Latin, or at least to start with. After a while they sometimes go back to their native tongues, or just become impossible to understand. My theory is that they capture soldiers on the other side of the river, where they're supposed to be safe, knock them on the head and spirit them across the river in small boats. After all, what's one man going missing each month when you consider how many we lose to desertion? We've not lost a single man in all our time manning this shithole outpost, but my lads are all fucking terrified, and no wonder.'

He shook his head angrily.

'We should just march back over that fucking bridge and burn it down to the water, but we're not allowed to because that would make it impossible to gather the taxes that the governor's expected to deliver to Rome.' He spat on the ground in bitter disgust. 'If it were left to me we'd put half a legion together and burn out every fucking town and village for ten miles, but all I get from command is that we've got no proof of any of what I've told you. And of course any proper punishment would upset the local tribes, and get in the way of trade, wouldn't it? But one of these days, you mark me, we'll get a legatus with some balls who'll tell the governor to go and fuck himself, and turn us loose on that scum.'

Cotta nodded in genuine sympathy.

'And on that day I'll be cheering you on. No wonder your boys are scared shitless.'

The centurion looked at the veteran and his comrades with a sad expression.

'And so should you be. They'll greet you with indifference at first, ignore you and spurn your attempts to sell to them, but that's the easy part. It's what happens later, after dark, that I'd be worried about if I were you. Want my advice? Don't hang around any of their villages after the sun's down. Make your excuses mid-afternoon at the latest and head for the next village, only actually don't go there, vanish into the forest and hole up somewhere hard to find. And don't leave a fire burning after dark.'

He looked at the swords that the party had strapped on before leaving the mansio, raising an eyebrow at Lugo's heavy iron war hammer.

'Know how to use those?'

Sanga shrugged, his disdain for the officer's nervousness barely concealed.

'We've done our fair share.'

The centurion nodded.

'I'm sure you have. Well, you'd best be on your way, if you're going to have time to see their capital and find a hidey-hole in the woods. Open the gate!'

He watched as they walked out between the gate's heavy doors, calling after them as they headed away down the road to the east.

'Are you sure you can trust that German? Only I could always just cut his throat for you if you're too attached to him to do it yourselves!'

By the time the sun was clear of the horizon the detachment were already on the move through the forest. Dawn had found the Tungrians awake and ready to march, the morning's dew shaken off their cloaks and a hurried handful of bread taken to sustain them for the first part of the day. Scaurus had gathered his officers and the guide to him, looking at each man in turn as he issued his orders for the day.

'The same as yesterday, we advance at the pace of a cautious Hamian. Nobody hears us and nobody sees us. Until we take this priestess from her tower we need to be nothing more than silence in the forest, if we're going to get out of this with our skins. Oh, and Gunda?'

The scout raised his eyebrows in question.

'Make sure we keep well clear of that sacred grove this morning, eh? The priests may be putting the final touches to their display of last night's victim, and while there's little that would give me greater pleasure than providing that hapless individual with a little revenge on the men who tortured him, the uproar that would follow might prove problematic.'

He pointed to the path, dismissing his men to their places in the march formation, until only Marcus remained.

'Is it really that horrific, Tribune? Given all we've seen on the battlefield?'

The tribune shrugged.

'Not in terms of the simple physical reality, no. One headless corpse with its guts torn out is very much like any other, I suppose. But it's not what they do to their victims that bothers me as much as the way in which they do it. And right now that poor dead bastard we heard screaming last night is no more than just another poor dead bastard, no matter how hard his exit from this life was. It's always easier to take when the victim's anonymous.' He looked at Marcus for a moment with eyes that were suddenly empty of all emotion. 'It's a different matter when it's your best friend.'

Cotta and his companions walked along the road east from the Novaesium bridgehead with a mixture of curiosity and foreboding, the four soldiers looking around them at the open farmland to either side of the road. Arminius grinned at their evident surprise at the landscape, spreading his arms to encompass the cultivated ground to either side.

'Not what you were expecting? Wondering where all the mountains and bogs have gone?'

He laughed at their confused expressions.

'Sure, the lands on this side of the Rhenus have mountains, and bogs, and forests that go on forever, but wherever a tribe makes its homeland you will find farm land. How else can they feed themselves?'

Morban shrugged and turned back to the road.

'So you lot are a nation of farmers? Doesn't seem likely.'

The German shook his head.

'Your problem is that the Romans have long since forgotten what it is to work the land. Your masters are town dwellers, and they use slave labour to run their farms. Which means that you soldiers have often never lived on the land. You might be drafted in to collect the harvest every now and then, but that's not the same as living on the soil that feeds you, suffering through the winter and sweating through the summer. I grew up on land like this, where the people know how to farm *and* how to fight . . .'

He looked out over the fields affectionately, pretending to ignore Sanga's snort of disapproval.

'Fucking onion-munchers. So if we're here, where's the centurion then?'

Arminius pointed away to the south-east, where a forest's dark mass ran down the shallow hillsides to meet the cultivated land.

'There. Somewhere in that forest, under the oak trees' canopy where the sunlight is more green than gold, where the wild pigs grow to the size of this old girl . . .' He slapped the mule's rump, provoking a surprised whinny. 'And where the tribal priests have their sacred groves, holy places where even the bravest men shrink in terror from entry without invitation.'

'It's so bloody quiet I think I can hear my damned heart beating.'

Varus's whispered comment made Marcus smile as he took his next slow, careful pace along the ill-defined track as it rose slowly towards a ridgeline lost in the forest's jumble of trees.

The detachment was strung out along the hunting path with two paces between each man, each of them watching a different direction in turn to ensure that an approach from anywhere would be detected with enough time to send the Tungrians into cover. He stepped forward again, flicking his glance down to ensure that his footfall would touch only clear earth, and that no twig or pebble could make a noise or unbalance him, then looked up again as his boot touched the path's grassy track, searching the trees away to his right. A bow borrowed from Qadir rested easily in his right hand, the arrow nocked to its string tipped with a heavy-bladed three-lobed arrow designed for the express purpose of either killing its target outright through shock and blood loss, or by opening an unhealable wound in a man's body that would eventually kill him through sepsis.

'If we go any slower we'll start moving backwards.'

Marcus grinned, as much at the tone in which the complaint was made as the words themselves.

'A little patience will go a long way in this place.'

Varus snorted quietly.

'Patience? I wasn't born with very much of that commodity.'

Fifty paces up the column Dubnus raised his hand to indicate a halt, and the detachment's men went to ground, alternately facing left and right to ensure continued vigilance. Marcus and Varus went forward to join their friend, finding him conferring with Scaurus and Gunda over what was effectively a crossroads in the forest, a track crossing their path from east to west in a wide clearing that had been cleared in the forest's heart.

'Where does it lead to, Scout?'

Gunda pointed his hand to the east.

'In that direction there is little more than an empty expanse of forest and, eventually, the Marsi tribe.'

'And to the west?'

The tribesman looked down the path for a moment before responding.

'That way leads to one of my tribe's sacred groves.'

'Where they were torturing whoever it was we heard doing the screaming last night.'

The scout nodded.

'Undoubtedly.'

Scaurus looked at Marcus with a calculating expression.

'I've been thinking, Centurion. It *would* be useful to know what the local tribal priests are up to in their sacred groves, although I've no desire to give them any hint of our presence here. So, given that you seem in good humour this morning, I wondered if you might care to take one of our sharper-eyed men with you and take a look? Quietly, and without managing to betray our presence out here.'

Marcus nodded levelly.

'There are good days and bad days, Tribune, and today that sounds like a good idea. And if I might be permitted to suggest that I be accompanied by—'

Scaurus nodded with a wry smile.

'By all means take Centurion Varus with you. Anything to reduce the risk of his *whispering* frightening every beast within a mile into blind panic . . .' He cocked an eyebrow at Varus, who had the good grace to look vaguely embarrassed. 'Just remember, Vibius Varus, that if you end up roped to an altar with a saw-wielding lunatic standing over you, I'm unlikely to be able to do much about it.'

Varus frowned.

'A saw, Tribune?'

Scaurus shook his head, turning to Qadir with an expression of apparent despair.

'I think we'll have a *pair* of your archers to escort these two young gentlemen, Centurion, the stealthiest men you have, to compensate for our colleague's constant urge to express himself verbally.' He turned back to Varus, tapping him on the breastbone. 'This, young man, is too thick for a knife to cut with any ease, and protects that which a barbarian priest covets most, once he's had the low-hanging fruit of your eyes, your tongue and most likely your sexual organs. So to get at your heart he'll use a saw, a horrible, locally made thing with the crudest of teeth to be fair, but still a saw for all that. And he'll hack away at your chest for all he's worth, cutting a slot in your ribcage until he can crack it open and pull your heart out, with you conscious for the whole time if he's any sort of artist, given that no major blood vessel will be disrupted by his excavations until he actually pulls the heart out. So if you don't want to find yourself suffering that sort of indignity, I suggest you keep your head down, your ears open and your mouth *shut*.'

'Thusila? What the fuck does that mean then?'

'Roar.'

Morban turned to stare at Arminius with a look of disbelief.

'Roar? They call their city "*roar*"?'

The German shrugged, looking down the hill's slope at the sprawl of huts and wooden buildings that almost filled the space between the river that flowed through it, a tributary of the Rhenus, and the forest.

'Both river and city. What you see there is the home of a tribe that four generations ago was almost wiped out. Attacked by two neighbouring tribes who saw their opportunity, or more likely had it put under their noses by the Romans. Reduced to a few thousand wandering women, boys and old men, their warriors either slaughtered in a one-sided battle or enslaved and sent to Rome to feed the arena. When the Marsi allowed them to settle here it was an act of charity, but they underestimated what was left of the Bructeri. Whoever it was that led that tattered remnant here from the battlefields to the north wanted some measure of dignity for what was left of their people, so they named their new tribal capital after the noise made by the river that runs through it.'

Sanga cocked his head to one side, listening ostentatiously.

'*Roar?*'

Arminius shrugged.

'You have to exercise a little imagination.'

They marched down the gently sloping road's gradient past

the outlying buildings, noting with seemingly casual glances the stares that greeted and followed them in their progress. Saratos looked about him with a look heavy with the promise of violence.

'Like he say, nobody happy to see we.'

Morban shook his head in apparent disgust.

'To see *us*, you barbarian. And I couldn't give a fuck whether they're happy to see us or not as long as they show a little respect. I didn't fight long-haired cunts like this lot all the way across the empire and back again to have my dignity spat on by the likes of this unwashed rabble.'

Sanga grinned at his back.

'As it happens Morban, you didn't actually *fight* your way across anything more fucking dangerous than the mud between a tavern and a whorehouse, you usually stood behind us men and squealed every now and then when the barbarians got close enough for you to smell them.'

The standard bearer stopped and fixed a stare on Sanga that made the soldier suddenly acutely aware of the older man's role in controlling his portion of the century's burial club.

'But as it happens I can pretty much see your point. Although I think you're going to be disappointed when it comes to the spitting on your dignity thing.'

'It's not exactly subtle, is it?'

Marcus nodded grimly, looking up at the bleached skull of a bull, complete with horns, that had been nailed to a tree adjacent to the almost invisible track the four men had cautiously followed away from the point where the two paths crossed, stalking with slow and deliberate care towards the apparent source of the previous night's screams. He gestured the other men closer, speaking in a soft voice barely louder than a murmur.

'They do it to scare off the locals, which means we're getting close. From here we're silent, right? Move slowly, be careful with your feet and don't even breathe hard.'

He gestured to Husam to lead them on down the path's slight gradient, following the Hamian's example and examining the ground before him with exaggerated care before stepping forward, the arrow nocked to his bow ready to loose in an instant. As the four men drew closer to the grove, the number of bull's skulls set to warn off the unwary multiplied, drawing nervous glances from the easterners, while a faint buzzing sound caught their ears. Marcus raised a hand to his companions, gesturing for them to stop and hold their positions. Laying down his borrowed bow, he lowered himself to the forest floor and crawled forward down the path with slow, careful movements, pausing every few feet to listen for a moment before resuming his cautious progress. Twenty paces from what was apparently an entry to the grove, the trees on either side intricately carved with runic patterns, he slid off the path to the right and resumed his progress with such caution that he barely seemed to be moving. Worming his way between a pair of bushes, he found himself at the edge of a patch of forest from which all undergrowth had been stripped, towering oaks looming over the open space that was apparently deserted. He waited, breathing shallowly to avoid disturbing the leaves through which he was staring, grimacing as he realised that his assumption as to what was generating the pervasive buzzing sound was uncomfortably accurate.

In the middle of the grove a massive block of stone reared out of the ground, a huge boulder of white rock that had been cut down to form a flat surface and then painstakingly carved across every inch of it with runes of unknown purpose, the primitive symbols made distinctive by a dark brown inlay that made the ornately decorated rectangular slab's purpose horribly familiar to the Roman. His prone position prevented him from seeing exactly what rested across its horizontal surface, but as he considered moving to a better viewpoint a crow swooped down from one of the trees, sending a cloud of flies up into the air above the altar and alighting atop what Marcus could only assume was the priests' victim, pecking vigorously at the unseen body. Realising that the grove had to be deserted for the carrion bird to be so brazen, he pushed through the bushes' cover and cautiously got to his feet with one hand on the ground, ready to thrust himself upright, the other gripping the hilt of his sword.

The sight that greeted him was horrific, if no more so than he had expected. The corpse of the sacrificial victim was stretched out across the altar's smooth surface, black puddles of dried blood beneath the body apparently the remnant of what had pumped from veins opened during the unknown man's torture. His eyes had been torn from their sockets, leaving only bloody pits in which flies were swarming, and his nose had been hacked off, leaving a repulsive opening in his face that turned the Roman's stomach. His face was pocked with bloody craters where, Marcus suspected, the crows had feasted on his pallid flesh, and the skin that remained was tinged blue from the blood loss that had occurred prior to the man's untimely death. His legs were twisted into unnatural lines, clearly broken and the injuries used to torment him, and their skin was covered in a dozen and more burns whose shape looked dreadfully familiar to the Roman. Stepping forward with the same deliberate care that he'd used to approach the grove, he struggled to ignore the horror as he looked slowly around the tribal shrine, trying to absorb every minute detail to recount later on. The trees were decorated with human skulls, dozens of which had been nailed to the trees, and by fragments of armour and helmets of a variety of ages and models, some almost rusted away, others still relatively new, testament to the tribe's continuing enmity with Rome. Some of the prizes were accompanied by rusted swords and spearheads. Satisfied that there was no threat to him, he turned his attention to the dead man, frowning as he reached out a hand to touch the tunic that had been cut open to allow the priests' knives easy access to his penis and testicles. The wool was finely woven, a high quality and expensive weave for a tribesman or slave to be wearing, and his expression hardened with anger as he turned the dead man's arm over to look for proof of the suspicion that had formed in his mind. The corpse's hand whipped out, clutching at his arm with the strength of despair, and the tongueless mouth moved in a silent entreaty from between his blue lips.

Resisting the urge to scream in horror the Roman pulled his arm free and whipped his hand up, reflex overcoming his sudden overwhelming feeling of being no more than an onlooker, detached from the scene before him, pinching the dying man's throat closed and standing stock-still as the sacrificial victim shuddered, straining against the ropes that still restrained his body. With a final racking spasm the dying man contorted, his spine arching, then sank back onto the bloody altar, his death rattle almost inaudible with his throat still pinched shut. Marcus allowed a long, slow breath to escape his body, putting a hand out to steady himself as the shock of what had just happened washed over him. While he stood braced against the altar a quiet muttering from somewhere close to hand reached his ears, and he reflexively sank into the shelter of the massive stone block, looking about him with his sword half drawn.

The sound came again, and with a start Marcus realised that the source was so close that it seemed as if he could reach out and touch the speaker. Sliding the gladius from its scabbard, he stepped quickly and quietly round the altar to stand behind the dead man's head, looking about him in mystification, then advancing around the stone again as the slurred, unintelligible words were repeated. Looking down as he rounded the block's corner, the Roman raised his blade to strike, then realised that the man at his feet posed no threat, as a gentle snore escaped from his twitching mouth. The priest, his long black hair shot through with streaks of grey that had fallen to partially cover a face deeply scored with the creases and lines of age, was asleep, blissfully unaware that a cold-eyed nemesis was standing over him, his blade stayed only by the struggle between a need to take revenge for the dead man and his orders to leave no trace of his presence. The Roman stared down at him for a long moment, calculating the hue and cry that must surely follow what he was contemplating, at the same time almost willing the man to wake, and give him an excuse to put the blade through his throat. The sleeper shifted uncomfortably against the altar's side, muttering more unintelligible words, then let out another snore, and Marcus backed slowly away with his eyes searching the trees around him as he retreated back towards the path.

Turning away from the grove, he hurried back up the slope to where he'd left Varus and the Hamians, raising a hand to forestall their questions.

'Not now. You can hear the story when I tell it to the Tribune.'

5

'What a waste of time and effort.'

Cotta looked about him with an air of exasperation.

'This lot wouldn't give us so much as the steam off their piss.'

The neutral expression Arminius had been careful to maintain since they had walked into the settlement was unchanged, but the German's voice was rich in irony.

'I can see what my master was thinking when he sent us here, but he has reckoned without the long-standing enmity these people have for your empire. That centurion was right, we need something to get past the barrier of their hatred, or we might as well go and shelter in the forest and try to find our comrades tomorrow.'

Morban's rejoinder was morose, and edged with fear.

'We should go and find Lugos, dump the cart and get the fuck out of here before they decide we're the next offering to their gods.'

Cotta opened his mouth to speak, then closed it as Sanga and Saratos rounded a corner and sauntered over to join them.

'You're looking smug Sanga, what have you been up to? Even you can't have managed to persuade one of this lot to open her legs for you already, not unless you were paying in gold. And you haven't got any gold.'

The soldier's grin silenced him, a gap-toothed smile that narrowed the older man's eyes.

'Go on. Spit it out.'

'We need an angle, that chosen man said, a way to break the ice with this set of sulky bastards, right?'

'Yes. And?'

Sanga smirked again, pointing back the way he and Saratos had come.

'And I reckon we've found it. Might get a bit messy though. And I think this might just be what you brought Morban along for.'

'You're sure you weren't seen?'

Marcus nodded grimly.

'The priest was sound asleep after his hard night's work.'

Scaurus snorted without mirth.

'And the man on the altar was Roman? You're sure?'

'He was trying to ask me to kill him, I could see his lips forming the words. And he was wearing a fine woollen tunic, the sort of thing an off-duty soldier might wear for a night in the vicus . . .'

He fell silent, lost in the memory of the moment when the mutilated corpse had come to life at his touch. Scaurus put a hand out and touched his arm.

'And . . . ? I'm sorry Marcus, but I have to know everything.'

'I stopped his windpipe. After all the punishment he'd taken in the night he was so close to death that it only needed a gentle nudge to put him over the edge. Most of his blood was spread across the altar, although there was enough of it scattered about the grove that the priest was probably using it to anoint his followers.'

Scaurus looked pointedly at Marcus's left hand.

'You seem to have brought some of it with you.' Marcus lifted his hand and looked at the palm, realising that when he'd steadied himself against the altar he'd put his fingers into a patch of drying blood. 'Do you think you left a mark?'

The Roman nodded slowly.

'It's likely. But I doubt they'll think anything of it.'

Scaurus mused for a moment.

'So they're abducting our soldiers for the purpose of sacrifice.' He paused for a moment, studying the look on his friend's face. 'But there's more to it than that, isn't there? Something you've not told us yet?'

Marcus looked up at the trees' canopy.

'You're going to say that I'm imagining it.'

Scaurus raised an eyebrow.

'You've just told me that the Bructeri are kidnapping our legionaries, bringing them out to a clearing in the forest and then torturing them to death piece by bloody piece. I can't see what else you might have in mind that's any more disturbing than that particular set of revelations.'

The younger man shook his head.

'I might be wrong . . . but there were burn marks on his body that looked exactly like . . .'

He frowned, pulling the memory of the distinctive markings to the front of his mind.

'Like what?'

'An eagle, a legion standard.'

Scaurus's eyes narrowed.

'You think he'd been tortured with an *eagle*?'

Marcus nodded in silence, aware that every man within earshot was staring at him.

'But . . .' The tribune shook his head in rejection of the possibility. 'It can't have been. The eagles lost in the Varus disaster were all recovered, and we've not lost a standard in Germania since then. I really don't—'

'Yes, you have.'

All eyes turned to Gunda, who was looking at the tribune with a confident expression. Scaurus shook his head.

'No, we haven't. Lost eagles are one of those things that every young officer learns about, usually from the senior centurions to whom that sort of thing is really important, not for career reasons but because for those men the eagle is an object of worship, the heart of the legion. They teach you that the eagle always, *always* comes first, no matter what the personal risk. Eagle bearers are invariably the best men in the legion, trusted to carry the legion's soul into the heart of the battle, and they usually have a century of the nastiest men available as their personal bodyguard, men whose motivation goes beyond fanaticism. Trust me in this, the only eagles that Rome has lost since Varus are two in Judean revolts, one in Dacia before Trajan conquered the province, and one in Parthia, the Ninth Legion from memory.'

Gunda shrugged.

'I am forced to disagree with you. There is a story that has been passed down from father to son for generations in our tribe that tells a different story.'

He held Scaurus's stare until the Roman nodded slowly.

'Tell us your story then, German, and allow us to consider what you say.'

The guide looked around at his audience, sensing their fascination.

'It's a short enough tale. There was a time, so long ago that my father's father's father was not yet born, that the Batavi, a warlike tribe who had given long and faithful service to your empire, thought better of their place in the world than to serve a master who continually abused them. Your people called them Batavians, and for a time respected them as the bravest and the best of their allies, but over time this respect turned to contempt between their soldiers and yours. The relationship began to rot, and there was open fighting between Romans and Batavi in the taverns and streets of your fortresses. And just when the relationship was at its worst, a priestess of the Bructeri foretold a Batavi victory over Rome in battle . . .' Scaurus exchanged glances with Marcus. 'And so, encouraged by these visions, they went to war with your people, and with them – and this is the important part . . .' he paused, smiling at Scaurus, '. . . went the Bructeri, my people. And, with one thing and another, the war went badly for Rome, and well for the Batavi. At least for a time.'

Scaurus nodded.

'It was a time of civil war, a year when four men sat on the throne in one year, which meant that the empire's attention was distracted from events in Germania. Two legions managed to get themselves bottled up in the fortress that was all that was left of Roman rule on the Rhenus, a fortress called Vetera. They held out for a time, their walls of stone being too strong for the

Batavians and their allies to defeat, and they were even relieved once, but due to a combination of miscalculation and plain stupidity they were forced to surrender for lack of food, when they had been reduced to eating their horses and mules.'

Gunda bowed to him.

'It seems your people have this story too, perhaps written in those books you love so much. The two legions agreed to surrender, leaving all of their weapons and gold behind, in return for safe passage away from the fortress. And so they marched out, trusting to their captors' good nature, which, as every man of my tribe knows, is a foolish choice to make when dealing with the tribes to our north.'

He shook his head at the folly of the decision.

'Better for them to have taken their own lives. They were attacked a short distance from the fortress, and slaughtered, their officers enslaved and given to the priestess who had predicted their defeat to be her servants.'

Scaurus stood, stretching his back.

'All of which is known, and true, but the legions' eagles were safely removed from the fortress when it was relieved for a short time. They—'

He fell silent under the guide's stare.

'Was this a time of great disasters, Roman? A time when the loss of not one but two of your eagles would have been a grievous insult to the dignity of a new emperor?'

'Yes. I cannot deny it.'

'And did the Batavi leader perish, when his tribe was finally defeated, silencing him forever?'

Scaurus nodded.

'That does seem to have been the case.'

Gunda spread his arms.

'Even I can see how that worked, and I'm just a simple tribesman. The eagles were captured, one of them falling to the Bructeri, and your rulers decided to quietly ignore the fact as it was simply . . .'

He looked up, fishing for the right word.

'Inconvenient?'

The German turned to Marcus.

'Indeed, Centurion. Inconvenient. And so. Romans, whether you believe me or not, it is my belief that it is quite possible for my tribe to be in possession of one of your beloved eagles. I cannot claim to have seen it, for I left the tribe as a young man, too young to have participated in the ceremonies where it would be shown to the warriors as a valued prize, and perhaps used to torment our captives. But I have heard tales of its existence, and that it is kept hidden in the king's treasury for the most part and only brought out for such special occasions.'

Scaurus gestured to Marcus.

'Thank you for your frankness, Gunda. Walk with me, Centurion.'

He led the younger man away from the detachment until they were out of earshot.

'You're sure about this?'

Marcus thought for a moment, his face etched with the stress bearing down on him.

'Completely sure? How can I be? I saw nothing more than burn marks on a man's legs, and I was somewhat preoccupied at the time. But do I think they were put there by an eagle that had been heated over a fire? Yes Tribune, I do.'

The older man looked up at the trees for a moment before speaking again, his voice tense with frustration.

'We could be back in that grove in minutes. put the priest to the sword, perhaps even find this eagle, and vanish into the forest to the east as if we were never here. But . . .'

'That's not the task we were given.'

'No. And worse than that, if that German's story is right we won't even be thanked for returning it to Rome. After all, the empire had its revenge on the Batavians once they'd been beaten on the battlefield, and you heard what the governor's secretary told us about the way Rome encouraged neighbouring tribes to push the Bructeri off their land, and almost destroy the tribe. I don't think we're going to be thanked for throwing away the job we've been given to do to recapture an eagle that's never actually been acknowledged as having been lost.'

The younger man nodded.

'And yet . . .'

'Exactly. Every time that eagle's used as part of some filthy sacrifice it demeans every man in the army, whether they know it or not. And worse than that, they're abducting soldiers to torture and murder, and presumably using the eagle as part of the ceremony. If we took it back, perhaps it would stop them.'

Scaurus looked down the path again, then back in the direction of the sacred grove.

'No. There's nothing I'd like more, but we can't do it. Or at least not yet.'

He turned away, signalling to Dubnus to get the detachment moving again.

'Consider it unfinished business, if you like. I will.'

'Gods below, but he's a big bastard!'

Cotta craned his neck to see over the crowd that had gathered on the slopes of the city's fighting pit, a shallow arena dug into a small hill overlooking the Bructeri capital. He stared down at the man Sanga had pointed out to him, an unnaturally tall and massively muscled tribesman with the hard eyes of a professional fighter beneath a thick head of red hair which was tied in a plait that reached the small of his back. Big enough to rival their friend Lugos in size, and clad in a simple belted tunic, he dominated the space about him with his size and sheer presence. The white-haired man who was evidently either his trainer or owner moved around him with the innate caution of a wild beast trainer, taking ostentatious care to approach him from the front, fussing with his champion's belt and offering him a drink of water.

Sanga spoke quietly in the veteran centurion's ear as they watched the giant's unhurried preparations.

'I might not speak their language, but it's not that hard to figure out having watched a couple of bouts. The man who puts him on his back and keeps him there long enough gets paid a decent purse, but he has to pay a bronze for the chance to win it, which is how they make their money. That and the gambling, obviously.'

The soldiers watched in silence as a fresh challenger was brought forward, stepping into the ring already stripped to his loin cloth, his limbs glistening with freshly applied oil. A well-muscled specimen, with the lithe grace of a boxer, he danced easily from foot to foot as the giant got to his feet with an air of bored disinterest, shaking his hands and then clenching them into fists.

'This one looks handy enough. Perhaps he'll be able to tire the big man out with all that fancy footwork?'

Saratos snorted mirthlessly.

'Same as last one we see. He dance for twenty heartbeats, then he carry out asleep.'

Sanga nodded, not taking his eyes off the circling fighters, the challenger moving nimbly around his opponent as the giant stepped stolidly forward. Clenching his fists he looked up at the sky and let out a roar of challenge that the crowd answered by baying at the two men, clearly recognising it for the sign that the fight was on. With a sudden rush the smaller man stepped in close, hammering a powerful fist into the redhead's stomach and then moving back quickly to avoid his retaliation, although the punch's impact seemed negligible as his opponent stepped ponderously towards him in a display of blank-faced menace that sent shivers up Cotta's spine. His opponent repeated the move, darting in to land another punch, only to be met by a devastating counter-punch to his face that momentarily staggered him, leaving him wide open to the looping hook that followed. Spun a full circle by the blow's force, he tottered for an instant and then slumped headlong to the dirt floor, his eyes rolling upwards as he lost consciousness. A pair of men stepped into the ring and dragged the defeated challenger away while the crowd shouted and hooted abuse at him, those among them who had been foolish enough to put money on him shaking their heads in disgust as the big man's owner dropped their money into his leather purse. He shouted above the crowd's hubbub, and Arminius translated his words for them.

'Are there no more challengers for the Beast? No man who believes he can be the hero of the day, and win a handful of Roman silver?'

He looked about him in apparent disgust.

'No? Very well, I can see we're going to have to raise the stakes! Not five silver coins for the successful challenger! Not ten silver coins! The man who can put the champion down and keep him down will win a Roman gold aureus!'

He raised a hand to display the coin, provoking a flurry of excitement in the watching crowd, looking around at them in simulated frustration.

'Is *nobody* else here tempted to try their luck?'

Sanga looked at Cotta with an expression the older man knew from experience.

'So, that big lump wanders up to whoever's stupid enough to face him inside the circle, takes a punch or two, which he barely notices, then puts the poor unfortunate to sleep with a slap or two? Or at least that's all that's happened so far.'

'You're not thinking . . . ?'

Sanga grinned.

''Course I am. How else are we going to get under this lot's skin, eh? The man who puts him on his back and wins the gold is going to be famous for the rest of the night, and therefore the object of admiration and quite possibly lust. Some of which may rub off on his mates.'

'And you think that you—'

The Briton barked a cynical laugh.

'*Me?* Fuck no! *I'm* not that stupid! But I know a man who is . . .'

They looked around at Saratos, who shrugged and looked over at the brawler with an untroubled expression.

'He a big man. Fall hard, slow to get up.'

Cotta looked at the Beast, then back at Saratos with a sceptical expression.

'You're *sure* you want to fight him?'

The Dacian nodded, turning to Morban.

'You give me price of entry. I win fight, I keep gold—'

He raised a hand to pre-empt the avaricious standard bearer's protest.

'You want gold, *you* fight. I win, I keep gold. You gamble, like you always is, make good money.'

He paused to allow Cotta the time to work it out. The older man grimaced at him disbelievingly.

'And you really reckon you can win?'

'Give coin. We soon find out.'

The veteran nodded, turning to the man beside him.

'Right Morban, this is what you do best. Go down there and skin that white-haired old bastard alive.'

Stripping to the waist to reveal a sinewy, hard-muscled frame that was the product of years of soldiering since his capture by the Tungrians, the Dacian stretched and warmed his muscles in the company of Sanga, nodding as his friend talked incessantly at him, encouraging and cajoling him and plying him with advice as to how he could best fight the massive German. After a few minutes he declared himself ready and made his way down to the fighting ring with Morban walking behind him in imperious fashion, attended by Arminius as his translator, ignoring the muttered comments and dirty looks that he was getting. The giant's trainer spat a stream of German at them, then nodded as Arminius told him what it was that the Dacian intended.

'He says that Roman money is as welcome as any other, although for you the price will be higher. Two denarii.'

'Two *denarii*? The greedy bastard's only been charging these hairy-arsed fuckers a bronze apiece and he wants two silvers out of me!'

The German shrugged at him, understanding the Tungrian's outrage despite lacking any apparent ability with Latin, and then grinned as Arminius translated his response.

'He says you'll understand that he's likely to be taxed harder by the tribe's chief for allowing a Roman to fight in the pit. And he wonders if you really think this streak of piss and gristle will provide any more sport for the crowd than his oldest daughter could?'

Saratos stayed stony-faced, staring at the far wall with the look of a man whose mind was elsewhere, and Morban nodded slowly.

'Tell him that I'm open to a side bet if he feels so sure of his man.'

The German grinned hugely, having got the reaction his insult was intended to draw, nodding vigorously without waiting for Arminius to translate. Morban fished into his purse, making a show of poking around in it before pulling out a gold aureus. Arminius translated the startled trainer's response with the ghost of a smile.

'He says you must be fucking mad, or that's the closest I can get to what he actually said. He'll cover you at two for one, given the size of your stake, which he will hold for you until the result is clear.'

Morban winked at the trainer and flicked the coin towards him, nodding as the other man took it out of the air with expert fingers.

'Tell him he just accepted the worst bet of his life.'

He turned away, calling back to Arminius over the crowd's renewed baying as Saratos stepped into the ring, his face still vacant and apparently lacking any interest in the coming bout.

'And stay close to him, I don't want him trying to do a runner with my money when the big man goes down.'

He turned back to look at the expression on the German's face.

'You *might* not speak Latin, but you understood that well enough, didn't you, you wrinkled old fart?'

The trainer scowled at him, spitting a string of instructions and warnings at his fighter as the giant stepped into the ring to face the waiting Dacian, instructions that were clearly being ignored as the massive redhead clenched his fists and inflated his chest to issue his usual roared challenge, throwing back his head and bellowing defiance at the sky above. At the instant he looked up, Saratos moved, sprinting forward with the urgency of a man who knew that this was his best and quite probably his only opportunity to take control of the fight, covering the five paces between them before his opponent's bellow had exhausted itself.

The German's gaze snapped down onto him as he belatedly realised what was happening, but before he had time to react his opponent was upon him. Rather than strike what would almost certainly have been an ineffectual blow at the big man's stomach or face, Saratos lunged feet first into a sliding tackle that entangled his legs with the giant's, then twisted his body violently to topple the ponderous German. Hitting the ground hard, his opponent grunted with the unexpected impact, flailing his arms in an attempt to push himself upright, but the Dacian was swifter to react. Thrusting his body into the air, he slammed a braced elbow down into the momentarily helpless German's sternum with his full weight behind it and then, as the breath left the big man's lungs in an explosive rush, swung the same arm's fist down in a hammer blow to his crotch with the speed and skill of a seasoned street fighter. Rolling away he readied himself to strike again, waited for his groaning opponent to get halfway to his feet and then turned swiftly through a full circle to deliver a back-fisted blow to a spot just behind his left ear. His eyes rolling up as he lost consciousness, the German slumped back onto the dirt floor in a boneless flop that betrayed his sudden and complete loss of consciousness.

For a moment the crowd gathered around the fighting pit was silent, and in that instant before they had the chance to turn ugly at the shock of the champion being defeated by a Roman, Arminius took his chance, bellowing at them in their shared language.

'The Dacian wins! Free beer for every man here to celebrate!'

Taking the German's trainer firmly by the arm, his knife out and pricking the man's ribs beneath the cover of his cloak, he dragged the older man alongside him and set off downhill, repeating the cry as the crowd regained their wits and stared at him in amazement.

'Free beer! Follow me!'

Torn between the prospect of violence and alcohol, the Germans wavered momentarily, then as one man surged after Arminius and his captive while Morban stared at them in horror.

'*Free?*'

Saratos strolled over to him, still breathing hard from his violent exertions, crooking a finger to lead the horrified standard bearer back over to the corpse-like form of the defeated giant.

'Is not to worry. I watch them before, see, and more than one time I see trainer check that this belt still good. Make me wonder what is point of belt when rope better in fight, give less for enemy to grip. We look, yes?'

Sanga and Cotta had joined them, the pit now completely deserted by the men streaming back toward the settlement's centre.

'Let's see if your guess was right, eh?'

He unbuckled the German's belt, pulling it free and hefting the thick strip of leather in one hand.

'I'd like to have seen the cow that gave its life to provide leather this heavy!'

He turned the belt over, using a fingernail to dig into what looked like a coating of hide glue, probing its reverse in search of something not immediately evident.

'What the—'

Morban fell silent as the soldier grinned triumphantly.

'Got you!'

Sliding the nail into a long cut in the leather's surface he peeled back a layer of hide to reveal a string of circular depressions that had been painstakingly scraped into the belt beneath that thin layer.

'Must be a dozen of them. Right now this one's owner thinks he's spending our winnings to buy beer for anyone that can drink it, and all the time he's counting on this being here when this lump wakes up. Thinking all is not lost.'

Morban reached out a hand for the belt.

'But it fucking well is! That's my stake, and my winnings!'

Cotta put out a hand to stop him, taking the belt from Sanga and fastening it about his own waist.

'The tribune's winnings, given you were betting with his gold, and, more to the point, *safe*. And we're not done getting our "edge" yet, so that small fortune is best kept hidden. And now we'd best go and see how a German tribe behaves when provided with unlimited free beer!'

The Tungrians went forward at the same cautious pace for the rest of the morning, stopped for a brief rest when the sun, or what could be seen of it through the trees' thick canopy, was at its highest point, and then resumed their slow, patient march through the forest.

'I swear this is worse than a thirty-miler. At least you can get your head back and get stuck into a proper distance, but this . . .'

Qadir, having joined Marcus at the front of the column, nodded, his head turning slowly from side to side as he scanned the forest before them. His voice was soft as he replied.

'For myself I have to say that this method of progress is entirely more suited to my abilities than your constant emphasis on charging around the countryside with your boots on fire. It does a man's spirit good to . . .'

His eyes abruptly narrowed, the bow's wooden frame creaking as he drew back the arrow that was already nocked to its string, pausing for an instant with the missile's fletching barely touching his ear, then releasing the string and reaching for another arrow. Marcus looked frantically for a target for his own bow, but the forest was silent, the only movement the stirring of the trees' higher branches by the wind.

'A man, on the path.'

The Hamian's quiet comment was all it took to break the moment's spell, and the heavy cloak of lassitude that had settled over Marcus fell away with the rush of blood as he hurried forward in a half-crouch with his bow still ready to shoot, Dubnus at his heels with his axe in one hand and a sword in the other. They found Qadir's target a hundred paces up the track, a roughly dressed man whose knuckles were white around the grip of a bow, leaning against a tree while his life blood pumped out around the shaft of the Hamian's arrow. He looked up at the Romans with eyes already glassy with his impending death and reached out an imploring hand, too badly shocked even to know what had happened to him.

'I doubt he even saw us.'

Marcus put the borrowed bow aside and drew his gladius, swiftly and efficiently putting the point to the stricken German's chest and pushing it between two ribs to stop the dying man's heart just as the head of the detachment's column reached the scene.

'He was alone then.'

Marcus nodded at Scaurus's question.

'If he'd been accompanied we'd have spotted anyone else as they ran. The question is what do we do with him?'

'Bury him deep.' They turned to find Gunda looking down at the dead man dispassionately. 'If you leave him to lie in the open the animals will tear him to pieces quickly enough, but the bones will be scattered, and the risk of another hunter finding them is too great. This man needs simply to disappear. He will be missed, of course, but it is not unknown for hunters to travel deep into the forest in search of game for days at a time.'

Dubnus took over, issuing a swift order to Angar, who selected four of his axemen, leading them as they picked up the body and carried it away from the path.

'They will find a quiet spot and bury him deep enough to keep his body safe from the wild beasts, then follow us down the path.'

Scaurus turned to Qadir.

'A pair of your archers to watch over them might be a good precaution, Centurion.'

He pointed down the path's track to the north.

'Gunda, how much farther must we walk to be close enough to Thusila to effect the next part of our plan?'

The guide thought for a moment.

'Another two miles.'

'In which case, gentlemen, I suggest we get back on the move, but with the same caution as before. I want to be in position by nightfall, but I don't want to risk discovery now we've got so close.'

As the evening sun dipped towards the horizon, a party of twenty armed and armoured legionaries made their way along the Rhenus fleet's quayside in column, two-men wide, a centurion at their head and another half-dozen men in formal togas bringing up the rear, followed in turn by a solitary figure dressed in the full ceremonial armour of a Roman senator. Ordering the column to halt alongside the fleet's flagship, the centurion shouted to the men manning the vessel's rail to fetch their commanding officer. Summoned to the vessel's side, Varus's cousin found himself looking down at governor Clodius Albinus, accompanied by his full official retinue of lictors, each with his bundle of rods and axes held across his body in an ostentatious display of power that he very much doubted was anything but intentional.

'Greetings, Prefect.'

The naval officer inclined his head.

'Governor.'

Albinus looked up and down the dock at the sailors loading baskets of food and sheaves of arrows onto the decks of the three ships that had been pulled down the slope from their storage sheds into the water of the basin and were now arrayed alongside the provisioning quay.

'It looks to me, Prefect, as if you're making preparations to sail.'

The naval officer considered the question for a moment before making a reply.

'Indeed, Governor. I plan to take three ships on a routine patrol as far down the river as Novaesium, poking about on the eastern bank as usual to make sure that the Germans are behaving themselves.'

Albinus smiled thinly.

'A good defence never sleeps, eh Prefect? It's heartening to see that we have alert and diligent officers such as yourselves in *my* German fleet. Indeed I share your interest so deeply that I thought I'd come along for the ride. When do you plan to sail?'

'At first light, Governor. Our preparations are more or less complete.'

The older man nodded, already very well aware of the ships' state of readiness, having taken steps to determine the prefect's most likely next steps the previous day, when their role in the Tungrians' insertion into Bructeri territory had become plain.

'In which case I'll come on board now. A night of some slight discomfort will be a small price to pay for the professional satisfaction to be had from patrolling the empire's borders with a renowned officer such as yourself.' He smiled at the prefect again, clearly enjoying himself. 'Obviously my lictors will have to accompany me, and my private bodyguard, but we'll do our best to keep out of your way. Perhaps you could redistribute your marines around the other ships, just to make a little room for us?'

The prefect inclined his head in agreement, his smile of acquiescence as thin as the governor's apparent good humour.

'Of course, Governor. It will be an absolute privilege to have you along for the ride.'

'I had no idea this lot could drink so fast!'

Morban looked around the crowded tavern with growing alarm, watching the delighted tribesmen swigging their beer with the dedicated abandon of men who saw their chance to achieve oblivion without having to spend so much as a single coin. But if he was dismayed at the frantic pace with which the rapidly growing band of drinkers had been consuming the tavern's supplies throughout the afternoon, all recognising that either beer or the money to pay for it might well run out at any moment, his consternation was nothing in the face of the German trainer's abject misery as the contents of his purse went down their throats. To the Tungrians' surprise, clearly unable to tolerate the injustice of the situation in silence, he suddenly burst into a tirade directed at Cotta, his Latin all but fluent.

'What are you bastards playing at? You beat my boy, I would have paid out the prize and settled the wager! But this?'

Sanga leaned in close, his conspiratorial wink doing nothing to ease the man's anxiety, pointing at the belt around Cotta's waist, almost hidden under the fold of his tunic.

'Nothing personal mate, we just thought it'd be good for you to experience a little disappointment for a change.'

The trainer's face fell further as he recognised the belt.

'You thieving f—'

Cotta wagged an admonishing finger at him.

'We'll have a little less of that, thank you. Accusations like that can only draw attention to your favoured manner of transporting your winnings around the countryside. Surely you don't want this lot to realise that your man routinely carries enough gold to fund a solid month of drinking and whoring for enough men to overpower the pair of you. Half a dozen big lads for him and an old woman to deal with you.'

His face a map of misery, the German reached for a mug of beer, shaking his head in disgust as he took a sip of the bitter brew.

'I should have told the lot of you to fuck off the moment I laid eyes on you. You've got the looks of thieves alright, especially you, you tub of lard.'

Morban bridled, while his companions exchanged looks which mutually conceded that the comment, if harsh, was still a fair one. But before he could even begin to attempt a rebuttal the tavern doors were thrown open, and five heavyset men wearing swords marched in, four of them wearing identical iron helmets while the fifth was bareheaded and dressed in the furs that indicated noble birth. Their presence rapidly cleared a path to the bar, and the bareheaded man looked about him until his eyes settled on the trainer, his sneer accompanied by a guttural verbal assault in his own language.

'When I heard there were men drinking for nothing in here I should have known *you'd* be involved in it.' He pointed a hand back through the tavern's doors. 'There are drunkards roaming the streets making improper suggestions to respectable women and openly pissing in the gutter, and who do I find at the heart of it but *you*, Lucius the Roman.'

The object of his ire spread his hands wide with an outraged expression.

'I have nothing to do with this, Gernot, I've been fooled by this band of robbers!'

Gernot's attention switched to the Tungrians, his eyes narrowing as he looked them over.

'I see. And that, presumably, would make a good enough tale for the king to hear. All of you can follow me.'

Cotta looked at Arminius questioningly, and the German shrugged back at him.

'It seems we've attracted a little more attention that might prove healthy.' He gestured to the door. 'Follow those men, or you may find them lacking in patience.'

Gernot turned back towards him with a frown.

'More Romans? It seems we're suffering an infestation. Come, you can explain yourselves to King Amalric, and then he can decide what to do with you.'

The Bructeri king lounged in his heavy wooden chair, playing a slow stare across the Tungrians with the look of a man who wasn't overly enamoured of what he saw. A man barely out of his teens, he nevertheless exuded the confidence of a man born to rule, even in his reclining position, and his eyes were bright in a face that combined a noble aspect with more than a hint of brutality.

'I'll speak Latin, since none of you seems to have gone to the trouble of learning our language other than you, Lucius the Roman, and even then it is a poor broken thing in your savage mouth. So, to ensure we're clear, I'm told that you,' he pointed at Saratos, 'managed to defeat the monster that Lucius the Roman has been parading around the tribal lands for the last five years. Is that right?'

'Yes, King.'

Gernot scowled at him from his place behind the throne, and Arminius translated his barked orders for them.

'When you address my beloved nephew the king you are to bow, and show appropriate respect!'

The king looked at him with a raised eyebrow.

'And how do you come to be associating with these Romans? What is your name?'

The German bowed.

'Great King, I am Arminius, son of Raban, of the Quadi tribe. I was captured in battle ten years ago during our war with Rome, and I am sworn to give service to this man until he chooses to free me from my slavery.'

Amalric looked at Cotta and then back at Arminius with a smile that was more disbelief than welcome.

'*This* one? He captured you?'

'I was knocked senseless, great King. When I recovered my wits I was already in chains. The Romans wage war for gain, not for honourable reasons.'

The king nodded grimly.

'That is true, and better understood by the Bructeri than most other tribes. Perhaps I should free you, and make him and these other men who accompany him your slaves?'

Cotta opened his mouth to retort, but closed it again as Arminius tapped him lightly on the arm.

'There is no need, great King. In truth he is a decent master, and I have grown accustomed to his ways.'

Amalric shrugged.

'I have heard that after a time the slave becomes dependent on the master. So be it. And you, master of this slave, what brings you here?'

Cotta stepped forward, bowing low.

'I am Cotta, a trader, King Amalric. I simply seek to make a living by trading with the peoples of the lands I travel through. I have recently returned from the distant east, and—'

'Where in the east, Cotta the trader?'

'Parthia, great King.'

Amalric sat forward in his chair, his interest suddenly piqued. 'And you have silk to trade? Spices?'

'Unfortunately not, great King, the people of Rome were far too eager for me to have retained any stock of such luxury. On hearing of the wonders of Germany I decided to reinvest my profits into trade goods, and to make a venture across the mighty river Rhenus to see if what I had been told was true.'

'And you bring . . . ?'

'Knives of high quality, linen, Samian pottery—'

Amalric grunted and sat back.

'Just the usual then. And where exactly is your stock, trader?'

'Waiting for us at the forest's edge, guarded by a barb–, by a warrior from Britannia who is also in my service, a man by the name of Lugos. He is a man of exceptional size and strength, and should be approached with caution.'

Amalric leaned back and spoke to Gernot, who nodded and left with half a dozen of the helmeted warriors who, Arminius had muttered as they were escorted into the king's hall, were likely to be part of the king's personal retinue, sworn to his service until death.

He looked at Saratos and Sanga.

'And here, unless I am mistaken, we have the victorious boxer and his trainer. A rarity, in that you of all men have defeated the beast of a man who's been terrorising the arenas of half a dozen tribal capitals for the last five years. How did you do it?'

Sanga stepped forward, bowing deeply.

'If I might be so bold, Great King, I am Sanga, and I am indeed this man's trainer. We are discharged soldiers, and we travel with the trader in return for food and coin, to keep him safe on the road.'

'I see. And how, then, did your friend defeat Lucius's monster?'

Sanga drew breath, but before he could speak the king raised a hand and spoke again.

'You have the look and indeed the sound of a talkative man, and my patience is being drawn thin by this protracted explanation of who you all are. Try not to test my patience.'

Sanga bowed again.

'I shall be as brief as possible, Great King. When I saw my man's opponent it was clear to me that only by taking him to the ground could any man hope to triumph over him.' Amalric nodded at the truth of his words. 'And so I told my fighter to go for the trip before the fight could start in earnest, and not to allow the big man to get back to his feet.'

'And this tactic clearly worked. You . . .' he pointed past Sanga to Saratos. 'You are a champion indeed, and deserving of our respect for your skill in the ring.'

The Dacian bowed deeply, and the king looked back at Cotta.

'But with the champion defeated you had your slave lead the onlookers back into the town, in order to get them drunk with Lucius's money. What was the point of that? Was there perhaps some gain to be made from such an action?'

After a moment's thought the veteran decided not to lie, encouraged by the hard stare that the king's uncle was giving him.

'You have seen through my plan, great King. My aim was simply to get Lucius here away from his fighter, so that we could liberate their gold from its hiding place.' He waved Saratos forward, indicating the heavy leather belt. 'There are a dozen gold coins hidden inside this belt, great King. I needed to remove the chance of anyone spotting us taking the belt.'

Amalric nodded, fixing a hard stare on the trainer.

'I've long wondered how it was that you were able to display so little money when the time came for you to be taxed. You must have tricked me out of a great deal of your takings over the years.'

He looked at Cotta and Lucius with equal distaste.

'So, one of you has defrauded me over a long period, the other sought to rob a man of his possessions while under the rule of my people's laws, and the justice which I and I alone administer on their behalf. Laws that are firm on the subject of theft, and the punishments to be applied in the event of a thief being captured. And, worse than that . . .'

He fell silent for a moment, leaving the two men hanging on his next words.

'In this case the gold in question was in point of fact never subjected to taxation by the Bructeri throne, taxation that should have been carried out every time Lucius entered this city. Which means that *you* . . .' He looked directly at Cotta. 'Have admitted to stealing from *me*, a crime for which there is a penalty of death by beheading.'

The veteran nodded grimly and bowed his head in acceptance of the judgement, while the king addressed Lucius.

'Whereas you, Lucius the Roman, are guilty of failure to pay taxes, which is also theft from the throne, pure and simple. By rights I should have you both killed, and your headless corpses thrown to the dogs.'

He looked at them both for a long moment before speaking again.

'Fortunately for you we are celebrating the birth of a son to my wife, and I am therefore minded to be lenient. I see two men with the same mixture of cunning and venality, and the fact that I have the means of inflicting a punishment on you that will sting you both deeply provides me with the means of doing so. You, trader, bring me that belt.'

'How close are we to Thusila?'

Gunda shook his head at the question.

'A mile, as you ordered. Too close.'

Scaurus looked up and down the gully the detachment's Hamian scouts had found, the grassy trench down which rainwater would flow in winter almost filled by the weary Tungrians, most of whom were already asleep.

'It'll have to do. We'll overnight here while you go into the city and make contact with Morban and his men.'

The scout started, turning to look at the tribune with wide eyes. '*Me?*'

The Roman raised an amused eyebrow.

'And who else do you think we should send? An Arab? A six-foot-wide axeman spoiling for a fight? Or a man of the tribe, capable of passing unnoticed in such a large town?'

Gunda stared at him for a long moment, tapping the tattoo on his forehead.

'You may recall, Tribune, that I am not on the best of terms with my tribe. I was forced to leave after doing something I am not proud of, but which I was both unable and unwilling to deny. If I am captured by the king's men I will be killed for having returned, there is no doubt of that. And this mark on my face does tend to be something of a giveaway.'

The tribune waved a hand at the detachment's resting soldiers.

'I sent Cotta into Thusila, assuming that he's managed to reach the city, with orders to find out where the priestess is to be found. He'll need to be located and brought here so that he can pass on the intelligence he's managed to gather, because without knowing where to find her we might as well skulk away into the forest and wait for Varus's cousin to come back and pick us up. So I need you to go and get him, if my mission is to succeed.'

He looked at the obstinate German for a moment.

'Very well, another two gold aureii.'

Gunda raised an eyebrow.

'Four.'

Scaurus laughed softly.

'And so the fate of my mission, my career and quite possibly my life, depends on a negotiation with a German who expects to live forever.'

Gunda shrugged.

'Nobody lives forever, Tribune. But not all that many men leave this world with the Hand of Wodanaz hacking into their chest to get at their beating heart.'

'The Hand of Wodanaz?'

'The King's most senior priest. They call him that because he has sent more men's spirits for the god to escort to the under-world than any other man in the tribe. He was only just forty years of age when I was exiled, and as far as I am aware he still holds the position despite the frequent and violent curses his juniors are reputed to make against him in the hope that he will drop dead and provide one of them with the opportunity to practise his butchering skills on a real live Roman legionary.'

The tribune nodded slowly.

'I see your point. But my best offer is three aureii. You can either like that sum or you can do without the gold altogether.'

'Bet you never expected this, eh Cotta?'

Sanga took another swig of his beer, grimacing momentarily at the taste, then slapped the beaker down and ripped another chunk of bread from the loaf on the table between them. The veteran centurion sipped his own drink, shaking his head at the turn in their fortunes.

'Did I expect an idiot to come up with an idea that would put me on my knees before a king from whom I'd just stolen enough gold to have him seriously considering my execution? And was I expecting to have our cart, its contents and all the money that the tribune gave us confiscated as a consequence of another idiot's decision to make sure we attracted the attentions of the king's attack dogs by getting half the city pissed up?'

His comrade blithely ignored the acerbic note in the response, taking another mouthful of beer.

'This stuff might taste like dog piss, but the more I drink the more it grows on me. Eh, Lucius? You must have had enough time to get a right old taste for the stuff!'

The trainer fixed his stare on the table before him, disconsolately sipping his beer with an expression that made his distaste for the brew evident. His fighter, however, having recovered from his temporary state of unconsciousness, had revealed himself to be a comparatively cheerful individual by the name of Magan. Apparently blessed with a personality quite at odds with his persona in the ring, he was happily engaged in a discussion with Saratos on the subject of his many and varied fights. Sanga looked at the giant for a moment and then asked the question that had been nagging at him from the moment he'd set eyes on the two men.

'How did you end up with that monster, eh Lucius? What good fortune was it that brought the two of you together?'

The trainer stared at him for a moment, then put his beaker down with exaggerated care, sighing with exasperation.

'If I tell you the answer to that question will you get off my fucking back for the rest of the night?'

Sanga shrugged, nodding his agreement.

'Right. He's my son. That enough for you?'

The Briton's eyes widened in amazement.

'What? That . . . giant of a man?' He raised his beaker to the giant. 'That's supposed to be *your* son?'

Lucius rolled his eyes up to the ceiling.

'Every time! Every *fucking* time I tell someone my story they just look at me like I'm mad.' He shook his head angrily, clearly seriously provoked by the Tungrian's amusement. 'Look, it might surprise you, but I was a soldier too—'

'Under which emperor? Hadrian!'

The older man ignored the jibe.

'You asked, so I'm telling you. Shut the fuck up or I'll have *my son* put you to sleep for a while.'

Sanga nodded graciously in acceptance of the other man's eloquently made point, and Lucius resumed his story.

'I served in the Thirtieth Legion, the good old Ulpius Victorious, did my twenty and got out just before the war with the Marcomanni and the Quadi got going, which was a stroke of luck. In those days relations with the other tribes were a good deal more friendly than they are now, so I bought a plot of land on the east bank of the river, married a local girl I'd been seeing for a while and settled down to be a farmer. The locals tolerated me well enough, although that was the Usipetes, not these miserable Bructeri bastards. She got pregnant and everything looked rosy until the birth. She had to be opened up to get Magan out, as you can imagine, and well . . .'

He stopped speaking for a moment, and the Tungrians waited for him to resume the story, respecting the moment of reverie.

'She died. Leaving me with an infant to bring up and a farm to run. Damn nearly killed me, I can tell you.'

He looked around at the listening soldiers.

'I know, how does a man *this* tall father a man *that* tall? Or that wide? And the truth is that I'll never know. He's a throwback, I guess, some freak combination of our ancestry that came up with all of the tall and wide we both had in us. By the time he was fifteen he was routinely smacking seven shades of shit out of the local kids when they tried to have a go at him for having a Roman for a father, even when they ganged up on him, but it wasn't until one of their fathers had a go at me and the boy laid him out with a single punch that I realised what I had in him. It would only have got worse, that much was obvious, and ended up with one or both of us getting killed one dark night, so I packed up and sold up, and we went on the road. Been doing the same thing for the last five years, more or less, travelling from town to town and making money on the back of the boy's sheer power. Until you cunts came along and took away the fruit of all that work.'

Cotta nodded sympathetically.

'Sorry about that. If there was a way to make it up to you . . .'

Lucius snorted.

'Which there ain't. I'll just be grateful never to see your fucking faces again. Promise me that and we can agree to put the . . .'

He fell silent as Gernot appeared behind Cotta, easing his big body onto the bench next to him, putting a mug full of beer down in front of him and playing a hard stare around the table.

'Just so there are no misunderstandings—'

'You speak Latin!'

The noble stared pityingly at Sanga.

'Of course I speak Latin, you fool. All of the king's nobles speak it, so that we can deal with the officers at the fort on the river. I only use it when I choose to, and I'm choosing to use it now so that what I've got to say sinks into your tiny minds. Got that?'

The soldier nodded, keeping his mouth shut in a rare demonstration of good sense.

'Good. You idiots have been luckier than you know. You . . .'

he pointed at Lucius. 'You have been stealing taxes from the king for years, and presumably from all the other tribes whose men your son's been knocking about. You may find them better informed from now on.'

Lucius lowered his gaze to stare down at the table, slowly shaking his head as the implications of the threat sank in.

'And you, *trader*, or whatever you really are, you're not welcome here after tonight. The king's merciful decision not to kill the pair of you is good until dawn tomorrow, at which point it will be rescinded. When this feast is over you can sleep here for the night and get out of Thusila first thing in the morning. If I see your ugly faces, any of you, after the sun's above the horizon tomorrow, then you'll wish you'd never been born. There are men of the Bructeri who would like nothing more than to see a Roman spreadeagled across an altar, with our chief priest summoning Wodanaz to witness our revenge on you for everything you've done to us since the first time your legions crossed the river. Do you take my meaning?'

Cotta nodded slowly.

'We'll be sure to take your advice, Lord. I wasn't staying here in any case, I'm looking for a priestess of whom I've heard stories, about how she can see a man's future, and tell him what lies in store—'

'*No!*'

The emphasis in Gernot's voice was reinforced by a heavy slap of the table with his palm, making the beakers in front of them jump.

'Forget any ideas of bothering our seer with your petty concerns. She has more important matters to be considering, and the risk of any detail as to her whereabouts getting back to your people is not one the king can afford to take. We know your ways of interfering in the affairs of your neighbours, and for all I know you're nothing more than a spy, sent to find out where she resides in preparation for some sort of attempt to abduct her. In fact perhaps I should simply take a knife—'

The veteran raised his hands wearily.

'No need, Lord. We'll be away first thing, and I guarantee that you won't ever see us again!'

The German stared at him for a moment, then nodded slowly, holding the gaze until Cotta was forced to look away.

'Very well. You have been warned.'

He drained the beaker and stood up, walking away to rejoin the royal party watched by every man at the table.

'I knew there was something wrong about you lot.'

The Tungrians turned to Lucius, who was looking around the table with an expression of sudden revelation.

'You're not retired,' he pointed at Saratos. 'You're too young, for one thing, and there's nothing wrong with you that would be a reason for early discharge. And you . . .' he turned to Sanga, 'you're every arsehole big-mouthed mule I ever served with rolled into one. And you're not retired either. Know how I can tell?' He paused rhetorically. 'I can tell because you're just as sharp and nasty as he is, in your own quiet way. Retired soldiers sit around drinking and talking about the good old days, and slowly but surely getting fat. And you don't have an ounce of fat anywhere on your body.'

He looked at Morban for a moment before cracking an evil smile.

'And you? A trader? You're no trader, you're more like a book-keeper, all percentages and calculation. More like a . . . a standard bearer? Not a proper standard bearer, they're all muscles and glory, more like one of those older men who carry round the fist and discs for their century when they're too shagged out to fight.' When Morban said nothing Lucius grinned triumphantly at Cotta. 'And you're no trader either, you've got centurion written all over you. The way you struggled to control the urge to sneer at Gernot then was classic. I've fucking got you, haven't I? You bastards aren't trading, you're spy—'

He froze, as the point of a blade tickled the base of his spine.

'You forget that there are six of us, *Roman*. He . . .' Arminius tipped his head to Lugos, who had been walked into the city at the point of half a dozen spears an hour earlier, 'is the man most likely to rip you limb from limb, if I tell him to. And *I'm* the man with the least regard for human life among us, having seen so much of it wasted over the years.' Lucius twisted his head to meet Arminius's flat stare, the blood slowly draining from his face. 'If your boy so much as twitches a muscle at me I'll cut his throat, here and now so that you can see him go to meet Wodanaz before you. So keep your voice *down*.'

An uneasy silence reigned for a long moment, Lucius breaking the spell by placing his hands on the table in front of him.

'You'll get no trouble from me, Quadi. See, I'm not interested in handing you in to these maniacs, 'cause I know too well what'll happen if I do, and it won't go well for any of us 'cause they'll just assume I've got some part of it.' He shook his head, staring across the table at Cotta. 'No, I'm offering you a trade, *trader*. Money for information. You want to find out where the king's got his favourite seer hidden, for what purpose I couldn't really give a shit, and me, I just want to get my money back. So just how much does Rome want to know that information, eh?'

Cotta opened his mouth to reply, but the words went unheard as a commotion at the hall's door drew their attention. A pair of uniformed Roman cavalrymen were handing over their weapons amid a hubbub of tribesmen calling out abuse and threats, their voices silenced by a sudden rapping of steel against wood. The king had got to his feet, and continued banging the table with the flat of his sword until the hall was silent.

'These men have come in peace! They have surrendered their weapons and wish to impart news of the greatest importance to our people, news sent to us from Rome itself! If they offer me or the tribe any disrespect then they will forfeit my protection, but until then you will remain *silent* so that I can hear their message!'

Disarmed, the soldiers approached the royal table and bowed deeply. The older of them stepped forward, addressing the king in a respectful tone that was nonetheless loud enough to be heard around the hall.

'Great King, I am Decurion Quintus Matius Dolfus, sent by

the governor of Germania Inferior! I thank you for your hospitality and for choosing to ignore our peoples' differences on this occasion! In return I offer you tidings from Rome of the greatest importance! My master the governor has ordered me to warn you of an attempt to rob your royal treasury, an attempt that he believes to be imminent, and which will be perpetrated by Romans, men who have chosen to ignore the delicate balance of our current peace! Men who may even be among you now!'

The Tungrians froze in horror at the cavalryman's words, and as Cotta looked about him he realised that while their attention had been focused on the speaker, half a dozen armed warriors had positioned themselves behind them.

'Oh *fuck*.'

'I told Cotta to wait for you at the edge of the town, and that you would guide him back here. With a little smile from Fortuna you'll be in and out well before dawn.'

Gunda nodded curtly, the gesture almost invisible in the near darkness, and Scaurus turned to Qadir who was standing behind the German in silence, a pair of his archers waiting with their usual blank-faced patience in his shadow.

'Accompany the scout to the edge of the forest, Centurion, and wait for him to return. If he does not return by the time it is light enough to see the town clearly then you are to return here without him, remaining undetected. And no, Centurion Varus, before you ask, you may not accompany the scouting party. What we need here are men who know how to move with stealth and subtlety, not an aristocrat with an apparent death wish.'

Qadir saluted the tribune and gestured to the scout, following him away down the path that led to the tribal capital, barely a mile distant, while Scaurus put a hand on the young Roman's shoulder.

'If you want to do something that will help, then go and keep Marcus company. He's not sleeping well, and I'm guessing he's nothing better to occupy his mind than brooding on the two men he killed today. He says that he has good days and bad days, but

I'd be willing to bet that the best of his nights are more of a trial to him than his worst days.'

'Well this just gets better and better, doesn't it?'

Lucius stared angrily at the Tungrians, pointing to the bruises that were evident beneath both of his eyes even in the hut's moonlit half-light. Where the soldiers had had the good sense to co-operate with their captors, recognising that their strong desire to inflict violence on such hated enemies was barely held in check and riding the kicks and punches that were aimed at them as they were taken from the king's hall, Lucius had chosen to protest his innocence. With Magan rendered impotent by the threat of a dozen spear blades, his father's protests had been silenced with swift and brutal simplicity, and they had been pushed into a stoutly built hut clearly intended for the imprisonment of offenders, under the watching eyes of the decurion who had betrayed them.

Cotta shrugged.

'You quacked at the wrong time, and as an-ex soldier you should have known better, shouldn't you? Besides, you'll get out from under this once the facts are clear . . .' He shook his head. 'Which is more than you can say for us. We're going out the hard way, I reckon, unless we can find some way to get out of this shithole before dawn. Once that lot have sobered up they'll have us away into the woods to one of their sacred groves, and that'll be the last anyone sees of us. Unless . . .'

'Unless what?' Sanga lifted his head and laughed curtly. 'Unless we manage to break down the door and do for the men they'll have left to guard us with our bare hands?'

'Door too strong. Not even Magan break.'

The soldier looked over at Saratos with a pitying smile.

'I know the fucking door's too strong mate, I already had a good look at it.'

The Dacian ignored him.

'So if door too strong, door need open by guard.'

Cotta and Sanga looked up at him with something close to

shared amusement, but it was Morban, previously silent and seemingly lost in his own thoughts, who voiced their disbelief.

'You mean we should hammer on the door and shout for help until they open it, and then we take them on with the advantage of surprise? And you really think they'll be that stupid?'

Sanga joined in with the standard bearer's argument in a rare display of agreeing with the older man.

'They'd come through that door with swords and spears ready for us, give us a good hiding for disturbing whatever games they'll using to pass the time, then lock us up again, nothing changed except for a fresher and more expensive set of lumps and fewer teeth for the priest to pull out once he gets down to the serious business. Face it boy, we're dead meat. If I had a blade I'd slit my own wrists and leave them with a smiling corpse to do their worst with.'

The Dacian snorted.

'You so bothered, you kill self with teeth.'

'With my fucking teeth?'

Lucius nodded sagely.

'We used to have the same discussions when I was a legionary. What's worse, to have your eyes pulled out, your ears and nose cut off, not to mention your cock and balls, and then some dribbling old bastard take an age to get your heart out, all while a pack of mad German cunts scream at you and spit in your face.'

Sanga frowned.

'Or what?'

'Or show some balls and do the job yourself.'

The Briton shook his head in bemusement.

'I know. But with my teeth? How does *that* work?'

Saratos sank into a sitting position.

'Is easy. Is blood here . . .' he pointed to his arm, just above the crease of his armpit. 'You bite, hard enough to find blood, and the rest easy. Just lie down, go sleep.'

Morban nodded.

'To be fair, I've heard the same, more or less.'

Sanga looked about him aghast.

'You're all fucking mad! I'm not going out by biting myself to death, I'll fight the bastards and make them put me to the sword.'

'Except they won't. They'll just tap you on the head to quieten you down and then tie you up. The next thing you'll know will be the tickle as some mad old sod starts carving you up for the entertainment of his followers.' Morban shook his head. 'No, I really do think that a nice quiet suicide might be the better way to go.'

6

With the feast's inevitable and messy degeneration from celebration to orgiastic drinking frenzy, Gernot had given the command for guards to be set on all of the tribe's most important places. The roads in and out of the city to the south, west and north, the grain stores and the tribe's treasury, all were to be manned by men whose lack of fortune in the traditional drawing of lots had resulted in their being excluded from the feast other than a quiet mug of beer taken out of sight of the celebrating tribesmen. Not for them the long evening and early morning of drinking that would inevitably result in most of the tribe's warriors lapsing into insensibility and sleeping where they fell, but instead the honour of ensuring that the Bructeri's most sensitive spots were guarded by men possessed of sharp iron and the wits to use it.

The young warrior standing guard on the treasury paced from one end of the short corridor that led from the palace quarters to the massively beamed and heavily nailed door that secured the repository of the tribe's gold and silver, still glowing with the pride of having been given such responsibility by Gernot when there were men far better experienced and deserving of such an honour than he. On pointing out his unsuitability for the task in the face of his betters he had been heartened to hear his lord's reply.

'Consider this as a reward for your hard work on the training ground over the months. Other men may be better prepared, but none has worked as hard or improved as quickly. Another will stand guard tomorrow, but for tonight the honour is yours.'

Pacing up and down the long corridor his heart swelled with

the pleasure of it, the pride that his father, himself a warrior in the king's household, would be enjoying now, perhaps raising one last beaker of beer to his son's rise in their lord's estimation before falling into the drunken stupor that was the aim of every man present at the feast. As he reached the treasury door and started to turn, he heard a footstep behind him, and spun, swinging his spear down from its place at its shoulder to bear on whoever it was that was approaching him from behind without warning. Seeing a face not only familiar to him but revered, he lowered the weapon's point to touch the ground as the newcomer stepped close, bowing his head deeply.

'My—'

The knife struck once, swiftly and with all the power that the other man had at his disposal, its blade punching into his stomach and its point thrusting upwards to find his heart, stilling its rhythm with a cold, harsh kiss that sent his lifeblood spraying briefly across the corridor. Opening his mouth to speak, to ask why, he found the strength to do so absent, fled from his body with the blade's implacable theft of his life, and slumped against the strong room's door frame with his consciousness already absent and his life not far behind it. His killer bent over him for a moment, pulling the largely ceremonial but still completely functional key from around the dead man's neck, opened the door and slipped inside.

'This is the place.' Gunda's whisper was so quiet that Qadir had to lean close to him to make out the words. 'Wait here. I will whistle before I rejoin, so that you don't put an arrow in me.'

The Hamian nodded, and before he had the chance to reply the scout was gone, away down the path that led into the town below them, a track so heavily used that it was wide enough for two men to walk abreast, and utterly devoid of any hint of grass.

'We do not want to be here after daybreak.'

The centurion nodded at Husam's blunt statement.

'I agree. You heard the tribune's order, we are to leave before the sun is above the horizon.'

'He is a wise man, and he cares about the men who serve under him. We are lucky to have come under his command.'

Qadir smiled in the darkness.

'Lucky? As you have said yourself on more than one occasion, being under his command could soon enough prove to be our death sentence. Do you never wonder how it is that we are forever being sent to perform just one more "impossible task"? His birth, his disregard for the niceties of his situation . . . his protection of our friend Centurion Aquila, all calculated to make him easily disposable, should such a sacrifice be required. And in that event . . .'

'We would die with no little honour. That we know. But have you forgotten your vow to the Deasura, our goddess Atargatis, three times blessed be her name?'

'The goddess . . .' Qadir sighed, and Husam frowned at his centurion's weary tone of voice. 'In a world where the gods are so frequently used as a loin cloth to disguise the naked evil that lives in the hearts of men, I do find myself questioning the validity of all such idols when I hear a man being tortured to death in the name of a god. And I wonder why a god, were he – or she – to exist at all, would wish for that man to die in such a degraded manner.'

The chosen man almost hissed his reply, whispering despite the lack of any audience beyond the third member of the party, a stolid man entirely trusted by both of them.

'Do not say such a thing aloud! Do not even allow yourself to consider such a thought! Question the German gods all you like, but you doubt the existence of our Deasura at your peril!'

Qadir smiled at his friend.

'We are among friends, Husam. None of these men is likely to censure me for the crime of being godless.'

Husam's reply was indignant, his shock at the centurion's admission evident in his hushed voice.

'I care not what these Tungrians think of such a thing, but only what the Deasura herself might do were she to believe that your faith in her was lacking. You know as well as I do that she is a jealous goddess, and demands the total loyalty of her followers!'

Qadir shrugged.

'So we are told by the priests, who instruct us in these matters from such an early age that we never think to challenge their preaching.'

'You cannot think . . .'

'That they may tell us the things they do, as to the fate of unbelievers, in order to ensure that we follow their teachings, and make our gifts to their temples. Perhaps I do.'

An uneasy silence fell over the trio, Qadir musing on his growing feeling of disassociation from the goddess he had for long venerated with every ounce of his being, while Husam puzzled as to how he was to stop his friend from voicing such terrible doubts.

'You still recall the vow we both made to the goddess the day we joined the army, that first day when the centurions roamed our ranks with their vine sticks beating any man who gave them the faintest hint of an excuse? That we would live *and* die with the same honesty and cleanliness of purpose, in her sacred name?' The chosen man snorted dark amusement. 'And after all, given our current position, it would hardly be surprising if our time to die was close at hand, would it? Perhaps you should avoid antagonising the goddess, at least until we are once again on the safe side of the river?'

The second archer shifted his position fractionally, easing the strain on his knees. Older than both Qadir and his second in command, he was stoic by nature and perhaps the steadiest of Qadir's men, given to saying little unless he had something to say.

'Better to make the other man die, I would say. And better to use the sharp ears that the Deasura gave us for the purpose of detecting movement in the dark rather more, and the tongues that we are supposed to use for the purpose of communicating with our fellow men, rather than idle chatter, somewhat less.'

Both men grinned at his dour chiding, respecting his wisdom, and silently nocked arrows to their bows, settling in for a long silent wait in the forest's darkness.

Moving with slow, exaggerated grace, Gunda eased himself into the shadow of the first house that overlooked the path, now grown in width until it was practically a road, walking slowly down its length until he reached the end of the rough-walled building. Slowly leaning forward, he carefully observed the sleeping town, remembering his maternal grandfather's frequent admonishment against making any sudden movement while stalking a beast in the forest, a lesson that seemed equally appropriate as he gambled his life on his skills to avoid detection by the tribe's warriors. In the absence of a father, the older man had taken on the task of educating his grandson in the skills of a hunter with a combination of straightforward instruction hammered home by straightforward punishment of any error.

'Your eyes should dart here and there as swiftly as a rat's, boy, but your head needs to move as slowly as a bull's! Your eyes are more like your grandmother's first thing in the morning, staring at nothing for moments on end, and your head's no slower than a weasel's when it scents rabbits!'

He grinned at the memory of the old man gripping a wooden switch, the end flicking out to sting his ears whenever his movements were anything less than slow and smooth, then pushed the memory away to focus on the present. Somewhere close by a dog was asleep, the faint whimper of its dreams priming him for flight until he realised with a flood of relief that the animal was dreaming rather than growling a warning. The potential for any faint noise to wake the animal redoubled his awareness of the peril he was courting as he slowly settled into the building's cover and slowed his breathing, listening for any hint of the men he was expected to meet.

The faint scrape of boot leather on the hard ground caught his attention, and he sank deeper into the cover of the building's shadow as first one shadowy figure and then another pair of men detached itself from the darkness of the forest to his left. Standing stock-still, the newcomer stared about him with a slow sweep of his head and then, satisfied that he was unobserved, started forwards, moving stealthily into the settlement's dark streets with his escort close behind, passing within a dozen yards of the crouching scout who slowly turned his head to the wall to prevent his being betrayed by the shine of his eyeballs. Holding his breath, he waited until the other man was safely past him before exhaling slowly, watching as the dark figures vanished into the shadows. Something in the first man's gait had pricked his memory, and he stared into the gloom into which the half-seen intruder had vanished, his lips moving with a silent expression of amazement.

'Surely not . . . ?'

Slipping through the darkened streets of the city, the decurion called Dolfus stood for a moment on the corner of a building overlooking the king's great hall before gesturing to his men to stay in the shadows, then crossed the road and entered the building through a door that had been left ajar. Inside the large wooden structure he paused for a moment to allow his eyes to adapt to the almost complete absence of light.

A figure stepped out of the shadows with a bulky object in one hand and the blade of a long knife protruding from the other.

'You've got balls of solid iron, Roman, to come here so brazenly.'

The man who had been waiting in the great hall's shadows whispered the agreed challenge, then stepped forward to reveal himself to the waiting Roman. Dolfus stood stock-still at the sight of the long knife in the other man's hand, its blade still wet with blood, and eased his arms away from his body to demonstrate that he represented no threat. Pitching his voice low, he replied to the challenge with the words that had been agreed years before.

'Without risk, there can be no reward.'

The Bructeri nodded, handing an iron-bound wooden box to the decurion.

'Your message gave me little time. To bring this here I took a risk that will see me cut to pieces on my tribe's altar if it is ever discovered. No man could be allowed to live after such treachery, not even a man of my exalted rank. I can only hope that the end result will justify the risk into which your master has forced me.'

Dolfus bowed his head in respect for the evident danger to which the German had exposed himself.

'This is the eagle?'

'It is. It was taken when a legion was defeated in our war against the Romans alongside the Batavi, and claimed by my people as a prize of battle.'

Dolfus looked down at the wooden box, opening its lid to reveal the symbol of Roman power it contained, a once proud legion eagle fashioned of solid gold, although its surface had long since lost the brilliant shine that had once graced its outstretched wings.

'A thing of beauty, is it not? And yet the best use we can put it to is to use it to torture the legionaries our warriors capture and bring across the river, heating it in a fire and branding them with its image while they are tied to our altar. A dangerous game, which must one day result in a punitive raid by your army that will leave this city a smoking ruin. And I will share their fate were my part in this theft ever discovered. Rome would lose a friend within my tribe, and a rare friend at that. Few other men have the sort of influence that I can wield.'

'The eagle will be returned to your treasury soon enough, never fear.' Dolfus closed the box, extending a hand to point at the Bructeri's garment. 'There is blood on your tunic.'

The other man looked down at the spots of blood that had been sprayed across him during his murder of the man who had been guarding the royal treasury.

'It is of no matter, a clean tunic will be no great surprise the morning after a feast of that magnificence. We proceed as you proposed, in the message your men delivered to me earlier?'

Dolfus nodded.

'Yes. The eagle's loss will be discovered, and suspicion will naturally fall upon them, suspicion they will very shortly be doing their best to encourage by riding for our bridge over the Rhenus.

You must ensure that the king's household pursues them to the gates of the fort that guards the crossing to demand the eagle's return, at which point the plan will unroll just as I have proposed. You will be rid of the two men who have the most to gain from continued conflict with Rome, and Rome will have the prospect of an ally where there was previously only enmity. If we both follow our roles then mutual benefit will be the outcome.'

The Bructeri nodded tersely, his face set hard.

'Let us hope so. My people need a change of fortune, and that can only be achieved by removing those who preach violence against your people. There will never be a better opportunity.' The noble nodded to Dolfus and turned away, then stopped and looked back at the cavalry officer. 'The Romans you betrayed are imprisoned close by, and I made sure that your men were allowed to witness their incarceration. Whether you choose to free them or leave them to suffer the tribe's revenge for what is soon to happen is entirely your decision.'

He vanished into the shadows, leaving the cavalryman looking after him for a long moment before he too padded silently away from their meeting place and back out into the night.

'What that?'

Sanga raised his head, looking at Saratos quizzically.

'What's what? You still hoping to overpower the—'

His friend put out a hand and placed it over his mouth, putting a finger to his own lips while his expression became one of warning that the Briton had learned from experience not to ignore. From outside the hut came the faintest of noises, a coughing grunt that was cut off almost as soon as it had been uttered, and then silence fell, only the minute scraping of boots in the dust betraying the presence of men outside the building. With a sudden heavy thud the bar that secured the hut's entrance tumbled to the ground, and the door itself slowly opened, to reveal a single figure standing in the frame with a drawn sword, the blade dark with blood.

'*Wait!*'

His whispered imperative stopped them in their tracks, as every man in the hut tensed himself to make a dash for it, and as they paused two more swords emerged from the darkness on either side of their apparent rescuer, the men wielding them instantly recognisable. He walked forward into the shaft of moonlight, revealing a face whose eyes were hard and intent on the men before him, his stance that of a man ready to use the blade in earnest.

'Nobody leaves until we've got a few things straight. Which one of you is Cotta?'

The standard bearer stepped forward.

'That's me. Centurion, apparently condemned to a slow and horrible death as a result of being betrayed to the king of this particular shithole by men dressed just like you. Have you come to finish the job?'

The other man's expression didn't change.

'If you're Cotta then you're the man I'm extracting from this mess, you and whoever you vouch for.'

The veteran bridled.

'This *mess*?' We were doing fine until some prick calling himself Dolfus marched into the feast and sold us out!'

The swordsman shook his head.

'I doubt it, and I've got a good deal more experience of the way these people think than you do. I think it entirely more likely that the king's nobles were planning to have you quietly killed later in the evening, or perhaps they'd have just thrown you in here until their priest was ready for you. But that is of little consequence. I'm here with orders to get you out, and take you to your comrades in the forest, wherever it is you're planning to meet up with them.'

Cotta shook his head, feigning ignorance.

'Friends in the forest? What—'

'There's no time for denials, Cotta, the man I'm working for knows everything about your mission to abduct the priestess, and he wants it to succeed just as much as the men who ordered it. So while Governor Albinus thinks he sent me out to betray you all to the Bructeri, to further some little spat he's having with your tribune, I'm acting under orders from someone whose authority is somewhat stronger than his. So you can either come with us or I can just lock you back in to wait for the man I believe they call the Hand of Wodanaz to get round to putting you on his altar. You choose.'

'My King! Wake up!'

Amalric rolled over in his bed and stared uncomprehendingly up the man standing over him, shaking his head as he fought to focus.

'What?'

'The treasury, my King! The treasury has been opened!'

Surging from his bed, suddenly, horribly, very much awake, the king pulled on a tunic and followed the man's lead to the massive wooden door that was the only access to the stone staircase that ran down to the underground chamber where the tribe's wealth was stored. Slumped against the door's wooden frame was the body of the young warrior who had been tasked to guard the treasury the previous evening, his chest covered by a thick, dark red bloodstain. Offering a swift prayer for the dead man's spirit before taking a torch from the wall sconce, the king strode down the stairs and into the repository of his tribe's wealth, looking about him with a growing sense of relief.

'Whoever they were, and however they managed to open the door, they don't seem to have taken any—' He stopped in midsentence as his eyes alighted on the spot where the tribe's most valued spoil of war should have stood proudly in pride of place along the gold and silver plate, neatly stacked bags of coin and other valuable items. The words hissed out of him, amazement robbing him of any more than a whisper. *'The eagle . . .'*

'My King?'

He swung to face the man, spittle flying from his lips as rage rose within him.

'The eagle has been taken! Call for the men of my household!'

Gernot appeared at the slave's side, his appearance as crisp as ever despite the hour, and his face grim.

'I've already called for your warriors, my King. The men standing watch on the road to the south were ridden down a short time ago, and the Romans are not in the quarters we provided for them. It seems fair to assume that their presence here was always aimed at this theft, and that their condemnation of the trader and his men was simply a cover for their plan.'

Amalric snarled his fury at his closest advisor.

'Very well! Have my household mounted and ready to ride at first light! I'll show those thieving, murdering usurpers the limits of a king's patience!'

Gernot nodded and turned away, careful to conceal his slight smile of satisfaction until his back was turned to the king.

'As you command, my King.'

Cotta's party and their rescuers were most of the way to the city's eastern edge when a hissed challenge from the shadows froze them in their tracks. The armed men turned to face the potential threat.

'*Cotta!*'

A figure detached from the shadows of the closest building with empty hands spread wide, his voice no more than a faint whisper.

'Your tribune sent me to guide you to the meeting place.' He looked more closely at the men around him, tilting his head in question. 'Dolfus? It *was* you . . .'

Cotta turned to face the subject of his question.

'Dolfus? But—'

'Keep your fucking voice down. Yes, I'm Dolfus.'

'But if you're Dolfus . . .'

'Save it.' The command implicit in the whisper was unmistakable. 'Yes Gunda, it's me. You'd better get on with what you came here for, hadn't you?'

The scout nodded, turning away wordlessly and leading them past the last of the houses and up the wide track that led into the forest.

'But if *he's* Dolfus . . .'

Sanga shrugged in reply to the veteran's baffled question.

'Fucked if I know. It'll all be clear soon enough, so until then I'm just going to work on not getting recaptured by those barbarian bastards.'

Saratos leaned over their shoulder.

'Is easy enough. More than one man call self Dolfus.'

Dolfus himself chuckled quietly.

'At least one of you has a brain then? Now shut up and follow the scout, the sooner we're in the trees and out of sight the better. It'll be dawn soon enough.'

Amalric looked out over the ranks of his household companion warriors, gathered before the King's Hall dressed and equipped for war, their iron helmets and spear heads gleaming dully in the dawn's cold light.

'These Romans have gone too far! They have stolen our eagle! The prize that our ancestors fought and died to protect as we were driven from our tribal lands by the Chamavi and the Angrivarii! The trophy that is the symbol of the Bructeri people's survival in the face of overwhelming numbers! And we will not tolerate this! *I* will not tolerate this!'

An angry rumble greeted his outraged statement of intent, the warriors raising their spears and calling for him to lead them in pursuit of the Romans.

'Follow me, my brother warriors, follow me and we will recover what has been stolen or take the flame of our anger to these thieves!'

He looked at Gernot, who nodded approvingly at his words before turning to face the assembled warriors.

'I stand with my king! I will fight with my king! And if necessary I will die for my king!' He turned back to Amalric with a deep bow. 'My King, your orders?'

The younger man took the reins of his horse from the man waiting with the beast, disdaining the offered hand up into the saddle and springing up onto the horse's back, reaching down to take the spear that was held up for him.

'We ride for the river!'

Gernot's mouth split in a ferocious grin.

'We ride on Rome! We ride!'

'Men coming in!'

The hissed warning brought the detachment to a state of readiness to fight that showed no sign of either fatigue or hunger, Dubnus's axemen crouching in the cover of the gulley's lip, their evil-bladed weapons at the ready for a sprint at whatever enemy might have discovered them, while the Hamians nocked arrows and peered out into the gloom. An owl hooted mournfully twice, and Dubnus tipped his head on one side, waiting as the silence strung out.

'Perhaps it really was just an ow—'

The call sounded again, and the big Briton snapped out a terse order for the men of the detachment to stand down. Gunda was the first man to materialise out of the dawn's murk, stepping down into the gully with the look of a man who was grateful for the completion of his night's work. Cotta and his companions followed close on his heels, their progress a succession of snapping twigs and rustling leaves where the German had been all but silent, but it was the next man over the edge of the tiny valley that got the officers' startled attention. Unused to having to look up to any man other than the giant Lugos, Dubnus stared in amazement at Magan for a moment before finding his voice, his father's arrival almost going unnoticed.

'What the fuck is *that* . . . ?'

The question froze on his lips as Dolfus made his entrance behind the trainer, still carrying the box containing the Bructeri eagle, and even Scaurus was now starting to look more than a little perturbed. The various parties were still eyeing each other speculatively when Qadir and his archers stepped down into their midst.

'So go on then Cotta, tell us who your new friends are. No, don't tell me – Morban won them in a wager.' The standard bearer shot Dubnus a poisonous look, but the big centurion had known him too long to be impressed. 'I've told you before not to try eyeballing me, standard bearer—'

'I knew that prick was a statue waver!'

Lucius refused to be cowed by Dubnus's swift glare, and Cotta sighed, stepping forward to make the introductions to a clearly bemused Scaurus.

'The big lad's called Magan, Tribune, and this former legionary is his father. He goes by the name of Lucius, and he tells me that he knows where the German woman is to be found.'

'His father?'

'Unlikely as it might seem, yes. And as to how we met them . . .' He shook his head with a wry smile. 'Even I'm struggling to believe it. The thing is, the Bructeri hate us, they loathe us so badly that we weren't getting anywhere with pretending to be traders.' He held up thumb and forefinger with a minute gap between the two digits. 'I was this far from giving up on the whole scheme when this one . . .' he waved a hand at Sanga, 'saw that monster taking on the locals for money, and had the idea of getting his Dacian bruiser to smack the boy about a bit as a way of getting the Germans' attention. But we did too good a job of it, and got dragged into their king's feast so they could keep an eye on us. And then . . . *he* happened . . .' He indicated Dolfus, who stepped forward and saluted Scaurus, who returned the salute with a look of growing incomprehension. 'Or at least his men there did. They betrayed us to the Bructeri, who locked us up ready for execution, and then a couple of hours later *he* killed the guards and released us.'

Scaurus looked at the cavalry officer with his eyes narrowed in calculation.

'You can explain this, I presume? Your actions might easily be construed as verging on treasonous. Your name?'

Dolfus snapped to attention.

'Decurion Quintus Matius Dolfus.'

Scaurus looked him up and down.

'Gods below, as if I wasn't already laden with one thrusting young gentleman without another one dropping into my life just when I'm trying to pull off something that requires a bit of subtlety. So what are you doing here sticking your nose into my delicately poised mission, Decurion? Are you one of those sons of privilege who found life in Rome insufficiently challenging and volunteered to join the occupants of the Camp of the Foreigners? You are a Grain Officer, I presume, despite the lack of any insignia to that effect?'

A dozen pairs of eyes hardened at the suggestion, men who'd already seen the damage that one of the emperor's private army of spies could wreak at close quarters, but to Scaurus's bemusement Dolfus shook his head and chuckled.

'A fair guess, Tribune, but a fair way from the truth none the less. My profession is aligned with the men you've mentioned with such disdain, but our recruitment is a good deal more select. And our activities are a little less murky from a moral perspective too, I'd have to say . . .' he paused for a moment, 'or at least most of the time they are. My orders are to do whatever I see fit to ensure that your mission is a success. In the pursuit of which I had one of my troopers here pretend to be me and betray your men to the Bructeri, which by the way might well have kept them alive longer than had I failed to do so, but mainly in order to procure this from the tribal treasury . . .' He offered the iron-bound box to Scaurus, who opened it, staring at its contents for a long moment. 'The absence of that highly prized item is currently distracting King Amalric in quite a dramatic style, since he's chasing two more of my men all the way back to the Rhenus and thereby giving you the time you need to achieve your mission and make your escape, *if* you get down to it immediately.'

He fixed a level gaze on Scaurus.

'Although once I've briefed you properly as to the governor's intentions, you may have cause to make a few small alterations to your plans.'

'They knew we were coming!'

Gernot nodded grimly at Amalric's angry words as he trotted his horse alongside his king's mount towards the bridge fort's towering wooden walls. The ramparts were lined with men, at least half a dozen centuries of legionaries interspersed with clusters of easterners whose differently shaped helmets made their presence obvious as, he guessed, was the intention. He had chosen to ride to the Novaesium bridgehead with all forty of his companion warriors at his back, far too few to offer any real threat to the fort that guarded the crossing, but enough to make it clear exactly who he was, to be escorted by so many men bearing such a precious weight in iron. Where most of his men fought with a spear, and a shield with an iron boss if they could afford it, the men of the king's household, the tribe's fastest and strongest warriors, were lavishly equipped by comparison with bowl-shaped iron helmets that protected the tops of their skulls, and long swords of sharp iron.

'Certainly, my king. They will have been warned by the thieves.'

Reining their mounts in a dozen paces from the gate, they looked up at the defenders for a moment in silence before the king spoke again.

'They look scared to me.'

Gernot smiled up at the legionaries.

'Consider it from their perspective. They hear their fellow soldiers being tortured in the night, distant howls and shrieks of pure agony, and the chanting of our warriors as your priest sends their spirits to Wodanaz. They know we hate them above all others, and that if you were to throw the strength of the tribe at that fort it would be a burned-out shell before nightfall, populated only by their corpses. They have good cause for fear.' He looked up at the men on the wall above them. 'Shall I address them, my king? To do so is beneath your dignity.'

Amalric dipped his head in acknowledgement, and the noble straightened his back, calling out to the men on the wall closest to where they sat.

'Soldiers of Rome, is this any way to greet the leader of a tribe with whom you claim to have friendly relations? My king has suffered the theft of something that is very dear to his tribe, and has come here with all speed to request your assistance in its return, only to find himself faced by a wall of spears! I suggest that you put this presumably unintended insult to one side, and that we speak man to man with your commander!'

A grizzled centurion stared down at them for a moment and then turned away to speak to someone inside the fort. After a moment's discussion he turned back and called out a reply.

'Our prefect will come out to speak with you! Twitch in the wrong way while he is outside these walls and you two will be the first to die!'

After a moment's pause the fort's northern gate swung outwards, a file of legionaries issuing through the opening and fanning out to either side to form a ten-man escort for the officer who followed them. Looking up, Amalric saw that the easterners now had arrows nocked to their bows, while the fort's bolt throwers had swung down to point at them in an ostentatious display of threat. The prefect strode forwards confidently enough, but as his questing eyes looked beyond the two horsemen to size up the threat posed by the men of the king's household, both of the Germans could see his awareness of the situation's delicacy. He stopped walking when he was five paces from their position and bowed, the minimum diplomatic gesture of the respect that could be expected by a king, then looked up at Amalric from beneath his helmet's brow guard.

'Your Highness, this is an unexpected pleasure.'

Gernot laughed out loud.

'Apparently neither unexpected not pleasurable, for you to have all these men out of their beds and, as you like to say, ready for war!'

The Roman nodded his acceptance of the fact.

'It was pointed out to me yesterday that I might be receiving just such a visit, although the circumstances were not made entirely clear. It seems that the advice I was given was well founded.'

'Advice given to you by a man who goes by the name of Dolfus?'

The Roman sniffed.

'My informant didn't identify himself. He was passing through the fort into your land on a mission for the governor, with four of his men.'

Amalric frowned.

'Four?'

'You were sent by the governor to wreck our mission.' Scaurus raised his eyes to look at the iron-grey dawn sky. 'That man's idiocy seems to have no limit! But instead, and acting on the orders of a *higher* authority, you've rescued my men from the Bructeri, stolen a captured legion eagle that's a sacred tribal relic, and sent their king off chasing those of your men you've used as decoys.'

Dolfus nodded equably.

'That's it, Tribune, more or less.'

'A higher authority? Higher than the *governor*?' The younger man looked back at him in silence. 'You're trying to tell me that you've been posted to the province by the same people who appointed Clodius Albinus, with instructions to subvert his orders should they run counter to whatever it is that your masters think should be happening?'

The cavalryman raised his eyebrows without saying a word, and Scaurus shook his head in frustration.

'I gather you don't feel able to comment.'

'No.'

The tribune walked away for a moment, then turned back, a decision clearly made.

'Dubnus, get the men fed and ready to move.' The Briton nodded and turned away to his task. 'Centurions Varus and Corvus, accompany the decurion and me down the gully a way and bring the giant's father with you. And Qadir . . .'

The Hamian came to attention.

'Tribune.'

'Make sure our guide is *closely* observed at all times by men with arrows on their strings. He looks nervous to me, and I don't want him vanishing off into the trees. We'll never find him if that happens.'

He led the three officers and Lucius away from the detachment, until they were out of earshot.

'You served with the legions?'

The older man saluted.

'Yes, Tribune sir. I was a legionary with the Thirtieth Legion, before I retired on this side of the river to be with the woman I loved.'

I see. And you're sure you know where this priestess is to be found?'

Lucius nodded.

'She's right under your nose, Tribune. There's a hill to the east, less than five miles distant, where Amalric keeps her safe and sound, guarded by his men.'

'To the east.' Scaurus's tone was suddenly hard. 'One minute.'

He turned back to the detachment, calling up the gulley.

'Centurion Qadir, I've changed my mind. Bring my scout here please.'

They watched in silence as Gunda was escorted, stony-faced, down the gully to where they stood. Scaurus stared at him for a long moment, and when he spoke his voice retained its iron-hard tone.

'I asked you where the path to the east went, yesterday morning. You told me that it was just a hunter's trail, and you led us away from it as quickly as you could. That wasn't true, was it?'

The German shook his head, his face downcast.

'No.'

'Where does it lead?'

After a momentary pause the guide sighed.

'To the place where my people keep my sister.'

'Mithras help me . . .' Scaurus shook his head. 'This priestess is your *sister*?'

Gunda looked up, his expression suddenly hard enough to match the Roman's.

'Yes. My *sister*. I was expelled from the tribe for killing a man who threatened her, when one of her prophecies wasn't fulfilled exactly to his liking. I told you that she sometimes only sees a part of what is to come, and this was one such case. She fore-told a male child for the wife of one of the tribe's noble warriors, but when the child was born it was evident that he was not the father. He threatened to kill her for misleading him, and I took my sword to him in her defence. The old king was merciful, partly for love of Gerhild and partly because the man in question was dangerously quick tempered, but he had to send me away if only for my own protection from the dead man's brother Gernot. Ever since that day the kings of the Bructeri, old and new, have both kept Gerhild safe from harm in the tower where she has lived for the last fifteen years, a prisoner in a fur-lined cage. When you told me that you planned a mission into my tribe's territory so close to Thusila, it didn't take much intelligence to work out what your purpose was, and so I was even more determined to come with you if only to make sure that she wasn't harmed.'

Dolfus and Scaurus exchanged glances before the latter spoke again.

'And why is it that you think I won't just kill you, here and now, and leave your body for the pigs? There's going to be a lot of death in these woods today, so another corpse wouldn't trouble me overly.'

Gunda looked back at him, shaking his head slowly.

'Two reasons. Firstly, Tribune, because you're not that sort of man. And that's not a guess, it's a fact. I may not be my sister, but I never fail to judge a man correctly. It's a gift, compared to what might be said to be her curse.'

'And the second reason?'

'If you kill me, she'll know. Don't ask me to explain it, just believe me when I tell you that we have some sort of connection. If I die here then you'll find her less than co-operative. And I wouldn't want to be subject to my sister's anger, not if I were you.'

Scaurus looked at him for a moment.

'That's a first. I'm being threatened, it appears, with the retribution of a woman who doesn't even know I exist.'

The scout smiled back at him.

'I wouldn't be so sure about that if I were you, Roman. She sees *everything*.'

'I see.' Scaurus shook his head in disbelief. 'This day is rapidly descending into farce, so I think it's time we took control of it back from the Fates. I presume it's a fair assumption, Decurion, that this . . .' he gestured to the eagle inside its box, 'is going to bring the Bructeri after us like a pack of wild dogs, once they get so much as a hint that we're in the forest?'

'I'd say that's a safe assumption, Tribune. And it can only be a matter of time before they reach that conclusion. The decoys who led them to the bridge will have fulfilled their purpose very soon now.'

The tribune nodded decisively.

'In that case I think we need to strike fast and hard, with as much distraction as possible, get what we came for and then get back to the river and the warships that are waiting for us. Once we're under the protection of their archers and bolt throwers we might as well be on the far side of the Rhenus as far as the Bructeri are concerned.'

'This man Dolfus brought *four* men with him through your gates yesterday?'

The fort's prefect nodded tersely.

'And two men came back through them this morning?'

'Yes.'

Amalric looked at Gernot in puzzlement.

'Those two men . . .'

The noble's face darkened, as he drew the same conclusion to that which his king had already reached.

'Were decoys! Intended to draw out our strength and send us chasing shadows!'

The king looked down at the Roman officer, who seemed none the wiser.

'Was either of these men carrying a wooden box, bound with iron and big enough to hold your dagger in its sheath?'

The prefect turned to the senior centurion who had walked out alongside him with the look of a man spoiling for a fight.

'First Spear?'

'No Prefect. I watched them come back in myself, given the unusual timing of their arrival. They had nothing more than their standard equipment.'

Gernot looked down at him for a moment, then pointed back the way they had come.

'If he's telling the truth then we've been lured away from Thusila while the other three men who didn't declare their presence last night are somewhere back there, doing who knows what!'

The king turned his horse in a whinnying half-circle.

'And they still have the eagle!'

Marcus and Dubnus ran back down the track in the direction from which the detachment had marched the previous day, a mixed group of axemen and archers at their heels. Scaurus's last words to the Briton had been stark in their intent, his face set hard as the detachment readied themselves for the fight.

'Do two things for me, Centurion. Make me a diversion, something to get the Bructeri's attention and lead them in the wrong direction. And make sure the man who's been torturing our soldiers isn't ever going to do it again.' The two men had saluted and turned away, only for the tribune to add an afterthought. 'Oh, and gentlemen, make very sure that anyone who fancies their chances of taking on this priest's mantle as "the Hand of Wodanaz" has a *very* clear understanding of what Roman justice looks like.'

They stopped running a hundred paces from the clearing, taking a moment for their breathing to return to something close to normal before proceeding at a slow, careful pace with arrows nocked and ready to fly on either side. Pacing stealthily towards the grove's entrance Marcus flicked a pointing finger to either side, waiting as the two axemen, chosen for their rare ability to move quietly in the forest, vanished into the foliage on either side of the path and were lost to view. The remaining members of the party sank down into the bushes' cover and waited while Dubnus and Marcus silently counted down the agreed three hundred heart beats. Looking at each other they nodded, rose from their crouches and walked slowly and quietly towards the arch of trees. Stepping into the clearing Marcus eased his gladius from its scabbard with an almost silent hiss of metal and oiled leather, raising the blade to point at a figure busy at work on the grove's far side with his back to them, his hands raised in the act of tying a fragment of plate armour to the tree before him. Ghosting forward with one hand up to ensure that his companions held their positions, he was less than ten paces distant from his quarry when the tiny sound of his hobnails scraping against a pebble gave the priest the slightest of clues that he was being stalked.

Whirling, his decorative task instantly forgotten, the German was in flight even as his eyes registered the Roman's presence, making a bolt for the glade's western entrance with a surprising turn of pace for a man of his age. As he passed through the arch the biggest of the pioneers stepped from cover, ducking the wild punch thrown at him by the fleeing priest and hammering a big fist squarely into his gut, leaving him coughing and gasping for breath on his knees in the path's dust. At Dubnus's command the two axemen swiftly pinioned the priest before pulling him to his feet and dragging him back to face the two centurions. Wild-eyed, his tunic and cloak filthy with dust, the German railed at them all in his own language, struggling as vigorously as he could against their iron grip.

'What's he saying?'

Arminius smiled darkly.

'It may be better you never know, Dubnus. That sort of curse can get to you, given enough time to think about it. Although quite a lot of it seems to be him asking if we have any idea just who he is?'

The big Briton snorted, snapping a fist out without any warning and rocking the priest's head back in a spray of blood that spurted across his tunic in a wide fan.

'Tell him I know exactly who he is. Tell him that he's about to find out what it feels like to receive the sort of special attention he specialises in.'

The holy man's face took on an affronted expression as he began to gabble at them again, a new note of outrage in his voice. Arminius sighed.

'Seems he didn't take you seriously. Now he's threatening that his master Wodanaz will call upon his brother Thuneraz to punish you with his mighty bolts of lightning.'

The Briton shook his head disbelievingly, unsheathing his dagger.

'Bring him over here and let's put that theory to the test.'

He gestured to the pioneers to follow him to the altar, with the furious priest powerless to resist. Reaching out, he took the holy man's right hand and forced it down onto the altar. The German stared at him in horrified realisation as he pulled the dagger from his belt, holding it up to display the small blade's keen edge.

'A lot of men don't like the idea of doing harm to a priest. After all, almost everyone believes in some sort of god.' The Briton waited while Arminius translated. 'My friend here is a follower of Mithras, I'm a worshipper of the hunting god Cocidius. And that sort of devotion makes your sort believe you're in no danger from dangerous men like us, because you believe we'll be too afraid of the revenge of your god if we do you any harm.' He grinned, shaking his head. 'The problem is, priest, while I have no special urge to mutilate a man, I'm under orders to send a message to your people by making sure you exit this life with as much pain as possible. Just like you've been doing with our soldiers, eh? So while I'd rather just put this knife through your throat and leave you to die, that wouldn't really do my orders justice, would it? My orders are to make sure that anyone finding you is terrified that if they take on your mantle they're going to end up in the same sorry state. So I'm afraid that this is going to hurt . . . a lot.'

He waited until Arminius had translated for him, then put the dagger to the German's little finger and cut down into the first knuckle joint, eliciting a muffled, snarling growl of pain as the digit came free. The German struggled against the hands gripping him, the pain lending him fresh strength that was nevertheless ineffective against the two pioneers' firm grip. The Briton worked swiftly and without any let up, cutting away each of the priest's fingers with firm strokes of the knife, ignoring the German's frenzied, muffled shrieks of pain and the thrashing of his feet against the altar stone as his blood spread across its blackened surface.

'There, you'll never hold a knife again, that's for certain. But that's hardly enough of a message, is it?'

'That's the place? That's where the Bructeri are holding your sister?'

Gunda nodded. Scaurus peered through the thin foliage that straggled across the forest's edge at a stone-built tower that occupied the centre of a wide-open area, the trees having been cleared for fifty paces in all directions. The ground around the building was neatly kept, largely turned over to what looked like an extended vegetable plot, and the scent of aromatic herbs was carried to the watching men on a slight breeze.

'The king has told his men that no effort is to be spared in keeping my sister content. She may be a prisoner, but the cage bars have been gilded.'

The bitterness in the scout's tone surprised Scaurus.

'But why hold her prisoner, I wonder? I had been led to believe that she was the tribe's most valuable asset?'

'True, but she is a prisoner nonetheless. The king keeps her counsel for himself, and for himself alone.'

'Why?'

Varus's question drew little more than a shrug from Gunda.

'I could not say, I only hear snippets of gossip from time to time. But whatever it is that she tells him is clearly not for the ears of his people as far as Amalric is concerned.'

The young aristocrat looked to his tribune.

'Perhaps she foretells another uprising?'

Scaurus shook his head.

'More likely she predicts another defeat at the hand of Rome. That would probably be enough for any king to want her voice to go unheard, I'd have thought. But that's enough speculation. Let's go and see who's at home, shall we?'

They stepped from the trees, pacing across the open space in a line which interspersed archers with axemen. The air was heavy with silence, no call of bird or animal to be heard as the Tungrians slowly, deliberately, advanced though the vegetables and herbs with swords drawn and arrows nocked. With a creak of ungreased hinges a door opened on the other side of the building, and the sound of a man breaking wind with gusto made the advancing men grin despite the tension. Scaurus raised a hand, sinking down into a crouch to give his archers a clear shot just as the tribesman came round the tower's curved side, still too sleepy to see what was in front of him until it was too late. At Qadir's hissed command the Hamians loosed their arrows, dropping the Bructeri guard into the dirt with no more noise than the thumping impacts of a pair of iron arrowheads and the grunt as they drove the breath from the German's lungs.

'*Move!*'

Whispering the command to attack, Scaurus led the dash for the tower's door with Varus at his heels, the two men rounding the building to find that the dead tribesman had left it wide open. Varus lunged in through the opening, coming face-to-face with another Bructeri who had seemingly just climbed from his pallet bed, alerted by the noise of their feet on the hard-packed dirt around the building. They stared at each other for an instant that seemed to last an eternity before Scaurus threw the unprepared warrior back against the room's rough stone and followed in with his blade, stabbing the point into the warrior's unprotected chest with such force that it unintentionally lodged between two of the hapless tribesman's ribs. Struggling to free it, as Varus hacked down another of the priestess's guards to his right, he was taken unawares by an attack from his left, out of the darkest corner of the room. Releasing the sword's handle he reached for his dagger, but had the weapon no more than halfway out of its sheath when the half-seen figure punched at him, a sudden intrusion of cold pain that sent him staggering back with his right-hand side suddenly numb.

The tribesman snarled, baring his teeth and stepping in close again, raising the blade to strike with the wild-eyed expression of a man who knew he was about to take a life, then went down under the axes of a pair of Dubnus's men as they rampaged into the fight. Varus stepped over the corpse of his man with a look of concern.

'You're wounded.'

The tribune nodded, grimacing at the pain in his side, already wet beneath the torn mail.

'He put the point through my mail. You . . .' he pointed to Gunda, 'fetch your sister.'

The young Centurion helped him out of the building and back out into the watery sunlight, then lifted the tribune's mail shirt and looked unhappily at a slit in the tunic that lay beneath it, dark red blood already staining the material down to its hem.

'We need to get that bandaged.'

Scaurus shook his head decisively.

'No time. We need to . . .'

He fell silent as Gunda reappeared through the door, leading a woman by the hand with a piece of cloth tied over her eyes. Copper haired, her willowy frame was clad in a simple woollen tunic, a string of stone beads hanging around her neck the only obvious form of decoration. The scout gestured to her, his face creased in a sad smile.

'My sister.'

The priestess shook her head in protest.

'There was no need for the blindfold. I've seen those men die more than once, in my dreams. There is no horror left in their deaths for me.' The soldiers looked at each other in disbelief, but before any of them could comment, she continued. 'That's a nasty wound, Tribune. He twisted the blade as it went in, I believe.'

'How did you . . . ?'

She reached up and removed the cloth bound over her green eyes, playing her penetrating gaze across the men around her as she answered in a patient tone, her Latin perfect and almost unaccented.

'I told you. I have dreamed this moment a hundred times, this and others yet to come. The wound will need treatment, but there is indeed no time now, if you are to evade the attentions of my king. There are horses, tethered in the woods over there . . .'

She pointed to the forest opposite the point where the detachment had entered the clearing.

'And while you fetch them, gather me some herbs with which to prepare a balm for that wound. Sage, thyme and lavender will be enough, but I'll need a large quantity of each, and the purple flowers over there.'

The soldiers looked at each other in confusion, and after a moment she shook her head in amusement.

'It seems I'll have to do this myself. Perhaps one of you could fetch my iron pot from the tower?'

'Varus.'

Scaurus called out to his subordinate, and found himself both amused and irritated by the fact that his centurion's attention was fixed on the woman as she swept away towards the herb garden.

'*Varus!*'

The young centurion snapped his attention back to his tribune.

'Yes, Tribune.'

Scaurus grimaced as he pointed at Gerhild, who was now crouched over a plot thick with herbs and flowers.

'We have no time to waste. Detail some men to fetch the horses, send a man to fetch her bloody pot and set a guard on the witch. Make sure she doesn't make a run for it, and watch what she gathers. I don't want to end up with a belly full of hemlock, should we manage to give this Amalric and his men the slip.'

*

'I have to admit it, you're a tough little bastard.'

The priest stared up at Dubnus through a mask of pain and hatred, then looked down at his ruined hand, still held firmly against the altar stone. Flies were already buzzing around the finger joints that had been severed, one at a time, to lie discarded on the ornately carved stone.

'Yes, I can't deny it.' The Briton nodded sombrely into his captive's agonised glare. 'You've handled yourself with some dignity, but then all I've done so far is take off a few fingers.'

He waited for Arminius to translate, then lifted the sacrificial bone saw from its place on a shelf beneath the altar.

'When my tribune told me to make an example of you I decided to cut off your ears, your lips, your nose and your balls, and leave them laid out for the men who find you, ruined but still alive. I even wondered if I might use this . . .' he held the saw up before the priest's wide eyes, 'to carve your heart out, like you do with those poor bastards, but now that the moment has come I can't bring myself to do it. Because when it comes down to it, I'm not an animal wearing a man's body like you are.'

He watched a triumphant expression spread across the priest's face as Arminius's words sank in, and nodded slowly in response, bending close to the stare into the German's eyes.

'Yes, you've won, I give up. I'm not going to torture you any more.'

As Arminius explained the meaning of his words he looked intently at the priest, waiting for the moment when the tribes-man's believed his victory was complete. For an instant the German's guard relaxed, and in that moment Dubnus had what he wanted.

'No. I'm not going to torture you, because that would be lowering me to your level. I've got something a lot purer in mind for you.'

The priest frowned, and the Briton gestured to his men.

'Fetch the wood.'

The priest's expression crumpled, and Dubnus bent close to speak into his ear as the Tungrians hurried to pile kindling and firewood onto the altar's flat surface, taking it from the neat stacks of aged timber at the grove's edge.

'I never held with human sacrifice myself. My people used to practise it in secret, back when I was a prince of the Briganti tribe, when they thought the Romans weren't looking. I always considered it a waste of a human life, personally, but of course there's always someone happy to leave this world in search of someone they've lost. A slave wanting to follow a dead master, or a wife looking to see her husband again. Our priests were kind when it came down to it, always trying to make sure that even if the sacrifices weren't allowed to be dead when they went onto the pyre, they were already most of the way across the river, with poison or bloodletting to weaken them so much that it took no more than a gentle push to finish them off, but every now and then they'd get it wrong and put someone on the sacred fire with the wits to realise what was happening and the strength to fight it, once the flames reached them. And that, let me tell you, was never nice to watch. A man who knows that he's about to burn to death – there's a man who'll fight like an animal to escape. They screamed, they strained against the ropes, and then, when the fire took them . . .' he paused, shaking his head, 'they just weren't human any longer. Their screams were those of animals, dying in agony. I used to hate watching it then, but in your case I expect I'm going to find it . . .' he paused, searching for the right word, then nodded with satisfaction, 'ah yes. I'm going to find it . . . *just.*'

He gestured to the hulking men of his century who had gathered around them.

'Tie him up so tight that he can't move a muscle, then get him on top of the altar. And try not to scatter the wood when you put him up there, eh lads? This is one sacrifice where we want a nice strong fire.'

Scaurus looked back at the men running behind the horses, their heads thrown back to gulp in the cold morning air. The movement made him wince, as a bolt of pain shot up his side.

'Tribune?'

Varus was riding alongside him with a look of concern, one hand ready to reach out and steady his superior if necessary.

'You should be focusing on the witch, Centurion. I can keep this up all day.'

The younger man nodded, allowing his horse to drop back down the column to where Gerhild was riding her own white mare with the confidence of an accomplished horsewoman.

'You have no need to worry, Centurion. He won't fall off his horse until *much* later in the day.'

He stared at her for a moment before replying, unsure of how best to deal with her complete self-possession, even in the face of enemies who had abducted her with violence.

'You have dreamed that as well?'

She laughed at him, her green eyes seeming to sparkle.

'No, Centurion, but I can read a man. Your tribune is made from stronger iron than most, and he will stay in that saddle, no matter how painful the ride, until he passes out from loss of blood. When next we stop you will persuade him to allow me a short time to apply a bandage, and that will enable him to stay in the saddle for a good time longer than if he continues bleeding from an unstaunched wound.'

Varus stared at her again, then nodded brusquely and dropped back to encourage the runners. After another mile of riding they reached the point where the path crossed the main trail, and Scaurus reined his horse in, looking to the north hopefully.

'No sign of Marcus and Dubnus. I'd hoped they would be here by now.'

The centurion looked at his thigh, dark with drying blood from the wound hidden beneath his chain mail.

'The woman wants to bandage your wound. And I think she's ri—'

Scaurus shook his head brusquely.

'There's no time.'

Gerhild climbed down from her mount, the tone of her voice making the words something between encouragement and a direct command.

'On the contrary, Tribune, you have more than sufficient time for me to dress the wound. Your men won't be done with burning the Hand of Wodanaz for a while yet. Now get off that horse and have these men help you out of your mail so that I can make sure you don't succumb to its effects. How else am I going to ensure that you fulfil your destiny?'

'Bring me that torch.'

Two of the Hamians had busied themselves with flint and iron while Dubnus's axemen were busy trussing the priest up so tightly that he was completely unable to move, and manoeuvring him onto the firewood that now covered the altar to a depth of three feet. The priest's outrage had long since become simple terror in the face of his impending immolation, and his eyes followed the Briton's movements as he took a burning brand from them and approached, holding up the blazing torch for the German to see. Reaching out, he stripped the crude woollen gag from the helpless priest's mouth, waiting in obdurate silence as the doomed man babbled a stream of invective, curses and entreaties at him. At length, raising a finger to silence the captive's abuse, he spoke in a matter-of-fact tone.

'You murdered our soldiers. Men who had never harmed you or your tribe were tortured, maimed and then cut open while they were still alive, the beating hearts ripped from their bodies.' He paused, lifting the torch to shoulder height. 'And now you pay. Roman justice has been delivered. Feel to free to shout that fact at the sky as you burn. The more of your people who hear you, the better.'

Pushing the brand into the heart of the kindling he waited for a moment while the twigs and leaves took light, then walked around to the other side of the altar and repeated the process. Leaving the brand in place he reached for the saw, pulling his arm back to hurl it far into the forest.

'Don't throw it away.'

The Briton turned to find Marcus with his hand out to take the evil little tool.

'*This?* You want to keep something that's killed so many men?'

His friend nodded, reaching out to take the cold metal from his hand.

'Yes. Don't ask me why, because I couldn't tell you.'

Dubnus shrugged and turned back to the now frantic priest, wriggling and writhing fruitlessly against his bonds.

'Now it comes down to it I find I have no desperate need to watch this bastard fry. Do you?'

Marcus shook his head and turned away.

'No. Knowing that he'll burn is enough for me.'

Calling to the soldiers who were standing watching the helpless priest's fruitless struggles, as the flames from the kindling began to play on the wood on which he lay, Dubnus led them from the grove while Marcus paused for a moment at the clearing's entrance and locked eyes with the helpless torturer. With a sudden burst of fire the stacked timber underneath his head ignited, the flames catching his greasy hair and burning it away in a sudden gout of flame that provoked a falsetto scream of agony from the priest, his entire body straining hopelessly against the bonds that would secure his body until their destruction by the hungry flames. The Roman turned away and followed his comrades up the path without a backward glance.

7

Amalric and Gernot found Thusila much as they had left it, both men dismounting outside the king's hall and hurrying inside while the men of the king's household waited alongside their beasts. Amalric ran to check his family while Gernot strode swiftly to the treasury only to find it secure and under a redoubled guard, the previous sentry's body and the bloody evidence of his murder having been removed in their absence. Frowning, he retraced his steps to find the king standing outside the hall.

'They're safe?'

Amalric nodded tersely.

'Nobody has seen neither hide nor hair of the Romans since we rode out.'

The two men looked at each other for a moment before the king spoke.

'Five Romans entered our land yesterday, but only two of them came here. They warned us of a plot to rob our treasury, provoked us to lock up a ragbag collection of idiots and former soldiers who may or may not have had any connection with them, and then stole the tribe's eagle in the middle of the night. They made a run for the Roman bridge fort and led us away chasing shadows, while the other three freed the same men their comrades had incriminated and escaped into the forest, presumably with my eagle.'

Gernot looked at his king with a growing light of certainty in his eyes as Amalric continued.

'One group of two men to distract us with their claims of a threat to our treasury, and then to steal the eagle. Although it puzzles me that the man guarding the treasury didn't raise an alarm before he was killed.'

The noble nodded, grim-faced.

'And another party of three, who entered the city during the night, received the eagle from the thieves, freed the Roman captives, and then used the distraction caused by the theft to do . . . what?'

They looked at each other for a moment, Amalric slowly shaking his head as if to dispel an idea that had just occurred to him.

'Surely not.'

He stared out over the forested hill that rose to the city's east. Gernot followed his gaze, his eyes narrowing as he realised the conclusion to which the king had suddenly sprung.

'You don't think . . . ?'

The king pointed a finger at the trees, his eyes widening in horror.

'Look!'

A thin plume of black smoke was rising through the forest halfway up the hill, thickening as they watched, as the fire's grip of whatever it was burning intensified. A sudden piercing shriek rent the morning's calm, audible despite the distance over which it had carried, the sound of a man undergoing mortal torment, and Amalric started.

'Is that . . . ?'

Gernot turned to the closest of his men.

'Summon the men of the city! The enemy are in the forest!'

'Did you hear that?'

Dubnus nodded grimly at the question, his chest heaving from the mile they had already run since leaving the sacred grove to reach the main track. A horn was sounding off to the north and west, its brazen note rendered thin and insubstantial by distance, but its meaning was no less clear for being distant. After a moment another blaring note joined the first, their urgent sound clearly a call to arms for the Bructeri tribesmen within earshot.

'Horns. And horns means that they've woken up to the fact we're out here, most likely.' He turned to the men of their small party. *'Run!'*

They had covered the best part of another mile when the

axeman bringing up the rear called out a warning, turning and setting himself for combat while he took great whooping breaths to steady his trembling frame. Shrugging his shield's strap off his shoulder, he lifted the oval board into the fighting position, glaring over its hide-clad rim at the horseman whose appearance had prompted him to turn and fight, his axe held ready to strike while his fellows hurried to his side. Nocking arrows, the Hamians looked at Marcus for the order to shoot, but the rider, having taken a swift look at them from the vantage point of a rise in the ground, had already wheeled his horse about and disappeared. Dubnus shook his head in disappointment.

'Gone to fetch his mates. Which means we'll be thigh deep in the bastards before long. Keep moving!' They ran again, Marcus blowing his horn in the agreed signal for the rejoin every five hundred paces. Behind them the sound of horses, at first distant and almost unreal in the absence of a visible presence, quickly grew louder.

'We'll be fighting in a moment! Archers, take position to shoot and get your breath back! Axes, to me!'

The detachment stopped running at the burly Briton's command, the Hamians dividing their numbers either side of the track and taking up positions with clear shots back the way they had come, sucking in air to calm their heaving chests while each man pushed his arrows' iron heads into the ground next to a tree behind which they could take shelter from any return shots. The Tenth Century men stepped into a wall of shields, two on either side of their centurion, blocking the path with their armoured bulk.

In a flurry of hoof beats the Bructeri were visible, half a dozen riders crouching low over their horse's backs as they galloped at the waiting Tungrians.

'Loose!'

The archers let their first arrows fly, dropping the leading horseman's mount and hurling its rider into the undergrowth, the horses behind the fallen beast balking as it kicked and writhed before them.

'Again!'

Another volley of missiles found targets along the struggling riders, picking one from his saddle with arrows in his chest and throat, another stepping off his mount as it staggered sideways into the forest and collapsed with feathered shafts protruding from its broad chest. The remaining tribesmen took flight, the unhorsed man grabbing onto the last horse's saddle and running alongside it with exaggerated strides. The Hamians looked to their officers, but Dubnus shook his head.

'We're going to need every arrow if we're going to get back to the river! Prepare to move!'

Dubnus detached himself from his men and walked across to his friend.

'That was just the hotheads, right?'

The Roman nodded.

'From what Morban was telling us about the state they were in last night I'd imagine they're still trying to slap some sense into the city's warriors, and doubtless their king felt he had to do *something*. That was probably just a roll of the dice aimed at finding out if we could be ridden down without much effort.'

Dubnus grinned humourlessly.

'Well, they know the answer to that one, sure enough. Let's get out of here before the rest of them come for a try at dealing with us the hard way.'

Gernot turned away from the horsemen who had returned from the first abortive foray against the intruders with a grim face.

'Romans. Archers, and brutes with axes, from what they saw. Horsemen aren't going to be enough, not without any more room to manoeuvre, and the forest paths are just too narrow.'

Amalric nodded tersely, his face a mask of fury.

'They have the eagle, our sacred grove is burning, and if what I fear was their true purpose in worming their way into my kingdom, my seer may be their captive! I want these men's corpses nailed to the trees around our sacred grove and their heads thrown over the walls of Novaesium, to remind the Romans who rules on this side of the river! Make it happen, Gernot, and spend whatever lives are necessary to deal with these thieving animals!'

The noble bowed and turned away to the city's warriors, many of them still half asleep from their celebrations of the previous night, issuing a flurry of orders.

'Two spearmen to every horseman! Spearmen, you will hold the horse's saddle and run alongside. Nobody drops out! If you have to puke, then puke, but keep running or you'll have me to deal with!' He looked around at his men with a forbidding expression. 'Horsemen, no faster than a trot to ensure the spearmen can hang on. There's no need for us to ride any faster, these intruders aren't going anywhere with the river at their backs.'

He waited while the foot soldiers paired up with riders, each man readying himself for the run through the forest with one hand clutching the horse's saddle straps and the other holding onto his spear and shield for grim death, each of them clearly praying not to lose their grip and fall under the hoofs of the animals behind. It soon became clear that there were over a dozen horsemen either without any spearmen at all, or only a single man.

'You, and you, go and find riders who need another man. You riders without spearmen, dismount and come here.'

'What do you intend?'

He turned to find the king at his shoulder.

'A dozen men won't be sufficient to kill these Romans, but it will be enough to stop them running, and force them to defend themselves while we cover the distance between us. And who can tell how the gods might favour such a gamble, or the men who undertake it?'

Amalric thought for a moment and then nodded.

'I will speak to them.' He waited until the riders had gathered, then addressed them directly. 'Men of the king's household, you are indeed fortunate to have the chance to strike a first blow at these intruders, and to help speed the rescue of the most precious prize of war our tribe possesses. You will ride forward ahead of our main body, and as fast as you can safely travel, you will find the Romans and you will offer them battle. Hold them in place for me, and I will bring your brothers in arms to the fight to stamp them flat for having the temerity to attack us here, in our home. Ride before us, find these Romans, and teach them what it is to incur the rage of the Bructeri!'

'What happened to the tribune?'

Marcus and Dubnus's party had rejoined that led by the tribune moments before, only to find Scaurus stripped of his armour and tunic, and lying flat on his back while the woman who had been the target of their mission treated a wound in his side. Dubnus had stalked away to organise their defence of the clearing where the two paths met, arraying his men along its southern side to maximise the archers' shooting time if an attack started while they were held static by Scaurus's treatment. Arminius tapped Lupus on the shoulder and pointed to the clearing's western edge.

'Go and practise your spear work over there, and if anything happens get down and stay down until it's all over.'

Scaurus scowled up at Marcus and Varus, craning his neck to see past the priestess bent over him.

'I was stupid enough to stop a Bructeri dagger wielded with enough strength to put the blade through my mail, that's what happened! And you don't have to ask Varus, you cheeky young whelp, Valerius Aquila! I may have incurred a nasty little puncture but I can still talk for myself!'

'You will lie back and allow me to work!'

The woman's tone brooked no argument, and he subsided back onto the ground while she arranged a pad of linen over the wound, tying it in place with a longer strip of the same material.

'There. Now rest awhile and gather your strength. There is a long way to ride, and difficult ground to cross, before you will be safe.'

Marcus looked at Varus questioningly, and the younger man led him away out of earshot of the woman before speaking again.

'It seems that we won't be—'

Dubnus strode up to them, cutting across the discussion and pointing at the pair of archers they had left watching the path on the far side of the clearing.

'There are more of them coming! Horsemen!'

Having signalled the Bructeri approach, the two archers standing guard on the clearing's far side were shooting as fast as they could, their arrows flicking away into the forest. As the sound of the oncoming horses' hoofs grew louder they started looking back between shots, clearly attempting to gauge the right moment to make a run for the safety of the detachment's line, such as it was. Loosing one last arrow apiece they turned and ran, one of them darting away to his right into the undergrowth while the other pelted directly towards the safety of his fellows. Bursting from the narrow path's confines into the open ground, the Bructeri riders fanned out to either side, and were immediately engaged by the eight archers waiting on the clearing's far edge. While the sleet of arrows took a rapid toll of those riders who guided their horses to right and left, a pair of men took it into their heads to ride down the fleeing archer and were protected to some degree by the man they were pursuing, his fellow bowmen unable to shoot at the mounted tribesmen for fear of hitting their comrade.

His vision fixed on the running archer, the leading horseman came on at the gallop, triumphantly spearing him ten paces short of the Tungrian line, the stricken soldier's back arching as the long blade punched through his body. A pair of arrows sprouted from his mount's chest, and, stricken, it half-cantered and half-staggered towards the Tungrians until one of Dubnus's axemen stepped forward and swung his curved blade in a flickering arc to sever one of its front legs, sending the beast crashing to the ground with an awful scream of agony. The rider, pitched over the beast's head by its headlong plunge, was thrown violently into a tree's thick trunk and flopped lifelessly to the ground to stare vacantly at the sky above. His companion, realising the danger into which he had driven his mount, had started to wrestle his beast around when a broad-headed arrow loosed at close range plunged deep into its chest and stopped its heart in an instant, dropping the horse in the length of a single stride and sending him spinning away from its death throes. Rolling to his feet he looked about himself wildly, spotted a gap in the encircling Romans with only the boy Lupus to beat and ran for it, stabbing out with his spear at the boy only to find his thrust competently parried and the youth's framea pointed squarely at his chest, Lupus himself rooted to the spot as the warrior bore down on him. Committed to his headlong charge the German almost fell onto the blade, gasping as it slid between his ribs and took his life in a single heartbeat, snapping the spear shaft as he collapsed lifelessly onto it and fell at the momentarily paralysed boy's feet. An axe rose and fell, putting a merciful end to the maimed horse's piteous attempts to regain its footing, and suddenly the clearing was silent again except for the sound of the handful of horsemen who had escaped death making a hasty retreat back down the track, the wheezes and piteous whinnies of their wounded mounts slowly dying away.

Scaurus got to his feet with Arminius's assistance, white-faced from the loss of so much blood, his wound heavily padded with moss held in place by a strip of cloth that Gerhild had wrapped around his body. He gestured for the German to help him back into his tunic and armour, looking about him at the corpses of Bructeri warriors and their horses scattered across the clearing.

'And with that, gentlemen, I think it's time we were on our way, don't you? I expect the next attack will be somewhat better thought through.' He pointed to the boy, still staring down at his dead German with an open mouth. 'Fetch the child, Arminius, he'll stand there all day if you don't pull him away.'

He gathered the officers around him, wincing while his mail was pulled over his head and dragged down into place, Gerhild's hand on the padding over his wound preventing it from being pulled free by the armour's weight.

'Thank you, Madam. Centurion Varus, we'll do this just as we discussed it.'

The younger man saluted and took the woman by her arm, drawing her away from the group while Scaurus turned back to the men of the detachment.

'Now then, gentlemen, I think we all know what we have to do, but for those of you who live for the idea of burying an axe in a barbarian's head . . .' he stared at Dubnus for a moment before continuing, 'this will be a tactical retreat to the river with our bows and axes combined, one axeman to accompany each archer for their protection while they use their bows to keep the Bructeri at arm's length. Centurion Qadir, ensure that your men shepherd their remaining arrows carefully, and only shoot when they have clear targets. You must not let them get carried away and leave the detachment without any means of keeping the enemy's heads down.'

Qadir nodded his understanding.

'And you, Dubnus, your axemen are to fight going backwards, and only to step onto the front foot if necessary to preserve a tactical advantage. When not engaged hand to hand, I want them to concentrate on using their shields to protect both themselves *and* the archer with whom they're paired.'

Dubnus nodded curtly.

'Yes, Tribune. They'll defend their brother soldiers to the last man.'

Scaurus smiled wanly.

'I know they will. Very well then gentlemen, get your men moving. We're still a long way from the river.'

'What happened?'

The oldest of the three riders who had survived the ill-fated attack on the Romans shook his head, his face grey with shock and exhaustion. Amalric had found them at the side of the forest track, staring down at one of their number who was clearly close to death, his breathing shallow and eyes glassy, a pair of arrows protruding from his chest, and had halted the Bructeri main force's column to question them.

'It was a slaughter. Their archers shot us to ribbons.' He pointed down at the dying man. 'He was hit before we even saw them.'

'How many are they?'

The man looked up at him, shaking his head again as he tried to gather his wits.

'Twenty? Perhaps thirty?'

The Bructeri noble turned in his saddle to face the king.

'Thirty men at most, and we have eighty spearmen *and* half as many riders! We should pursue these Romans until we catch up with them, then dismount and overrun them. Thirty men will never stand against this many warriors!'

Amalric nodded his consent, and the noble raised a hand to order the advance. He led the column to the south at a slow trot, eyes scanning the forest to either side of the track, until the clearing where the Romans had offered his horsemen battle came into view, with its grisly scattering of dead men and horses. Gernot shouted a peremptory command over his shoulder, knowing that some of his warriors would have recognised brothers and cousins among the fallen.

'Leave them! We hunt Romans!'

They trotted on for another two miles before a flash of sunlight on iron alerted Gernot to the presence of armoured men ahead of them, the backs of the fleeing enemy giving him fresh purpose.

'There, my King! There is your enemy! We must attack them on foot through the forest, the leading horses will never survive an attack down the path and the rest of us will be trapped behind the first beasts to fall.' He turned back to the men behind him. 'Dismount!'

The oldest and youngest among them led the horses away while the remaining warriors pressed in around their king, looking to him for leadership. A rider galloped up from behind them, jumping from his saddle and hurrying to Amalric, whispering urgently in the king's ear. Amalric nodded at the messenger's words, staring grim-faced around the tribesmen's tight circle.

'They have my seer! Gerhild has fallen into their filthy grasping hands! And I swear my revenge to Wodanaz!' He drew his sword and raised the point at the sky. 'My brothers! Men of my household! Men of my city! These Romans have stolen our pride away this day, through lies and deceit! We must bring them to bay, and then we must show them how the Bructeri deal with those who set foot on our soil without our leave to do so! If you have no choice then they are to die, but every one of them we take alive is worth a gold coin to the man who captures him, and five for an officer! I will take these captives to the Roman fort by the river, and I will put them to death, within clear sight of the soldiers who guard the bridge! Their screams will be heard in Rome itself!'

Gernot nodded, pointing at the distant Tungrians with his sword.

'Run, brothers! Now we take this war to the men who started it!'

'Here they come!'

Still a mile from the river, the detachment turned to fight in the way that Scaurus had prescribed once combat was inevitable, the bowmen laying out their arrows for rapid shooting while one of Dubnus's men took his place beside each of them with their shields raised against enemy archery. Dozens of Bructeri warriors were advancing towards them through the trees, clearly already well aware of the Hamians' threat as they moved from tree to tree and kept their bodies low, hoping to use the cover of the forest's ferns and bushes to disguise their advance.

'Wait!'

Qadir's shouted command was obeyed with absolute discipline by his men, despite the increasing number of arrows flying past them, still mostly above head height as the few Bructeri archers loosed swift shots before diving back into cover. A handful of the younger tribesmen were loosing sling stones at them from the flanks of the war band's advance, the improvised bullets hissing past them unseen and occasionally smacking into a man's shield with a loud click. The pioneers pulled their Hamian comrades into cover as the volume of harassing arrows and sling stones increased with the Bructeri warriors' confidence, more than one of them flinching despite their collective vow to show no fear, as arrows punched into the layered wood of their shields and were prevented from penetrating only by the layers of leather and silk that overlaid the wood, a trick that had saved more than one life in the battles of their eastern campaign. The enemy warriors were closing in, no longer distant figures flitting between the trees but individuals, the fear and determination on their faces visible as they shouted encouragement to each other, collectively readying themselves to storm the detachment's line while behind them someone was shouting commands and driving them forward. With a sudden spur of collective determination they lurched forward, eschewing the protection of the trees for a straightforward charge towards the hated Romans, those men with shields leading the assault. Qadir swept his arm forward.

'*Loose!*'

The Tungrians unleashed their arrows, shooting quickly into the mass of men running at them, three volleys in the space of five heartbeats, their deadly missiles hammering through the illusory protection of the leading warriors' shields to pierce the bodies behind them. Loosing again, and again, they reaped a savage harvest of the poorly protected Germans, and with every man that fell the remaining warriors crouched a little closer to the ground, their headlong charge becoming little more than a shuffling, zigzagging trot from the cover of one tree to another. Qadir and Dubnus exchanged glances, both men nodding to affirm the plan that they had agreed minutes before. The Hamian shouted the command for which his men had been waiting.

'*Archers . . . Cease!*'

Dubnus's men clenched their hands on the grips of their shields and the handles of their axes, knowing that their turn to bleed the enemy was at hand. Their centurion bellowed the command they were waiting for, slipping their collars to send them at the wavering Bructeri.

'*Tenth Century! Advance!*'

He strode out at their head with his face set implacably, a warrior chieftain come for vengeance at the head of men whose devotion to him was absolute, striding purposefully at the enemy with their shields and axes raised. Dubnus was the first into the fight, stamping forward to attack a pair of warriors who threw themselves at the armoured giant with suicidal bravery. Turning the spear thrust at him from the left with his shield and following through with a punch of the iron boss that sent the warrior staggering backwards, he sidestepped the other man's stabbing attack before spinning to deliver a vicious chopping axe blow that hammered into the Bructeri's chest, kicking the dying warrior off the blade in a spray of blood and turning on the first man with a snarl of triumph, looping the axe high to smash the spike on the reverse of its heavy iron blade down into his head. On either side his men waded into the enemy with equal fury, their shields and armour protecting them from the enemy's spears while every swing of their axes did grievous damage to the men who were still attempting to resist their advance. One of the pioneers staggered from the fight with a spear wound to his thigh, and while he was reeling, a quick-witted archer lurking behind the Bructeri line put an arrow into his throat, but the roar of triumph from the warrior who'd managed to stab beneath the hem of his mail was short-lived, as the Tungrian fighting next to the dying man stepped forward and swung his axe in a flat arc, slicing off the top six inches of the German's head and leaving his corpse to crumple limply to the ground. As those warriors who chose to fight rather than back away from the rampaging pioneers grew fewer, Dubnus realised that the Bructeri were collectively retreating before the Tungrian onslaught, no longer seeking to fight the armoured monsters whose axes were likely to be the ruin of any man who confronted them, and were instead consolidating their scattered force into a hedge of spears.

'*Tenth Century! Disengage!*'

As one man they stepped back, retreating from the baying Germans without turning their backs, raising their shields against the threat of Bructeri arrows and sling stones as they pulled away from the line of spearmen. A scattering of dead and dying warriors marked the limit of their brief advance, their bodies wrecked by the axes' awful blows, the spectacle they presented so terrifying that the enemy warriors standing and watching the Tungrians walk backwards out of the fight were unwilling to advance past the ruined bodies of their comrades in search of revenge for them. When his men were twenty paces from the enemy line Dubnus turned and flicked two pointing fingers towards the riverbank, still half a mile distant.

'*Tenth Century, at the run!*'

Jogging past the archers he nodded to Qadir, who was already shouting the command for his archers to resume shooting. As the Bructeri regained their will to go forward, shamed by the imprecations of their leaders and heartened by the Tungrians' retreat, those men who were the first to step forward became the targets of a fresh volley of shafts, precisely aimed shots that dropped several more men writhing and kicking at the pain of the iron arrowheads lodged deep in their bodies, and sent the remainder into cover once more. Seeing the enemy momentarily cowed, the Hamian centurion made a swift decision.

'*One more arrow! Pick your targets!*'

The Hamians nocked one last time, selecting their marks with care to send shots into the mass of men attempting to shelter from their cold rain of iron behind their shields, then looked to their centurion for his next command.

'*Disengage!*'

Waiting while his men hurried after Dubnus's retreating axemen, he settled into the cover of the tree next to him, knowing that he needed to give them a few moments of grace to prevent the Bructeri bowmen targeting their retreating backs. Nocking an arrow he pulled it back until the flight feathers were level with his ear, waiting motionlessly with the bow pulled taut for a target to reveal itself. After a moment an archer stepped out from behind the tree he'd been using for cover, putting an arrow to his own bow and raising the weapon to loft the missile at the retreating Hamians' backs. Qadir waited for an instant, holding his breath to steady his body, until the Bructeri bowman had his bow bent almost to its fullest extent, then killed the man with a clinical shot and reached back to his quiver for another arrow.

He waited for a long moment for another target to present itself, but the remaining Bructeri seemed intent on keeping their skins intact, and the Hamian smiled wryly as he stood, backing cautiously away from the tree with the arrow still nocked in case of a sudden change of heart by any of the Germans. When he had paced backwards a dozen times he removed the arrow from his bow's string, sliding it back into the quiver on his right hip, then turned to lope away in pursuit of his men.

With a dull clang, a sling stone struck the back of his helmet with enough power to dent the iron bowl, sending him sprawling unconscious to the sun dappled forest floor.

'I have an idea, my King! Give me thirty men and I will break this resistance for you!'

The Bructeri had followed up on the retreating Romans eagerly enough until the retreating soldiers had formed a rough defensive line. Having turned to face the tribesmen they crouched behind their shields in small knots of men, clearly waiting for the tribesmen to advance upon them in another charge that could only end the same way as the last, in the face of their enemy's viciously effective archery and brutal axe-work. In the distance behind them Amalric had twice caught a flash of blue among the forest's more sober shades, fleeting glimpses of Gerhild's distinctive cloak as her captors hurried her away towards the river.

'What do you plan, Uncle?'

He threw an arm out to indicate the Roman left flank.

'There is a weakness in their position, too much ground cover on our right for their archers to see us coming. You keep their attention and I will overrun them from the right. When they turn to face me you will have your moment of glory! Then you must charge!'

Amalric nodded, and Gernot pointed to two of his senior warriors.

'Bring your men! We go to claim the victory!'

He bounded away to the west in a long, looping run that took his small force out of sight of the Romans, and as he threw his head back to suck in the cold morning air, he wondered briefly if anyone on the other side had seen their departure, and whether they would make the connection between the unexpected departure of so many men from the Bructeri line and the lack of clear ground for shooting on the Roman left. Concentrating on the uneven ground before him, wary of turning an ankle in a rabbit hole and losing the fight before it was properly joined, he dismissed the concern without a second thought. If Wodanaz willed it, his would be a mighty victory, a song to be shouted at roof beams studded with new heads, and the weapons and armour of the men he was about to tear apart with his audacious strategy.

'Have you seen Qadir?'

Angar shook his head, staring out at the Bructeri war band less than two hundred paces distant, drumming their spear shafts against shield rims in a rhythmic pattern that was slowly increasing in tempo. Dubnus cursed and looked about him, shaking his head at his comrade's disappearance. Angar pointed at the waiting Germans, hefting his blood-slathered axe, ready to fight again.

'Never mind Qadir, his boys will cope without him. Concentrate on dealing with this lot, there must still be nearly a hundred of them.'

The big centurion nodded, scanning the battlefield with the seasoned eye of an old campaigner, his eye coming to rest on the far left of the small field of battle.

'I don't like that left flank, and I could swear there are less of them than there were last time I looked, so perhaps they've spotted it too. Take two men and reinforce it, I'll manage this.'

Angar nodded and called to two of his remaining eight men, hurrying along the detachment's short line to find a pair of archers nervously staring at a wall of foliage less than a hundred paces from them. With a sudden roar the Bructeri's main line was lurching forward, the tribe's warriors reflexively starting forward after a single man whose will to stand and wait in the face of the Romans' rhythmic drumming had suddenly and decisively snapped, sending them forward at their enemy in an involuntary, screaming charge. As the chosen man watched the Hamians unleashed the full power of their long years of practice on the oncoming warriors, each men calmly and systematically nocking, drawing and loosing a shaft once every two heartbeats, their arrows hammering into the Germans' shields and finding the gaps between them while Dubnus readied his remaining axemen.

'They won't even reach us, look, they've already lost a dozen men.'

Angar turned to speak to the retired legionary Lucius, standing alongside his son and watching the Bructeri suffer as they came on, but a faint movement in the bushes to their left caught his attention for an instant.

'What the . . . ?'

'We must attack!'

Gernot nodded grimly at the warrior's outburst, peering through the bushes behind which his small party was regaining its breath from their swift run. The main attack was already faltering, slowing under the Romans' unceasing barrage of arrows. Every step forward took them closer to the Roman line, increasing the force with which the missiles' wicked iron heads slammed through their raised shields to maim the flesh behind the layered wood, or pierced unprotected legs and arms, and a disquietingly large number of men lay silent or screaming in the wake of the advance.

'Some idiot . . . decided to go . . . too soon . . . and those fools . . . followed him!' The Bructeri chieftain sucked in one last breath. 'Our time is here! *Follow me!*'

He burst through the bushes, praying to Wodanaz that his men were following, raised his sword and charged, too badly out of breath to shout a war cry.

'To the left! Shoot to the left!'

The two archers in front of Angar took a moment to realise their deadly predicament, then swivelled and loosed their next arrows into the twenty or so men running at them in ominous silence, nocking and loosing again, but the pioneer officer could already see that the tribesmen would overrun them before they had time to shoot more than one more shaft apiece.

'Ready!'

His men stepped alongside him, both tensing their bodies to fight, and the civilians made ready alongside them, the retired soldier exchanging a knowing glance with him while his giant of a son flexed his muscles and roared a deafening challenge at the Bructeri. Each of the archers managed one more arrow apiece, then were beaten down by the oncoming Germans before they could nock again, both men dying with spears through them as the Bructeri took their savage revenge for the punishing damage the Hamians' bows had done to their brothers. The axemen charged into the melee, separating themselves widely enough that they could swing their axes with complete abandon in the manner demanded by the odds against them, arcs of blood flying as their brutal weapons hacked a path into the enemy. One of them went down with a spear blade in his foot, and Angar flung his axe in a wide arc into a hastily raised shield to smash down the man wielding the spear, knowing that he would be unable to reach his man before he died under the blades of the warriors gathered over him, only to goggle as Magan waded into the fight. Ignoring a stabbing attack that opened a wound in his side, he grasped two warriors by their heads, smashing them together and dropping them senseless to the forest floor. Another spear stabbed into his back, but, turning as if nothing had happened, he took the man who had inflicted it by his throat and squeezed, his knuckles white as the flailing warrior's larynx collapsed under the pressure.

Angar found himself facing an older man, clad in furs and wielding a sword, parrying the German's first stabbing lunge with his shield and sweeping the axe down while the weapon was still outstretched, snapping it in two close to the hilt and grinning ferociously as the swordsman backed away with a look of consternation. Two tribesmen were stabbing at the giant now, their spears bloody as they thrust and wrenched the blades free, and stabbed again, and then, as he tottered on the edge of collapse, his father was among them with a bellow of horrified rage at the blood streaming down his son's body, gutting one with a lunge of his sword and distracting the other for long enough that the axeman who had fallen with a pierced foot could swing his weapon in retaliation from the spot where he lay, hacking the man's back foot in two and leaving him screaming his agony at the forest's canopy, his arched body open for the retired legionary's death blow. And then the remaining Bructeri were gone, half a dozen men falling back, most of them wounded, while Angar and his remaining soldier bellowed imprecations after them.

Dubnus ran up with another two men, and Angar looked over at the main Bructeri force to find them in retreat, more corpses and struggling, kicking, arrow-shot men littering the ground before them. The chosen man spat on the forest floor, examining his axe's notched, bloody blade.

'Looks like you handed me the short straw.'

The centurion nodded dourly.

'You held though. The Hamians?'

'Died like men. Must have taken some balls to stand and keep shooting while that lot ran them down.'

They turned to look at Lucius, who was cradling his son's bloody body as best he could, tears washing down his cheeks as he mourned the giant's loss.

'He had no idea . . . He was just a boy, really . . .'

The two men looked at each other for a moment before Angar spoke.

'He saved us though, distracted enough of them for long enough that they couldn't mob us. And died like a man. You can be proud.'

Lucius looked up at him and nodded, wiping his eyes with the back of his sleeve.

'I can't leave him. He's my son. I have to bury him.'

Dubnus shook his head peremptorily.

'You can't. They'll tear you to pieces once we pull back to the river, and we can't carry him.'

'Then . . .' Lucius nodded to himself, hardening his face. 'Send me with him. I have nothing to live for now that he's gone. At least we can be together when we cross the river.'

Angar looked at Dubnus, nodding his head.

'I'll do it. You get the men ready to move. You . . .' he pointed to the remaining soldier from his small party, 'help your brother get back to the river, and tell the Hamians to come and get their mates' arrows, there must be a hundred or so unspent in their quivers.'

'They can't escape! Their backs are to the water, we just have to wear them down!'

Several of the spearmen closest to Gernot cheered lustily, but their advance remained as careful as before, moving from tree to tree and keeping the protection of the thick wooden trunks between them and the deadly archers who were doggedly retreating before them. An arrow sighed past his head, and he reflexively ducked into the cover of a sturdy oak, looking to either side and realising that most of his men were doing just the same thing.

'We *have* to charge them again!' Looking over his shoulder he found Amalric a dozen paces back, crouched at the base of a tree and pointing forward at the Roman line. 'They are only one hundred paces ahead of us! If we attack together we will smother them with our numbers!'

The nobleman pursed his lips, unable to shake the memory of the horrendously mutilated corpses that were the remnant of the last charge he had led at the deceptively small enemy force. To his horror Gernot had been forced to tolerate the ignominy of retreating from their deadly axes with his remaining men while knowing that their number should have been sufficient to deal with a handful of equally tired Romans. Crouching behind their shields his men had backed away from the blood-soaked enemy, pursued by their taunts and shouts of derision as the Romans retreated towards the river. They were calling out to the tribesmen now, while their archers, retreating from tree to tree, shot arrows at anyone who showed themselves for more than a brief moment, taunting his warriors for their timidity in their rough version of the Roman tongue. Running the gauntlet of the archers once more he zigzagged his way back to the tree behind which the king was sheltering, ducking behind its trunk as another arrow struck the wood with a heavy *thwock*.

'My King, we have already spent the lives of fifty and more of your warriors attempting to break their resistance!' He lowered his voice, the words for his king's ears alone. 'And I do not believe that many men here will respond eagerly if I call on them for another attack. They know that if we charge again more of us will fall to their bows, and as many again to their axes. And, my King, the Rhenus is close at their backs now and will prevent them from running any further. We should simply follow them, until they reach the river's bank and realise that they have nowhere else to go. When their archers run out of arrows, and they tire for lack of food, *then* they will either surrender or fall to our spears.'

Amalric reluctantly nodded his consent, and Gernot gave the order for a slow, cautious advance, directing his men to spread their line out to the right, ready to form a wall of spears between the retreating Romans and the bridge fort. As the tribesmen warily followed the intruders in their retreat, the number of arrows being loosed at them began to perceptibly reduce, as the forest's gloom grew lighter with the proximity of the river's wide open space. Amalric grinned at Gernot triumphantly, as the nobleman pointed at the withdrawing Romans, disappearing over the last crest and down the slope that led to the river's bank and the expanse of impassable water.

'You see, my king? We have them now! They have nowhere left to run, and their supply of arrows appears to have been exhausted!'

Amalric snarled exultantly, raising his sword to urge his men forward.

'The time has come, my brothers! Bructeri!' He hammered on the boss of his shield with the blade of his sword. 'Bruc-ter-i! Bruc-ter-i!'

The men closest to him joined the chant, some of them instinctively drawn to the comfort of its collective strength, others clearly more predatory in their intent, eager for revenge on men who had sought to kill them, and had left dozens of their brothers dead and wounded. They rose from cover, advancing towards the top of the shallow slope that fell away towards the river, their continued chanting bringing no more reaction from the Romans than a few hurried glances back at their oncoming line, as the last of the enemy vanished over the crest and made their way down towards the river bank that would be the scene of their final bloody stand.

Dubnus looked grimly across the river's grey water at the warships anchored fifty paces from the shore, then back up the riverbank's slope to where the Bructeri tribesmen were gathering for their final assault. The remaining men of the detachment were gathered about him, the seer's blue cloak barely visible among their armoured bodies, archers stringing the last of their missiles and lofting the shafts speculatively up the hill at those of the enemy who were visible on the crest while his pioneers stood with their shields raised against the occasional incoming arrow.

'Kasim!'

The archer loosed the arrow he had been holding on a taut bowstring, ready to release, and turned away from the enemy to find the big Briton close behind him, his face set in worried lines.

'There's still no sign of Qadir. What was the last you saw of him?'

The Hamian shook his head unhappily, looking up at Dubnus and trying not to be intimidated by the big centurion's blood-slathered armour and weapons.

'He ordered us to retreat after the first time we held them off, Centurion, and stayed for a moment longer to keep their heads down. I made the mistake of not stopping to watch his back as he followed us.'

Dubnus shook his head incredulously.

'So he's either dead or captive.'

He turned away and looked back across the river again, the sides of the warships seeming to ripple with movement as their marine archers readied themselves for action, shaking his head in frustration.

'Shields to the rear!' The men of the detachment looked round at him, the pioneers instinctively obeying the command and hurrying to face the river. 'And get down behind them, all of you! The men on those ships are about to turn this slope into a butcher's back yard, and I for one don't much fancy getting one of our own arrows stuck in my back!'

The first of the Tungrians had come into view from the prefect's flagship a few moments before, one of the big axe-hefting soldiers who had marched from Claudius's Colony three days before supporting another man able only to hop on one foot. The pair were closely followed by the remainder of the detachment as they retreated down the slope and into view, no longer hidden beneath the canopy of trees that crowned the hill, the archers shooting carefully aimed arrows back up the slope at their pursuers while the axemen protected them from the occasional return shots with their shields. At their commander's order, bellowed loudly enough to be heard on the other two ships, the vessel's archers raised their bows and pulled back the arrows ready to loose, as those Tungrians who had made it back to the river huddled into a tight knot, shields presented towards the ships in a gesture of self-preservation that made the naval officer's mouth twitch with amusement.

The governor's next pronouncement wiped the smile away in an instant.

'I'm half tempted to leave them to it, you know.'

The prefect frowned momentarily at Albinus's words, then turned to his navarchus.

'Hail the squadron. Archers are ordered to commence shooting when our bolt throwers engage the enemy.'

'After all, even ignoring all those times in the past when that insubordinate shit Scaurus has sought to put me down, he has rather made a mess of it this time. I wouldn't imagine it's going to do him very much good when my report reaches Rome and details his refusal to follow my suggestions, and the all-out war with an otherwise neutral tribe that's resulted. Perhaps the best outcome of all this would be for them all to die, and the problem to quietly disappear.'

The prefect's mouth tightened to form a line, his jaw muscles hardening as he turned to his superior.

'On the other hand, Governor, imagine the political consequences that would ensue when my family discovered that you'd abandoned one of their sons to the degradation and torture that we know these barbarian animals routinely practise with their captives. Not to mention the more *meaningful* consequences.'

Albinus raised an eyebrow at him, his mouth tightening into an angry line.

'Consequences, Prefect? Am I to consider that a threat?'

Varus stared at the governor for a moment, then shook his head slowly. When he spoke again his voice was soft, barely audible to Albinus who was forced to lean closer to hear his words.

'A threat, Governor? Of course not. I will execute any legal order you give me, as is my duty. But I can't vouch for the considerable number of men in my family who are likely to feel less bound by imperial duty and rather more by their familial obligations. I know what my responsibility to my cousin would be, were I in their place.'

'And?'

The prefect shrugged.

'I expect it's a moot question, Governor, since I'm sure you have no intention of following through with such an unlikely course of action. And now, if you'll excuse me.'

He strode down the rail, staring across the fifty paces of water that separated the three anchored warships from the river's bank. On the slopes above the tribesmen were gathering for the kill, coming out of the shelter of the trees as the Tungrian bowmen stopped shooting and sought the cover of the last feet of dry ground, advancing down the slope with murderous intent. Nodding to his Navarchus he snapped out the order that the captains of his engine crews had been waiting for.

'Engage!'

The older man dragged in a lungful of air, then lunged forward to point at the advancing enemy in an unmistakable gesture.

'Bolt throwers – *shoot!*'

Amalric raised his sword, lowering its point to aim at the Romans.

'We have them now! Kill them all! With me, my brothers, with me!'

The Bructeri spearmen responded to their king's enraged command with a sudden rush down the hillside, eighty men with Amalric at their head, their spear blades raised and eager for blood, and Gernot followed in the body of his warriors. Their charge down the slope suddenly slowed, and, craning his neck, the noble realised that the men leading the charge had found their path down the hill obstructed by the branches of several trees that had been felled and dragged into position with their tops pointing towards the river, presenting a more or less continuous barrier of branches with only one clear path through around which the war band was unavoidably bunching, almost fighting to get through the gap that would let them at the cowering Romans crouched at the river's side.

Looking up, he started as he saw the wooden hulls of three ships anchored close to the shore, and with a horrible lurch in his guts realised in an instant the nature of the trap into which they had been lured. He bellowed a warning at Amalric, but the shout was lost in the general cacophony as the tribesmen vied for position at the opening in the unexpected obstacle.

'My King! The ships! This is a tr—'

The man alongside him opened his mouth to bellow at the trapped Romans cowering at the water's edge and then suddenly wasn't there, the salt sting of his blood monetarily blinding the noble as his men's roars of impending vengeance became a cacophony of screams.

*

The fleet's bolt throwers spat their bolts into the milling warriors, perfectly presented to their eager crews by the tactic that had been agreed with the detachment's tribune two days before, trees expertly felled to present the Bructeri with a near impossible obstacle and with only one clear path through to the river's bank. Varus nodded to his fleet captain, and the grizzled veteran pointed at the bank again, raising his voice to bark a fresh command.

'Archers – *shoot!*'

Thirty archers lined the rails of the vessels to either side of the Mars, and at the navarchus's command they unleashed a volley of arrows that sang across the space between ship and shore in an instant, their arrows lancing down into the Bructeri war band in a new and unexpected savagery.

Gernot looked around, momentarily puzzled, then found the man's corpse a dozen paces behind him, the body only recognisable by the heavy silver torque around its neck, a heavy iron-tipped bolt having reduced the warrior's face to no more than a bloody crater in the front of his head. Looking up, he stared at what had been concealed from them by the trees until their charge had taken them close to the water's edge, a trio of Roman warships moored so near to the bank that he could see the individual archers' faces as they bent their bows, waiting for the command to shoot. Another bolt had pinned a man to the tree behind him with his feet dancing on thin air a foot above the ground, his lifeblood sprinkling the earth beneath him as he twitched and shuddered in his death spasms. And then, with an eerie sigh that made the hairs on the back of Gernot's neck stand up, a flight of arrows fell across the Bructeri in a volley, a deadly sleet that peppered the hillside and took men's lives as indiscriminately as the wrath of a vengeful god.

The tribesmen dithered momentarily and then ran for cover, cringing as another flight of arrows tore at them, men falling with leg wounds that reduced their attempts to flee to no more than frenzied crawling. The noble ducked into the cover of a tree, watching in horror as a wounded spearman no more than five paces from him was struck by a succession of arrows, his attempts to find shelter from the murderous rain of iron weakening with each impact until, with five shafts protruding from his back and legs, he slumped face down into the slope's earth and stopped moving altogether.

Looking around he found Amalric staring at him grimly from the cover of a felled tree further down the slope, a grievously wounded tribesman hunched over the feathered shaft of an arrow beside him. The king made a gesture for him to stay where he was, a suggestion whose common sense was reinforced by the abrupt despatch of a man whose nerve had broken, his frantic attempt to flee up the hill's difficult slope being terminated by a pair of feathered shafts that sprouted between his shoulder blades in swift succession and dropped him writhing to the ground.

'*Stay where you are, Gernot! This battle is lost!*'

Squinting around the tree's bole the noble watched as the Tungrians climbed into boats that had been lowered from the warships, cursing volubly as he saw Gerhild's blue cloak among the men boarding the first of them. He looked about him frantically for one of the tribe's archers, but the only man with a bow that he could see was already dead, the weapon's limbs protruding out from beneath his body. Unable to watch any longer as the boat pulled away from the shore, he sank back into the tree's cover and closed his eyes, listening to the groans and cries for assistance from the tribe's wounded as the arrows fell in a harsh iron sleet, the marine archers shooting at anything that moved across the slope's deadly killing ground.

Clodius Albinus watched with scarcely concealed delight as the first of the boats rowed back towards the *Mars*, its steersman under strict orders that the Tungrians were to be delivered to the flagship. It bumped against the warship's flank, and a pair of crew members assisted its passengers up and over the vessel's side, the first of them a pair of Hamians who stood blinking in the late morning sun after so long in the forest's gloom.

'Fuck me, look at the pair of 'em! All that's missing is them holding hands! I reckon they'll be toss—'

The suggestive nudgings of Albinus's bodyguard were silenced by the appearance of one of Dubnus's men who heaved his massive frame onto the deck with a grunt of effort, closely followed by another, equally impressive in his muscularity. Both men's armour and skin were blasted with blood, their axes brown with the drying remnants of other men's lives, and even the less experienced men aboard the *Mars* could see that they were still twitchy with the aftermath of mortal combat, their bodies almost shaking with the need to do violence. Looking about them with the expression of men who had discovered excrement on their boots, they turned and assisted the primary subject of the governor's interest aboard. Clad in an ankle-length cloak of bright blue, the seer's face was hidden by the garment's hood, but Clodius Albinus was undeterred by the apparent attempt at modesty. Advancing across the vessel's deck, he essayed a bow, holding out a hand to the new arrival.

'Good morning, my dear, and welcome to . . .'

Looking up, he choked on the words as the subject of his address swept back the hood. After a moment's horrified silence, as the governor stared in undisguised amazement, the man who had been wearing the cloak greeted him cheerily with a smart salute.

'Good morning, Governor! Tribune Scaurus sends you his greetings, and his regrets that he won't be able to join you today. He—'

'What? You're . . .'

Albinus groped for the name for a moment before the fleet's prefect put him out of his misery. The fleet prefect shook his head in apparent disgust.

'Gods below, Gaius, I knew there was something wrong with you, but I never expected it to be the wearing of women's clothing!'

The governor stared, aghast, as the younger man took off the cloak to reveal his armour and weapons.

'Forgive me, Governor, but I had strict orders from the Tribune to make sure the Bructeri saw a figure in a blue cloak make its way from the shore to this ship while he rode away to the north with her. Clever thinking too, I'd say.'

Albinus stared at him with narrowed eyes for a moment before replying.

'So the Bructeri king believes his seer has boarded a Roman ship, and therefore gives up on the idea of getting her back.' He stared at Varus with thin lips. 'Whereas in truth your tribune clearly thought he had good reasons for not doing so, despite the fact that by failing to deliver her to me he has risked the success of his mission just at the point when it was set to be successfully completed. Why do you think that might be, Centurion Varus?'

The young aristocrat shook his head, his expression guileless.

'I really don't have a clue, Governor. It's quite unusual for a centurion, and a junior centurion at that, to be invited to share the deliberations of his senior officer.'

'I see . . .' Albinus shook his head slowly at the frustration of having been outmanoeuvred once again. 'So Scaurus gave you no clue as to where it was that he was taking the German woman?'

'None at all, sir. The first thing I knew about the change in plans was when he rode away to the north, rather than falling back to the river with the rest of us.'

'And who was with him?'

Varus looked up at the sky in an apparent effort to recall the moment's detail.

'Our Bructeri scout, who by somewhat of a quirk of fate turns out to be the seer's brother, centurion Corvus and the veteran Cotta, the tribune's slave Arminius and a boy he's training to manhood, a pair of Qadir's archers, the seer, of course, and three cavalrymen whose names I'm not aware of, Governor. They joined us as the result of a scouting mission into the Bructeri capital. It seems they were there on some kind of imperial business.'

The governor's eyes narrowed again.

'*Dolfus?* That insubordinate bastard has just signed his own death warrant.' He looked up at Varus. 'And Rutilius Scaurus has done the same for every man of his detachment. You, given your social rank, and the fact that Scaurus chose not to involve you in his crime, will come back to Claudius's Colony with us. But *every* other man of his misbegotten command will be put back in the boats and rowed back to the . . .'

He turned to Varus's cousin, whose ostentatious throat-clearing was evidently intended to draw his attention to something. While the governor had been apprising himself of the facts around Scaurus's apparent decision to ignore the pre-arranged method of escape from the Bructeri, the remainder of the Tungrian detachment had boarded the flagship. Dubnus stood before them, the gore-slathered head of a heavy axe resting on the warship's otherwise pristine deck, and to either side of him stood three of his pioneers, each of them a head taller than every other man aboard, while behind them stood half a dozen archers with their bows held loosely, hands resting idly on the arrows that remained in their quivers. The prefect stepped forward until he was within two paces of the Tungrian centurion.

'I'd be grateful if this could be resolved peacefully, Centurion?'

Dubnus nodded, his expression an unchanging mask of contempt directed squarely at Albinus, and the prefect turned back to face his superior with raised eyebrows.

'It is my estimation, Governor, that these men are somewhat dismayed to hear you suggest that you might consider putting them ashore. So before you consider turning that suggestion into an order, I'd be grateful if you were to consider the alternative.' The Tungrians watched the men around them with hard, uncompromising eyes that played across Albinus's bodyguard dismissively, looking around themselves for a genuine threat to face down while the naval prefect continued speaking. 'An alternative which in simple terms is to pull up the anchor and sail back up river.'

He swivelled back to face Dubnus.

'Lost men, have you, Centurion?'

The big man nodded slowly at the prefect's question, which had been asked in a suitably respectful tone, then looked down

meaningfully at the liberal quantity of blood and other uniden-
tifiable substances that had been sprayed across his armour during
the fight in the forest.

'Five dead and one who may not walk again, since you ask,
Prefect. And one of our officers is missing. Hopefully dead . . .'

Varus looked at Albinus for a moment before speaking.

'Soldiers recently out of combat aren't often feeling reasonable,
Governor. I'd say that any attempt to put these men ashore would
be likely to result in unpleasantness. And quite possibly even
more blood on my deck for some poor bastard to wash off.
Perhaps even mine. Perhaps even *yours* . . .'

The commander of Albinus's bodyguard dropped a hand to
the hilt of his sword, the dozen men behind him shuffling and
setting themselves for combat at the minute but significant movement. Catching the shift in their stances from the corner of his
eye, Varus stepped forward and raised a hand, his voice changing
from reasonable persuasion to a harsh command in an instant.

'Stand *down*, you fools! I don't care how many of you die, but
I do care how many of my men might get caught in the middle
of the slaughter you're intent on starting.'

He turned back to the governor.

'It's your choice, Governor. Either we transport these men
back to the city or your fool of a guard captain can take on half
a dozen bloody-handed men in armour with shields and axes
and see how far it gets him?'

Albinus's face twisted with frustrated anger.

'I'll have you both dismissed, you and your cousin, I'll see you
both . . .'

He spluttered into outraged silence, and Varus filled the gap
in a tone that oozed patrician confidence.

'Broken? Disgraced?' The prefect laughed at him softly. 'Of
course, that's something that *may* be within your power, although
without the German woman you'll have less leverage with the
imperial chamberlain than perhaps you'd hoped. But I promise
you this, Decimus Clodius Albinus: raise a finger against either
of us and you'll rue the day you choose to make an enemy of a

family as well connected and numerous as ours.' He waved a dismissive hand and turned away, catching his navarchus's eye. 'I've got a squadron to get turned around and heading back up the river, now that the barbarians seem to have got bored of being used for target practice.'

The return of Qadir's consciousness was a slow, patchy thing, the dull ache in his head matched by an inability to move his limbs to any greater degree than a twitch. He lay in the shadow of an uprooted tree's root crater staring up at the forest's canopy, and the sunlight that was lancing down through the leaves, wincing with each fresh flash of light that found his eyes. As reason returned he realised that he was lying prone on a battlefield, probably in the midst of his enemies, and that, if the tribune's plan had succeeded, he was very much alone. Lying back against the tangled roots beneath him, he closed his eyes, listening to the forest's unnatural silence that told him the Bructeri were still in the vicinity even if their advance had probably passed the spot where he lay in pursuit of his fellows.

Raising his head fractionally to look about him, his heart leapt as he realised that his body was cushioned from the root ball's knobbly surface by a thick carpet of fallen leaves, enough having drifted into the depression left by the tree's collapse to cover a man, he calculated. Squirming deeper into their soft camouflage, he forced his right arm to move, sweeping a handful of the forest's detritus across his legs to obscure his knees, then repeated the movement with his left, pushing more handfuls across himself until his chest was invisible to all but the most careful of observers. Wriggling carefully, mindful of the need to minimise the amount of noise he was making, he eased his left arm and shoulder beneath the carpet of leaves, using his right to complete the concealment of his upper body before brushing more across his helmet's polished iron bowl, leaving only the arm and his face exposed.

A voice spoke, terrifyingly close to hand, and he pushed his right arm slowly beneath the surface of his camouflage and froze, trusting in the leaves' concealment. If he could avoid capture then his ability to live off the forest's flora and fauna would enable him to make his return to the safety of the other side of the Rhenus at leisure. A tribesman stepped into view, speaking to another man as he bent to pick something up from the ground at his feet. The Hamian groaned inwardly as he saw his bow in the German's hands, not only for its loss but for the risk that its presence would betray him, willing himself to immobility as the tribesman looked around him for the body to which the discarded weapon must surely belong. His gaze swept across the centurion's hiding place in a long, slow appraisal, but, just when Qadir was sure he was discovered, shook his head and turned away.

Allowing the breath to seep slowly from his nostrils with relief, he started involuntarily as the Bructeri whipped back round, tossing the bow aside and levelling his spear as the realisation of what it was he'd been staring at registered in his mind. Raising the weapon above him in a two-handed grip, he stepped forward, his knuckles whitening as he readied himself to thrust the blade down into the helpless Hamian.

8

The remaining Bructeri gathered at the top of the slope that ran down to the river's edge, protected from the warship's archers and artillery by the cover of the trees' foliage. Amalric stood in the middle of his warriors, looking about him to take stock of their mood with the keen eye of a man who knew that no king could consider his position safe after such an abject and abrupt defeat.

'They'll get over it.'

He turned to find Gernot at his side, the older man's gaze equally as calculating as his own.

'They well might. But the doubt inspired by this . . . *disaster* . . . will remain in their minds, and every man who journeys to Thusila will hear that doubt in their voices. It will spread across my kingdom like the disease that killed so many of the tribe in my father's last days.'

'You chased the intruders to the very banks of the river. Were it not for their ships we would have gutted every last one of those pigs.'

The king shook his head bitterly, his face reflecting the bad news the men sent to secure the sacred grove had given him only moments before, information not yet known to his warriors.

'Which was all well and good, but they have taken my seer from under my nose! And they burned my chief priest on his own altar, burned him *alive* so that the woods echoed with his screams! And to deepen my shame they have the captured eagle that has been our prize for over a hundred years. Be clear, Gernot, this insult cannot go unanswered if I am to close my eyes for sleep without the fear of a blade in the night.'

The noble nodded slowly.

'I see your argument, my King, but . . .'

Amalric rounded in him with sudden vehemence.

'Do you not see? Only the gods can save me now! They must provide me with some means of rescuing my kingdom from the jaws of these Roman wolves. I do not know how, but without a miracle of some sort my days are numbered.'

He frowned at the sight of a horseman leading his beast into the gathering with a body slung across his mount's back.

'As we need the sight of any more corpses.'

Opening his mouth to shout a challenge at the man, he closed it again as the rider called urgently for assistance, telling the men around him that his brother had seemed a dead man and yet still lived. Exchanging puzzled glances, monarch and noble strode across to the spot where the injured man had been laid out on the forest floor, his eyes wide open and staring at the trees above, his body so still that even the rise and fall of his chest was barely discernible.

'He seemed dead, when you found him?'

The rider turned and bowed to them in turn.

'Yes, my King. I was about to throw his body onto the horse when he spoke. I almost soiled myself, I was so surprised. And then I realised that you had to hear his words.'

Amalric and Gernot nodded, looking down at the comatose warrior.

'He fell in battle?'

'Yes my Lord. He was the bravest of us, and charged his horse straight at the enemy. One of their archers died under his spear but his horse was felled, throwing him into a tree. I saw him fall, but my horse had an arrow in its side and was close to dropping. I barely escaped with my own skin intact.'

'And so you went back to find him when the battle moved on?'

Mindful of the criticism in Gernot's voice the horseman bowed his head in contrition.

'It seemed that you had the fight won, my Lord, with the Romans backing down the slope into the river. And . . .'

'And he was your brother.'

'Yes, my Lord. I—'

Amalric cut off the attempt to apologise with a curt gesture.

'And these words I have to hear?'

The man on the ground started speaking, his words almost inaudible as his lips barely moved, the effort evident in his eyes. The two men knelt beside him, each of them bending close to hear what it was he was trying to say.

'*The woman . . .*'

'Gerhild?'

The eyes swivelled to stare up at Gernot.

'*Yes.*'

'What of her?'

'*Rode north.*'

Amalric shook his head, placing a hand lightly on the stricken warrior's shoulder.

'No, brother. She boarded a Roman warship, I saw it with my own . . .'

He fell silent, looking up at his uncle with a sudden flash of insight.

'What did we see?'

'My king . . .'

'What did we *see*, Gernot, when the Roman warships were killing anyone who showed himself, and the men we were chasing reached the water's edge?'

The noble stared back at him.

'We saw Gerhild get in a boat that took her away to the biggest of the ships.'

'And how did we know that was Gerhild?'

'Because she was wearing her blue cloak.'

The king smiled tightly at his uncle as the realisation started to dawn on the older man.

'We saw *someone* in a blue cloak get into the boat. But we have no way to be sure it was Gerhild. And now this man is telling us, with what might be his last breath, that he saw her ride north at the fork in the path that leads to her tower. And beyond her tower is . . . ?'

Gernot nodded, his lips pursed.

'Is open land and forest. No barrier to someone who knows the ground.'

'*Gunda.*'

'What?'

Both men's attention snapped back to the paralysed warrior.

'*Saw Gunda . . . and the Roman . . .*'

The king's face hardened into cruel lines that Gernot knew only too well.

'Which Roman?'

'*From feast . . .*'

'I should have known it.'

Amalric nodded at his uncle's flat-toned verdict.

'How many were they, brother, apart from Gerhild?'

'*Ten . . . my King.*'

Putting a hand on the man's shoulder, the young king looked down into his face.

'You have earned the gratitude of both your king and the entire tribe. You will be cared for until your time comes, whether that be today or fifty years from now.'

Gernot stepped close to the king, speaking quietly in his ear.

'They have an hour's start on us, my King, no more. You must gather the remaining men of your household who are fit to ride and have them mounted on the freshest horses. And fetch your huntsman, he knows the ground to the north of here, and the paths that are known to Gunda, along which he will lead these thieving animals to safety unless we catch them first. We must be after these Romans before the sun is overhead if we are to catch them. If our men need any encouragement you can tell them that when we catch the Romans every single man in their party will be sacrificed to Wodanaz by your new priest.' He grimaced at the human wreckage strewn across the riverbank's slope. 'And slowly. *Very* slowly.'

Both men turned at the sound of a growing commotion, a dozen or so warriors surrounding a pair of men who were half leading and half dragging a semi-conscious figure between them and holding off their brother warriors with the points of their spears. Gernot put his hands on his hips and looked up at the sky as the two men waited for the brawling group to reach them.

'Perhaps the gods heard your plea, my King?'

Amalric strode forward, scattering the men who were attempting to get their hands on the prisoner with the flat of his sword, bellowing at them to get back until only the dazed Roman and his captors stood before him, tribesmen surrounding them in a tight circle with murder in their eyes. The older of the two tribesmen released his grip on the prisoner's arm, leaving him to sag against his comrade, bowing deeply to Amalric and Gernot.

'A captive, my King, a Roman officer! My son wanted to kill him, but I heard you offer a gold coin for each Roman we captured, and five for a centurion, so I made him be satisfied with knocking the man about for a while.'

Gernot looked past him at the prisoner, who was swaying on his feet with the look of a boxer who had taken one punch too many, his face puffy with fresh bruising.

'A centurion? This is no centurion. Look at him . . .'

The speaker's son shook his head.

'He is, my Lord! He was the man shouting orders at their archers when first we attacked them!'

One of the men circling with evident blood lust spoke out, his voice an angry growl.

'I saw this fucker put an arrow in my cousin Hald's throat while the rest of those dogs were retreating from us, and he was the man telling them when to shoot and when to run! I say we gut him open and leave him here to—'

'No!' Amalric's eyes blazed. 'If there's any butchering to be done then it will be performed in the right way, by a priest and on an altar sworn to Wodanaz! I am your fucking king, and you will obey me in this! If any man wishes to disobey my command, he can draw his sword and challenge me, but if none of you have the nerve to fight me then back away!'

He stared about them for a moment, the wild fury in his eyes making more than one man take a step back. With his men cowed he continued in a more rational tone.

'This man may be the key to understanding what game these Romans are playing. They have taken Gerhild to the north, doubtless running to the safety of the Angrivarii. I will pursue them, and I will take him with me. Should . . . *when* we catch these animals, he will provide a sacrifice whose bloody horror will make their blood run cold. So you can be sure of one thing, my brothers – this man is going to pay for the number of our people he killed today with a slow and agonising death. Bring him!'

Dubnus stood staring out over the bow as the warship *Mars* led the small squadron up the Rhenus past the walls of Claudius's Colony, looking round as Varus joined him.

'They'll be safe enough. There's no way that the Bructeri could know that Rutilius Scaurus has taken the witch to the north, and even if they did know they're not going to catch a man like Gunda, who knows every blade of grass between the river and the northern edge of their kingdom. Our friends are long clear of any danger.'

The Briton nodded, still staring out over the river's green water.

'I suppose you're right. But I wasn't thinking about them, I was trying to work out the last time I saw Qadir alive.'

Varus thought for a moment, cursing his insensitivity.

'I'm sorry, I should have realised that the loss of your comrades would be hurting. And when did *I* see him last . . . ? I think it must have been just after your first counter-attack, when his archers were shooting to cover your retreat. I heard him order them to pull back, and I didn't hear his voice again after that. What do you think happened to him?'

Dubnus shook his head, turning to face the Roman.

'Who knows? He's face down in the forest with a gang of Bructeri pissing on his corpse, if he's lucky. Or a prisoner if he's not. And we've both heard what they do to prisoners.'

'Centurions?' Both men turned to find the most senior of

Albinus's lictors standing before them with a scroll in his hand.
'Forgive me, gentlemen, I hardly like to intrude on your loss.'

Varus raised a patrician eyebrow.

'Yes?'

'Well, forgive me for being the bearer of unwelcome news . . .
the Governor has instructed me to summon the centurion here
to an investigatory meeting once we're safely ashore.'

'And not myself?'

'No, Centurion. You are deemed to be . . .'

'Too well connected to act as a lightning rod for the governor's
ill will?'

The lictor shuffled his feet.

'I'm sure I couldn't comment, Centurion.'

Varus shook his head in disgust.

'I'm sure you couldn't. Not that it's any fault of yours.' He
shot the man a conspiratorial glance. 'So tell me, and bearing in
mind I know enough about Clodius Albinus to have a fairly good
idea in any case, perhaps you could give us some clue as to the
likely outcome of this investigatory meeting.'

The lictor stared at him for a moment before speaking, lowering
his voice almost theatrically.

'You know that I'll deny having told you this, don't you?'

Varus nodded impassively.

'Of course. But that's immaterial, because you have my word
as a gentleman not to repeat anything you tell us.'

'In that case I can tell you that it's already been decided. The
governor will ask your colleague here a few questions of little
import, and then no matter what answer he gets he will then
decide to have your detachment ordered to a fort so remote that
he'll expect your tribune to utterly fail to find his men, if he ever
returns, especially once all records of the matter have been
destroyed.'

The Roman clenched his fist in anger.

'And he expects me to allow such an injustice to pass?'

The lictor shook his head, passing him the message container.

'He doesn't expect you to have any view on the subject, Vibius

Varus, because you won't have any awareness of it. You're ordered to ride to Rome with this despatch . . .' He handed over the watertight message container. 'And given that your senior officer has absented himself from his command, it is not an order you can legally disobey. You're to ride immediately, the moment we reach the city, and not to deviate from roads that lead directly to Rome. You are to deliver the despatch directly to the imperial chamberlain.'

The young aristocrat looked down at the sealed container in his hand in disgust.

'Amazing. And there was I thinking the man was merely a small-minded careerist. This proves that he's something far worse than that.'

'We'll get a fire set, and organise a watch. You look after the tribune.'

Marcus nodded to Dolfus, who turned away to issue commands to his own men and the two Hamians who had been detailed to accompany the party by Qadir, then looked up at his superior who was still sitting in his saddle, his eyes closed and his face grey with exhaustion. For the last hour of their ride he had swayed in the saddle like a man who had ridden for two straight days, and while there had still been an hour of usable daylight, Dolfus had made the decision to find a sheltered spot in the hills through which they had been travelling, rather than push on to the river that flowed across their path only a few miles further on. He had gestured to Gunda, inviting the German to agree with his decision.

'Another mile or so and it's all downhill to the River Reed. And as I'm sure your guide will agree, the last thing we want is to spend a night in the open on the edge of *that* quagmire.'

Marcus touched the swaying tribune's foot lightly to get his attention.

'Tribune? You'll feel better once the fire's lit and you have some food inside you.'

Scaurus dismounted slowly, every movement evidently painful as he roused himself to a semblance of consciousness.

'Mithras, but that hurts! I feel as if I've fought that German giant and lost. Twice.'

Marcus helped the tribune to ease his body into a sitting position against the bole of a tree, seeing the pain of the day's ride etched in the lines of his friend's face. Their path had covered mile after mile of forest tracks, difficult going once they were away from the heavily used hunting ground around Thusila, and the bumpy ride had taken its toll on the wounded man. He looked across at Gerhild, who had climbed down from her horse's saddle and was speaking quietly with Gunda.

'Lady, your assistance in redressing the tribune's wound would be greatly appreciated.'

Touching her brother's cheek she made her way to where Scaurus stood.

'Help him to remove his armour.'

Marcus lifted the mail's dead weight from the exhausted tribune's shoulders, smiling wanly as Scaurus sank back against a tree trunk with his eyes closed. Gerhild put a hand to the blood-soaked tunic, pursing her lips at what she felt.

'The wound is hot, I can feel it through the bandage and his tunic. Fetch my pot.'

Emptying her water skin into the iron bowl, she erected the tripod that suspended it over the makings of a small fire, which she built with the skill of a born woodsman while Marcus watched, intrigued.

'You've never seen a fire being constructed, Centurion?'

'Never with quite such skill.'

She flicked a glance at him, her eyes hard.

'And by a woman, as you tactfully did not say.'

Her words opened the wound of his memories as deftly as her Bructeri guard's blade had torn Scaurus's body.

'My wife was a better doctor and surgeon than any man I've met before or since. I'm the last man to seek to denigrate a woman's skills.'

Gerhild looked up at him as she tore up the herbs that would make a herbal tea with which to treat Scaurus's wound.

'*Was?*'

'She was torn from this life by the depravity of a deranged emperor and the incompetence of an inept doctor.'

The woman's face softened.

'I am sorry for your loss. You have children?'

'A son.'

An uneasy silence settled on them as Gerhild built the fire's base with twigs and dry grass.

'There is more to your story.'

The words were a flat statement of fact, but in the seer's mouth they were both soothing and an encouragement to talk.

'There is. But this is not the time for me to tell it.'

She nodded.

'I understand. This loss has dealt a blow to your soul from which there is no easy recovery. But I know in my heart that when the time comes, you will speak of it, and unburden yourself of the weight that bears down on you.'

He stared at her for a moment before nodding curtly and standing.

'If you will excuse me?'

The woman smiled again.

'Of course. Your tribune will sleep for a while, and I will not need your help to administer the herbal tea until the pot has boiled and then cooled.'

He walked away, shaking his head at the moment of compulsion he had felt to tell her his story, of his father's murder and his own escape from the throne's hunters, of the vengeance he had wreaked on the men responsible and the love that had been destroyed by the actions of powerful and perverted men.

'My sister has that effect on most men.' He looked up to find Gunda waiting for him by the horses, watching as Dolfus and his men started to build a camp fire. 'She gets inside their heads just by speaking with them, without effort or artifice. That was what upset the man I was forced to kill in the act of protecting her. That and the fact she foretold he would die very soon, which was the reason for his attack on her.'

His smile was ironic, and Marcus found himself warming to the man.

'You led us well today. How much further do we have to ride?'

'Tomorrow we cross the Reed River, *if* I can find a place to ford it after all these years. Then we will ride north, past the remains of your fort at Aliso until we reach the borders of the Bructeri and the Angrivarii. We can only hope that they will be as friendly as Dolfus seems to believe will be the case.'

'Centurion?'

Marcus turned, to find Munir, the Hamian watch officer, at his side.

'Yes?'

'We have seen something of which we believe you will wish to be aware.'

He followed the Hamian to the edge of the slope, looking out across the land to the south. Husam beckoned to him, gesturing for the Roman to keep low, and Marcus crawled the last twenty paces to the spot Husam had chosen from which to watch the ground across which they had travelled.

'There.'

Following the older man's pointing arm he saw what it was that had excited their attention, a long column of horsemen winding their way down a hillside in the distance.

'You are to be congratulated on your eyesight, Husam. Munir . . .' He looked at the younger man. '. . . run and tell Decurion Dolfus not to light his fire, and say the same to Mistress Gerhild. Quickly.'

The Hamian was away at the run, leaving Marcus and Husam staring across the valley at the German horsemen.

'How many, would you say?'

'Thirty men, Centurion. And, if my eyes do not deceive me, one prisoner.'

'So tell me, Centurion, exactly what it is that your tribune thinks he's playing at with this latest escapade?'

Dubnus considered the governor's question with a neutral

expression on his face, standing to attention with his helmet under one arm. The expected summons to an audience had been delivered to him by one of Albinus's lictors soon after the Briton had settled his and Qadir's men into their temporary quarters within the fortress, barely giving him time to get medical attention for his wounded man and find a new tunic in anticipation of the meeting. While the Briton was managing to keep his disgust at the senator's obsession with Scaurus and his doings from betraying itself in his voice, the emotional hangover of the day's events and the urge to do violence as a result was proving harder to control.

'I can't say, Governor. I wasn't part of the discussion around the change of plan.'

Albinus leaned back in his chair with a sour grimace.

'No. I'm sure you weren't. So tell me this, Centurion, who *was* part of the discussion? A certain decurion was certainly involved, that much I do know.'

The big Briton stared impassively at the wall behind the governor's head, ignoring the predatory stares being directed at him by the bodyguards arrayed behind their master.

'I'm sorry, Governor, I was too busy killing tribesmen at the time to pay it much attention.'

'You saw nothing?'

'No, sir. Killing tribesmen does tend to be distracting.'

Albinus stared hard at him for a moment, and the Briton cast his mind back to the moment when Scaurus had made the decision to drastically change his plan.

'It seems that our party trick with Centurion Varus's cousin isn't going to work as well the second time around. Decurion Dolfus here was obliged to report it to the governor, and when his messenger passed on the news Clodius Albinus was highly vocal on the subject, to say the least. Apparently he won't be allowed to make quite so free with the fleet which, the governor was at pains to point out, reports to him operationally.'

The tribune had shifted his position fractionally, wincing at the pain as the blood drying around his wound was pulled by the movement.

'You expect him to seek to prevent Prefect Varus from collecting us?'

Dolfus had shaken his head at Qadir's question.

'Your orders come from Rome, and I doubt he'd go so far as to block the will of the man behind the throne. But I do think . . .' he smiled wryly, 'or rather I should say that the man I work for thinks, that he'll seek to compensate for not having predicted such a move in the first place by ensuring that he's on board the flagship this time round. He'll bring his lictors along to demonstrate the power of his office, and his bodyguard to provide enough men to take the woman off your hands, especially with the tribune wounded and therefore dismissible as unfit to command. Then he'll send Gerhild south to Rome, and keep Tribune Scaurus hospitalised here for long enough that she'll have been paraded in front of the emperor before he's even allowed to get out of his hospital bed. With Clodius Albinus as the architect of the whole thing, I'd imagine. Putting it bluntly, if you board those ships your cause is as good as lost.'

Albinus stared at the Briton standing before him in obvious disbelief.

'Really? You expect me to believe that your superior officer took it into his head to abandon a means of escaping from Bructeri territory, and instead rode off into the wilderness with this Bructeri witch, and barely enough men to form a legion tent party, on a *whim*? And that he didn't bother briefing you as to why he would make such a decision? Do you think I'm *stupid*, Centurion?'

Given the opening, Dubnus was unable to resist the opportunity.

'No sir, I don't *think* you're stupid . . .'

He left the other half of the statement unspoken, but the scowl on the governor's face deepened as he realised the implication of the Briton's words.

'You insolent *dog!* Get out of my sight! You and your barbarian soldiers are confined to barracks pending transfer to a more suitable duty than you've performed to date. I'll bury you so deep that in the unlikely event of Rutilius Scaurus surviving his latest mad escapade, he won't find you in a lifetime of searching!'

'Feed him? Why would we feed him, Gernot? He's going to be screaming his lungs out within a day or so, once we've caught up with his fellow murderers. Food would be wasted on him.'

Qadir was careful to keep his head down, knowing that the slightest reaction to the Bructeri king's dismissive answer might well give away his ability to understand their discussion. The older man shrugged, his response framed in a tone the Hamian suspected was deliberately light.

'As you wish, my King. My only concern was to ensure that he doesn't delay us by being so weak from lack of food as to be unable to ride. But, as you say, he'll—'

'You're right, as always.' Amalric nodded his agreement with the older man's words. 'You, give the easterner a piece of that bread, and some dried meat, too. And make sure he eats it. If he falls from his horse tomorrow as the result of hunger and delays us, then it will go ill with *you*.'

The Hamian looked up in feigned surprise as a hunk of bread was shoved into his bound hands, nodding his thanks into a hostile expression but remaining silent. The pursuit of his comrades had taken most of the morning to organise, with the fetching of food and organisation of the men left behind to collect and bury the bodies of the fallen warriors, and the afternoon had passed in a blur of forest paths, hills and open land, farmed for the most part unless too marshy to support a crop, across which the king's men had ridden at a deliberate pace with the king's huntsman at their head, two magnificent dogs ranging alongside him. From time to time he had stopped to examine the ground in front of them, clearly finding encouragement in whatever it was that he was seeing that they still followed the trail of the Romans who had abducted Gerhild. For Qadir himself the ride had been a waking nightmare, a continual struggle to avoid the loss of consciousness that beckoned him so seductively, the men around him using the butts of their spears to enliven him whenever he started to slump in the saddle. With the coming of night the thirty-man column of horsemen had halted and made camp, gathering firewood and making no attempt to disguise their presence despite knowing that the light of their encampment would serve to warn the fleeing Romans of their pursuit. The king had laughed at his uncle's concern that their quarry might exploit the warning by escaping in some way.

'Let them know that their doom is hard on their heels! How far ahead do you believe they are?'

Gernot shook his head.

'Not far, my King. Perhaps two hours. And tomorrow they have to cross the river of reeds. Even Gunda may struggle to find the right place to get across the stream, given how long it is since he was exiled, whereas your huntsman has roamed these parts most of his life. I think it most likely that we'll find them on the southern bank of the river, still hunting for a ford.'

Amalric grinned wolfishly.

'Not one man of them is to die when we take them, not if he can be captured. Wodanaz is waiting eagerly for sacrifices to restore our tribe's lost honour, soiled by their destruction of our sacred grove and the murder of my priest. And if we fail to take them tomorrow then perhaps I'll give him this one, once the sun has set, wielding the knife myself in my role as the tribe's first priest. I'll open his chest with my sword and pull out his heart. That'll be a nice surprise for him.'

He stared at Qadir hungrily, and the Hamian cast his eyes down in the manner of a man who knew better than to present his captor with any challenge, locking his face into what he hoped was an immobile mask.

'See, he has no idea? I wonder when he'll start screaming?'

Gernot laughed softly.

'They say the Romans' eastern soldiers have different gods to ours. Perhaps the moment that he'll start screaming is when he realises that he's about to meet whoever it is that he worships.'

*

'*Centurion.*'

Dubnus turned to seek the source of the quiet greeting, finding only an empty street in either direction, dimly lit by the guttering flames of a solitary torch. Half expecting that he would be set up for a beating on his disconsolate walk back from the governor's residence to the transient barracks, he had already slipped a set of viciously studded metal knuckles out of his belt purse and settled them over his right hand, his fingers reflexively tightening on the thick bronze loops as he scanned the street for threats.

'*Centurion. Here.*'

A door was ajar in the building closest to him, the fortress's headquarters, and a man dressed in the simple tunic of a slave was beckoning to him.

'What the fuck do you want?'

The beckoning figure put a finger to his lips and gestured again. Shaking his head in bemused irritation the Briton strode up the building's steps, raising his beweaponed fist into clear view.

'If this is some sort of game to lure me in there for a kicking, then you're going to be the first man whose jaw I break.'

The answer was couched in the same quiet tones, accompanied by another summoning gesture.

'*No harm will come to you, Centurion. Follow me.*'

Readying himself for violence, the Briton stepped in through the open door, raising an eyebrow at the sight of a pair of impassive legionaries standing guard over the entrance.

'What the *fuck* is this?'

The slave walked away into the building, gesturing wordlessly once more for the Briton to follow. Curiosity overcoming his reluctance, Dubnus followed him past another pair of men standing sentry duty over the chapel of the standards, the strong room where the legion's eagle slept when it was not in the hands of its standard bearer. Turning a corner, his guide pointed to a heavy, nail-studded door.

'Enter, Centurion. My master is waiting for you.'

Opening the door the Briton stepped through, braced for

violence, but instead found himself in a lamplit office, whose opulence was at once apparent from the massive polished oak desk behind which stood a single figure. His face was almost invisible, the lamps arranged behind him to cast shadow on his features, but his gesture for Dubnus to take a seat was clear enough, his voice both cultured and direct.

'Sit, please, Centurion. And you might as well divest yourself of the bronze knuckles, you'll struggle to hold a cup with that monstrous thing on your hand.'

Taking a seat the Briton slipped the weapon back into his purse, staring in mystification at the other man as he poured two cups of wine, sipping from his own as he pushed the other across the table to the Briton.

'It's a fine vintage. I'm of the opinion that life's too short to drink poor wine, and I make a point of offering my guests nothing less than would satisfy my tastes.'

Looking down at the cup before him Dubnus shrugged, taking a mouthful of the wine and savouring the taste for a moment, raising the cup in salute.

'It is good. In fact it's the first good thing in an otherwise shit day. Thank you . . . Legatus?'

The other man laughed softly.

'No, Centurion, I'm no legion commander. A man has to be born to enormous wealth if he's to command one of the emperor's eagles, and my birth was as far from that exalted station in life as can be imagined. In truth, Dubnus, prince of the Brigantes, you had an infinitely better start to your life than I. I was born to a slave, although I had the good fortune to be delivered to my mother in Rome, and to be the illegitimate son of a powerful member of the court of the emperor Marcus Aurelius, the current emperor's father. By combination of fortunate circumstance and my own intelligence I managed to prove my value to the throne, and was eventually freed from my servitude and put to work here, on the frontier. My name, should you be curious, is Tiro.'

'So how do you come to be sitting behind the legatus's desk, Tiro?'

The other man shrugged.

'He lends me its use, every now and then, when I wish to impress upon a man the real nature of imperial power in this province.'

Dubnus's eyes narrowed.

'He *lends* you the use of his office? The *legatus?*'

Tiro smiled, the expression barely visible.

'Indeed, Centurion. Allow me to explain.' He sipped at the wine again. 'The legatus, as you're very well aware, is a member of the senatorial class, a man who either has inherited or will inherit an enormous sum of money, and who has been smart enough, or lucky enough, or perhaps simply not *quite* rich enough, to avoid being branded as a traitor in order for that wealth to be confiscated by the imperial treasury. Being emperor is such an expensive business, what with thirty legions to pay, and the cost of all those games and circuses, not to mention the bread that keeps Rome fed and content. But then you know this, given your friend Marcus Valerius Aquila's recent experiences of imperial justice.'

Dubnus frowned across the table.

'How—'

'How do I know these things? Because it is my job to know them, Centurion, because a man in my position needs to know every little fact that could make the difference between success and failure. Perhaps it would help if you understood my role here a little better? Let me explain it this way . . .' He sipped the wine again, refilling his own and Dubnus's cups before continuing. 'There is, as a general rule, a lifespan for everything in this world. For everything and everyone and, for the purposes of this discussion, every family too. A great man arises, from nowhere, with a combination of ancestry that unlocks a genius, perhaps for warfare, perhaps for business, or perhaps simply for ruling other men. Sometimes, in the genuinely terrifying examples, for all three. His light burns brightly until he dies, revered by all, to be succeeded by his son who, everyone agrees, may not have quite his father's brilliance, but who nevertheless performs his role well enough to bring honour to the great man's legacy. But after him comes the third generation, with the founder of the dynasty's genius so diluted by the introduction of other men's blood to the mix that, unless by some quirk of fate or calculation new genius is introduced by marriage, he will be but a pale shadow of his grandfather. And so the dynasty crumbles into insignificance, or in the worst cases to ignominy and shame. Consider the fall of the first family, from the Emperor Augustus's glorious forty-year reign to the disaster of his great-grandson Caligula's short span of three years on the throne. Only a few decades later the Emperor Vespasian's younger son managed to destroy his father's inheritance in only a single generation. And so it goes. It is simply the way things are, Centurion.'

Dubnus nodded.

'I have seen this for myself. But why are you telling me this?'

The other man leaned back in his chair, his face invisible in the office's shadows.

'The answer to that question is more straightforward than you might think, and concerns both the first and third generations of our hypothetical family. As I said a moment ago, the legions are commanded by Rome's masters, the senatorial class who bow only to the emperor himself, and as a rule the provincial governors are for the most part chosen from among the ranks of successful legati, or those whose family have the most influence with the emperor. Which of course presents the emperor, or rather those men who make the decisions for him, with a limited choice of men from whom to choose, some of them brilliant, some rather less so. And, of course, even the smallest of frontier provinces will have legions, powerful tools in the wrong hands and even more so when, as has happened, two or three governors in adjoining provinces make the decision to join forces. So, what's to be done if a province falls into the hands of another Julius Caesar, a man with the skills of a great general and the unmitigated bravery required to mount an assault on the throne? Or another Varus, with the abject lack of imagination and leadership required for another Teutoburg Forest? Whether in the hands of brilliant minds or fools, the use and the maintenance of such power needs to be assured by the presence of men with undoubted loyalty to the throne, if attempts to take the throne or military disasters are to be avoided. And so each major province has a man who can be trusted posted to a position of apparent mediocrity, men who can quietly steer around such potential disasters by means of a deft touch here, a swift bloodletting there. Men whose successes in avoiding either outcome can be ascribed to others, so that they can remain hidden in the shadows.'

'Men like you?'

'You have it, Centurion, I knew you were more than a scowl on a particularly muscular stick. Men like me. I watch over Clodius Albinus from the shadows, ensuring that everything he does is free from risk or, when I am unable to prevent him from acting in a manner more likely to further his own aims than those of the empire, I do whatever is needed to put right what would otherwise be wrong. Like sending a message to an enterprising young tribune to suggest that he might not want to risk boarding a naval vessel whose mission had been suborned by a man who considers him a mortal enemy.'

Dubnus's eyes narrowed.

'Dolfus is *your* man.'

The other man nodded.

'Of course he is. All it ever takes is a short and meaningful discussion about potential future careers, and the display of my imperial warrant, for men like Dolfus to give me their unconditional loyalty. The decurion is a man of good family, and he knows full well that his first duty is to the empire and not to any individual, no matter how exalted.'

'And it was your idea for my tribune to take the German woman to the north, rather than boarding the warships?'

Tiro nodded.

'It was. I expect him to successfully evade any Bructeri pursuit, unlikely though such a pursuit may be given the quiet exit I hear the tribune and his party made before the Germans caught up with you. I plan to journey north tomorrow myself, and to meet

Scaurus and his men on the northern border of the Bructeri lands, and ensure that the Angrivarii grant them safe passages. Perhaps you'd care to accompany me?'

The Briton drained his cup.

'Of course I would. But my men and I are ordered to remain in barracks, pending a posting to some shithole or other.'

The freedman smiled beneficently.

'Then it's a good thing that I have the ability to make you and your men vanish into thin air, isn't it? As far as Clodius Albinus will know, he's had you posted to dig latrines in a fort so distant that he'll never think to check on the veracity of the records. Have your men ready to ride at dawn. And draw yourself a vine stick and a helmet crest from the fortress stores, the time for your status to be concealed is long past. Where we're going, the more imposing you both look, the better.'

Dubnus nodded, putting the cup down on the desk before him, then frowned as a thought struck him.

'There is another problem.'

The other man smiled at him knowingly.

'Young Gaius Vibius Varus and the governor's message? There's no problem there . . .' He raised his voice. 'Is there, Vibius Varus?'

The door behind him opened, and Varus stepped through it in a clean tunic and freshly polished boots.

'No, Tiro, I don't believe there is.'

'But . . .'

Both men smiled at the bemused Briton.

'The message?' Tiro shook his head. 'Opened, read, filed for future reference and forgotten. The governor will entertain fond imaginings as to what's going to happen when his rather idiosyncratic version of events reaches Rome, and only in the fullness of time will it dawn on him that the lack of response indicates that it might not have arrived after all. I've taken the precaution of substituting a rather more factually based summary of events to date and ordered its delivery to Rome with all speed, just in case he has second thoughts as to the reliability of young Varus here and decides to send another.'

He stood, indicating the room's door.

'And now, gentlemen, there's just one thing I need from you. Gold.' The two men stared at him in bemusement, and he laughed, shaking his head. 'Come now, you can hardly expect me not to have heard the governor's frequent complaints about the amount of freshly minted coins that managed to get stuck to your tribune's fingers in the process of it being used to enable the imperial chamberlain to make his bid for power? I know for a fact that Scaurus's travel chest contains enough wealth to fund what I've got in mind with the Angrivarii, and their neighbours the Marsi to the east, whose lands we'll have to travel through to reach the border with the Bructeri. So off you go and dig the chest out, and I'll be along shortly with a smith to crack open the lock. I'm sure your superior won't complain, given that without his money he might well end up exchanging death on a Bructeri altar for the same fate at the hands of another tribe!'

'You're sure?'

Husam shook his head.

'No, Tribune, I am far from sure that these Germans have a prisoner, but I think it very likely. And I believe I know who it is.'

Scaurus stared at him in tired disbelief.

'But they were what, half a mile from your position when they stopped to camp for the night? How could you know?'

The party had relocated another mile towards the river when it became clear that their pursuers had decided to camp on a small tributary of the Reed River, putting enough distance between them that the glow of their fires would be completely hidden by the trees. The Hamian inclined his head respectfully, but he wasn't so deferential as to back down in the face of Scaurus's scepticism.

'Every other man in their party was wearing a helmet, Tribune. Only sufficient iron to cover the top of their heads, but every man wore this protection.'

Dolfus nodded.

'It's the distinguishing mark of Amalric's household guard. They all wear it.'

'But one man was not wearing such a helmet. Nor was he carrying a weapon, unlike the men around him. And when he dismounted, two of them stayed close to him. I could not see if they were using their spears to keep him subdued though.'

'So, perhaps the Bructeri have one of our men. Perhaps. The more important thing is that . . .' Husam raised his hand with a deferential expression, and Scaurus, clearly still in pain, restrained himself from the volcanic loss of his temper that he was aware was building within him as a reaction to stress and exhaustion.

'Yes?'

'Forgive me, Tribune, I do have one more observation to share with you.' Scaurus waved his hand, looking at the man with an expression verging on the predatory. 'When the man I have assumed to be a prisoner dismounted, his head was at the same height as the horses. This appeared to be a tall man.'

'And? Our detachment contained several such men, more than half of us, in fact.'

The Hamian spread his hands in polite agreement, but continued despite the tribune's obvious ire.

'Just so, Tribune. But this man was not powerfully built, his stance was not that of an axeman. He was of a more normal build, although he did have broad shoulders. Perhaps from use of the bow.'

He fell silent and lowered his head in deference to the senior officer.

'You're telling me that the Bructeri have a prisoner, and that you think it's Centurion Qadir?'

'I cannot make such a bold assertion, Tribune. But the man I have seen was certainly a prisoner, in my view, and his build and stance were at once familiar to me. I have said enough, and wasted enough of your time. Forgive me for . . .'

Scaurus raised a hand.

'No, you must forgive me for being short-tempered with you. I am tired and in pain, which is only a partial excuse. Now we must discuss your suggestion, and decide what we must do. Thank you.'

The Hamian chosen man bowed and turned away, Scaurus waiting until he was out of earshot before speaking again.

'The centurion is a dead man, if Husam is correct in his identification. They have brought him along with them in order to torture him to death at the right time, hoping to unnerve us.'

'Or to bargain for his life with hers?'

Dolfus looked over at the woman, busily tending the iron pot over her small fire.

'We cannot make such a bargain. And they will know that, or at least suspect it. No, our main focus now must be on these pursuers. How is that they come to be so close behind us, and how did they even know that we didn't board the warships?'

The decurion grimaced.

'Perhaps they overcame your men before they could reach the river, or perhaps the ships didn't arrive at the right time. Either way they would be able to count corpses, and look for the bodies they would have expected to find, those of the woman and myself. They will quickly have worked out that we must have run, fearing such a conclusion to the fight, and once that was their belief it wouldn't need a genius to work out where we would be heading.'

'Or perhaps a man who fell in battle with you lived while he seemed dead, and saw us ride north.'

They looked around at Gerhild, who was still tending her pot, dropping crushed herbs into the bubbling water.

'But all the men who fell at the crossroads were dead. Not one of them moved with a knife stuck into his arm or leg.'

'Indeed that is true, Tribune, for I watched your men perform their grisly test of life. And yet . . .'

'And yet what?'

She smiled a quiet, private smile.

'And yet who is to know what strangeness might have overcome a man who was thrown headlong into a tree?'

Dolfus looked at her for a moment and then shook his head.

'Whatever the cause of their pursuit, putting some distance

between us is my main concern. In the morning we must cross the Reed, and quickly, if we're not to find ourselves staring down twice our strength in spears. What do you say, Gunda?'

The scout grimaced back at him.

'I say that the Reed changes its course almost every year, as the marshes that fringe both banks grow and shrink, and become more solid or more liquid as if on a whim of the gods. We might find a workable ford before the sun has risen far enough to warm the day, or it might take all day. The morning will reveal our fate.'

'In which case, gentlemen, I suggest that we eat and get some sleep. Post two men to watch, and make sure that they are changed regularly. I want everyone clear-headed tomorrow.'

Scaurus turned away only to find the woman standing behind him.

'If *every* man is to be clear-headed then I will need you to drink this.' She passed him a wooden cup, smiling as he looked down into it with a dubious expression. 'It is a herbal tea, Tribune, lavender, sage and thyme, and the purple flower that we call The Healer, all boiled in water. It will soothe your mind, and help your body to make good the damage that the knife wrought on you. You will sleep well, and, with the blessing of Hertha, heal faster.'

He looked down into the cup again and then took a tentative sip, pulling a face at the slightly bitter taste.

'It tastes . . .'

'Natural. If I had a little honey I would sweeten it for you, but the bees will all be asleep by now and impossible to find, so the unsweetened version will have to do. Drink it. When the remainder has cooled I will use it to clean your wound, before I dress it with clean cloth.'

Scaurus stared at her for a moment longer and then drained the cup.

'Thank you. Your solicitude is appreciated.'

'I would do the same for any man with such a wound. Even if you bore me malice which, despite calling me a witch, I sense you do not. Sleep, Tribune Scaurus, and let us see what the morning brings us.'

The Roman nodded and turned away, leaving her standing alone. Returning to the pot she refilled her cup, calling to her brother who was setting out his blanket a few feet away.

'Come here and take a drink, Gunda. You of all people will need to be alive to the possibilities that the morning will bring.'

'Where the fuck are you lot going at this time of the night?'

Dubnus stepped forward from the ranks of his men. Realising that he was addressing a centurion, as the Tungrian's crested helmet became apparent in the dim torchlight, the sentry snapped to attention and saluted, looking down at the wax tablet in the officer's hands. Tiro had given Dubnus the orders the previous evening, raising a sardonic eyebrow as he had passed the tablet across the table.

'I'll see you down the road from the eastern gate at dawn. You and your men, Centurion . . .' He had looked at Dubnus with a cautionary expression. '. . . would be well advised to leave barracks quietly and with care not to attract any attention. No shouting of orders, and no hobnails crunching on the flagstones either, make sure your boots are muffled and leave those men who might be interested in such an unexpected movement on your part to enjoy their sleep. And you, Vibius Varus, you'd be best marching as a common soldier in what's left of your detachment, so roll your new crest up in your blanket to keep it out of sight. Keep your head down and your mouth shut, so that the gate guards don't pass word back to the governor's residence that you were seen disobeying his orders. I've no desire for him to chase us down the road to the fleet headquarters in a fit of bad temper, as that would force my hand to an act that, while I've often fantasised about it, would only serve to make things more complex. After all, having men of Clodius Albinus's stature killed does entail a very great deal of paperwork.'

He had shrugged, pointing to the tablet.

'So, give the gate guards that and you should be allowed out of the fortress without much ceremony. I've made the "orders" it contains nice and wordy to put the gate guards off actually reading it, but the seal's genuine enough.'

The Briton held out the tablet, grunting out the tired and bored response of a man who had risen too early to perform a task for which he had little enthusiasm.

'Governor's orders. We're to march south to a fort in the hills and become the permanent garrison.'

The soldier holding the tablet turned to face his watch officer as the senior man walked up, jumping to attention as his superior took the tablet and turned it to the torchlight with the expression of a man absorbing its contents.

'So what's this then?'

'Watch Officer, sir! This centurion has orders to ride to a fort in the hills to the south to join the garrison, Watch Officer, sir!'

His superior saluted in turn, taking the tablet from his soldier and holding it up to the light of a torch to better see the words scratched into the wax surface, and the seal pressed into a corner next to its wooden casing. Standing in the rear rank among Dubnus's remaining archers Varus suppressed the urge to smile with difficulty, realising that neither man could actually read. The watch officer stared at the tablet in his hands for a moment longer, then nodded decisively, clearly unwilling to appear either indecisive or less capable than his soldier.

'Looks to be in order to me. That is the governor's seal.' He looked at the soldier, who nodded vigorously, knowing his superior's hatred of being gainsaid once he'd made a decision. 'Very well, on your way.'

Dubnus took the tablet and stepped back into the detachment's front rank, waiting impassively while the fortress's eastern gate was opened for them.

'March!'

Having discarded the rags that had been tied around their boots before they approached the sentry, the Tungrians stepped out with the characteristic crunching sound of hobnails on the road's hard surface, marching out of the fortress and into the pre-dawn gloom at a brisk pace. A mile down the road they found Tiro waiting for them, getting to his feet as the detachment approached and looking up at the rapidly lightening sky above.

'It's going to be a fine day, which is good for us but, I suspect, not so good for your tribune and his men. They'll be praying for mist and rain, I'd imagine, if there's any chance that they were followed.'

He led them down the road at a good pace, marching along-side Dubnus with an easy gait that belied his apparent age.

'Don't look so surprised, Prince of the Brigantes, you're not the only man here who knows what it means to march thirty miles and then offer battle to an enemy who's sat waiting for you in the shade of their shields all day.'

Varus had ranged up alongside them having tied the new crest onto his helmet, and his intrigued question echoed that on the tip of Dubnus's tongue.

'Really, Tiro? Where did you have the honour of serving?'

The response was a bark of laughter.

'The honour of serving? You've not been doing this long enough, have you, Vibius Varus? I had the misfortune, young man, to be attached to the Second Italian legion when the emperor Marcus Aurelius led us against the Marcomanni, in what those writers who don't know any better call the German War. My gift for languages and my apparently barbarian features caught the eye of the emperor's spy master.' He shook his head in wry amuse-ment. 'As a consequence of which I was eventually selected for what was euphemistically called "detached duty", which in reality meant roaming the lands to the west of the theatre of war, and encouraging those tribes who were predisposed to support us to keep doing so, for reasons of greed for our gold or fear of our iron, and discouraging the rest from taking their spears against us for fear of what we'd do to them if they did. I led more than one clandestine mission to quietly make a hostile king disappear, and put a more amenable man on the throne in his place, and did things that the gods will doubtless judge harshly when my time comes to enter the underworld. And as if that wasn't enough I did the empire's dirty work on this frontier for so long that I became indispensable, too precious an asset to be allowed to return to Rome when there's always a situation to be dealt with somewhere among these barbaric animals. The Bructeri are just the latest in a long line of tribes who have needed to be shown their place in the natural order of things. Who knows, perhaps you'd make a fitting apprentice for me, eh young man? I could see a man of good family who's stupid enough to serve as a centurion, rather than stay safe and well provided for in Rome, taking to this role's danger and uncertainties like a fish to water.'

'You horrible bitch.'

Gunda looked out across the river's grey expanse, water as yet untouched by the sun's warmth and only dimly illuminated by the half-light that was gradually permeating the sky above.

'You dislike the river?'

The guide chuckled grimly at Marcus's question.

'Every time I cross her waters I come to hate her a little more. On one occasion it took me two days, and a dozen attempts, and yet another time I was successful in less than half a morning, and on only my second try at crossing. The current is so slow at this time of the year, and the reeds so thick, that in a very few places where the water is shallow a man can walk from one side to the other with nothing worse than wet calves to trouble him, if he is strong enough to jump the channels that thread through the vegetation. But for men on horses the problem is a different one, whether the animal will be able to make any progress through the marsh without its feet becoming stuck in the bog beneath the reeds. And we dare not leave the horses behind us.'

'And you think that this is a good place to cross? You led us here without a moment of hesitation.'

Gunda shook his head with a bemused look, as if he were asking himself the same question as that posed by Scaurus.

'In truth, Tribune, I cannot tell you. When I awoke I knew where to bring our party this morning, as if a god had whispered in my ear while I slept, and, more than that . . .' He pointed across the river at a stunted tree, its roots wrapped around a large boulder on the far bank. 'I knew I was in the right place as soon as I saw that tree, and yet I have no idea how.'

'You've not used this crossing point before?'

'I haven't even *tried* to cross here before, never mind succeeded or failed. And yet . . .'

Gerhild smiled at him beatifically from her saddle.

'And yet it seems to you that you have been drawn here, does it not?' Both men turned to look at her. 'In which case, brother, perhaps you should test that *unexplained* urge.'

She turned and walked away to her horse, leaving the two men looking at each other in silence. Gunda shrugged and mounted his own beast, urging it forward into the shallows with gentle nudges of his heels. The horse bent its neck to drink for a moment and then stepped into the river's flow, apparently untroubled by the reeds, which looked no thinner at that point than anywhere else in what they could see of the river's vegetation-choked course. Scaurus looked up at the rapidly brightening sky, then pointed at the scout.

'Follow him across. Archers first, in case there's a threat on the far bank. Husam, set yourself and Munir up to shoot back across the river in case our pursuers arrive before we're away. You two centurions can escort the witch across. Dolfus, I have an idea.'

The decurion listened for a moment and then issued a swift order to his men, both of whom handed the reins of their horses to the officer and waded into the stream while he led the beasts past them in Scaurus's wake. Scooping handfuls of river mud from the stream's bed the two cavalrymen carefully poured it across the hoof trail left in the bank's soft mud, carefully flicking it off the few blades of grass that grew at the river's margin, then washed water across their handiwork to blend it in seamlessly. Within minutes all trace of their passage had been erased, the wet mud almost invisible in the dawn's gloom, and the two men washed away the dirt from their hands and arms before remounting and following Dolfus across to the far bank.

'Hear that?'

A horse whinnied in the dawn murk somewhere close, and Scaurus waved his arm at the waiting riders.

'Get into the cover of those trees. Centurions, take my horse and make sure that the witch doesn't announce our presence.' He turned to the archers and gestured to the bank's thick crop of reeds. 'Into concealment, gentlemen, and shoot anyone who puts a hoof in the water where we crossed.'

Sinking into the reeds beside them, he ignored the tugging sensation in his side as the first of the Bructeri appeared out of the trees that ran down almost to the river's bank, watching as the man looked up and down the reed-choked river in both directions. Husam and Munir slowly eased their bows up, arrows already nocked to the strings, waiting patiently for the enemy warrior to give them a reason to loose their missiles.

In the trees behind them Dolfus and his men had swiftly arranged feed bags for the horses, counting on the beasts' preoccupation with their oats to prevent them from betraying the party's whereabouts by whinnying at the wrong moment.

'Do you still doubt the power of the goddess, Centurion?'

Marcus looked over at Gerhild, who was soothing her mount with long, slow strokes of its head and neck.

'Have I been given reason to ease my doubts, Madam?'

She smiled at him, secure in her belief.

'You'll have to be the person to make that decision. But can you not see how we have been aided this morning? My brother drank the herb tea I made, imbued with the earth goddess's blessing, and today he rode straight to what might well be the only crossing point for miles, guided by nothing more substantial than a dream.'

'Coincidence?'

'You could view it as such. And now I need a moment of silence, if you will. There is a man whose perceptions I wish to influence.' She closed her eyes, bending over the horse's neck and moving her lips silently in some arcane prayer while the two officers watched her in bemusement.

'Can we cross here?'

Amalric's huntsman stepped forward, eyeing the river unhappily.

'The Reed is a changeable river, my King. A place where a horse may cross one year will be impassable the next, and a tangle of grasses today may be a clear passage in a week.'

The king nodded impatiently.

'I am aware of the river's challenges. My question was simply whether we can cross the river *here*? For all we know, the men who hold my priestess hostage are already across, and riding north with nothing to stop them reaching the borders of our lands with the Angrivarii, and their escape from the punishments that I plan to heap upon them.'

His servant looked up at him with an earnest expression.

'The land to the north of here is far from easy riding, my King, especially if a man has not travelled it recently, a maze of marsh and forest. A few hours lead into the jaws of that monster will be of little aid to your enemies when they are wallowing in a plain of mud so deep that even a horse will not cross it.'

The king reined his temper in by force of will.

'Nevertheless I wish to cross this river before them, if I can. So . . .'

The hunter bowed, wary of his king's swift temper.

'I understand, my King. Allow me to consider the river for a short time and you will have your answer.'

He dismounted and walked down to the Reed's bank, staring across the expanse of grasses that choked the river's course, then knelt to examine the water close to the bank.

'Wait.'

The Hamians' bows were fully bent, needing only the smallest of movements to send a pair of arrows at the men now gathered around the kneeling scout, and Scaurus's harsh whisper was seemingly all that stood between the Bructeri and his death. When Husam spoke his voice was as taut as the string in which the strength of his body waited, controlled only by the fingers of his right hand.

'He will see the traces of our crossing.'

Scaurus raised a hand in caution.

'And if he does, he will be the first to die. Now wait.'

The huntsman paused a moment longer, his head seeming to momentarily dip toward the water, then rose from his crouch, apparently satisfied with whatever it was he had been searching for. He pointed at the river's bank as he walked back to the group of warriors waiting for his words, and Scaurus leaned closer to Husam, his voice iron hard in the Hamian's ear.

'*Wait.*'

'The reeds are too thick, my King. A horse's hoofs will be fouled by them.'

Amalric looked up at the grey sky in frustration, then scowled down at the hapless scout.

'Did you find any sign of the men we are pursuing?'

The older man shook his head.

'Nothing, my King. I knew Gunda as a friend, before his expulsion from the tribe, and this is not a part of the river he knew well. It is more likely that he would look to cross further to the east, where the Reed is a little narrower, and flows faster.'

The king exchanged glances with Gernot before speaking again.

'Very well. Lead us to a crossing place where you are confident that we will succeed in passing this obstacle. I wish to set my wolves loose on these thieves and traitors, and see their blood run across my tribe's altar.'

'I have their king within the reach of my iron, if you wish him dead, Tribune?'

Scaurus was silent for a moment.

'My orders do not extend to killing a tribal king.'

Husam grunted dismissively.

'One death might end all thoughts of pursuit.'

The tribune turned and looked at him with a raised eyebrow.

'One death might result in a tribal war that could set the entire country to the east of the Rhenus alight. And I seem to recall that it is customary for a common soldier to speak to his officers with somewhat more respect. Clearly I shall have to have a serious discussion on the subject of military discipline with your centurion.'

He fell silent as he realised that the archer was staring across the river.

'My centurion is *there*, Tribune.'

Following the Hamian's stare he started, as he realised that the subject of his last words was mounted on a horse in the middle of the Bructeri tribesmen.

'Could you hit him through that pack of men?'

The archer nodded slowly, easing the point of his arrow to the left as the Bructeri rode slowly to the east along the Reed's bank.

'If you order it, Tribune.'

Scaurus stared bleakly at his officer for a moment, then came to a decision.

'I will not order his death. Not when he may yet have the chance to escape.'

Husam allowed his bow to unbend in a long, slow easing of the strength he had forced into its wooden frame, as the Bructeri rode away to the west, the breath sighing out of him as he put his head down and stared at the ground beneath his feet.

'I could have hit him. It would not have been a very difficult shot. But the act of actually releasing the arrow would have been the hardest thing I have ever done.'

The three men remained silent until the Bructeri riders were lost to view, each of them alone with his thoughts.

9

'I'm starting to have the feeling that my fleet has come to be regarded as little more than a means of transporting soldiers of dubious origins . . .' Prefect Varus shot his cousin a grin. 'Present company excepted, of course . . . to places where they can do their utmost to piss off the locals, thereby leaving my command to cope with the risk of anything from the odd sly arrow from the far bank to outright enmity and open attack.'

He folded his arms and stared down at Tiro, who returned the gaze without the slightest sign of being intimidated. Behind him waited his fleet navarchus and over a hundred sailors, summoned in readiness to drag whichever vessel was deemed appropriate for the new mission's requirements from its boat shed and down the muddy slipway to the fleet's basin, a lake by the side of the river.

'Whereas, Prefect, in reality the emperor's provincial fleet of the Rhenus is nothing more or less than a tool of imperial foreign policy. Most of the time that policy consists mainly of sailing up and down the river, demonstrating that the empire has eyes on its borders, and will not suffer any form of incursion without exacting a stiff price. That, and endeavouring not to sail into the bridges if it can possibly be avoided, of course. Occasionally that role requires you to act in support of the army, carrying troops and providing artillery support to actions that occur close to the river. And, even more rarely, the emperor's will is that you should use your powerful ships and undoubted naval skills to further the less orthodox aspects of that foreign policy.'

'And this is one of those rare occasions? Less than a day after the last one?'

The freedman smiled up at him.

'Quite so, Prefect. After all, you know how this sort of thing works just as well as I do. You wait decades for such a thing to come to pass and then, before you've even had the chance to sigh with relief that the whole ghastly business is done with, you're being asked to do it all over again.'

Varus shook his head slowly in evident resignation.

'Very well, but only if they take their boots off. My navarchus is still giving me shit about the mess their hobnails have made of the *Mars*'s deck.'

He turned away and spoke briefly to the aforementioned senior captain, who stared at him for a moment before turning away and issuing a string of orders in a tone bordering on irascible.

'He's not happy.'

Tiro turned to Dubnus, his smile if anything broader.

'Imagine if you were in his place. Indeed the description I had of you tells me that you have been, more or less? You were senior centurion of a legion cohort, were you not, when your own first spear was promoted to run the Third Gallic legion in Syria, under Tribune Scaurus?'

'I was.'

'Then simply imagine your disgust if I had appeared out of nowhere, unexpected and most certainly unwanted, and told you that your duty for the next few days would be to set your men to digging up onions, in their full equipment mind you? No man likes to see the command he's worked hard to bring to a peak of efficiency in its defined role turned to something he regards as less than appropriate, especially if doing so risks degrading the perfection to which he has elevated it. I doubt that having a gang of dirty soldiers roaming the decks of his ships . . .' He broke off, looking over the Briton's shoulder at the ship that was emerging from the nearest of the fleet's sheds. 'Ah, not a cargo vessel, Prefect. Where we're going we'll need something rather more imposing to back up a somewhat interesting negotiation.'

*

Waiting until the Bructeri hunting party had ridden out of view, the detachment remounted and rode north in silence. After a mile or so Cotta called forward to the scout, who was trotting his horse at the column's head.

'Where are you taking us now, Gunda?'

The German allowed his mount to drop down the column until he was riding alongside Marcus and the veteran soldier.

'To an old fortress that was built by your people in the time before the battle that destroyed three of your legions. It was used after the disaster to support the war to punish the tribes, but then for some reason, when it seemed that all hope was lost for our peoples, your armies left and never came back.'

Scaurus joined the conversation from behind them, his voice betraying the weariness that made him slump in the saddle despite a full night's sleep under the influence of Gerhild's medicinal tea.

'There was a new emperor on the throne. Augustus died two years before we had our revenge on Arminius and his followers, and once the traitor was dead at the hands of his own people, and the tribes had been beaten back into their place, his successor Tiberius decided that pacifying Germania was a step too far for the empire.' He shifted uncomfortably in his saddle, clearly favouring the wounded side of his body. 'My Greek tutor was of the opinion that Rome can only easily conquer peoples whose way of living is focused on towns, making them easy to control and indoctrinate to the imperial religion, whereas in the absence of organised slave labour and large estates most of your tribes' peoples are distributed across the country to farm their land, making them hard to influence to our way of thinking. Perhaps he was right, but whatever the reason the decision was made to leave the Germans to stew in their own juices, weakened by internecine warfare and the occasional military expedition, and overseen by a succession of ambassadors and spies to prevent any attempt to unite their forces.'

He shifted again, his eyes slitting with the pain.

'This fortress you're taking us to, Gunda, what is its name?'

'It was called Aliso, in the days when it was occupied.'

'And why there?'

'Because it is from there that the wooden road your people called the long bridge once ran to the north east. It is the fastest way that we can travel to the Angrivarii's lands across a wasteland of marshes.'

Cotta looked at the scout for a moment.

'How can you be sure that this other tribe will welcome us with open arms? Aren't they just as likely to take the opportunity of a small party of Romans to have their fun with us?'

Dolfus spoke up from the front of the column.

'That all depends on whether my master gets there before us. Roman gold can be a powerful motivator.'

The veteran raised an unconvinced eyebrow.

'And if he *doesn't* get there in time?'

The decurion shrugged.

'Then we might be as well not announce our presence too loudly, for fear that we'll be screaming it at the sky shortly thereafter.'

Dubnus and Varus looked out over the prow of the *Mars* at the riverside community that was the warship's evident destination, the Briton shaking his head at the meagre scattering of buildings lining the river.

'We're going to land there? It looks like a complete shithole.'

'It is.' They turned to find Tiro standing behind them. 'And while it isn't the closest landing place to their tribal capital, it's suitably small for our purposes. This land is controlled by the Marsi, a tribe with whom Rome's relationship is, shall we say, ambiguous at best?'

'Ambiguous?'

Varus smiled at his fellow centurion.

'I think what our colleague Tiro is trying to say without actually saying it is that we've played the roles of both friend and enemy to this tribe on so many different occasions that they won't know whether to greet us warmly or take us by the throats.

Which means that coming ashore somewhere where there *aren't* hundreds of warriors sitting around with nothing to do but dream of gutting Romans can only be a good thing?'

Tiro nodded.

'I told you, you're a natural for this line of work, Vibius Varus. That is *exactly* my reason for choosing this place to come ashore in the land of the Marsi. And this is what I plan to do, once we dock next to that particularly disreputable-looking fishing boat . . .'

Wide-eyed fishermen stared up at the warship as the navarch bulled his vessel in towards the dock through the scattered boats that were working the river's waters. Both bolt throwers were manned, cranked and ready to shoot, while half a dozen archers lined each side of the vessel with their weapons very evident. Tiro looked out at the cowed Germans with a grim smile, nodding his approval of the highly visible precautions.

'There's no harm in a bit of a show of muscle when dealing with any of the tribes. For one thing it's all they respect, and for another you can never tell when some stupid bastard might take it into his head to take us on single-handed. Experience has taught me that a man who's been ripped apart by a heavy bolt is the best possible deterrent to anyone else harbouring the same idea. Are your men ready, Centurion?'

The warship coasted in towards the shore still carrying rather more momentum than the men lining the rough wooden quay thought was safe. Backing away from the dock with expressions of consternation they watched in awe as, with the bellowing of a string of commands, the warship's rowers abruptly backed their oars to kill the vessel's momentum in half a dozen strokes, another order turning her until she was drifting onto the wooden pilings at less than a man's walking pace. As the ship's side touched land, men leapt ashore at bow and stern with ropes and strained to control its last vestiges of momentum, while the Tungrians disembarked with less grace but equal purpose amidships, axemen planting themselves in a short but ugly line of muscle and iron, eyeballing the nervous Marsi with expressions that promised violence at the slightest provocation. Tiro was the last man off the warship, strolling past Dubnus's men with an insouciance that was calculated to communicate his utter confidence with the situation. Pointing at the nearest of the bemused Marsi, he barked out something that sounded very much like an order in the man's native tongue, then turned away and looked up and down the line of axemen with a satisfied expression.

'Very good, Centurion. I can see that your men have been practising their forbidding expressions for long enough that they come naturally and without any conscious effort. Whatever else we achieve today at least we're not likely to lose one of the emperor's more fetching warships to attack by a few dozen indignant fish-gutters.'

He waited in the morning sunshine until the village's head man arrived in the company of several poorly armed and somewhat intimidated spearmen, all of whom, to judge from the aroma they were giving off, had been preparing their catch only moments before. Pacing forward with nervous glances at the Tungrians, he raised an admonitory finger and essayed an attempt at taking the initiative back from the Roman before him, but before the first word was even formed in his mouth Tiro stepped forward and pressed a small leather purse into his hand.

'Greetings, and my humblest regards to your most exalted position as the ruler of this hub of the local fishing industry! Here is a small expression of Rome's gratitude for your kindly allowing us to moor our warship alongside your dock, a few meagre coins but hopefully enough to express our thanks to you.'

The German opened the purse, his eyebrows rising at the sight of the gold within. Tiro leaned forward and lowered his voice conspiratorially.

'I included a few silver denarii as well, just in case they might be useful in persuading your comrades to aid our cause.'

The head man looked up at him with new-found respect, nodding his head in agreement.

'We pleased to host you visit! But you do not come to see fish,

I sure . . .' His expression changed to one of calculation. 'Tell we, how we help you?'

Tiro smiled, inclining his head in apparent respect for the other man's swift perception.

'I see you're ahead of me. We wish to travel to your tribal capital, for an audience with your king. And, I can quickly assure you, given that I have another larger purse for him, he will wish you to assist us in our travel. Indeed the only possible way you can incur his wrath is to be seen to hinder our swift arrival before his throne.'

'You want to go city. Meet king.'

'Indeed I do, and I wish to take with me several of my companions. Which means that apart from granting me free travel across your land, I will need you to sell me some horses.'

He looked back at Dubnus and Varus with a knowing expression. The head man's smile broadened until it seemed the top of his head might detach itself from his jaw.

'Sell horse? I sell you best horse in all Marsi land! Wait here, new friend!'

He hurried away, and Tiro watched him go with amused patience.

'What will follow now is, for those of you who've never purchased a horse from a German, a swift but unavoidably painful negotiation, conducted with smiles and good nature on both sides, at the end of which I will have reduced his price for a handful of decidedly average beasts from the downright outrageous to the simply extortionate. He knows I have no choice in the matter, and that my only negotiating point is the fact that my not buying the horses from him may come back to him in a painful manner, were his king to find out who prevented the gold I've promised from reaching him. We'll be on horseback within the hour gentlemen, and in the tribal capital by nightfall, the gods willing.'

'This was a legion fortress, nearly two hundred years ago. Now look at it.'

The remnants of burned and decayed timbers poked out of the ground along the one-time camp's defensive perimeter, while the buildings that had once crowded the interior behind the palisade were identifiable only by the darker lines of their foundations. The ruins of a small vicus told their own story, of a civilian population that had accompanied the legions, drawn by love, money or simple duty, but which had either retreated back down the river Lupia with the soldiers when the decision was made not to hold territory in Germania or had paid a high price for staying. Dolfus had taken Gunda and his men on up the road to the north to scout their path, leaving the remainder of the party to snatch a short rest from the rigours of the march and water their horses.

Scaurus sighed wearily, even though the afternoon was still young.

'We'll rest for a short time, then press on. The Bructeri won't be far behind us.'

He climbed down from his horse, but as his feet touched the ground it was as if a sword had been plunged into his injured side. Groaning in pain he sank to one knee, holding a hand to his wound in a vain attempt to stem the agony he was so clearly feeling. Marcus and Arminius ran to him, catching him as he slumped forward in a dead faint. Gerhild hurried to join them, putting a hand on the tribune's forehead and nodding as if her expectations had been fulfilled.

'Get his mail off, I need to see the wound.'

Pulling the heavy iron mail shirt over Scaurus's head, the two men watched as she peeled away the bandage that covered the tribune's head. Where the perforation in his flesh had been an angry red it was now more of a dirty yellow, the skin around the wound swollen and discoloured.

'The wound has gone bad, I thought as much. He must rest, and have it treated.'

Marcus shook his head.

'You heard what he said. If we stay here and the Bructeri find us, then we're all dead.'

She looked up at him with a quizzical expression.

'Do you want this man to die, Centurion? I can replace the bandage to allow us to ride on, if you think he can stay in the saddle for very much longer, but if I do not treat him then his death will come swiftly. You choose.'

The two men exchanged glances.

'We cannot simply press on and have him die in the saddle.' Marcus nodded slowly at the German's words.

'How long will you need?'

Gerhild looked around her.

'Long enough to build a fire, heat water, gather some fresh lavender if it is to be found, grind it into a little of the horse feed and then mix what you Romans call a *pultes*. I must draw the infection from the wound before we can consider moving him.'

The Roman nodded decisively.

'Arminius, get the men working to do what she needs as quickly as possible. I'll take the Hamians and watch the ground to the south. At least that way we'll have some warning if the Bructeri have found their way across the river and are at our heels.'

'I have found a way through the reeds, my King.'

Bowing his head, the hunter waited for a rebuke, or worse, at the number of attempts that had been required to find a crossing point that would allow a horse to wade the river unimpeded, but Amalric's anger at their seemingly interminable delay had long since exhausted itself.

'Good. Lead us across.'

The older man turned back to the river with his dogs capering beside him, eager to resume the hunt, and the young king watched as the first of the men of his household nudged their horses into the water, following the huntsman's lead into the field of reeds that choked the river's bed.

'They will be long gone by now, I expect.'

Gernot was silent for a moment.

'I wouldn't be so sure about that, my King. Consider where

they can run to, in reality. To the west are the Chamavi, our enemies it has to be said, but no great friends to Rome either. To the east are the Marsi, neutral to Rome but allied with ourselves and so unlikely to knowingly allow a party of fugitives to enter their land. But between them are the Angrivarii, forever our enemies, and if I were this man Dolfus, and whoever it is that stands behind him, I would be looking to them to provide me with shelter from our anger.'

'And that means . . . ?'

'If I were running for our border with the Angrivarii, my first stop would be their ruined fortress at Aliso, to use the road of wood, or what little remains of it.'

Amalric stroked his chin.

'It would be something of a gamble to assume that this will be their route. If they realise how obvious it seems, then surely they might pick another road to throw off our pursuit?'

Gernot shrugged.

'They may not have any choice in the matter. If this Dolfus has been told to make for the frontier with the Angrivarii, he has no option but to ride in that direction. If we ride swiftly we may yet take these Romans unawares.'

'These Marsi clearly don't trust their neighbours.'

Tiro nodded his agreement, leaning back in the saddle that had been provided as part of the price of the horse he was riding to ease the pain in his buttocks. Leaving the remainder of the detachment behind them to safeguard the warship, Tiro and the two centurions had ridden north for most of the day. Now the Marsi capital was before them, heavy earth walls protecting the city from any potential aggression from the tribes that bordered their land.

'There isn't a single tribe on the eastern bank of the Rhenus that trusts any of the others. Fortified cities like this are commonplace for the protection of their major settlements, and a symbol of status as well. It is a continuing mark of the ignominy to which the Bructeri were subjected after their war with the Angrivarii and the Chamavi that they still are not allowed to build similar defences.'

The village's head man had sent one of the younger men riding ahead of them to warn the tribe's chief of the Romans' approach, and a party of warriors resplendent in red tunics and wearing swords were waiting for them, drawn up in a line across the road that led to the city's main gate. Tiro turned in his saddle to face the two centurions.

'We should now dismount, to show the king the appropriate respect. And take your swords off, both of you.' They climbed down from the horses, and Dubnus pulled a pained face as he lifted his scabbard's leather strap over his head, moving his hips in discomfort much to Tiro's amusement. 'Piles, Centurion? Perhaps when we meet the Bructeri woman she can make you an ointment for them, I hear she's quite the healer.' He saw the king approaching, and raised a finger to them. 'You two concentrate on keeping your expressions respectful, and I'll do the talking here. The men with the swords are mainly there for show, and to let the king tell his people that he doesn't roll over to have his belly tickled when the big boy from across the river turns up, but a few words out of place might just give them cause to air their iron. And if it looks like getting aggressive, whatever you do, don't react. If this lot decide to kill us then let's face it, we're dead whatever happens.'

He dismounted and strode forward, stopping at a respectful distance from a man clad identically to the warriors on either side, but whose size and bearing immediately marked him out as their leader. Bowing deeply, the Roman spread his arms to indicate that he was unarmed.

'Greetings, King Sigimund. I come before you without sword or shield, empty-handed in the pursuit of a peaceful resolution to a dispute between Rome and the Bructeri tribe!'

The king looked back at him for a moment before speaking, and when he did respond his tone was sardonic, reflective of an apparent amusement at Tiro's unexpected appearance at the gates of his capital.

'So, Tiro, once again you arrive unbidden, and doubtless seeking a "small favour" from the Marsi. And whatever this request entails, I feel certain that were King Amalric here he would even now be railing against you. Word travels swiftly when you Romans decide to interfere in the affairs of any of the tribes, because what you will do to one of us today will become your accepted way of keeping us all in our place tomorrow.'

Tiro shrugged, apparently unabashed.

'What can I say, your Highness? Kidnapping the woman Gerhild would not have been my favoured approach to the problem.'

Sigimund laughed.

'I'm sure it wouldn't! Your way would have involved a few well-placed bribes and a small but deadly dose of poison, I expect! So, now that you know that I'm already very well aware of your theft of Amalric's seer, what is it that you want from me?'

'Only a small thing, your Highness. I ask permission for my comrades and I to cross your land as far as the point where the Angrivarii hold sway.'

Sigimund raised an eyebrow.

'And that's the full extent of your request? I'm surprised, given that my headman's messenger told me that you have a bag of gold with which to purchase my favours.'

Tiro conceded the point with a gracious half-bow.

'As ever, King Sigimund, you have seen through my attempts at diplomacy. I do have a small gift to offer you, a token of Roman friendship with the Marsi, although there is a good deal more than this to be had . . .'

He passed across the purse, watching hawklike as Sigimund weighed it in his hand. His disappointment on forcing Scaurus's chest open had been evident, finding only sufficient gold to pay off the local head man at their landing point and fill the purse he had just handed to the Marsi king.

'I wish to enter the kingdom of the Angrivarii in order to welcome a few of my men who have chosen to ride north from the Bructeri land, rather than—'

'No!' Sigimund shook his head in amazement. 'You mean

to tell me that your kidnappers are bringing the Bructeri woman out to the north, across their own land? Even I am amazed at the lengths you people will go to in order to put an enemy back in his place. Amalric will be humiliated in the eyes of his people and those of the tribes that surround them, when the news of such audacity becomes public. Having lost her to the unexpected intervention of your ships would have been one thing, but this? This is something much, *much* worse. Such a loss of face could see the man killed by his own nobles just for the shame of it.'

He walked out of the line of his warriors, gesturing for them to stay in their places, stepping to within a foot of the Roman and bending to speak more quietly in his ear.

'And if you need me to grant you leave to ride across my land in one direction, surely you'll need the same favour to come back the other way with your men?' He paused for a moment. 'And with Amalric's witch, I presume?'

Tiro stared back at him unflinchingly.

'You have the nub of it, Your Highness. In return for which I am empowered to offer you a further payment of one hundred gold aureii.'

The king looked away for a moment, considering the offer, then raised his voice indignantly, poking a finger into the Roman's chest to emphasise his point.

'You ask me to betray the friendship of a fellow king! For a purse of gold? You should have a higher regard for the Marsi, an honourable people!'

He leaned closer, lowering his voice to a whisper that was loud enough to be obviously venomous while too quiet for the words to carry, continuing to stab his finger at Tiro's chest as if to reinforce some dire threat.

'Two hundred. And fifty. To be paid *before* the woman leaves Marsi territory. The woman *not* to be visible to my people, and to travel by boat for as much of the distance as possible. I must be able to tell Amalric that her feet never touched Marsi soil, understood?'

Tiro nodded almost imperceptibly and, stepping back, Sigimund struck a decisive pose.

'I will, for the sake of good relations with our powerful neighbour in the west, accept your offer of gold for the Marsi treasury, but that is as far as I can go in the name of our mutual friendship. You will be allowed to cross our land until you reach that of the Angrivarii, and after that your welcome here will be at its end. Do you understand me?'

Tiro bowed deeply again.

'Completely, King Sigimund. My humble apology for having made such a gross assumption that your goodwill could be bought, and my thanks for allowing myself and my companions to cross your land. I would be grateful for the chance to feed and water our horses, and perhaps take a bite to eat and sleep for a few hours, if that were possible?'

Sigimund nodded regally, waving a hand at one of his men to make the arrangements, and Tiro turned back to the watching centurions with an inscrutable expression, speaking quietly as he took the reins of his horse from Dubnus.

'And that, gentlemen, is how business is done with the Germans. They'll stab a brother in the back for enough coin, but they always want to be able to tend his wounds afterwards, and offer their heartfelt condolences. So not a twitch of the lips from either of you, eh? Just remember that we've just been soundly embarrassed, and we're not happy. Bear that in mind while we're inside those walls, unless you want some bad-tempered Marsi warrior asking what the fuck you're smiling at?'

'He's still sleeping?'

Gerhild looked up at Marcus from her vigil over the tribune's comatose body, swathed in several layers of blankets despite which his body was trembling as if chilled by a cold wind.

'He is fighting the infection from the wound. Until he either wins this battle or loses it we cannot move him.'

Dolfus walked up, his gait and expression bespeaking a man whose patience was close to exhaustion.

'We have to leave *now*! The Bructeri can't be far behind us, and I'm under strict orders not to allow her to fall back into their hands.' He paused for a moment, one hand clenching at his side. 'I don't want to take a sword to you, lady, but if I have to . . .'

Gerhild smiled up at him.

'Do not worry, Decurion, it will not be your hand that takes my life, on the field of bones and gold.'

The Roman stared at her for a moment in exasperation.

'Leave him here, if he can't ride. I'll take you north to the Angrivarii, and the centurion here can protect Scaurus.'

She shook her head again with a gentle smile.

'I cannot leave him. The point will come, sometime in the night, when he needs protection that none of you men can give him.'

Marcus and Dolfus exchanged looks before the former spoke.

'We could make you leave him. I won't harm a woman, but you could not resist us if we chose to take you north by force.'

She stood, her eyes hard with determination.

'You won't.'

She looked down at Scaurus, cocking her head as if she were listening to something faint and far away. After a moment she looked up again, her expression deadly serious.

'I have been blessed with three gifts from the goddess, as foretold by my tribe's holy woman at the time of my birth. The least of these, sometimes unreliable, is on occasion to manipulate the minds of men, as you saw at the river of reeds when the king's huntsman failed to see the path across the river.'

Dolfus shook his head in disbelief.

'You expect us to believe that you prevented him from seeing the—'

She cut him off with a curt gesture, a subtle flicker of fingers that seemed to leave him abruptly speechless.

'I am also gifted, or possibly cursed, with an ability to see what is to come, days or years from the present, in my dreams. It is by this means that I know only too well that neither of you will raise a hand to me. The other, the gift I treasure over everything else, is my ability to heal both body and mind, sometimes with nature's remedies, sometimes with the touch of my hands, and sometimes with the help of the goddess herself, acting through me. With your tribune's wound I am going to have to use all three, so we must all both stay here until the moment comes for me to act.'

She stared up at him with flint-hard eyes.

'Understand me clearly when I tell you that the man shivering and twitching beneath these blankets will play a role in events that are yet to occur that will shape the destiny of your empire. He *cannot* be allowed to die here.'

Dolfus frowned.

'Events that are yet to come? What does that mean?'

Marcus shook his head at the decurion.

'Were you not listening? The lady believes that she sees the future in her dreams. And you've seen the tribune in those dreams, have you, madam?'

The seer nodded solemnly.

'Yes, Centurion, I have. When five men claim the ultimate prize, he will be the man who holds the balance between the final two contenders.' She waved her hand again, and Marcus felt giddy for a moment, Dolfus taking an involuntary step back at the same moment. 'But I've said more than enough on the subject. You will both forget my words, but you will remember, and believe, that his time to die has not yet come.'

'We must camp for the night, my King. Without the light of the moon I can no longer follow the trail.'

Amalric shook his head in frustration at the supplicating hunter who was cringing in the expectation of a blow for his temerity.

'Your dogs still have the scent?'

'Yes, my King, but . . .'

'Then we can still follow their trail. By the light of torches if need be!'

Gernot leaned out of his saddle to whisper in the king's ear.

'Perhaps we would be better halting for the night, my King?

The light of torches would be visible for miles, and might enable the Romans to set up an ambush. Their archers could take a heavy toll of our numbers were we to be so illuminated, and perhaps even threaten your own life.'

The younger man looked at him for a moment, then came to a decision.

'Very well, make camp.'

He climbed down from his horse and strode away into the half-darkness to relieve himself, the men of his household busying themselves hobbling the horses and gathering firewood while there was still a vestige of light in which to do so. Walking back into their midst he stood and watched their hurried preparation for the night, aware that most of them were avoiding his eye for fear of his evident ire.

'We'll catch them, never fear. They have wounded, we know that much, and the last time your man had their trail we were still finding blood spots every hundred paces or so.'

Amalric nodded at the truth in his uncle's words. His huntsman's dogs had been wild with excitement at their detection of the first of the blood drops, and the marks had provided them with a reliable guide as to the fugitives' direction of travel which, as Gernot had predicted, was clearly heading for Aliso.

'How far are we from the Roman fortress?'

Gernot called the huntsman across and repeated the question.

'An hour's steady ride, my King, less if you were to put your heels to the horses.'

'So close . . .'

Dismissing the tracker with a smile of thanks the nobleman leaned back, watching as his men worked to build up the fire that they had coaxed out of twigs and leaves. When he spoke again his voice was almost smug with certainty.

'So close that their escape is almost impossible, my King. Consider this: they have at least one wounded man, and have chosen not to abandon him. Any man losing blood during a day in the saddle will have needed treatment, and while we both know that Gerhild will insist on healing him, even her abilities cannot repair that sort of damage in one night. With such a burden they will be easy enough to find in the morning.'

Amalric nodded morosely, watching as the fire took hold of the logs that had been placed across the initial blaze, sending sparks into the dark night sky in a series of pops and cracks as the wood split in the blaze's heart.

'Sound counsel. But I burn with the need to do something. My tribe's honour has been spat on and trampled into the ashes of a fire set on our sacred altar to Wodanaz, and here I sit powerless to do anything other than wait for the dawn.'

Gernot looked pointedly across the clearing at their captive, sitting between a pair of men who had been set to guard him on pain of their lives.

'If you need to demonstrate your vengeance, my King, why not do so with the Roman?'

The king's gaze rose to dwell on the prisoner, and his eyes narrowed at the thought of bloody revenge.

'Bring him to me.'

He pulled out the hunting knife that lived on his right hip while Gernot crossed the encampment and gestured for the Hamian to be brought before the king, testing its edge and point against the heel of his palm. The prisoner was pushed to his knees in front of him, staring into his eyes with a disconcerting lack of fear.

'You presume to stare at the king as if you were his equal? Avert your eyes!'

Gernot raised his foot to stamp on the kneeling Roman's leg, but Amalric shook his head and raised a hand to forestall him.

'No, my Lord. Obeisance given under duress is no obeisance at all. Allow the man his moment of defiance, he will regret it soon enough.' He stared back into the Hamian's eyes with a trace of amusement. 'So tell me, Roman, what it is that gives you the right to eyeball me with such insolence? Don't you know that I am a king, and the chief priest of my tribe, anointed by the gods?'

The captive centurion wearily leaned back on his haunches, still staring directly at Amalric.

'I respect your position as the leader of your tribe, King, although much of that respect has been beaten out of me over the last two days. But I cannot claim to respect your position as a priest, for it seems to me that the gods have long since forsaken this world, if they ever even existed in the first place.'

Amalric looked up at his chamberlain, who shook his head and shrugged.

'The man is godless. We should end his misery and kill him now. Unless, of course, he lies in the hope of avoiding death on the altar of Wodanaz.'

Qadir laughed softly and shook his head.

'I never lie. I have this past year come to question the existence of the goddess to whose service I have been sworn since boyhood. And as to the imperial deities . . . They were men, no more and no less.'

Amalric leaned forward, evidently fascinated by the man before him.

'Why? Why should a man like you, a centurion sworn to the service of your emperor, betray everything that he believes in, everything that makes him what he is? How can you spit on everything that your life has been built upon?'

The Hamian looked him in the eyes for a moment, then lowered his gaze.

'Truly, King, it feels to me more as if everything I have built my life on has betrayed *me*. I have watched men die in such a variety of manners, and for such meaningless reasons, that I no longer find it possible to discern any pattern to our lives. If the gods do exist then they are too savagely cruel for me to consider them as deities worthy of my worship. And if that results in my being killed for the crime of godlessness, then I will accept that death as a means of achieving peace from this world's incessant horrors.'

Amalric stared at him for a moment, then stood, gesturing to the captive.

'This man is not to be beaten. He will eat the same food that we eat, and will be allowed enough privacy to empty his bowels without being leered at by his guards. It seems me that any man who will abandon his gods and his people so easily would make a poor sacrifice to Wodanaz, but I will hold him prisoner until such time as my new priest is able to make an opinion on the subject of how best to sacrifice a godless man who lacks even the dignity of loyalty to his tribe. Unless of course his death will return my eagle and my seer to me. In which case I will say the prayers and cut his throat myself.'

'An escort, your Majesty?'

Sigimund nodded, taking a swig of beer before answering. Tiro and the two centurions had been invited to join the king at his high table, and the envoy had accepted the invitation on their behalf without a second thought, breezily reassuring the two centurions.

'As I told you, if he wanted us dead there would be a dozen easier ways to make it happen without resorting to poison.'

The king wiped his mouth, gesturing with the half-eaten rib bone of the wild boar that had been roasted for the feast.

'I'm willing to tolerate your presence on my tribe's soil, Roman, but I'm not likely to allow you free rein to go wherever you fancy, am I?'

Tiro bowed his head in acceptance of the German's decision.

'Of course, your Majesty.'

Sigimund raised a jaundiced eyebrow at him.

'I think you miss my point, Tiro. I'm allowing you to ride to the border of my land with the Angrivarii, and then make the return journey back to the great river, but you will always be under the eye of my sons and their warriors. Any attempt to deviate from the route you have asked to follow will result in your being placed under arrest and returned here. Any attempt to re-enter our land at any point other than that where you left it, where my sons will await your return, will, when you are inevitably captured, result in your execution as oath breakers. This is one occasion when you will not be able to play your usual high-handed games with us, Tiro. Because to even attempt to do so will have the direct of consequences, both for you and these men who ride with you.'

Tiro nodded and bowed.

'As you wish it, King Sigimund. And now, if you will forgive me, I will sleep. We have an early start in the morning.' He turned to Varus and Dubnus. 'I would recommend the same for you both, gentlemen. Tomorrow will be a long day, and just as hard in the saddle as today was.'

He winked at Dubnus, who raised an eyebrow in return.

'I will take to my bed shortly, thank you, Tiro. A little more of the king's excellent wine might numb the pain in my backside to the point where I will actually be able to sleep.'

'Sit here with me for a while, Centurion, and help me watch over your friend.'

Marcus sat down on the other side of Scaurus's body from the seer, stretching out his legs wearily and accepting the bowl of meat stew that Husam placed in his hands, the archer having used the opportunity of scouting to the south to hunt and kill a boar, whose meat he was busy cooking in batches in the woman's iron pot.

'You saw nothing on the road, I presume?'

'No madam. It seems as if your king has encountered a good deal more difficulty in crossing the river than we did.'

Taking his turn at watching the road that led out of the south to the ruined fortress the Roman had seen nothing to excite any suspicion, passing the hours introspectively huddled into his cloak and pondering the previous few weeks' events.

'He will be across the water by now, and close at hand.'

He stared at her in the light of the fire, the sun having sunk below the western horizon an hour before.

'You seem very confident that our delay here will not result in our capture.'

Gerhild smiled back at him.

'I have told you, Centurion, that this is not my place or time to die. Or yours, for that matter.'

'I know. This is not your field of bones and gold.'

She nodded.

'Just so. See how your initial scepticism has become a grudging acceptance of my prediction?'

'I didn't say I believed your words, simply that I remember them.'

'And nevertheless, you want to believe. You are a seeker of truth, Marcus Valerius Aquila—'

He shook his head in bafflement.

'Why would you call me that when my name is Corv—'

'Because it is the name your parents gave you.' Her tone was patient as she interrupted him, warm with amusement. 'You may wear the name of the crow, but you do so unwillingly, as the price of survival. And as I was saying, you are a seeker after truth, and justice, although I sense that you have found that the justice you have administered of late has borne only bitter fruit.'

He looked at her for a moment, chewing on a mouthful of stew.

'I sought revenge for my father's murder, and took the lives of men who were instrumental in the fall of our family from grace, but the cost was too high.' Gerhild stared at him, her question unspoken but as clear as if she had shouted it at him. 'I . . . we . . . came to the attention of powerful men, and were sent to the east. And while we were there . . .'

He paused for a moment, on the edge of unburdening himself, then shook his head.

'I cannot speak of it. I lost the most precious thing in my world.'

'And the wound will not heal.'

Marcus looked up at her, his face bleak with loss.

'The wound will *never* heal.'

'But it *must*. Everyone experiences the death of a loved one at some time.' She leaned forward across the sleeping tribune and took his hand. 'May I call you Marcus?'

He nodded, lost in his misery.

'Marcus, the time for grieving varies with each of us, but the one undeniable truth is that it must come to an end. For a man to spend the rest of his days mourning the loss of a loved one is not right. Life must be lived, not simply tolerated in the absence of the one who brought life and colour to the days that went before. You will find a way to put her loss behind you, a better way than taking your fury out on men whose death will serve no purpose, other than to sate a lust for blood that will end with your losing yourself in wanton murder.'

He looked up at her empty-eyed.

'I cannot even mourn her properly. I've never once shed tears over her loss.'

'And you feel like an empty shell of the man you were. It *will* pass.'

She looked across the fire at the sleeping Lupus.

'Tell me, the child, has he too suffered loss?'

He nodded, relieved at the change of topic.

'First his father, lost in a battle in Britannia, then a soldier to whom he had grown close. Arminius is the closest thing he has to a father now, and my wife was the closest thing to a mother, until . . .'

'I see. But I sense there is more?'

Marcus nodded as the memory of Lupus's unexpected kill jumped into his mind.

'He was blooded in the battle to escape from your people. A man ran onto his spear and died so close to him that the boy saw the life leave his eyes.'

'And none of you has spoken to him of it?'

Marcus shook his head unhappily.

'None of us has the words.'

Gerhild stared at him in disbelief.

'You all have to go through it. You all kill for the first time, and learn to deal with the horror of taking a man's life, and yet none of you seem to have the wit to use that experience to help those who come down the same road behind you. If you'll excuse me, you can watch the tribune for a while. I have work to do.'

She got up and walked across to where the boy lay, shooing

Arminius to one side and taking a seat next to him. Then, with a tenderness that was at odds with her evident irritation, she eased the sleeping Lupus's head onto her lap and placed a hand on his temple, covering both of them with her cloak. Closing her eyes she became almost motionless, only her lips moving as she looked out across the fire's flickering light with eyes that seemed blank and unfocused.

'They were here.' Amalric looked down at the embers of a large campfire in disgust. 'Still warm. Someone was sitting here tending that fire only an hour ago. And now they run for the arms of our enemies.'

The Bructeri had been mounted and ready to ride before dawn, the young king casting anxious glances at the sky until enough light had crept into the eastern horizon to enable them to start their pursuit afresh. An hour's ride had covered the distance between their campsite and the ruined Roman fortress, but their eager haste had been in vain.

'They would have been mounted and away from here at much the same time we were.' Gernot had dismounted, and was examining the ground around the fire. 'Which means that they are only an hour ahead of us. Nothing has changed, my King, as long as we retain our hunger for revenge.'

Amalric looked back at the Hamian captive.

'Surely if we are to follow the Romans down this road of wood then we will make ourselves vulnerable to an ambush?'

The noble nodded.

'Possibly so, although any man who stays behind to launch an arrow at us is likely to pay a high price for his opportunity. But, to ensure that any such attack fails, I suggest that you ride at the rear of our party.'

Amalric shook his head with a hard smile.

'Your concern for my safety is gratifying, Uncle, but I cannot throw my men into the way of danger without accepting a share of it myself. I will ride in the front rank of horsemen. Now, we go!'

*

'I thought you said this was a road of wood? It's not much better than bog.'

Gunda twisted in his saddle to look round at Cotta, who was staring down at the surface of the path that stretched out before them in something akin to horror. Once a broad walkway of rough planks, suspended above the bog on split logs laid lengthways beneath them, and anchored with wooden stakes, built by invading Roman legions to allow them to penetrate the swamps that limited their ability to manoeuvre in the German interior, it had decayed badly in the years since the empire's retreat from the eastern side of the Rhenus.

'This road was built so long ago that the means by which it was kept above the water has long since failed, but the wood itself has not become rotten despite sinking into the marsh. Perhaps the water in the ground here protects them, but whatever the reason it is still there, just beneath the surface, and intact for the most part. Our horses can walk on the wood, if we take it slowly.'

'So we can only proceed at a walking pace?'

The guide shrugged.

'Yes, but then the same will be true for the men pursuing us. I've ridden this road before, and walked the marshes on either side. We could leave the road, but we'd have to abandon the horses, and if you think this is unpleasant then trust me when I tell you that you really wouldn't want to attempt the alternative.'

'So this is the pontes longi.'

They all turned to look at Scaurus, who was holding himself in the saddle by what appeared to be an act of will. Marcus, riding alongside him, asked the question that was on every man's lips.

'Tribune?'

The wan-looking senior officer raised an eyebrow at him.

'The long bridge. It is the wooden road that Ahenobarbus built. Forgetting your history lessons again, are you, Centurion?' He winced as his horse stumbled slightly on the uncertain footing, then regained his composure. 'Lucius Domitius Ahenobarbus was one of a long line of distinguished men who were nearly all consuls during the republic, and continued to be part of the ruling class under the emperors. He was the Emperor Nero's grandfather, which might explain a few things. He built this wooden road to allow the legions to deploy forward at speed from Aliso as far as the river Albis, during the conquest of Germany that made Augustus believe that a province of Magna Germania was possible, with all of the lands as far north and east as the Albis under Roman rule. It must have worked, because he got a good deal deeper into the country than anyone before him. He was a bit of a bastard, as it happens, made eminent men and women perform on stage like common actors and actresses when he was consul, and staged such bloody gladiatorial contests that Augustus had to publicly reprimand him. Which, given his successes as a general, must have been a bit tricky for both of them.'

He looked down the track's watery ribbon, then back at Gunda.

'Anyway, shall we get on with this? It isn't going to get any easier by our talking about it.'

He had awoken shortly before dawn, coming back to consciousness like a man surfacing from deep water an inch at a time, lying on his back with his eyes open but neither moving nor speaking for a while, eventually managing a question.

'What happened?'

Gerhild had been asleep at his side, waking as if on cue as his eyes had opened, and she had bent over him with a cup of water.

'You slept, Roman, like a dead man. Which, after all, is what you so nearly were.'

'The wound?'

'Was infected. I drew the poison from it with a *pultes*, then fed you a strong potion of herbs to let you sleep.'

He had digested the seer's statement for a moment before speaking again.

'My dreams.'

Gerhild had smiled, shooting a knowing look at Arminius who had spent most of the night watching his master.

'Yes?'

'I saw a woman. Beautiful. Terrible.'

'That was the goddess I serve, Hertha. She came to you in the night, to beckon you back from the underworld.'

He had stared at her in partial disbelief for a moment before rolling onto his side with a grunt of discomfort.

'In which case she seems to have done the job well enough, for as you see I live to suffer through another day of your mystical nonsense.'

Climbing to his feet with Arminius's help he had called for his mail, resisting her attempts to stop him from donning its burdensome weight, and had only allowed himself the indignity of being helped onto his mount when the two centurions had insisted upon it.

'How far is it to the border with these Angrivarii, Gunda?'

'Forty miles or so, Tribune.'

'And we can do no more than a walking pace on this surface, whether it be safer than the marshes to either side or not. Two days more march then?'

The scout nodded dourly.

'I would say so.'

'And what are the odds of the Bructeri overhauling us, do you think?'

Cotta leaned forward in his saddle to pose what he clearly thought was an obvious question.

'Surely they're subject to the same restrictions on their speed as we are, aren't they sir?'

Scaurus shook his head, too weary even to give the veteran the smile that was his usual accompaniment to a correction.

'You need to think less like a rational military officer, Centurion, and more like a desperate king who'll stop at nothing to recover his prestige, in the form of the witch and the eagle. We have one horse per man, and can afford to lose precisely none of these beasts to exhaustion or injury, since each horse lost equates to a man dead or captured, which are much the same thing. Whereas Amalric of the Bructeri has, by the estimation of the keenest eyes in our party, thirty horsemen. He can afford to lose ten of them and still have double our fighting strength, on top of which I am clearly unlikely to take part in any combat that may be required if and when he catches up with us, which he will know from the blood trail I've been leaving for the last day and a half. I'd say that the moment for him to gamble on those odds is upon him, wouldn't you?'

'It doesn't look like we'll be going anywhere without an escort, does it?'

Dubnus eyed the waiting Marsi horsemen dubiously, but Tiro spared them no more than a glance.

'See it from his perspective. He's going to allow us to cross his land, in return for a small fortune in coin and one or two favours, which have been left carefully unspecified, but the last thing he wants is for us to leave here and vanish off into the wilderness to perpetrate who knows what and who knows where. So yes, he's detailed two dozen of his fiercest warriors under the command of his two oldest sons to make sure we behave ourselves until we're off their hands and somebody else's problem.'

'And there's something that prevents them from killing us all out of hand once we're far from civilisation?'

The older man looked up at him with a straight face, lowering his voice so as not to be overheard.

'Not really. For a start, young Varus, nobody knows we're here apart from us. I couldn't exactly leave a note for the governor saying "we've gone to recover the missing seer, come and find us if we don't come back", because for one thing that would betray my position in the province, and, to be brutal about it, if the king were to have decided to do away with us then there'd be very little left of us for anyone to find. And rather a lot of barbarian Germania to search even if anyone were minded to do so. I suspect that the significant amount of gold I've promised him upon my safe return will be an incentive for them to keep us alive, but in the end we both know that things sometimes just don't work out the way that we plan them.'

He looked about their escort, flashing a broad grin at the unsmiling princes waiting on their horses at their head.

'And let's face it, my profession is, when all is said and done, not for the faint hearted. Of course I do everything I can to minimise the risks of being discovered by the officials I'm set to watch over, and to ensure that these sorts of jaunts into the unknown don't end up with my bones being picked clean by the crows on the side of some unnamed mountain, but in the end it's all a bit of a gamble. And we both know that you're a gambler, don't we? Why else would you have come here in the first place? And now it's time to go, I think. There's still a hundred miles of rough country to cover before we reach the edge of the Angrivarii lands.'

He extended a hand towards their horses, which had been fed and watered and now awaited them with their saddle bags already in place, then raised a finger to forestall the younger man as one last thought occurred to him.

'And from now, young man, consider this before you speak or act. At least one of these barbarians will speak Latin well enough to understand everything we say to each other. Our bags will have been searched while we were at the feast last night, and every word we say will have been overheard, considered and reported to the king. So relax, Vibius Varus, and give them no reason for suspicion that we're anything more than we've told them. If it helps you, tell yourself that you're riding out to hunt in these magnificent hills.'

'Is that what you do?'

Tiro laughed quietly.

'Gods below, no it isn't. The difference between us is that you're still young, with ambition and an eagerness to serve, your life ahead of you. Whereas I am older, my skin thicker and my perspectives those of a stoic, like the last emperor. After all, everyone dies eventually, so why *not* here, on a sunny hillside with the birds singing?'

He winked at Varus.

'Just don't say so in front of these barbarians, eh? They might take the sentiment literally.'

*

'You're quiet this morning.'

Lupus looked over at Arminius, who was riding alongside him.

'I slept well. All the things that have happened in the last few days seem . . . far away. I fell asleep with that German's face in my mind, all screwed up in pain as he ran onto my spear. But when I woke up I couldn't remember what he looked like.'

The German turned and looked at Gerhild, who simply stared back with her usual small smile.

'What else did you dream about?'

'My mother.'

Arminius raised an eyebrow.

'Your grandfather told me that your mother died when you were very small, and that you were brought up by her mother.'

Lupus looked at him levelly, his expression untroubled.

'It was my mother. I don't know how I knew it, but I was sure of it in my dream. She was with another woman, who brought her to me and then walked away. She held me, and told me she loved me.'

Arminius felt a tear pricking at his eyes, feigning a cough to wipe it away.

'Of course she does.' He looked at the spear held across the boy's body. 'We're a long way from being out of danger, Lupus. If the Bructeri find us then we'll have to fight again.'

The young Briton stared back at him, then raised the weapon to an upright position between their horses.

'You want to know if I can stand in line and use this to defend myself again?' His mentor nodded silently. 'I've been thinking about the moment I killed that man . . .'

Arminius prepared himself for whatever the boy might say next, ready to reassure him that not every man was a warrior, and that there was no shame in taking a life only to discover that doing so had deterred him from ever wanting to experience the terror of the experience.

'And I can see that I was lucky. My parry was good, but after that I just stood there looking at him. He should have killed me, Arminius.' His face hardened, and again the German had the feeling that he was watching the man beneath the boy's skin asserting his presence. 'And it won't happen again, I've promised myself that. From now we practise twice a day, mornings and evenings, whenever we can. The next time my spear takes a man's life, it won't be luck.'

'They went that way.'

The king's huntsman pointed north, down an apparently arrow-straight line of open ground just wide enough for a pair of horsemen to ride along.

'The Roman road of wood. I remember coming here with my father when I was a boy, and wondering at the sheer single-mindedness that led them to build it. He told me that when it was new the wooden surface was a foot above the marsh, and that a horse could be ridden down it with never any danger of losing its footing. And now . . .'

'And now the wood is just below the water, but still there, my King. If we take it steadily no harm will come to our mounts.'

Amalric stared up the road's visible length, stretching to the horizon in a glinting, watery ribbon that reflected the morning sun's rays in flashes of brilliance.

'But if we take it steadily, Gernot, will we catch the Romans before they fall into the arms of our neighbours, the Angrivarii?'

'My King?'

The younger man pointed to the road's wet surface.

'If we travel slowly enough to avoid the risks of a horse slipping on the wood below the surface, which must be coated with the bog plants that grow in this part of our land, then surely our enemies will maintain the lead that they were gifted by our inability to cross the river of reeds?'

'Whereas if we attempt to progress more quickly it is more than likely that we will lose horses to falls on the slippery wood.'

Amalric shook his head.

'You miss my point. I have thirty men at my back, whereas the Romans are not only less than a dozen in number, but have at least one wounded man. All we have to do, Gernot, is overhaul them with only twenty men and the fight will be over before it really begins. So whereas the loss of a dozen horsemen would leave us in no different a position than we enjoy now, even a single man unhorsed presents our enemies with a problem to which they have no solution, a rider without a mount who must either be left behind or slow them yet further. You were going to counsel that we should walk our horses, to allow them to cope with the conditions underfoot?'

The noble bowed his head in agreement.

'And you, my King, would have us move faster than that?'

'I would. A trot, and no faster, a calculated risk. If we lose too many horses too quickly then it will be easy enough to revert to a safer rate of progress, but not to take the risk is to guarantee our failure.'

Turning his horse, he walked it to the head of the war band's column, calling a command out across the waiting riders.

'We will ride this road of wood at a slow trot, fast enough to allow us to overtake these Romans and yet not so fast that our beasts will be unable to control their footing. Follow me!'

'Do you feel that?'

Cotta looked around at Gunda, having dismounted with the rest of the party to give their horses a brief rest before pushing on to the north.

'Feel what?'

The guide looked down at his feet, an inch deep in the water that coated the wooden boards, clad in light leather boots, then at the Roman's heavy nail-studded military footwear.

'A tremble in the wood.' He knelt, putting a hand to the road's surface beneath the water that barely covered the split logs. 'There, I can feel it properly now.'

He got to his feet and mounted his horse, looking back down the path.

'I can't see them, but the king's men are back there and *they're* not walking their horses.'

The veteran centurion walked swiftly up the short column to

find Scaurus still mounted, unable to get down from his saddle without troubling his wound needlessly.

'The Bructeri are closing on us, Tribune. The scout can feel their hoof beats on the wooden road, and though he can't see them yet it can only be a matter of time before they overhaul us if they're risking a trot.'

Scaurus looked past the riders behind him and down the length of road they had already ridden.

'Which leaves us without any option. We'll have to follow suit.'

The older man nodded grimly, then smiled slowly as a thought occurred to him.

'I'll warn the rest of the party. And I've just thought of something that might slow them down a little.'

10

'Of course there was a time when the plan was for all of this to be part of the empire.' Dubnus looked at Tiro in disbelief, and the older man laughed at his expression. 'I know, it seems far-fetched, and it's not something that is discussed very much any more, but it was the Emperor Augustus's intention to incorporate all this into a new province. Magna Germania! Just another stage in the relentless conquest of the world, as he saw it, and a prudent step forward to prevent the barbarians from harassing our lands west of the Rhenus. After all, we'd dealt with the Gauls easily enough, and subdued those areas east of the Rhenus which could be reached by river.' He waved a hand at the wooded hills through which they were riding. 'This was in the days when the empire was young, of course, and nobody really knew quite how it actu-ally works. These days we understand much better how difficult it is to truly conquer a people who don't live in towns, and who can't have their way of civilised life changed to match ours.'

The Briton nodded thoughtfully.

'This is an interesting point. The people of my province live in towns in the south, but in the north, where we patrol the wall that was built by Hadrian, the tribes continue to resist, and in the mountains they cannot be beaten.'

The older man nodded knowingly.

'Towns are of course easier to control. Their inhabitants are concentrated, easy to influence and easily punished if they fail to obey their new masters.' He paused for emphasis. '*Vulnerable*. A careful mixture of stick and carrot, the building of baths and arenas when the population behave, and beheadings when they don't, soon brings most people into line with our way of thinking.

We match our gods up with theirs, encourage worship of each pair of deities together, and within a generation or two it is as if there was never any alternative way of living. But the peoples who live across the land this side of the river, that's a different matter. They're hard to reach in any numbers without using more legions than the land they populate can support, they fight like wildcats, deny our military strength by running away from it and are only too happy to put a dagger into our backs when we're least prepared. Why the divine Augustus ever thought we might subjugate them, or why it would be worth the effort, is still a puzzle to the people that care about those sorts of things.'

'Hubris.'

The imperial agent grinned at Dubnus.

'Well now, Briton, there's a word I wouldn't have expected from a provincial auxiliary, centurion or not.'

The big man shrugged.

'It's true that I do indeed come from just such a hill tribe, but my father the king was careful to see me educated, and it's hard to rub shoulders with the likes of Tribune Scaurus and my friend Marcus without some of their polish rubbing off on my rough barbarian manners.'

Tiro flinched theatrically with a self-deprecating smile.

'Ouch. And so perish all men who underestimate you, I suspect. And yes, hubris is certainly one word for it. Perhaps blind ambition is the simplest explanation. Certainly the imperial family seem to have been of the impression that they had some divine right to conquer everything between the Rhenus and the Albis. First it was Augustus's stepson Drusus who led the charge, defeating all manner of tribes across these lands before he was careless enough to fall off his horse and then, as if that wasn't bad enough, unfortunate enough to die as a consequence. Then his older brother Tiberius took over and did a good deal more of the same, easy enough to understand since they were cut from the same stone, so to speak, and all seemed assured until Augustus made the mistake of confirming your friend Gaius Vibius Varus's distant ancestor as commander of the army that was to complete the conquest of the planned province. Varus was an administrator and not a fighting general, although he does seem to have been an expert in the darker arts of suppressing an urban population in the way we discussed earlier. According to the histories he had two thousand men crucified in Judea to head off a rebellion before it could get properly started, so he wasn't exactly restrained in his use of the stick. And it seems he took that stick to the "pacified" German tribes with a vengeance, and they paid him back by allying with the traitor Arminius, and luring Varus and his three legions into a colossal ambush.'

'They were all killed?'

'Not at first. But they were broken by the initial onslaught, more or less, and then hunted and harried south over the mountain range and through the swamps that stood between them and safety. A handful of them reached the fortress at Aliso, but that was overrun in its turn soon after, and any plans to consolidate our grip of a pacified "Greater Germania" were at an end. There were punitive expeditions, of course, and the dead of the three legions were collected and buried, but the locals dug them up again as soon as the armies that had been sent in to take revenge were gone, and it all ended up with Tiberius making the very sensible decision to leave the Germans to stew in their own juice. You see . . .'

He lowered his voice to prevent their escort from overhearing him.

'It's really very simple. First we side with one tribe, and give them an incentive to attack their neighbours, and then we side with another and persuade them to attack the first. Keeping the Germans at each other's throats is the most effective way we can prevent them from ganging together and trying to cross the Rhenus, which means that we've had to get rather good at fomenting disputes between them.'

Dubnus looked at him for a moment.

'And there's a man like you somewhere in Britannia right now doing just the same thing?'

Tiro nodded with pursed lips.

'Yes. That's exactly the way it is. And it's not going to change any time soon.'

'We must be gaining on them!'

Gernot grinned at the king, having spurred his horse up alongside Amalric's mount, then stared out down the arrow-straight path that stretched to the horizon.

'Surely, my King! It can only be a matter of hours before we overhaul them, and then our rev—'

The scream of a horse behind them had both men twisting in their saddles in surprise, reining their mounts in to survey a scene of chaos. One of the men following behind them had been violently dismounted, and was lying prone in the thin layer of water that covered the track's wooden surface, his horse thrashing and bucking in apparent agony. Half a dozen of the riders following behind had been forced to ride off the path into the deeper water that lay on either side, and were struggling to persuade their spooked mounts to back up and regain the comparative safety of the wooden surface, while those further back had pulled up and waited helplessly, their way forward entirely blocked by the confusion.

Gernot slid down from his horse and strode back towards the apparently injured beast, eyeing its continued convulsions for a moment before coming to a decision, pointing at the fallen rider whose head was lolling at an unnatural angle.

'Get him out of the way!'

A pair of warriors edged forward and took hold of the fallen rider's clothing, dragging him clear of the injured horse, and the noble drew his sword, raising it in readiness to strike and waiting patiently for the right moment. The animal's struggles against the pain of whatever had caused it to stumble gradually calmed, and finally, shivering violently, it stood still with one hoof raised from the track's wooden surface. Pulling the sword back until it was almost behind him the noble struck, hacking a fearsome gash into the stricken horse's neck and stepping back as it staggered, blood gushing from the wound, sinking to its knees as consciousness faded from its brain.

'Quickly, get it off the track before it collapses!'

A dozen men rushed to join him, and their collective push toppled the trembling animal over the path's edge and into the knee-deep marsh water, where it lay twitching in an expanding cloud of its blood. Gernot leaned over to examine the foot that it had been favouring, reaching out and pulling at a hard metal object embedded in the centre of the hoof's underside. Turning, he held it up to Amalric with the bloodiest of its four points uppermost.

'A caltrop. It seems that our quarry isn't ready to be overtaken that easily after all.'

The king looked down at the pointed device in disbelief for a moment, then shook his head.

'No matter. One horse makes no difference either way, so nothing is changed.'

Gernot flicked a glance at his men, many of whom were eyeing the corpse of the dead horse's rider with evident dismay. He walked across to the king's horse, craning his neck to look into Amalric's eyes.

'You're sure, my King? There will be more traps like this. More men will die.'

The younger man locked down at him for a moment, then took the caltrop from his fingers, holding it up in plain view of the men of his household.

'Gernot warns me that there will be more of these. Look upon it, my brothers, and consider its nature as a weapon. Invisible until it strikes, murderous to man and horse, and easier to make than an arrowhead. If we ride on from this point it is likely that some of you will have your horses felled by these, assuming that our enemy has more of them. And so I ask you to choose whether you wish to ride on, or whether you will take the easier option, and turn your horses south, admitting defeat.'

He was silent for a moment, allowing time for his men to digest the awful choice.

'For myself there is no choice, but for each of you all that binds you to me are a few words that you spoke before the altar of Wodanaz when my father died, and I succeeded him on the tribe's throne.'

'A vow is a vow, my King!'

Amalric nodded, raising a hand in recognition of the outraged shout from somewhere near the back of his men.

'Trust me, my brothers, I have vowed to have these Romans' heads nailed to my roof beams, or else to die trying. And so I will be riding at the head of our column from now, taking as much risk as any other man. Who will ride with me? I will say again, any man who wishes may be released from his oath without fear of censure or punishment. Service of this nature must be given freely or not at all! Who will ride with me?'

A roar from his men and a thicket of spear heads punching at the air was his answer, and Amalric looked down at Gernot with a sad smile.

'I've just condemned who knows how many of them to die and they love me for it.' He tossed the caltrop into the water at the track's side. 'Have the dead man's body placed at the path side and we'll bury him with dignity when we return with the heads of the bastards who killed him. And then take your saddle, Gernot, we have Romans to hunt!'

'He's waking up. Let's try to get him upright.'

The Tungrians had been a dozen miles north of Aliso when disaster struck. Husam, riding near the head of the column, felt his horse stumble momentarily and then, just as he had thought the beast had regained its footing, found himself momentarily in the air before hitting the edge of the wooden causeway with a sickening crack. On coming to he had found several worried men gathered over him, their expressions becoming still darker with his frenzied reaction to their attempts to lift him.

'No! In the name of the goddess no!'

Two of the men standing over him were pushed aside, making way for the woman Gerhild who squatted next to him and ran her hands along the length of his twisted leg. She looked up at Scaurus and made to stand up, but Husam whipped out a hand

and gripped her arm with the wide-eyed strength of a man in severe pain.

'Tell me.'

She looked down at him until his grip loosened.

'Your leg is broken. You cannot ride and you cannot walk.'

He digested her statement in silence for a moment, then looked up at Scaurus, speaking with teeth gritted against the pain in his thigh.

'You must leave me, Tribune, or I will be the death of you all. I ask only that you stand me up and put a bow in my hand, and I will send a dozen of these Bructeri to the underworld before me.'

The tribune nodded.

'As you wish. But given that we have no time to spare I warn you that it will be painful in the extreme.'

Cotta squatted down next to him, taking one hand and holding out a piece of wood taken from his pack.

'Put this in your mouth and bite down.'

The Hamian opened his mouth and allowed the wooden dowel to settle against his back teeth, then nodded curtly. Pulling him to his feet as gently as they could, the men around him winced as he shrieked with the pain as the ends of his broken thigh bone grated together. Scaurus looked into the Hamian's eyes and nodded to himself.

'Hold him up. Arminius, fetch the vial.'

The big German nodded and turned away to his pack, returning with a small and solidly made green glass bottle whose stopper was sealed over with a heavy blob of wax and then wired for good measure. He raised a questioning eyebrow to his master, who nodded tiredly.

'Open it. If we don't use it now then we may never get the chance to do so.'

Stripping away wire and wax, Arminius pulled the stopper with delicate care, putting his nose to the bottle's neck.

'It smells sweet enough.'

Scaurus laughed.

'It tastes sweet enough too, especially once the contents have had time to take effect. Take a mouthful.'

The Hamian drank, licking at the residue that stuck to his lips. 'It tastes like honey.'

'It is honey mixed with wine, but with the addition of the milk of the poppy. I have given you sufficient to dull the pain, but not enough to completely remove it, as that would cause you to sleep. Now, we need to get you tied to something so that you can stay upright for long enough to make your arrows count.'

Cotta pointed to a sapling growing alongside the track.

'There? He'll have a clear view of the track.'

Scaurus nodded.

'Fetch rope. Husam, what is the distance of your best bow shot?'

The Hamian thought for a moment, lifting his head to look at the nearby trees for some indication of wind direction.

'Two hundred paces.'

Scaurus called after Cotta.

'And have the remaining caltrops laid out from two hundred paces back down the track.'

Biting down on the wooden stick again, the Hamian grimaced and shuddered while they manhandled him over to the young tree, then lashed his injured leg to its bole to enable him to stand upright on his remaining good limb.

'There. That should keep you standing long enough to put a few shafts into the air. Here, give me that stick.' Cotta extracted the wooden dowel from his mouth and then tossed it aside. 'Munir, come over here and sort your comrade out with his bow. And be quick about it, we need to be away.'

Scaurus stepped forward and took the stricken archer's hand, looking into his eyes with an expression of sadness verging on tears, and Husam laughed tersely, flinching at the pain in his leg.

'You can stop that.' Scaurus raised an eyebrow, but the archer shook his head dismissively. 'You heard me, Tribune. No sadness, not now. I'm going to die cleanly, and quickly, instead of suffering for hours and then dying from the barbarous attentions of the

Bructeri. I always knew that following your eagle would get me killed at some point, and all I ever wanted was for it to be a man's death, fitting for the service of the Deasura. So ride away now, before the Germans get here, and think of the harvest I'll reap from them as they come up that road. Now . . .'

He turned to Munir, who was waiting behind the officer.

'Give me my bow.' He took the weapon from the empty-eyed watch officer, hastily restrung with a dry string to replace its predecessor, which had been soaked by its fall into the marsh, and tested its draw with a critical expression. 'Perfect. Give me some arrows and I'll be ready.'

'I'm staying with you.'

Husam laughed.

'No you're not, my friend, because not only does the tribune have too much sense to let you throw your life away that cheaply, but I'm not letting you either. I'm your superior, and I'm telling you to give me some arrows, two quivers full, then get on your horse and get out of here.' Munir stared at him with eyes that were filling with tears. 'And *you* can stop that too, because I'm giving you a job to do that'll be a good deal harder than just standing here and putting some arrows into a hapless bunch of barbarians, right? At some point in the next day or two you may get a chance to put a shaft into Qadir, and when you get that chance you must send the arrow on its way with the Deasura's name on your lips in the hope that she will greet him into the afterlife despite his increasing lack of regard for her. Give him a merciful death, Munir, and when the time comes remember me and do not hesitate! Now be on your way, and leave me to commune with the goddess.'

His friend put a quiver of arrows over each of the Hamian's shoulders, making small adjustments to their positioning until the feathered shafts fell perfectly to hand, then kissed him on both cheeks and was gone, splashing across the submerged timbers to join the waiting horsemen. Husam saluted, lifting his bow in a gesture of defiance against the fates, and held it there while he watched them trot away to the north in showers of spray, as their horses' hoofs scattered the standing water in all directions. Lowering the bow he stared at it in bleak silence for a moment and then exhaled in a long, slow breath.

'Let us make ready.'

Licking a finger, he held it up to gauge the wind's strength and direction, smiling as he realised that it was at his back, a gentle breeze that would nonetheless help his shots achieve their best possible distance. Expertly plucking an arrow from the quiver, he put it to the weapon's string, lifting the bow to its optimum elevation. Drawing the string back to its maximum extent, forcing the power of his broad shoulders into the weapon, he loosed the arrow and watched intently as it first climbed to the height of its brief arc and then fell back to earth to impact the wooden track in a brief splash of water almost too distant to be visible, the white flight feathers no more than a dot in the landscape before him but nevertheless sufficient to give him an indication of the range at which he could begin to punish the oncoming horsemen. Relaxing for a moment he closed his eyes, imagining the carved statues of Atargatis, the goddess that the Hamians called the Deasura, the deity worshipped by every man serving under Qadir's command.

'Deasura, light of my life, I am about to undertake my last feat of arms, crippled and in agony, but still capable of putting the fear of your vengeance into the hearts of the unbelievers. Grant me the strength to wield my bow with the skill of my long practice, and the grace to accept my death when that time comes. Make my ending glorious, I humbly pray, and grant me the boon of a quick and honourable exit from this life. Do not allow your faithful servant to suffer the indignity of torture or mutilation, but rather allow me to enter the underworld entire and ready to serve you in whatever is to follow.'

He stood in silence for a moment longer and then spoke again, this time with less certainty and in something close to a pleading note.

'So much for my pleas for your favour. Now I must plead on the behalf of another man, my friend Qadir. I know that of late he has been less . . . attentive to your service than before. This is not from any lack of love and respect for you, but because he has seen and done many things that a man should perhaps not have to endure in the past few years. I know that he has become troubled by the taking of life, and I fear that he has become weary of this world. Please, I entreat you, provide him with the strength to master this weakness and return to his full powers as both a man and a soldier. I know that he will love you for it, and redouble his efforts to serve you as you demand and deserve.'

He opened his eyes, looking down the track's length and finding it still empty.

'It seems that I will have something of a wait before the time for my glorious death is at hand.' Closing his eyes, he pondered for a moment before speaking again. 'Forgive me, Deasura, for troubling you one last time. I speak on the behalf of a man for whom I have much fondness, an unbeliever, it is true, but a good-hearted man none the less, and another who has undergone more than his share of fate's insults and injuries. If you see fit, visit your bounteous favour on Centurion Aquila, and grant him some measure of peace from the furies that haunt him. I know that your favour would help him to return to his former self.'

He fell silent and opened his eyes, looking up into the empty sky.

'Enough. A man should greet his death with more dignity than to beg for assistance, even for a friend.'

Reaching down to the quiver with fingers that needed no instruction, he strung another arrow, tipping his head from side to side and back to front to warm the muscles that he needed to work perfectly one last time, stretching out his right arm and waggling the fingers in preparation for the feats of dexterity that would shortly be demanded of them, then looked down the track to see a minute speck of darkness on the horizon.

'Well it's about time. Come on then, you unenlightened barbarian scum. I'm ready when you are.'

*

Amalric rode in silence, brooding on the three horses that had
fallen to caltrops since their initial loss. Two of the riders had
emerged from their falls with nothing worse than minor injuries,
but the third had broken his arm on hitting the track's wooden
beams, and had been left propped against a tree with the promise
that he would be picked up on their return southward. All three
animals had been put out of their agony by Gernot, but each
fresh casualty had consumed enough time for their quarry to
have re-established a good half-mile or so of the lead that he was
attempting to haul in by means of his calculated gamble with
their pace. With each of the first two losses Gernot had urged
him to surrender his place at the head of the column to a man
whose loss would be less keenly felt, and each time he had
dismissed the idea out of hand, so that at the third stop the noble
had not raised the idea, but simply fixed his king with a lingering,
piercing stare that spoke eloquently as to his concerns.

Staring intently down the track he almost missed the small
fleck of white feathers as he rode past it, registering it out of the
corner of his eye as it vanished beneath the hoofs of the leading
riders. Just as he realised what it was that he had seen, a high-
pitched scream of equine pain sounded from behind him.

'This is the place your father named in his message to the king
of the Angrivarii?'

Sigimund's oldest son grunted, nodding dourly.

'He told them we would be here by the middle of the day.'

Tiro looked about him, finding only an empty landscape above
which clouds scudded slowly past.

'Well if they're here they're doing a remarkable job of staying
concealed.' He turned to Varus and Dubnus with a raised eyebrow.
'It seems my message to the Angrivarii has gone astray, but one
of the main tenets of the men I work for is to get the job done,
no matter what the circumstances throw in our way. Doubtless
the man sent to deliver my request for safe passage to the locals
is lying at the bottom of some ditch or other with a broken neck,
with the message still tucked away about his person. So, we have

a choice, gentlemen, to wait here until the Angrivarii do arrive, which of course might be a very long wait, or just to continue on our way without their assistance. Or their permission . . .'

Dubnus nodded slowly.

'And if they find us on their land without having granted that permission?'

The older man pulled a wry face.

'That depends on who does the finding. The tribe are still nominally our friends, but the discovery of Romans on their land unbidden might well result in our deaths before any sort of agreement could be reached.'

'And the same can be said of the tribune and his party?'

'Doubly so, for they have the Bructeri witch with them. My entire plan depended on our being able to recruit the Angrivarii to our cause, but without their co-operation there are several ways this can go bad.'

The Briton turned in his saddle to look at Varus.

'It seems to me that our only real option is to press on, find our brothers and bring them back here. Any other course of action seems likely to result in their capture and likely death.'

Tiro leaned back in his saddle, playing a hard stare on the centurion.

'You're more of a pragmatist than I'd expected, Prince of the Brigantes. Very well, since you've done my arguing for me, we'll risk the wrath of the Angrivarii and ride for the place I told Dolfus to meet us. I assume that you gentlemen will wait here for us?'

Husam watched the oncoming horsemen intently, the arrow nocked to his bowstring drawn and ready to shoot, gauging the balance between the urge to shoot with the Bructeri inside his longest range and the need to make every arrow count. A horse screamed, and the arrow seemed to spring away from the bow's string of its own volition, so swift was his reaction, aimed at the point in the enemy's column where chaos had erupted. With the first missile in the air he continued shooting for all he was worth, lofting shaft after shaft at the oncoming pack of horsemen, a target so densely packed that he knew that putting an arrow into their midst was likely to result in a hit. A horse had fallen just behind the horsemen's front rank, presumably to a carefully placed caltrop, and the ensuing chaos behind the fallen beast and those its fall had balked in turn was preventing most of the riders from either escaping from beneath the rain of arrows or attacking down the road. A rider whose horse had avoided the chaos put his head down and charged his mount forward, and Husam lowered his bow a little and put an arrow into the man's mount, cursing as the shaft struck deep into the beast's chest rather than hitting the man in its saddle. Killed in mid-gallop the horse simply ploughed into the track's shallow standing water, its rider managing to stay in the saddle long enough that when the beast's dead momentum was almost spent he was able to step off his mount and take shelter behind its massive bulk, safe from the Hamian's arrows.

The screams of wounded animals and their riders reached him, distant sounds of distress as his shafts hit targets that were so tightly grouped as to be unmissable. The Germans' forward momentum was clearly lost, fallen horses preventing the men behind from pressing through to get at the source of the arrows that were falling on them with terrible, brutal efficiency and burying their evil iron heads indiscriminately in man and beast alike. He paused for a moment to look down at his first quiver, tallying the number of shafts remaining, realising that a voice was shouting above the chaos of the trapped horsemen and their mounts, urgent, imperative commands that could only presage one action from the trapped Germans.

A handful of men had managed to fight their way through the milling chaos of the horsemen bottled up behind the fallen beasts, two of them dropping into the shelter of the king's dead horse twenty paces closer to the enemy archer than the main cluster of horsemen who were still suffering under his shafts, while the others fell flat in the marsh's fetid water to their right in order to avoid drawing the bowman's attention. The bigger of the two was a senior warrior within the royal household, a heavy bearded bear of a man whose greatest prize was a mail shirt he had taken from a Roman captive years before, and which he wore over a coat of thick hide so stiff as to itself resemble armour. He peeped over the horse's ribcage at the ground before them, and Amalric followed his gaze, his spirits sinking as the distance across which the archer was shooting struck home. The big man looked at him with a determined set of his jaw, knuckles white on the shaft of his spear.

'We must attack, my King!' Amalric nodded grimly, readying himself to join them in storming the lone archer, only to find a hand on his sleeve. 'Not you, Amalric. Your place is to lead our brothers and recover what has been stolen from us. Most of us who run at this man will die, but we give our lives for the good of the tribe. Praise our names, when the time comes for the songs to be sung of this day.'

Raising his voice the warrior bellowed at the men waiting in the swamp's water.

'Our king commands us to kill this archer! Are you ready to give your lives for the tribe?'

Their response was swift, if a little muted by the circumstances, a growled affirmation, and with a war cry that stood the hairs on the back of Amalric's neck the big man rose from cover, pointing at the lone archer and striding forward with his spear raised, then grunting in pain as an arrow struck him in the chest, staggering back with the force of the impact. After a moment's pause the man beside him leapt to his feet and vaulted the horse's body, joining the charge of the half-dozen men who had rallied to join the desperate attack. He took half a dozen swift strides forward, bellowing a war cry made ragged by exertion and fear, then stopped dead, sinking to his knees with an arrow's feathered shaft protruding from his chest.

Half a dozen men rose from the cover of their fallen mounts at an unintelligible bellowed command, clearly intent on overrunning

Husam's position, and with a savage grin that was half-exultation and half the agony of making any movement with his shattered leg strapped to the tree, the Hamian put an arrow into the first man to get to his feet, switching his attention to the next of them and dropping him as he stormed forward from the shelter of the fallen horse. The first man he had shot was back on his feet with no obvious wound, the arrow having apparently failed to beat whatever armour was protecting him, but the next shaft knocked him down again, apparently putting him out of the fight. A group of warriors climbed from the swamp beside the track and ran at him screaming their battle cries, and the Hamian switched targets, missing with his next shaft, as the warrior he'd targeted unwittingly weaved out of its path, but the next two shots both struck home, leaving only a pair of warriors baying for his blood as they came on in weaving, splashing runs, intended to throw his aim off. Behind them the first man was back on his feet, and Husam frowned at the realisation that two arrows had failed to stop the oncoming Bructeri, who was using the two men in front of him as unwitting cover. He lowered the bow, waiting for the runners to get close enough that their evasive changes of direction would cease to be of any protection against the lethal velocity of his arrows.

At fifty paces, as he raised the weapon to start shooting again, one of the runners went down clutching at his bloody foot in shock and agony, as he stumbled onto another one of the caltrops that had been scattered in the Bructeri's path. The Hamian shot the man who turned to look back at his maimed comrade for an instant, his pause all the opportunity the waiting archer needed. Nocking another arrow he drew it back as far as he could before releasing it at the sole remaining warrior, still stubbornly advancing despite having been struck twice, nodding his head as the shaft stuck in his target.

His small smile of satisfaction faded as the big German, having momentarily doubled up over the arrow's impact point, slowly straightened his body again, looked down, then pulled the shaft free of whatever had prevented it from piercing his body, tossing it aside. Raising his spear he stood still for a moment, coughing and spitting into the water, then grinned bloody-mouthed at the archer before he began to stagger forward again, still hunched against the pain in his body where three heavy iron arrowheads had struck with the power of spear thrusts, but clearly determined to use whatever magic was repelling the Syrian's arrows to close with his tormentor and put him down.

Waiting, partly exercising the patience that he had learned while hunting game in the German forests, partly through sheer curiosity, he watched with another arrow strung and ready to loose, shaking his head in amazement as the Bructeri mastered the crippling pain and walked towards him, his face contorted with the agony of his damaged body as he broke into a shambling run. At twenty-five paces distance he drew his spear arm back and, with an incoherent, pain-wracked bellow of rage in the face of Husam's raised bow, hurled his framea with a final roar, stopping with his hands on his knees to cough blood again as the spear whipped across the space between them in a short arc that seemed fated to strike the archer. Leaning his upper body to one side with a suppressed shriek of pain, Husam felt the wind of the weapon's passage on his face, then straightened his body with slow, agonised care, every movement sending spikes of red hot agony down his broken leg. He raised the bow, trembling with the pain, waiting as the big tribesman stood, staring back at him with blank eyes, nodded at the German in respect of his tenacity, and then shot him in the throat. He watched dispassionately as the tribesman sank to his knees and then fell face down into the track's water, nodding again.

'I'll be along to join you soon enough.'

Looking up he saw a lone figure racing forward out of the mass of horsemen bottled up behind the fallen beast, diving into the cover of a dying horse just in time to evade the arrow intended to kill him.

Staring past the fallen Germans he realised that the remaining warriors had gone to ground, and if any further attack on his position was in hand it was not yet evident. Drawing breath he bellowed a challenge at the men cowering behind the bodies of their dead and dying mounts.

'Are there no more of you with the guts to come and kill a cripple!'

Amalric stared bleakly at the bodies that littered the ground in front of him, then ducked below the flank of his horse, hearing the hiss of another arrow over his head, as Gernot dived into the cover beside him. In the silence that followed he could hear the distant archer shouting something in a language he didn't understand, his voice thick with anger.

'We have to get round him! That may be a single man, but this is a field of death! We have to get around him, there's no way we can go straight through him without losing too many men!'

The noble shook his head at his king's frustrated outburst.

'Impossible, my King. The marshes here are almost impassable unless you know the paths that give safe passage.'

Amalric nodded wearily.

'How many men have we lost?'

'At least five men lie dead and wounded behind us, and twice as many horses. Fortunately the rest had the good sense to pull back, out of the range of his bow. And here?'

Amalric waved a hand at the corpses strewn across the causeway.

'As you see, he killed six men of my household without any of them ever getting within touching distance of him. If we are to attack again, we will have to go forward with every man we have, and look to overwhelm him with numbers.'

The noble's mouth tightened in anger, and he turned to look back to where the prisoner squatted at the side of the track under the points of two spears.

'We would lose more men than we could afford, given the number already dead or wounded at his hand. No. I have a better idea. One that will see him out of our way without a single further death. Or perhaps just the one.'

*

'So where is it that we're heading?'

Tiro made another nervous scan of the horizon to their north and east before answering Dubnus's question, guiding his horse towards the cover of a copse several hundred paces distant.

'To a place I agreed with Dolfus would be our meeting place tomorrow. I chose it because it is rarely visited by the Angrivarii, who believe it to be haunted by the spirits of the legionaries who were killed as they fought their way across it, under constant attack by the men of five tribes led by the traitor Arminius.'

'Traitor?' The Briton frowned. 'He was a German, wasn't he?'

The older man shook his head.

'Only by birth. He was taken hostage at an early age, ransomed to ensure his father the king's support in the wars against the other tribes, which meant that he was given a Roman education and grew to manhood as a member of the civilised world. The emperor granted him equestrian status, and he proved himself to be an able leader of men. Too able, in fact. He performed well in the Pannonian war, and became so well trusted that the command hierarchy of the three legions campaigning on the eastern side of the Rhenus never for one moment considered him capable of betraying them. But he did, and twenty thousand men died as a consequence. Their bones are still scattered along the route they took to flee from the German attacks, for all the good it did them. Only a handful ever lived to see Aliso.'

Varus looked about him with a shiver.

'And the Angrivarii were part of this alliance against Rome?'

Tiro nodded, nudging his horse on with a touch of his heels. 'Both they and the Marsi were happy to take part, and even if they were whipped back into line by Tiberius and Germanicus they remain unpredictable and dangerous, which explains our somewhat ambivalent relationship with both them and most of the other tribes on this side of the river. I'm never sure whether they'll greet us with a smile or a drawn dagger.' He scanned the horizon again. 'Or both.'

*

Husam raised his bow once more, as a figure stood up from the cover of one of the dead horses, freezing with the arrow ready to loose as his preternaturally sharp eyesight identified his target, and the white square of linen that was held across his chest. Shaking his head in disgust he eased the last few inches of draw from the shaft, muttering to himself as he watched more Germans rise from their hiding places.

'I should have expected such a thing.'

Raising his voice to bellow a command, he lifted the bow to reinforce the threat behind his words.

'No more than three of you, or I will start killing you, white flag or not.'

Climbing carefully over the horse's corpse, Qadir walked slowly forward followed closely by three more men, each of them carrying a long spear ready to strike at the captive centurion. Walking steadily towards the crippled archer the centurion raised his voice to call out to his friend in Aramaic.

'Shoot me now, Chosen Man, while you still have the opportunity!'

Husam lowered his head for a moment and then looked up again.

'I know I should! I have ordered Munir to grant you that mercy, should he have the opportunity to send you to the arms of the goddess, but now that I have the chance I find my arm weak.'

One of the Germans walking behind Qadir barked out a command in Latin.

'No more of your eastern gabbling! Speak Latin!'

Husam laughed out loud, the sound ringing out across the corpse-strewn marsh.

'Fuck you, German. I have you under my bow, and given the slightest excuse I will put an arrow into the exceptionally small space between your balls! And that's close enough!'

The German moved sideways slightly, making sure he kept Qadir between him and the Hamian's bow.

'I am Gernot, Lord of the Bructeri, and I come only to talk. Will you shoot a man who speaks under a flag of truce?'

Husam shifted his good leg, grimacing at the pain that was now torturing both limbs, a combination of the injury and the discomfort of his position.

'Not if you stay where you are! But come any closer and you will test my patience just a little too much. As for talking, there is nothing to discuss! Simply turn away, and don't come back before dark unless you want to be dining with your ancestors this evening!'

Gernot shook his head, pointing to the tree that was holding the Hamian upright.

'I don't think so! You have a broken leg, which means that you can only shoot in this direction! All I have to do is send my men around you on either side and they will have you at their mercy! And mercy is a quality I'm not feeling inclined to at this point in time!'

Husam laughed again, calling out across the gap between them.

'You make it sound so simple! Whereas we both know that the ground to either side of this wooden road is an uncharted marsh, slow going to men who do not know it! If they are to avoid my arrows they will have to cast out far out to either side, so that by the time your warriors manage to get behind me the sun will be so close to the horizon that you might just as well have sat and waited for dark!'

The German shook his head in frustration.

'Then you leave me little choice, Easterner. Unless you surrender I will butcher this captive, here before your eyes! A man takes an uncomfortably long time to die with a spear in his liver!'

The Hamian altered his point of aim imperceptibly, loosing an arrow that flickered across the fifty-pace gap between them and stuck in the wood at Gernot's feet with a shower of spray that spattered across the man's legs. Another shaft was fitted to the bow's string before any of the Germans had time to react, Husam's iron-hard eyes waiting for any move.

'When you threaten to kill a prisoner you forfeit the right to any idea of truce! If you take your iron to my friend I will simply put an arrow through his chest to end his suffering, and then one more in your back when you turn to run!'

Qadir raised his voice, a note of anguish at his friend's predicament straining his words as the Bructeri behind him gripped his collar.

'Farewell Husam, best of comrades! Mention me to the goddess when you meet her!'

Gernot retreated stony-faced, pulling his captive backwards towards the place where his warriors waited, and Husam raised his voice to call after him.

'If you wish to save lives, Gernot of the Bructeri, you simply have to keep your men away from my bow! Send your warriors at me and I will kill another ten of you before they finish me, and I will die a happy man! It's either that or wait me out! When the sun touches the horizon I will give my life to the goddess Atargatis, but if you want me out of your path before then my spirit will be accompanied by a good deal more of your brothers than have already gone before me!'

'I gave the archer his chance to save this one's life. Now we must make our threat reality!'

Amalric looked up wearily at Gernot as the two men stood in the shelter of a grove of trees a hundred paces back from the point where the ambush had begun, both the track and the ground to either side littered with the corpses of horses and their riders. The remaining warriors were huddled on the track, Gernot's older warriors and the king's younger men talking quietly in their own groups as they waited for the sun to set.

'I cannot see a good reason to torture this man. It will not shake that archer's conviction that he must prevent our passage between now and the setting of the sun.'

Gernot shook his head impatiently.

'It will demonstrate that we mean what we say!'

The king stared at him for a long time before answering.

'It will prove that *you* mean what you say, Uncle, but I believe that he continues to be a potential hostage to use if we fail to rescue Gerhild by force. And I have decided to keep him intact for that moment.'

Gernot stared back at him incredulously.

'But my King . . .'

'You intend to tell me that this will be seen as a sign of weakness? Of an unwillingness to treat our enemies with the necessary harshness? I consider it to be an essential denial of our usual instinct to use these people for sport, recognising that I may yet need the bargaining tool of his life.'

'Have you forgotten the ways in which they have treated us, over the many years since our people and theirs first made war on each other? Enslaved, betrayed, murdered by the tens of thousands?'

Amalric shook his head.

'No. I have not. And nor have I forgotten our part in the events that have led us to this point. Our neighbours manage to maintain stable relationships with Rome, for the most part, some of them with histories of violence between them and the Romans that equal ours in some respects.'

His uncle stood in amazed silence for a moment.

'I would not have expected to hear such a sentiment from you, Amalric.'

The king nodded.

'Our views differ, Uncle. Let us agree to put these differences aside until this pursuit is complete. You can be very sure that I will fight tooth and nail to free my seer, and to return the eagle to its rightful place in our treasury, sparing no one who stands in my way. When that has been achieved let us speak again, and see if we can find common ground as to how we should approach the dangerous beast that squats on the far side of the Rhenus.'

'Dry ground? In this wasteland?'

Gunda raised a weary eyebrow at Cotta's disbelieving tone.

'Dry ground, Roman. The only dry ground large enough to take our numbers this close to the track for a day's march or

more. I have used it on several occasions, to get some relief from
the incessant soaking of my feet.'

Dolfus walked his horse alongside the two men's mounts.

'How far is it to Angrivarii territory?'

Gunda looked up the path's watery ribbon, tinged red by the
light of the setting sun.

'Ten miles further up this track there is dry land to be found
to the right, where the ground begins to rise towards the wooded
hills to the north. From there another five miles march will
bring us to the place you have asked me to find. We might
meet some of their tribesmen, although the Angrivarii tend to
avoid the place for fear of the spirits of all the men who died
as they fought their way across it, and rotted where they fell.
But any men we do meet will most likely only be farmers, and
not capable of fighting off thirty of my tribe's companion
warriors.'

The decurion shook his head with a snort of dark amusement.

'They won't be thirty strong now. The caltrops we scattered
behind us must have felled several horses, and that archer of
yours had the look in his eyes of a man determined to leave this
life the hard way, and take some of our foes with him. Tell me,
can you feel any sign of their approach in the wood?'

Gunda dropped lightly from his horse's saddle into the track's
dank water, putting a hand onto the rough wooden surface.

'Nothing. They must be far behind us.'

Dolfus nodded decisively.

'In which case camping for the night on this island of dry land
you describe must be the only sensible thing for us to do. Lead
us to it, scout.'

Gunda led the column away from the waterlogged track, and
along a narrow strip of soggy going for fifty paces or so until
their footing improved to dry ground, a small rise in the land
having created an island in the marsh approximately twenty paces
across. With the benefit of their slight elevation they were able
to see in all directions, the swamp's waters glistening with eye-
aching brilliance in the late afternoon sunlight, the landscape

around them devoid of any sign of trees in any direction for several hundred paces.

'A considerable improvement. And now I see why you had us carry firewood with us.'

Gunda nodded at Dolfus's statement.

'There are islands like this scattered around this area, but this is the only one for miles that can easily be reached from the road. The nearest that I know of is several hundred paces further from the road . . .' He pointed to the west. 'And the path to reach it is hard enough to find in the daylight, never mind after darkness has fallen.'

Gerhild stepped between the two men, gesturing to Scaurus who was being assisted from his horse by Arminius and Lupus, shivering uncontrollably like a man with a high fever.

'We need fire if we are to save this man's life. The sickness caused by his wound has come upon him again, having bided its time since the goddess defeated it last night.'

Dolfus set to organising the camp while Gunda collected the firewood that had been tied to each rider's saddle.

'There is enough for a small fire that will burn through the night, fed carefully.'

'Then light it now, do what you must for him while it's still light, and allow it to burn down to embers that can be hidden from the road with a shield. We will stick out like the balls on a sacrificial bull with a fire burning on this raised ground, and I wish to offer the men pursuing us no encouragement.'

The guide inclined his head in agreement with the decurion's command.

'As you wish.' He raised a hand to indicate the cloudless sky, and the quiet that had settled across the land, its oppressive quiet making the men of the detachment speak quietly despite the absence of any ears to overhear them. 'Although any approach down the track would be heard while the horsemen were still miles distant on a night like this.'

'So tell me again Briton, who went north with the priestess?'

Dubnus finished chewing the mouthful of the meat that he had cooked over an open fire.

'Your decurion and his two troopers, Tribune Scaurus, his German slave Arminius, a boy who's his pupil, and two Hamian archers. Two centurions also rode with the tribune, a retired veteran called Cotta and my comrade Marcus Corvus.'

Tiro nodded.

'Centurion Cotta is known to me. He has performed services for the empire before, services that involved shedding the blood of one of Rome's highest citizens to prevent an act of treason from turning into civil war. And even if it happened twenty years ago, he's still a man worth watching for any sign that his loyalty to the throne might be slipping.'

The big Briton shook his head.

'Cotta? The man's a loyal Roman to the core, a true centurion. If he spilled some senator's blood it will have been at the express orders of his superiors.'

The older man pursed his lips, leaning back against his saddle with a contented sigh.

'So I believe. But that isn't always how these things work, Centurion. A man who's killed an emperor once . . .' He paused, watching the Briton's face intently. 'Ah, so you do know what I'm talking about.'

Dubnus shrugged.

'I'd heard rumours, nothing more.'

Tiro smiled knowingly back at him.

'Rumours? Most of the work I do is concerned with the gathering and analysis of information that is mostly rumour, or no better than hearsay at best. Rumours kill, Centurion, and they tend to be somewhat impartial as to who gets caught in their net. Anyway, as I was saying, a man who's killed one emperor, even if his victim was a half-hearted usurper who accepted the purple under the misapprehension that the current emperor was dead and his son was unfit to rule, that's a man who won't hesitate to do it again. And in some rare cases even long-retired centurions can make excellent assassins, given the motive.'

He stared at Dubnus for a long moment, while the Briton stolidly chewed on another mouthful of meat and stared back flatly at him, ignoring the fact that his response to the older man's subtle interrogation was becoming overtly hostile.

'And as for your friend Marcus Valerius Aquila . . .'

'His name is—'

Tiro grinned wider.

'Corvus? Never try to lie to a liar, Centurion. Your friend is the son of a once highly respected senatorial family, is he not? Two brothers, both war heroes and very, very wealthy men, a dangerous combination when put into close proximity with an emperor prone to any insecurity as to his own position. After all, of the seventeen emperors we've had since the divine Augustus took the throne, at least three have died in circumstances where the senate's role was to say the least, somewhat dubious if not openly hostile. And so when our new, young, and very malleable emperor came to the throne to find the coffers bled dry by a decade of wars with the Marcomanni and the Quadi, it was both pragmatic and to some degree pre-emptive for him to deal with a few leading families, take their enormous wealth and remove them as threats. Not to mention cowing the rest of the senate into submission lest they join the list of proscribed names. But the Praetorian Prefect who was doing his bidding in this matter made one small but significant mistake in allowing Appius Valerius Aquila's son Marcus to escape, and from within the confines of his own camp to boot! We know he made it as far as Britannia, where he fell in with the army . . .' He stared hard at Dubnus for a moment. 'With a unit of Tungrians it was alleged, and vanished from sight. Attempts were made to find and deal with him, but the men sent to do the job clearly weren't up to the task, because they didn't come back and the next thing we know is that he popped up in Rome with some stolen Dacian gold which, it seems, was instrumental in both his revenge and the rise to power of the man who now issues me with my orders.'

He stopped talking and raised an eyebrow at Dubnus, who shrugged in return.

'That's quite a story. Like something out of a play.'

The older man nodded.

'Isn't it? Although not every story ends as prettily as the plays we watch at the theatre, with the hero and heroine reunited and everyone miraculously happy with their lot, do they? Never mind, that's what we're here for, isn't it? To make sure that your friends get out of the Bructeri tribe's territory safely, and that the Angrivarii don't cut them to ribbons the second they lay eyes on them. Never fear Centurion, we'll be there when they come up the road from Aliso, it's a short enough ride from here. And once we have Gerhild safely away from her people we'll all be able to relax, won't we?'

'One man.'

Amalric shook his head in disgust at the archer's blood-soaked corpse hanging loosely from the sapling to which he had been tied, turning back to stare at the bodies of those warriors who had fallen attempting to remove the Hamian from their path. Gernot nodded, reaching out and prying the bow from fingers already stiffening with rigor mortis. The dead man had cut his own throat with the dagger that now lay in the blood-soaked stagnant water at his feet, bleeding to death before the Germans had been able to reach the spot from where he had held them off for most of the afternoon.

'One man.' The noble nodded agreement, testing the bow's draw. 'But an archer of the highest possible skill, with targets forced to come at him from one direction. There is no shame to our having been delayed by this one man under these circumstances.'

Amalric shook his head, holding up what remained of the Hamian's quiver of arrows with a bitter smile.

'And he had no more than half a dozen shafts left. We could have rushed him at any time and cleared the road, whereas now all we can do is hope to find some dry ground on which to sleep, and renew our pursuit tomorrow morning.'

Gernot shook his head in disagreement, looking up at the evening sky with an experienced eye.

'No, my King, there is another choice. More risky, but with at least some chance of bringing these thieves to account. The sky is clear, as you can see, without cloud, and when the darkness falls the moon and stars will provide us with enough light to ride along this track, if we go slowly. If the Romans have ridden for an afternoon then perhaps the whole night will be enough time for us to catch them up. And even with our losses we are still twice their strength in numbers. We can attack in the time just before dawn, when they will be at their least vigilant.'

A thought occurred to him, and he beckoned the huntsman across to join them. His servant's already doleful expression had become one of misery with the death of both of his dogs, one pinned to the track by a chance arrow, the other killed instantly by a powerful kick from a pain-crazed horse, but he came to his master readily enough despite his evident dolour.

'Is there any dry ground up ahead, somewhere that Gunda might be tempted to halt for the night?'

The older man nodded vigorously.

'Yes, my Lord, ten miles or so from here. It would be no use as a place to hide though, for every tree for a mile and more has been cut down for firewood by those who use it as a place of refuge from the marsh over the years.'

'But it *is* dry?'

The huntsman nodded again.

'It stands half a man's height proud of the marsh, my Lord, and is large enough for a party the size of which you have described.'

'And you could find it in the dark?'

'I could, on a night such as this is likely to be, with a bright moon.'

Amalric stared down the track's straight line, mulling what the two men had said.

'So we might still catch them?'

Gernot grinned wolfishly.

'Better than that, my King. We might catch them sleeping. I

have one more idea that might give us an advantage that will allow us to take our enemies by surprise.'

'He looks like he's already dead.'

Dolfus stared down at Scaurus's recumbent form in the fire's flickering light with an expression that to Marcus looked more predatory than sympathetic. Gerhild looked up and shook her head at him brusquely.

'He will live. I know this because I have seen it. But he will not be able to ride in the morning, nor walk any distance.'

'I see.'

The decurion looked long and hard at the stricken tribune, then pursed his lips and walked away towards his men who were standing at the island's edge keeping watch to the south, staring back down the track's faintly visible line of reflected starlight. Squatting, he engaged them in conversation with his voice pitched too low for the words to carry.

'I don't trust that man. He sold us out to the Bructeri when it served his purposes to use us as decoys, and he'll sell us out again to complete this mission, with or without the tribune.'

Cotta's urgent whisper broke Marcus's contemplation of his superior, and he looked over to where the cavalry officer was speaking animatedly to his troopers.

'Do you think so? He delivered the warning that saw us run north, rather than surrendering the woman to Clodius Albinus.'

The veteran shook his head dismissively.

'And how good a decision does that look, now that we have the pleasure of considering it once more? Rather than being safely tucked up in a fortress on the right side of the river, with the tribune getting the medical attention he needs, here we are in the middle of a watery desert with a mad woman intent on making him drink herb juice at every opportunity. And with the apprentice of whichever bastard who wanted us to come this way, rather than just getting onto a boat, getting ready to ditch us. I don't think he was ordered to bring us out here to avoid our falling foul of the governor, *I* think he was told to get us away from the detachment and leave us to die in this swamp with some convenient story about how we died protecting the German woman.'

He fell silent as Dolfus turned away from his men, who resumed their contemplation of the twilight landscape while he made his way back to where Scaurus lay.

'We'll stay here tonight, but in the morning my men and I will be leaving with the witch. You can keep the eagle, for all the good it'll do you when the Bructeri catch up with you.' He looked at Marcus for a moment in silence. 'Given your somewhat dubious past it's probably for the best if you and your men stay here with your tribune. A quick and invisible death that will bring your family's history to its inevitable end would be the best for all concerned, I'd have thought.'

He turned away, leaving Marcus and Cotta staring after him, the veteran shaking his head at the confirmation of his suspicions.

'See? How could he know anything about you unless whoever he's working for has been briefed by Cleander? You and Rutilius Scaurus are just loose ends waiting to be tied up as far as that bastard is concerned, so why not order his man on the spot to quietly do away with you? We've been had.'

I I

'There. Do you see it now?'

Dubnus stared at the night-time landscape in the direction that Tiro was pointing until he managed to pick out the tiny mote of light that the spy was showing him, slightly lower than the invisible line of the horizon but clear enough in the gloom that had descended as the night had progressed, and a bank of cloud had slowly but surely obscured the stars and moon.

'It's a campfire, you think?'

'I'd say so. That will be Dolfus and your people, waiting out the night before travelling the last few miles to the meeting point.'

Varus frowned, his puzzlement invisible in the darkness of the hillside where Tiro had led the two centurions to look for signs of the detachment, away from their own fire's light.

'But if that fire is our people, then what are those?'

He was pointing to a spot well to the left of the original point of light, and Tiro stiffened as he realised that he'd missed something important.

'I can barely see them. They look like . . . torches?'

The tiny pinpricks of light were barely visible, the distance making them equally as hard to discern as the assumed campfire. Dubnus strained his eyes to make them out, trying to reckon the separation between the two points in the distant, dark landscape.

'They look like they're miles away from the fire. Could they be . . . ?'

'Some sort of pursuit?' A note of doubt had entered Tiro's voice. 'It's possible. If your tribune and his men were spotted making their escape from the battle then it's obvious that King

Amalric and his closest warriors would have given chase. And if it is a pursuit then there's no way we can warn them.'

'That may not be true.' Tiro turned to look at Dubnus in the near darkness, squinting at the object he was holding up. 'I put this into my pack because I wanted to hear it sound in battle one last time, if I knew that my time to die was at hand.'

The spy stared at the horn for a long moment.

'The problem, Centurion, is that the moment you blow that thing every Angrivarii for ten miles is going to know that we're out here.'

'And the problem, spy, is that if I *don't* blow it then there'll be no warning for the tribune and my comrades while whoever it is that's carrying those torches creeps up on them. They'll use the light to get within a mile or so, then put them out and cover the rest of the ground in darkness. And if they know what they're doing they'll wait until just before dawn, and attack without warning. It'll be nothing better than murder. Do you want your man Dolfus to die and the woman to be recaptured by her people when they're within sight of safety?'

'There it is again. Can you hear it this time? Come away from the fire, you'll not hear it over that crackling.'

Marcus listened for the sound that Cotta was describing, the distant, almost inaudible note of what sounded like a horn being blown.

'No. Can you describe it?'

'It's nothing Roman, that's clear. A metal horn would be higher in pitch. If I had to guess I'd say it was a bull's horn. And whoever's blowing it is a long way from here.'

The distant sound came to them again, and this time Marcus heard it, his face lighting up as he realised the source of the long, drawn-out notes.

'Dolfus!'

The decurion walked across the small camp at his beckoning, a questioning look on his half-lit face.

'You've mentioned having a superior giving you orders more

than once. Is that who we're meeting, once we get off this track?'

Dolfus nodded.

'Yes, not far from here where the land starts to rise, and form the Teutoberg forest.'

'And do you think we're close enough to hear a horn blown from that place?'

The decurion pondered for a moment.

'Possibly. If the man doing the blowing had strong enough lungs, and the wind was in the right direction.'

Marcus nodded decisively.

'Then your superior has my brother in arms Dubnus with him.'

The decurion thought for a moment.

'It's possible.'

Cotta shook his head, tapping his ear.

'It's more than possible, Decurion, I'd guarantee it. That horn you can hear blowing . . .' He fell silent for a moment, raising a finger as the clear but faint note of the horn sounded again. 'That's Dubnus alright, he's been blowing the blasted thing every night for the last three months, pretty much. And that call . . .' The sound came again, several long mournful notes so faint as to be almost ethereal. 'That's the legion signal to retreat. Wherever he is, he's trying to send us a message.'

Dolfus stared at the two friends in disbelief.

'You really think that your fellow centurion's out there blowing a *horn* to warn you about something? How would he know we're out here? And how could he see any danger in this darkness?'

Cotta waved a hand at the fire.

'This meeting place, it's on higher ground then this, right?'

'Ye-es . . .'

'Well then it's obvious. Dubnus, and whoever it is that he's with, can see our fire. And if they can see *our* fire . . .'

'That's close enough with the torches.'

Gernot dipped his blazing brand into the water that overlaid the track, extinguishing it in an instant, and a moment later the other torch-carrying warriors followed his example, plunging the Bructeri into near total darkness. The tribesmen waited in silence, knowing that only time could restore the night vision they had lost the moment they lit their brands.

'Good enough.' The noble gestured for his warriors to gather round, and when he spoke his voice was a harsh whisper intended not to carry in the still night air. 'This is our last chance to retake the eagle, and to rescue Gerhild from the Romans before they cross into Angrivarii territory and she's lost to us for good. Which means that we have two choices, my brothers. Either we turn back now, and return to our homes bearing the mark of shame for the rest of our lives, or we do whatever is needed to retrieve our lost honour.'

Holding up a hand to silence their protests at the idea of turning tail, he continued.

'We have left good men behind us, men with injuries, men with wounds and, may Wodanaz guide their spirits to the gates of the underworld, men who have died for the tribe's honour. I cannot consider the idea of betraying their sacrifice, and nor, I believe, can any of you.'

Their denials were instant, a rumbling chorus of assertion that they were all ready to fight and die for the tribe, for the eagle, for Gerhild, for their king. Gernot knew he had them now, had stoked the flame of their dismay at the Romans' theft of their dignity from a flame of anger to an incensed blaze, and knew that not one of them would step back from whatever was necessary to make this last throw of the dice work in their favour.

'Very well, my brothers. From here we walk in silence, one man behind another, and with as little noise as possible given that we still have to use this track until we are almost on top of our enemies. At the right moment we will turn off the track and circle round our enemy's camp, until we are in position to attack them from a direction they will never expect. Move silently, my brothers, silently and slowly, giving the Romans no clue that we are upon them until the time comes to strike.'

He waited a moment, allowing them to consider what would come next.

'But when you hear me call out the order to attack, make all the noise you can and move as fast as you can, for those few precious moments of surprise will be all the advantage we will have over men who stand on dry ground, and who may well expect us to make one last effort to overcome them.'

They were utterly silent now, considering the long, quiet approach march and the moments of gore-soaked mayhem that were to follow.

'Some of us are going to die today. It is inevitable that some of us will be greeted by Wodanaz when we leave this coming fight, and that he will lead us to dine with our fathers and their forebears. Some of us may find ourselves with a death wound, knowing that they cannot possibly live. If that happens to you, then you must sell whatever is left of your life at a cost that will punish these usurpers. Hurt them, my brothers, even in the moment of your death. Put the last of your strength into the point of your spear, and the point of your spear through a Roman throat. If your spear is broken, or lost, pull out your hunting knife and throw yourself at the Roman who has killed you, and make him pay a high price for your life. And if you have no iron left to fight with, trip a man and leave him open to the next man's spear, before you go to meet the god.'

He looked around the circle of men gathered around him and nodded slowly.

'I know that we will be brave beyond any comparison, my fellow warriors. I know that we will make our ancestors proud, and create a story that our sons will be proud to hear told. And I know that we will succeed. My King?'

Amalric stepped into the circle, turning a slow circle to look at every man present.

'I can add little to my uncle's words, other than to tell you that I have never been as proud as I am now, proud to share this moment with you all, and proud to have the opportunity to go into battle with men such as yourselves. Before he charged at the Roman archer, and fell after being hit by no less than four arrows, our brother Waldhar said something to me that still echoes in my mind. He told me that he was willing to give his life for the good of the tribe. And so am I. For the good of the tribe, my brothers. I will return with the eagle or not at all, and the ravens will have my flesh if I fail in this. I will have revenge, and right the wrongs done to our proud people, or I will have death!'

Gernot nodded his head, making a fist of his right hand and pushing it forward into the circle of men who, after an instant's pause, pushed their own clenched fists to join it.

'Revenge or death, brothers. Revenge or death.'

'And you, Centurion? How is your health? With all this concern for your tribune's survival, you seem to have been quite forgotten.'

Marcus rose from his place beside Scaurus, who was lying on his own blanket with those belonging to both centurions' covering him, bowing to the seer.

'I am well, thank you, Madam. My concern is entirely for my friend.'

Gerhild looked down at Scaurus with a critical eye.

'He will live, despite the fact that he will be as weak as a new born for the next day or two. No, you are the man for whom I have the most concern. Sit.'

The Roman sank back down onto his haunches, spreading his hands as Gerhild took her seat next to him, close enough for him to smell the sweat on her body.

'As you can see, I have neither wound nor injury. My health could not be any more robust.'

She smiled sadly at him, her eyes holding his with an almost hypnotic power.

'And yet there are wounds that you carry more savage than anyone could ever guess from an external examination of the flesh that houses your spirit, are there not? Injuries dealt to you by a hand of fate that seems destined to strike you down every time you attempt to climb back onto your feet? Good days and bad days, except that the bad days seem to come all too often, and the good days ration themselves with increasing strictness?'

He sat in silence, a tear glistening in one eye for a moment before running swiftly down his cheek as a tiny part of the defences he had built against the horrors he had seen and done cracked under the priestess's gentle but insistent questioning.

'You have suffered enough grief for one life, Centurion, and taken so many lives as a consequence of that suffering that the men involved have blurred into one in your memory. For a time it was enough for you to excel at the job of butchering your enemies, both those who had already destroyed your family and those who would have done the same to the members of your new familia had you allowed them to do so, but now even the exercise of your martial prowess is no longer enough to banish the melancholia that haunts you. Your spirit is close to death, choked by an uncontrollable growth of hatred which leaves you feeling little better than powerless on your ever rarer good days and crushed flat the rest of the time.'

'I—'

'There is no need to explain this to me. I feel your pain, it bleeds like an open wound and it prevents you from thinking or acting in the ways that were usual for you until the latest and worst blow you have suffered. And yet there is a moment fast approaching when you must be able to defend yourself, and those you care for the most, a moment that will find you wanting unless I can heal you.' Her gaze seemed to intensify as she raised her arm towards him. 'Take my hand.'

She sat stock-still, holding out her fingers to him, and Marcus suddenly knew compulsion of a sort he had never experienced before, a certain knowledge that if he reached out and touched the woman's fingers all might yet be put right. He felt his own hand rising from his side without conscious effort, watching as the trembling, scarred and calloused fingers rose towards hers.

'Madam . . .'

'Give me your hand, Marcus, and I will take your pain for

you. I will empty your mind of the hurt, and the betrayal, and the loss.'

His fingers were barely six inches from hers, and still slowly rising to meet them despite his bafflement.

'What . . . ?'

She smiled at him, her eyes boring into his.

'Trust me, Marcus Aquila. I have only one gift to give you before I am taken by Wodanaz, but you have to allow me to present it to you.'

Her hand closed on his, her touch warm and dry, and without warning a sensation like a sudden jolt stung his eyes wide, unable to pull away from her as the priestess closed her eyes and muttered an incantation in her own language. After a moment she released him, swaying as if tired for a moment before opening her eyes with a wan smile.

'So much pain. I could not take it all, for fear of losing myself to it, but I have done enough to allow you to find yourself again. You will need more than this to make you whole again, but time and the absence of conflict will allow you to deal with the remainder of what troubles you without my assistance. Now sleep, and when I call on you, wake with your palms itching for the feel of the hilts of those swords.'

She waved the hand at him, weaving a pattern in the air with her fingers and then standing up, touching him lightly on the head and pushing gently against his last physical resistance. His eyes closing, the Roman slumped to the ground next to Scaurus, already asleep.

'The fire. I see its glow.'

Amalric squatted down, hissing the command to halt and staring hard into the darkness in the direction that his uncle was pointing.

'I see it. Just a faint glow.'

'They have masked its light with their shields, my King.'

The Bructeri king stared at the place where their quarry had taken shelter for the night, calculating in his mind, then turned to the huntsman behind him.

'The fire is what . . . two hundred paces distant?'

'A little more, my King.'

'And you know a path by which we can approach this island in the marsh from the west?'

The hunter nodded.

'If the waters have not shifted, and covered the ground I have trodden before, then yes I do, my King. And with their fire so well masked there will be no light spilled upon us as we follow that path across the front of any watchers they have set to guard the approach from the south. *If* your men can walk in silence . . .'

Gernot grinned mirthlessly.

'The king has promised them all a great deal of gold from the king's treasury, if we win this fight, to make them bold, but I have told them that if we are to win then there is a time for boldness and a time for us to move slowly and quietly, with the patient skill of a cat hunting that mouse. Until the time comes to strike, that is.'

'At least we know they're coming. Without Dubnus's warning most of us would have been sleeping round the fire when the Bructeri struck.'

Dolfus grunted noncommitally, looking out into the darkness from their position next to the wooden road. Cotta had suggested that they should place men to watch the track and provide some early warning of an impending attack, and having volunteered himself for the first watch had been surprised to find the decurion accompanying him. He shifted position, grimacing at the water that once more filled his boots after the island's temporary respite, scratching at an itch on one of his buttocks as he pondered how best to ask the question that was at the front of his mind.

'So tell me, Decurion, how do you rate our chances?'

Dolfus gave him a long sideways look.

'What do *you* think, Centurion? There are precisely six of us who look like they know what they're doing in a knife fight like the one this will turn into. You and I, my two men, the tribune's

German slave, and perhaps that massive Briton . . .' He shook his head unhappily. 'The Hamian would be all very well in the daylight, positively murderous, but in the dark? Your friend Corvus, or whatever his name is, is a broken reed. Useless. The boy? He might have killed a man by mistake yesterday, but look what it did to him. He's no warrior. And Scaurus is nine-tenths dead. If he's not gone by the morning I can't see him making it to nightfall tomorrow. So, there are only six of us to fight off how many? Fifteen? Twenty? The numbers we're facing depend how many of them the Hamian was able to bring down before they put a spear through him, but I very much doubt it was enough to level the odds. I'd say we're dead men, *if* whoever was blowing that horn was right in thinking that they're coming after us in the dark.'

The veteran surreptitiously put a hand on the hilt of his dagger, ready for the reaction to his next question.

'That wasn't actually what I was asking.'

Dolfus's head swivelled back to face him, his body seeming to tense.

'And what *was* it that you were asking, Cotta?'

'You tell me. You seem very sure of yourself in most other respects, let's see if you can work out what's on my mind. Go, take a wild *stab*.'

The younger man stared at him for a moment before speaking.

'I see. Well there's probably no point in my denying it, is there, since your mind's clearly made up.'

He turned back to stare out into the darkness, and Cotta looked at him for a moment before speaking again.

'You're not going to deny it because you can't. Whoever this mysterious man is that you report to, he answers to Cleander. And Cleander wants us dead. We know too much about his rise to power, for one thing, and then there's the risk that one of these days that young man is going to come out of the stupor that he's been knocked into by the death of his wife, and go after the emperor. He'll become an assassin without fear of capture, or death, motivated by the rape of his wife and supremely gifted with weapons. And trust me, he's sudden death with any weapon, I made sure of that years ago. So you've been ordered to bring us out here, and make sure that we vanish without trace, eh? Come on Dolfus, we're all going to die anyway, the way you tell it, so why not unburden yourself and take a load off your spirit?'

The decurion shook his head slowly.

'Whether you believe it or not, Centurion, I'm not the killer here. You're not exactly without experience in that area of expertise though, are you, so perhaps you're judging me by your own standards.' Cotta nodded slowly, his mouth tightening as he remembered the moment that he killed and beheaded a man who had usurped the imperial throne ten years before. 'You smile, and when you do that you look just like my master. The same hardness around your eyes, the same stare, looking at nothing. You're probably fondling your knife even now, wondering whether to stick me with it?'

Cotta's gaze shifted, finding the younger man staring intently at him with both hands raised.

'Go on then. If you're so sure, air your iron and put it deep in my neck.'

The veteran shook his head.

'It doesn't work that way, youngster. I never killed a man that didn't deserve to die, and that includes Avidius Cassius.' He fell silent for a moment, staring at the cavalry officer thoughtfully. 'So if it isn't you that's going to kill us, it must be the man you serve.'

Dolfus laughed softly.

'Or perhaps you're just paranoid, Centurion. Perhaps Tiro is no more of a killer than I am, and you're just building a case based on your own expectations. I—'

He fell silent staring intently down the track's barely visible ribbon of darkness.

'Did you hear that?'

Cotta shook his head.

'No, but then your ears are sharper than mine. What was it?'

The decurion shook his head.

'Probably nothing. An animal of some nature, perhaps, whatever lives in this desert of water. It was out in the marsh over there . . .' He pointed to the right. 'Where only a fool would try to walk. They'll come up the road, that's obvious, form a line here and then charge us through what little standing water there is between here and the island.'

He stood.

'I'm going to go and make sure that the others are ready to fight. If you see or hear anything that looks like the Bructeri—'

'You'll be the first to hear about it, trust me. I plan to shout loudly enough for everyone for five miles to hear me.'

Sitting alone by the fire, with only the recumbent bodies of Scaurus and Marcus for company, Gerhild sat with her eyes closed and her lips moving silently in prayer. Dolfus stood over her for a moment, but if the seer noticed his presence in her half-trance she gave no sign of it, and the decurion's stare passed over her to the place where Marcus lay as still as a corpse, barely even seeming to breathe.

'As I expected – useless.'

He moved on, finding the closest of his men and squatting down on his haunches to wait for the coming attack with his sword drawn.

Gerhild's eyes opened, and she drew in a lungful of air as if surfacing from beneath deep water, looking around herself at the deserted fire and the two sleeping men.

'It is time then.' Looking over her shoulder she spoke a single word, the note of command in her voice almost palpable in the cold night air. '*Wake!*'

Reaching out, she took a handful of what firewood remained and placed it above the heart of the small fire's flames, staring down into the blaze with a rapt expression, her lips moving again. The wood caught light with a sudden crackle, each of the slim sections of tree branch igniting in swift succession and burning with a flare of light that threw shadows out across the marsh to the west. Another handful of wood flared up with equal speed, casting an orange light across the marshy landscape and revealing the scene that the seer had seen so many times in her dreams.

'What are you doing, woman!' Dolfus was suddenly standing over her with his sword drawn, his face contorted by anger. 'The light will—'

'The light will illuminate your enemies! They come from where you least expect it!'

As he stared at her, aghast, she took a handful of wool from the thick soldier's cloak she had been given to replace her own, painstakingly pulled to pieces during the night, and threw it onto the growing blaze with a swift incantation. The oil-soaked wool took light with a spectacular flare, sending a tongue of flame high into the air between them, and Gerhild pointed to the west with sudden vehemence that rocked the Roman back on his heels despite himself.

'Your enemy is *there*!'

'Just a few dozen paces more.'

Amalric nodded at Gernot's whispered comment, looking across the twenty paces of marsh that separated his men from the Roman camp. Their enemy's fire was now in clear view, no longer hidden from them by the shields that had been arrayed to prevent its light being spied from the track. Having followed the huntsman's lead away from the road to the west they had progressed in a wide arc around higher ground on which the Romans had taken shelter as predicted.

'There!'

The king stared as a figure crossed in front of the fire, a distinctive silhouette in Roman armour.

'There, my brothers. There are the men who stole our eag—'

He fell silent as the fire suddenly seemed to strengthen, and then grow brighter still as if new life had been breathed into its embers. A crackling noise was suddenly audible over the wind's soft moan, and then, with a sudden incandescence that made the warriors blink with the ferocity of its assault on their eyes, the fire grew from a blaze to a tongue of flame fully as high as a man, its brilliance illuminating the Bructeri and casting their long shadows over the abruptly lit landscape.

Gerhild threw another handful of wool onto the fire, and in the renewed blaze of light Dolfus saw what it was she was pointing at, a line of men splashing towards the island through knee-deep water, their swords and spears shining in the fire's orange light. Discovered, they roared their battle cries and came on at speed, wading through the muddy water in a fast-closing line of gleaming iron and snarling anger. The decurion raised his voice to call his men, shouting over the Bructeri's growing tumult.

'To me! The fight is here!'

Turning back to face the enemy he heard shouts and running feet behind him as the defenders realised their predicament and hurried to join him. Arminius ranged alongside him, his shield snatched from beside the fire and his spear held in a low guard, the boy Lupus beside him with a look so fierce that the Roman was almost moved to laugh, his two troopers along-side them and the giant Lugos at the line's far end, the huge Briton hefting a heavy wooden club. Then the Bructeri were upon them, straggling out of the water one and two at a time as the differences in their size and strength, and the deepness of the water told on each man's ability to get into the fight. Rather than charge into battle individually they paused to form a line ten paces from the waiting defenders, gathering their strength to attack as one, and Dolfus's heart sank as he realised that they outnumbered his men two to one. Gernot stepped out of the water into their midst, pointing his sword at the men silhouetted by the fire's light on the slope above him and bellowing a challenge.

'There they are, my brothers, there they are! They have *our* eagle! They have *our* priestess, *our* sister! Kill them all!'

They advanced slowly up the slope in a wall of spear points, weighed down by their sodden clothing but resolute, each man singling out one of the defenders, and in that moment Dolfus knew that fight was as good as lost, that for every spear thrust his men could make, two or three would come back at them, making any resistance they could offer doomed to fail.

'*Die hard, you fuckers! Make them pay!*'

He started at Cotta's furious bellow, as the veteran bulled his way into the line alongside him with his spear held ready to fight.

'You're a brave man, Centurion. I'd have been tempted to be away up the ro—'

Something whipped past the Roman and struck a man in the Bructeri line, a spear thrown from his right, and while the dying warrior was still tottering on his feet with the spear's blade protruding from his back, a figure bounded forward from out of the fire's incandescent glow, throwing himself down the slope at the enemy line with a scream of pure animal rage that raised the hairs on Dolfus's neck. Diving beneath the shocked tribesmen's raised spears he came to his feet against their shields in a whirl of polished iron, elbowing the warrior directly behind him in the throat and then backhanding the gladius held in his right hand down into another's thigh while hacking at the spear shafts to his left with the longer, pattern bladed sword to prevent them being turned on him.

'Throw your spears and get into them!'

One of the tribesmen had dropped his framea and drawn his dagger, and as he drew it back to strike at the Bructeri's assailant, Cotta hurled his own spear, spitting the man through his guts and dropping him kicking to the ground.

'*Throw!*'

The sight of the enemy warrior dying on his spear's shaft, and the whiplash of Cotta's shouted order galvanised them, more spears lancing into the enemy line to either side of the bloody-handed fighter, who had turned away a spear thrust with his gladius and countered with his long sword, severed fingers flying as the blade met flesh and bone.

'*Into them!*'

The defenders went down the slope at the run with their swords drawn, punching with their shields, stabbing with the points and using their momentum to push the Bructeri back into the water, leaving men bleeding where they had fallen. As the tribesmen struggled to fight back a man staggered from their line with an arrow in his chest, another dropping in the water at their feet a moment later with a bloody shaft protruding from his face, and as they wavered under the fresh attack a massive figure stepped into the marsh's water, Lugos swinging his club in a wide arc to land a blow against his victim's hastily raised shield that smashed the wooden board in two and flung him into the marsh water clutching at his wrecked ribcage.

Dolfus watched as the war band's remnant backed away from them into the darkness that was encroaching once more as the fire's momentary burst of flame died away, crouching behind their shields as another arrow took a tribesman's leg away from beneath him. Dolfus then turned to address the man who had unexpectedly turned the fight, only to freeze as a long, pattern-bladed sword pricked the skin of his throat.

'Aquila . . .'

'Hold this moment in your memory, Decurion. I have your life in my sword hand, and one swift movement would be all it would take to deprive you of it. Remember this the next time you think to decry any man whose experiences have left him less than the man he was.' He stepped back and sheathed the weapon, nodding to Cotta. 'It will be dawn shortly. I suggest we leave this place as soon as we have some light, and make our way to the decurion's meeting point before the locals come to investigate?'

'It's not very far now, a mile or so.' Tiro nudged his horse to the left, skirting a copse that loomed out of the dawn mist. 'I have to warn you that the meeting point I've agreed with my man Dolfus can be a little grisly at times.'

'Grisly, Tiro?'

'Yes. It was the site of a huge running battle between the men of three legions and five tribes. The legionaries came over a forested mountain over there . . .' He pointed to their right. 'With the tribesmen on them like wild dogs, snapping at them from all directions without any let up. They'd already lost one major battle on the other side of the range and were in full retreat, running for Aliso without very much of a semblance of discipline, although it was to get much worse as they got further south and the Germans just kept on coming at them all the way through the marsh. It was raining, pouring down if the accounts from the men that got away are to be believed, the ground was soft even this high above the marsh, the army had already been cut into two halves and men were starting to panic. They marched and fought or they died, it was that simple, and most of those who fought and marched still died. At one time there were bones and pieces of broken armour all over this area, where legionaries who chose to run, or fell out of their units with exhaustion, or just got lost in the bad weather were brought to bay and slaughtered, but most of what was scattered this far from the main route of retreat was collected and buried further down the hill.'

He grimaced wryly.

'Although once the avenging legions under Tiberius and Germanicus had finished slapping the tribes around for their temerity, and the new emperor had decided to make the Rhenus the permanent frontier, their remains were promptly dug up and scattered again, or used to decorate every sacred grove from here to the Albis. But that's not all that was scattered across these hills. There's a reason why the locals call this place the field of bones and gold.'

The mist had cleared a little, and the hillside before them was clear for several hundred paces. Tiro shifted in his saddle, looking about him with the air of a man disappointed at the absence of something or other.

'Bones and gold?'

He nodded at Varus, returning his attention to the story.

'Indeed. You see there's an instinctive reaction on the part of most soldiers to impending battle, especially when the fight looks like something of a lost cause, as it obviously was by the time the remnants of three legions were fighting their way down these hills in the teeth of constant tribal attacks. And that instinct is to hide one's most precious possessions, either to prevent the enemy from getting their hands on them or for later recovery, in the event that the individual in question manages to escape death. Sometimes men bury their gold, especially when they have too much of it to easily conceal, sometimes a more direct means of concealment is called for.'

'They swallow the coins.'

Tiro smiled at Dubnus.

'There speaks a veteran. Yes, a soldier in imminent danger does strange things, and sometimes one man's example can spread through a tent party, or a century, or even a cohort, like fire in dry grass. And on this hillside in the pouring rain and howling wind, with numb fingers slipping on sword hilts and shields so wet they weighed twice as much as usual, the soldiers simply swallowed their gold.' He dipped a hand into his purse and held up a gold coin. 'See, it's small enough to slip down easily enough. And in the course of what followed they were killed, for the most part, and left to rot where they lay, once they'd been stripped of their equipment and weapons. Of course their bodies were dragged about a good deal by the carrion birds and wolves, which meant that any gold in their guts was spread over a wider area than if they'd simply rotted away to bones where they lay. And so to this day there are still coins to be found, and the occasional bone for that matter, if a man has the nerve to brave the hillside, given it's supposed to be haunted by the spirits of the men who were killed here. Every now and then someone goes treasure hunting and doesn't come back, which is, of course, much more likely to be the result of earthly jealousy or simple robbery, but the more exciting explanation is usually the one that sticks in the minds of the impressionable. Speaking of whom . . .'

He rose up in his saddle looking around in search of something that wasn't readily apparent.

'Ah . . . Tiro? Those men of the Angrivarii tribe you're waiting for . . . ?'

The spy relaxed his thighs and sat back down on the horse's back, looking over at Varus with a raised eyebrow.

'Centurion?'

'I have a confession to make.'

'I see. Well I'm sure you'll be happier with whatever it is that's on your mind out in the open.'

'Indeed. Well, it's to do with the fact that you can't see the men you were expecting to meet here.'

Tiro raised an eyebrow.

'Is it? Should I be expecting to feel both a sense of respect for your abilities in the field of clandestine intelligence and just a little disappointment at being outwitted?'

'I'm afraid so, Tiro.'

The older man shook his head in disgust.

'It happens every now and then, usually just as I've convinced myself that nothing can go wrong. Go on then.'

'Are you sure you're alright with his weight, Lugos?'

The giant Briton looked down at Marcus with a sober nod.

'Can carry he all day if need.'

Scaurus had remained unconscious throughout their hurried preparation to move from the campsite, and the big man had ended the short debate as to what was to be done with him by scooping his recumbent form up into his arms and striding away to the waterlogged track while Marcus and Dolfus had stared after him. Walking their horses, now that the risk of being over-hauled by enough Bructeri to overwhelm them was no longer a threat, the party had made the three-mile march through a dawn rendered uniformly grey by the mist that hung heavily over the waterlogged land, with Munir walking at their rear alongside Arminius and Lupus, his bow strung and ready to shoot. After an hour's walk Gunda indicated that they should leave the path and strike off up a shallow, grassy slope studded with trees and bushes. A dark line of trees dominated the northern horizon, rising away into the mist, and at the edge of the forest three men on horses waited. When they spotted the detachment they trotted their mounts down the field until Marcus recognised two of the riders, standing with his hands on his hips and a broad grin as they dismounted to stand either side of a man whose face was familiar without his immediately being able to put a name to it.

'Your posture in the saddle looks almost natural, Dubnus. Perhaps practice really does make perfect?'

The Briton walked forward and wrapped his arms around his friend, looking him up and down.

'And you look like a man I used to know. What happened?'

Marcus tilted his head to indicate Gerhild.

'The priestess happened, it seems. One moment we were talking, and the next I awoke as if from a long sleep to find myself in the middle of a fight. And I am . . . myself, again, or perhaps just most of the man I used to be.'

The Briton stared at Gerhild for a moment, but her return stare was unabashed.

'A healer must heal, or what purpose does she serve?'

Marcus looked at Tiro again, his eyes narrowing in recognition.

'I remember you now . . . but ⸺ . .'

'But I'm the governor's secretary?' He shrugged. 'That is one of the roles I fulfil within the administration of Germania Inferior, but hardly the most important.'

Varus cut across the spy, his impatience evident.

'He spies on the governor for Cleander. And if your old friend Clodius Albinus has been somewhat amateur in his attempts to deal with the tribune, this man's efforts have been nothing other than entirely professional. We were supposed to be met here by a hundred warriors of the Angrivarii tribe who Tiro intended would take every man here other than himself and Dolfus into the forest and butcher them. Even these two.'

He waved a hand at the cavalry troopers, who shot their decurion venomous looks.

'And what about the priestess?'

The young Roman looked at Tiro with a questioning expression.

'Do you want to tell them, or shall I?'

The spy sighed.

'The witch was to stay here, with the Angrivarii, as a bargaining tool for them to use in keeping the new king of the Bructeri in his place. That was the price I offered them for their co-operation in killing all of you. But I'm still trying to work out how you know all this?'

Varus turned towards him.

'For a man who's so very well connected I have to say you seemed to have missed something rather obvious, Tiro. Even the governor knew that my uncle Julius had played a significant part in cementing relations with a number of tribes on this side of the Rhenus, including, should you still harbour any confusion on the matter, the Angrivarii. Apparently by the time he'd hunted and hawked with them, and fought their champion with naked blades to prove his manhood, the tribe's king was so taken with him that he named my uncle Julius as his brother.' He sniffed. 'I believe they went so far as to clasp bloody palms, or some equally barbaric ritual of unending friendship. Anyway, given that neither Dubnus nor I is foolish enough to take a man like you at face value, I was careful to speak privately with the Marsi king, when I got the chance. Apparently dear old Julius left his mark there too, and Sigimund was only too happy to discuss the state of the world with his friend's nephew once everyone else was abed. He showed me the message you'd written to the king of the Angrivarii, and upon the application of a suitable amount of gold he was more than happy to allow me to substitute a message of my own. A message from a close relative of the Angrivarii king's favourite blood brother, which effectively makes me some sort of adopted nephew, and therefore with my honesty and probity beyond question. A few months from now he'll be a hundred thousand denarii better off, small change to a family of our status, and everyone will be happy with their lot. The Angrivarii have been watching us, of course, Dubnus picked them out from the start, but they'll allow us free passage back to the Marsi, and the Marsi will of course honour their promise to you, delighted that Rome has seen better of the idea of transporting Gerhild across their territory while, of course, holding us to your side of the bargain. As I said, everyone will be happy except for *you*.'

Tiro shook his head in amazement.

'And you think you'll get away with flouting the authority of the imperial chamberlain? Cleander will have you hunted down, shipped back to Rome and torn apart by dogs in the arena. You, Varus, have condemned your entire family to liquidation, the men killed out of hand and the women made to suffer. Perhaps your sisters will be tied to posts in the Flavian Arena and left to the sexual depravities of intoxicated baboons, as I hear is the fate of many Christian women, now that a more relaxed regime has been restored to the people's entertainments by our rather enthusiastic young emperor.'

Marcus walked forward, nodding to Varus before turning to the spy, his eyes slitted with anger.

'You've chosen the wrong man to threaten with familicide. We only face that risk if there are any witnesses to—'

He turned to Dubnus, who had tapped his arm, then followed his pointing hand to see a small group of men walking up the slope from the marsh, a mud-stained scrap of white cloth held by the leader. The party stood and watched as they crossed the field, Marcus nodding slowly as he realised that the man holding the flag of truce was Qadir, and that he was followed closely by a man wielding a Hamian bow, an arrow nocked and drawn with its head pointed squarely at the prisoner's back. Turning, he shot Munir a swift glance, and the watch officer hurried back to a point with a clear view of the field, putting a shaft to his bow and then waiting, ready to draw and shoot.

'That's close enough!'

Qadir stopped, and the motley group of half a dozen men behind him followed suit. The warrior with the bow stepped alongside the Hamian, holding the bow across his fur-clad body and raising the arrowhead to his prisoner's neck.

'Which one of you commands this usurpation of my tribe's sovereignty?'

Marcus looked at Dolfus, who shrugged and gestured to the Bructeri.

'Be my guest.'

The Roman walked forward, stopping ten paces from his brother officer.

'Well met, Qadir. I'll confess I didn't expect to see you again alive.'

The Hamian smiled fleetingly.

'Or in one piece?'

'That too. But here you are . . .'

The bowman pushed on the arrow, drawing a trickle of blood from his captive's flesh.

'Here he is. Alive, for these few moments at least.'

Marcus shrugged.

'One of his archers is watching you from just over there, with an arrow strung and ready to loose. You could run a hundred paces and still be within his reach. Kill this man and you cut your own throat.'

The Bructeri smiled without humour.

'I am already a dead man. I am Amalric, king of the Bructeri, and when I return to Thusila without our tribe's captured eagle, without my seer, with most of the warriors of my household spent in their futile pursuit and with my uncle dead, there will be no future for me. My short reign will be over, and I will be killed by the tribal nobles, as will my wife and son. There is no mercy possible when failure is as complete as mine. Which is an irony, Roman, since my intention ever since my coronation has been to establish a less contentious relationship with our neighbour across the Rhenus, and given that, the most likely successor will be a man who will appeal to the hatred of your people that still runs deep in my people's blood.'

Marcus stared at him for a moment before speaking.

'How can you claim to seek peace? I have seen the results of your priest's sacrifices of Roman legionaries, taken from the western bank of the river and spirited back to your sacred grove to be maimed and physically ruined, kept alive for their sport.'

Amalric shrugged.

'What is your saying? Rome was not built in a day? These things, and more, were a regular feature of my father's reign, and

his father's before him, but they will *not* survive to be a part of
my son's. You have helped me in this by putting my chief priest
to death in the most appalling manner possible, a way that showed
he lacked the protection of the gods, and when I return I will
find a replacement who is a little less thirsty for the blood of
your people. But I will need your help if I am to succeed in this.
Will you bargain for this man's life with me?'

Dubnus walked forward with his axe hanging at his side, his
voice grating as he stared at the king.

'And what do you want in return for our brother?'

Amalric shrugged.

'The eagle, for a start. We won that sacred prize in battle, and
it is a symbol of the pride we still feel when we sing of that great
victory. I cannot return without it. And my seer, of course, she
must also be returned to her people. Nothing less will satisfy the
Bructeri's need to see their king return victorious over our oldest
enemy.'

Marcus shook his head slowly.

'All that? For the return of just one captive, however valuable
he might be to us?'

The king eased the tension off the arrow still strung to his
captured bow and pushed its iron head into the turf, then put
the weapon over his shoulder.

'I can also give you this.'

Putting out a hand he took a cloak-wrapped bundle from one
of the young warriors behind him, holding it out to allow an
object to fall out. Cotta started at the contorted features on the
severed head that came to rest staring sightlessly up into the grey
morning sky.

'Gernot.'

Amalric nodded.

'Ah, the trader. Yes, this is Gernot. My uncle, and with my
father dead the strongest believer in our state of perpetual war
with Rome, a belief they shared from boyhood. I always planned
to kill him at some point, but the opportunity was too strong
to ignore after our defeat in the swamp. I instructed the closest

members of my household to hang back, and allow Gernot's men to do the fighting and dying, which left him vulnerable to my sword when we retreated in defeat. This negotiation would have been impossible were he to have witnessed it, and I suspect he would have been the man to supplant me on the throne were I to have returned to Thusila empty-handed. He had to die.'

Marcus frowned.

'What of the men behind you?'

'Mine from their helmets to their boots. They are boyhood friends who grew to manhood with me, wenched with me, fought with me, laughed with me and drank with me. They will tell tales of my audacity in taking back that which was stolen from the tribe, and my people will love me all the more.'

Marcus shrugged and turned back to Dolfus.

'What would you do?'

The decurion opened his mouth to speak, but Tiro beat him to it.

'Spit on his bargain! The empire doesn't want peace with these people, it wants a state of perpetual war between them, alliances shifting at Rome's behest as it befriends first one tribe and then another. Keep the eagle, and the witch, go home and be heroes while this would-be *peacemaker* goes back to face his doom. I'm sure we can find some way to smooth over the awkwardness between us if—'

Dolfus cut him off with a wave of his hand.

'You asked for my opinion, Centurion?' Marcus nodded, and the decurion turned to Amalric. 'Then your bargain is accepted. On one condition.'

Amalric stared at him for a moment.

'Which is?'

The Roman pointed at Tiro, a look of disgust on his face.

'You will take this . . . *man* . . . with you as a captive. I don't care what you do with him as long as you ensure that he never escapes from his captivity. Use him as an advisor if you like, he's clever enough, although I'd counsel you to treat his words with caution. Or make a footstool of his bones and dried skin if you like, it matters little to me.'

Tiro took a step forward, his voice raised in outrage.

'You cannot do this! I am a valued agent of the imperium, a man—'

He crumpled to the grass like a puppet with its strings cut as Dubnus tapped him briskly behind the ear with the butt of his axe. Dolfus looked down at his sprawled body for a moment, then turned back to the king.

'But if he ever does escape I'll make sure of one thing . . .'

He stepped closer to the German, close enough to reach out and touch the king, his words spoken vehemently but softly enough not to be heard by the men behind him.

'I'll make very sure that your tribe find out that you're the man who stole the eagle from your own treasury and gave it to me, on *his* orders. I'm giving you your freedom from his intrigues, and those of the men who will inevitably follow him, if you'll let me do so. When I return to Claudius's Colony I will find your file, in his doubtless comprehensive records of who informs on who within the tribes, and who has been an agent of Rome, however unwillingly, however pragmatic their association with the empire, and I will destroy it. Take him away. And if I were you I'd bury him as deep as you can when you tire of his incessant smug prating and hand him to your priests to make reparation for the things he's done to your tribe and others over the years. He signed his own death warrant when he instructed the Angrivarii to kill my men.'

Amalric nodded, gesturing to his men to pick up the spy, then to Qadir with an open hand.

'You are free. But as the chief priest of my tribe I suggest that you reconsider your godless ways before they get you killed. There, I have fulfilled my part of the bargain, have I not?'

Marcus nodded, taking the iron-bound box from the trooper who was carrying it and holding it out it to the king.

'This eagle was never formally lost, so its return could only have been an embarrassment to be covered up. Swear to me that it will never again be used to torture any Roman.'

Amalric nodded.

'I swear to honour its capture in different ways.' He held out his hand to Gerhild. 'Come, sister. Your people await you.'

The seer frowned.

'But I dreamed that I was to die here, on the field of bones and gold.'

'Not everything you dream comes true. Or perhaps this is a prediction for another day? Until the day that Hertha claims your spirit you can make good use of the extra time you've been given by helping my people worship the earth goddess alongside their devotion to Wodanaz.' The king looked at Gunda. 'And you, brother, you have spent the last fifteen years roaming the frontier on both sides of the river. You will have seen and done things that we can only imagine. Will you return to my land, and share the wisdom you have gathered with me?'

The guide shook his head with a smile.

'No, my King. An order of banishment cannot be removed from a man's head once sentence is passed, and your priests would be duty bound to execute me for the sin of disobeying that order, would they not?'

Amalric smiled more broadly.

'Leave that problem to me. I am, after all, the king. I write the rules of our religion. And besides, when it becomes clear to our people that you, an outcast, still loved your people enough to become Wodanaz's chosen means of defeating our enemy by luring them out here, onto our ground, they will clamour for you to be forgiven. When they realise that the recapture of our eagle, whose theft was abetted by my uncle Gernot of all people, and the rescue of your sister from the clutches of Roman spies were both mostly your doing, I suspect that any resistance to your reinstatement as a member of the tribe will melt away. You have my word on it.'

Gunda nodded solemnly.

'Then I can only accept, my King.' He turned to Marcus and bowed. 'Give my thanks to your tribune when he wakes, Centurion. Tell him that I renounce my claim on the three aureii he promised me. I have earned something of much greater value in return.'

'You're telling me that the witch was actually the king's sister?'

Dolfus drank from his water skin before answering Scaurus's question, looking into the fire that lit the clearing in which they had made camp for the night before re-entering Marsi territory. The tribune had regained consciousness that afternoon after almost a full day of sleep so deep that his comrades had for a time feared the worst, but his recovery since waking had been swift. While the wound still troubled him it was now devoid of any sign of infection, and his demeanour was more or less back to its usual acerbic view of the world.

'Yes, Tribune. Tiro told me that Amalric's father was wont to use his prerogatives as the king to bed any female that took his eye, and long before his marriage produced any children he fathered Gerhild and Gunda as twins by one of his wife's serving women. It was all kept very quiet, of course, to avoid the risk of a bastard child contesting the throne, and neither of them had any idea of who their father was until much later, when Gerhild worked it out on her own. When the queen finally managed to turn out a male heir she insisted that Gunda be outcast when the opportunity arose, despite the extenuating circumstances, to finally remove any risk to her son's succession. And while Amalric's father agreed in order to keep the peace with his wife, he deemed the girl too valuable to the tribe to share her brother's fate, and instead had her incarcerated in the tower close to Thusila so that he could consult her on both his own failing health and her prophecies for the future.'

He drank again, grimacing at the memory of his service to the spy master.

'It was Tiro who put the idea of kidnapping her onto Cleander's desk. From what he told me it seems that he feared Amalric would seek peace with Rome, and in turn destabilise the tribes around the Bructeri. The Marsi, Chamavi, Angrivarii, and several others would all have had their noses put out of joint, whereas a hostile Bructeri would ensure the status quo in the region, and all at no more cost than the occasional soldier abducted and tortured to death. And of course he had leverage over the king, who had made his inclination towards peace clear to one or two Romans to whom he would have been better off saying nothing, including, ironically enough, your centurion's uncle.'

Scaurus shifted his position with delicate care for his wound, looking over at Varus with a questioning expression.

'And you, Centurion, actually had the balls to intercept Tiro's message to the Angrivarii and replace it with your own?'

The younger man shrugged.

'I suppose it's a question of that old adage, Tribune, it isn't what you know, but who you know. I've sat and drunk wine with my uncle Julius often enough to have heard all of his stories about the various tribal kings he met while he was ensuring that they would all keep their swords sheathed when Rome's attention was elsewhere. He might have been the quintessential man of action, but by the gods he could talk with a cup or two of good Falernian inside him. I felt as if I knew them all personally, so approaching the king of the Marsi wasn't quite as off-putting as it might otherwise have been. And knowing his strong motivation towards a certain yellow metal, it wasn't too hard to recruit King Sigimund to our way of thinking, once he had an even more significant purse than the one Tiro had given him in his hands.'

Scaurus lay back, looking up at the tree branches above his head.

'I suppose we can be grateful that Tiro wasn't sufficiently paranoid to make sure that neither you nor Dubnus were carrying any gold with which to effect such a change of heart.'

Dubnus laughed sourly from the other side of the fire.

'Has nobody told you? The devious bastard told us that he would need every aureus he could lay hands on, and demanded access to your private effects in order to ransack what was left of the gold that stuck to our fingers during our exposure of the praetorian prefect.'

Scaurus nodded.

'It was always my expectation that Cleander knew well enough we'd kept something back, even if Clodius Albinus wasn't shouting to that effect from the rooftops. I'd imagine he told Tiro to use us as a source of funds, not least to make sure such a useful asset was removed from my control. That's a pity, but unavoidable, I guess. So how did you manage to persuade the king of the Marsi to help you out?'

He looked expectantly at Varus, a familiar frown spreading across his face as the centurion's expression twitched with barely suppressed humour.

'With gold, Tribune.'

'But if Tiro had *our* gold . . . ?'

'Tiro had *some* of our gold. It was obvious to me from the moment he pulled me off the street and made it clear who he really was that he was likely to be serving only one interest, and that we couldn't trust him not to leave us face down in a ditch if the situation called for it. So I took the liberty of removing most of the gold from your chest.'

Scaurus frowned at him in disbelief.

'How? It was locked. You told me that Tiro was forced to break it open.'

Varus smiled indulgently.

'Your officers, Tribune, have long been less convinced of your immortality than you yourself seem to be. We copied the key to your chest months ago, with the assistance of a certain German, which made it the work of a moment for me to remove most of the coin and hide it about my person, and that of my colleague Dubnus, before Tiro made his move.'

The tribune looked from Varus to Dubnus, and then back again.

'About your persons? Does that mean . . . ?'

Dubnus nodded sourly.

'Yes. It does. And if you don't mind, Tribune, I'd rather not discuss it any further. I may never be the same again.'

Mastering his sudden urge to laugh out loud with a visible show of will, Scaurus nodded gracefully.

'Very well, we'll pass over the means by which you managed to preserve what was left of our gold . . .' A thought occurred to him. 'Is there any of it left, by the way, and if there is . . . where is it?'

Varus patted his purse.

'Enough to get us back across the Rhenus, and to take what's left of our men wherever we decide is the safest. But as to where that might be . . .'

Silence fell across the circle of men, broken at length by the tribune.

'And there's the rub. The decurion can probably get away with just returning to his unit, and telling anyone who comes asking that Tiro went across the border into Bructeri territory and didn't come back. Which is true, as it happens, even if it does omit a few details. But ourselves?'

Marcus poked at the fire with a stick he was holding before he spoke, his face illuminated by the blaze's orange light.

'It's hard to deny that Tiro's instructions to have the Angrivarii kill us all must have come from Cleander. Which means that any return to Rome would be risky in the extreme. It might be wise for us to find somewhere quiet and vanish for a while, the remnants of our detachment too, to avoid their being tortured for information if they're spotted returning to the cohort. In due course Cleander will probably fall victim to his own inflated sense of self-worth, and manage to get himself executed, at which point we can possibly risk coming out of hiding. Possibly.'

'But . . . ?'

The young centurion looked up at Scaurus, his expression sombre.

'But we'd be leaving Julius and two cohorts of good men at the mercy of Cleander's decision as to whether our disappearance is genuine or just contrived, since he won't get any reassurance on the subject from Tiro. Or anything at all, other than a bald statement from whoever he's set to watch his spymaster that Tiro crossed the river with us and nobody came back. And it won't take long for our association with our colleague's cousin and his fleet to make him start thinking, will it?'

Scaurus nodded.

'And if he suspects we've survived, he'll probably stop at nothing to find out where we are. That would put Julius and Annia at severe risk of falling under suspicion, and being tortured for our whereabouts. Not to mention your son. And of course there are two cohorts of men to consider. If he sees fit to do so, a man in Cleander's position could condemn them all to never seeing their homes and families again with the swift flourish of a pen.'

An uncomfortable silence fell upon them, each man reflecting on an unpalatable choice.

'Rome it is then.'

Scaurus nodded at Marcus's flat statement.

'Unavoidably so. I'm sure we can come up with some explanation or other for our deviation from the original plan to escape by means of the fleet, and justify surrendering the witch without making ourselves look like traitors.' He stared at the young centurion for a moment. 'And at least one good thing came of all this. It looks to me as if whatever it was that she did to you last night has burned away both your need for revenge and your sense of self-loathing at having taken it.'

Marcus stared into the fire as he answered, his expression unreadable.

'Possibly it has, Tribune. I no longer feel anything for the men I've killed, no remorse, no connection to them at all. It's as if all that death took place somewhere else, and I was simply an observer. But as to whether it has quenched the heat of my urge to revenge on the men who killed my wife?'

He poked at the logs again, staring into the flames as if seeing something there that held his attention for a long moment before he spoke again.

'Perhaps . . .'

Historical Note

When looking at the situation on the Roman empire's northern frontier in the late second century AD I find it difficult to get past comparisons with the British Empire in India in the second half of the 19th century. On the western bank of the Rhenus (Rhine) was order and prosperity, an imperial rule that had endured since the reign of Augustus almost two hundred years before, while on the eastern side of the river were a seething mass of unconquered and defiant German tribes, descendants of the men who had inflicted the first emperor's greatest defeat upon his hitherto ceaseless expansion of the empire. Like the British in India, in their relationship with the tribes of what we might loosely call Afghanistan, while Rome had the ability to mount incursions in strength, and to punish individual tribes through both the brutal application of military power and the slightly more subtle application of political persuasion to foster discord and internecine warfare, it lacked the means of lasting conquest.

I've used characters in this story to hypothesise some of the reasons for that failure to succeed in creating a province of Magna Germania – bloody-minded German resistance, the lack of any network of settlements to provide Rome with a 'soft' urban population that would be open to both bribery and coercion to comply with the imperial cult, and the unfavourable terrain that sometimes helped the less regimented German tribal armies, comparatively unsophisticated though they were. Whatever the reason, Rome glowered across the Rhenus at the province that never quite was for hundreds of years after the disaster of AD 9 (referred to in this book and described in much greater fictional detail by Ben

Kane's excellent *Eagles* series). Protected by a sizeable riverine fleet and by legions and auxiliary cohorts that studded the west bank in constant readiness to repel invasion or mount a local police action, the northern frontier was well secured against an enemy whose impetus to cross the river was hardly strong, given the absence of pressure from further east that was to be cause of so many problems in the late empire.

On the face of it, then, the German frontier in AD 186 was stable and even tranquil. And yet if the threat level in the immediate vicinity of fortress towns like Vetera (modern day Xanten), Novaesium (Neuss), Colonia Claudia Ara Agrippinensium (Cologne) and Bonna (Bonn) was low enough for substantial numbers of troops to have been posted to Britannia to help cope with an ongoing tribal rebellion in that troubled province, there were plenty of reasons for the governor of Germania Inferior (Lower Germany) to be nervous.

For a start there was the salutary lesson which Rome had learned from her subject peoples in the Rhine valley only a century before. The revolt of the Batavians, a German tribe who had become Rome's most favoured mercenaries to the degree that they provided the imperial bodyguard, shocked Rome's ruling class to the core. With a justified grievance that had swiftly ignited the tinder of a dozen tribes along the river's course, and which came at the time of a bloody civil war that had the empire's attention elsewhere, this dirty war resulted in a series of bloody defeats and legion mutinies that would have been required reading in an imperial Roman staff college had such a thing existed. Scattering the previously home-based tribal auxiliary forces across the empire had removed the threat of their rising in defence of their own people and interests – for a while, until they interbred and went native – but no Roman general could henceforth ignore the risk of a general German revolt on both sides of the river, with the ever-present spectre of both barbarian and (highly effective) Romanised troops on the other side of the battlefield.

And to the east (not all that far to the east either) a vicious fourteen-year war with (variously) the Chatti, Chauci, Langobardi,

Lacringi, Astingi, Iazyges, Victuali, Costoboci and, above all the Marcomanni and the Quadi, took advantage of an empire ravaged by plague brought back from the eastern campaigns against Parthia, putting hostile forces on Italian soil for the first time since 101 BC and winning several major victories over Roman armies. In the wake of this near disaster, a portent of invasions to come that would result in the empire's eventual dismemberment, 16 of the 33 legions were henceforth stationed on the Rhenus and the Danubius. So while the historical context of Germania Inferior in AD 186 might have been one of peace, Rome's watch on the tribes over the river would have been sharp-eyed and calculating.

And what of my other conceit in this book, the idea of there having been shadowy imperial appointees tasked with fostering discord and even war between the tribes? The British empire used political officers to influence those countries it couldn't or didn't want to subjugate, and I find it hard to imagine that Rome wouldn't have taken a similar approach to its neighbours. At least one tribal war – that which 'resettled' a devastated Bructeri tribe from their former homeland at the hands of the Chamavi and the Angrivarii in the last decade of the 1st century AD – was started with the direct connivance of Rome (as you'll see in the story), orchestrated by a Roman governor who was rewarded with a statue in the senate to record his achievement in getting some further measure of revenge on the tribe whose influence was a significant cause of the Batavian Revolt.

And the book I'd recommend you to read in connection with this story? You could do a lot worse than *The Roman Empire At Bay AD 180-394*, by David S. Potter, from which you'll gain a clear understanding of the increasing desperation with which Rome hung onto its frontiers from the time of this story onwards.

The Roman Army
in AD 182

By the late second century, the point at which the *Empire* series begins, the Imperial Roman Army had long since evolved into a stable organisation with a stable *modus operandi*. Thirty or so **legions** (there's still some debate about the Ninth Legion's fate), each with an official strength of 5,500 legionaries, formed the army's 165,000-man heavy infantry backbone, while 360 or so **auxiliary cohorts** (each of them the rough equivalent of a 600-man infantry battalion) provided another 217,000 soldiers for the empire's defence.

Positioned mainly in the empire's border provinces, these forces performed two main tasks. Whilst ostensibly providing a strong means of defence against external attack, their role was just as much about maintaining Roman rule in the most challenging of the empire's subject territories. It was no coincidence that the troublesome provinces of Britannia and Dacia were deemed to require 60 and 44 auxiliary cohorts respectively, almost a quarter of the total available. It should be noted, however, that whilst their overall strategic task was the same, the terms under which the two halves of the army served were quite different.

The legions, the primary Roman military unit for conducting warfare at the operational or theatre level, had been in existence since early in the republic, hundreds of years before. They were composed mainly of close-order heavy infantry, well-drilled and highly motivated, recruited on a professional basis and, critically to an understanding of their place in Roman society, manned by soldiers who were Roman citizens. The jobless poor were thus provided with a route to a valuable trade, since service with the legions was as much about construction – fortresses, roads and

The Chain of Command
LEGION

LEGATUS — LEGION CAVALRY
(120 HORSEMEN)

5 'MILITARY' NARROW STRIPE TRIBUNES ← BROAD STRIPE TRIBUNE

CAMP PREFECT

SENIOR CENTURION

10 COHORTS
(ONE OF 5 CENTURIES OF 160 MEN EACH)
(NINE OF 6 CENTURIES OF 80 MEN EACH)

CENTURION

CHOSEN MAN

WATCH OFFICER   STANDARD BEARER

10 TENT PARTIES OF
8 MEN APIECE

The Chain of Command
Auxiliary
Infantry Cohort

Legatus

Prefect
(or a Tribune for a larger cohort such as
the First Tungrian)

Senior Centurion

6-10 Centuries

Centurion

Chosen Man

Watch Officer   Standard Bearer

10 tent parties of
8 men apiece

even major defensive works such as Hadrian's Wall – as destruction. Vitally for the maintenance of the empire's borders, this attractiveness of service made a large standing field army a possibility, and allowed for both the control and defence of the conquered territories.

By this point in Britannia's history three legions were positioned to control the restive peoples both beyond and behind the province's borders. These were the 2nd, based in South Wales, the 20th, watching North Wales, and the 6th, positioned to the east of the Pennine range and ready to respond to any trouble on the northern frontier. Each of these legions was commanded by a **legatus**, an experienced man of senatorial rank deemed worthy of the responsibility and appointed by the emperor. The command structure beneath the legatus was a delicate balance, combining the requirement for training and advancing Rome's young aristocrats for their future roles with the necessity for the legion to be led into battle by experienced and hardened officers.

Directly beneath the legatus were a half-dozen or so **military tribunes**, one of them a young man of the senatorial class called the **broad stripe tribune** after the broad senatorial stripe on his tunic. This relatively inexperienced man – it would have been his first official position – acted as the legion's second-in-command, despite being a relatively tender age when compared with the men around him. The remainder of the military tribunes were **narrow stripes**, men of the equestrian class who usually already had some command experience under their belts from leading an auxiliary cohort. Intriguingly, since the more experienced narrow-stripe tribunes effectively reported to the broad stripe, such a reversal of the usual military conventions around fitness for command must have made for some interesting man-management situations. The legion's third in command was the camp **prefect**, an older and more experienced soldier, usually a former centurion deemed worthy of one last role in the legion's service before retirement, usually for one year. He would by necessity have been a steady hand, operating as the voice of experience in advising the legion's senior officers as to the realities of warfare and the management of the legion's soldiers.

Reporting into this command structure were ten **cohorts** of soldiers, each one composed of a number of eighty-man **centuries**. Each century was a collection of ten **tent parties** – eight men who literally shared a tent when out in the field. Nine of the cohorts had six centuries, and an establishment strength of 480 men, whilst the prestigious **first cohort**, commanded by the legion's **senior centurion**, was composed of five double-strength centuries and therefore fielded 800 soldiers when fully manned. This organisation provided the legion with its cutting edge: 5,000 or so well-trained heavy infantrymen operating in regiment and company-sized units, and led by battle-hardened officers, the legion's centurions, men whose position was usually achieved by dint of their demonstrated leadership skills.

The rank of **centurion** was pretty much the peak of achievement for an ambitious soldier, commanding an eighty-man century and paid ten times as much as the men each officer commanded. Whilst the majority of centurions were promoted from the ranks, some were appointed from above as a result of patronage, or as a result of having completed their service in the **Praetorian Guard**, which had a shorter period of service than the legions. That these externally imposed centurions would have undergone their very own 'sink or swim' moment in dealing with their new colleagues is an unavoidable conclusion, for the role was one that by necessity led from the front, and as a result suffered disproportionate casualties. This makes it highly likely that any such appointee felt unlikely to make the grade in action would have received very short shrift from his brother officers.

A small but necessarily effective team reported to the centurion. The **optio**, literally 'best' or **chosen man**, was his second-in-command, and stood behind the century in action with a long brass-knobbed stick, literally pushing the soldiers into the fight should the need arise. This seems to have been a remarkably efficient way of managing a large body of men, given the centurion's place alongside rather than behind his soldiers, and the optio would have been a cool head, paid twice the usual soldier's wage and a candidate for promotion to centurion if he performed well. The century's third-in-command was the **tesserarius** or **watch officer**, ostensibly charged with ensuring that sentries were posted and that everyone know the watch word for the day, but also likely to have been responsible for the profusion of tasks such as checking the soldiers' weapons and equipment, ensuring the maintenance of discipline and so on, that have occupied the lives of junior non-commissioned officers throughout history in delivering a combat-effective unit to their officer. The last member of the centurion's team was the century's **signifer**, the **standard bearer**, who both provided a rallying point for the soldiers and helped the centurion by transmitting marching orders to them through movements of his standard. Interestingly, he also functioned as the century's banker, dealing with the soldiers' financial affairs. While a soldier caught in the horror of battle might have thought twice about defending his unit's standard, he might well also have felt a stronger attachment to the man who managed his money for him!

At the shop-floor level were the eight soldiers of the tent party who shared a leather tent and messed together, their tent and cooking gear carried on a mule when the legion was on the march. Each tent party would inevitably have established its own pecking order based upon the time-honoured factors of strength, aggression, intelligence – and the rough humour required to survive in such a harsh world. The men that came to dominate their tent parties would have been the century's unofficial backbone, candidates for promotion to watch officer. They would also have been vital to their tent mates' cohesion under battlefield conditions, when the relatively thin leadership team could not always exert sufficient presence to inspire the individual soldier to stand and fight amid the horrific chaos of combat.

The other element of the legion was a small 120-man detachment of **cavalry**, used for scouting and the carrying of messages between units. The regular army depended on auxiliary **cavalry wings**, drawn from those parts of the empire where horsemanship was a way of life, for their mounted combat arm. Which leads us to consider the other side of the army's two-tier system.

The **auxiliary cohorts**, unlike the legions alongside which they fought, were not Roman citizens, although the completion of a twenty-five-year term of service did grant both the soldier and his children citizenship. The original auxiliary cohorts had often served in their homelands, as a means of controlling the threat of large numbers of freshly conquered barbarian warriors, but this changed after the events of the first century AD. The Batavian revolt in particular – when the 5,000-strong Batavian cohorts rebelled and destroyed two Roman legions after suffering intolerable provocation during a recruiting campaign gone wrong – was the spur for the Flavian policy for these cohorts to be posted away from their home provinces. The last thing any Roman general wanted was to find his legions facing an army equipped and trained to fight in the same way. This is why the reader will find the auxiliary cohorts described in the *Empire* series, true to the historical record, representing a variety of other parts of the empire, including Tungria, which is now part of modern-day Belgium.

Auxiliary infantry was equipped and organised in so close a manner to the legions that the casual observer would have been hard put to spot the differences. Often their armour would be mail, rather than plate, sometimes weapons would have minor differences, but in most respects an auxiliary cohort would be the same proposition to an enemy as a legion cohort. Indeed there are hints from history that the auxiliaries may have presented a greater challenge on the battlefield. At the battle of Mons Graupius in Scotland, Tacitus records that four cohorts of Batavians and two of Tungrians were sent in ahead of the legions and managed to defeat the enemy without requiring any significant assistance. Auxiliary cohorts were also often used on the flanks of the battle line, where reliable and well drilled troops are essential to handle attempts to outflank the army. And while the legions contained soldiers who were as much tradesmen as fighting men, the auxiliary cohorts were primarily focused on their fighting skills. By the end of the second century there were significantly more auxiliary troops serving the empire than were available from the legions, and it is clear that Hadrian's Wall would have been invalid as a concept without the mass of infantry and mixed infantry/cavalry cohorts that were stationed along its length.

As for horsemen, the importance of the empire's 75,000 or so **auxiliary cavalrymen**, capable of much faster deployment and manoeuvre than the infantry, and essential for successful scouting, fast communications and the denial of reconnaissance information to the enemy, cannot be overstated. Rome simply did not produce anything like the strength in mounted troops needed to avoid being at a serious disadvantage against those nations which by their nature were cavalry-rich. As a result, as each such nation was conquered their mounted forces were swiftly incorporated into the army until, by the early first century BC, the decision was made to disband what native Roman cavalry as there was altogether, in favour of the auxiliary cavalry wings.

Named for their usual place on the battlefield, on the flanks or 'wings' of the line of battle, the cavalry cohorts were commanded by men of the equestrian class with prior experience as legion military tribunes, and were organised around the basic 32-man **turma**, or squadron. Each squadron was commanded by a **decurion**, a position analogous with that of the infantry centurion. This officer was assisted by a pair of junior officers: the **duplicarius** or **double-pay**, equivalent to the role of optio, and the **sesquipilarius** or **pay-and-a-half**, equal in stature to the infantry watch officer. As befitted the cavalry's more important military role, each of these ranks was paid about 40 per cent more than the infantry equivalent.

Taken together, the legions and their auxiliary support presented a standing army of over 400,000 men by the time of the events described in the *Empire* series. Whilst this was sufficient to both hold down and defend the empire's 6.5 million square kilometres for a long period of history, the strains of defending a 5,000-kilometre-long frontier, beset on all sides by hostile tribes, were also beginning to manifest themselves. The prompt move to raise three new legions undertaken by the new emperor Septimius Severus in AD 197, in readiness for over a decade spent shoring up the empire's crumbling borders, provides clear evidence that there were never enough legions and cohorts for such a monumental task. This is the backdrop for the Empire series, which will run from AD 192 well into the early third century, following both the empire's and Marcus Valerius Aquila's travails throughout this fascinatingly brutal period of history.

EMPIRE
will continue.

In 2017,
THE CENTURIONS
will do battle.

Set against the fratricidal background of the Revolt of the Batavi in AD 69, the first book in a new trilogy is

BETRAYAL

Britannia, June AD 43

'It comes down to this then. All that hard marching from Germania Superior to the coast, coaxing the men to risk Neptune's wrath despite their terror of the open sea, all the marching and manoeuvring since we landed . . .' The speaker paused, staring down across the mist-shrouded valley, its contours delicately shaded by the faint purple light in the eastern sky behind him. 'It all boils down to this. A river, and an army of vicious savages determined not to let us get across it.'

Gnaeus Hosidius Geta looked down from the hill's summit at the legions waiting in the positions they had taken up along the river before dark the previous evening, almost invisible in the pre-dawn murk, then raised his gaze to stare across the river which snaked across the flood plain at the foot of the slope, and the dark mass of tribesmen on the far side, clustered around the pin-prick points of light that were their smoking camp fires. Although still remarkably young for a legionary legatus at twenty-three, he was already a veteran of a successful military campaign in Africa the previous year, and had lobbied hard to join the long-awaited mission to conquer the island of Britannia despite already having done enough to earn the highest position on the cursus honorum for a man of senatorial rank, that of Consul. The sole arbiter of every meaningful decision that would be made with regard to the conduct and disposition of Legio Fourteenth Gemina's five and a half thousand men and their supporting Batavian auxiliaries, as long as he operated within the plan that had been agreed the previous evening in the General's command tent, he clearly expected his men to see combat before the sun set on the field of battle laid out before them. His companion nodded, not taking his eyes off the vast army gathered on the river's far side, the fighting strength of at least half a dozen British tribes gathered in numbers that threatened a difficult day for both Geta's Fourteenth legion and his own Second Augustan, unless the plan in whose formulation they had both played a leading role worked as intended. When he replied the words were uncharacteristically quiet, betraying his nervousness with the coming day.

'Indeed. It all comes down to this. On the far side of the river there are a hundred and fifty thousand shaggy barbarians, while on this side we have less than a third of their strength. More experienced, better armed, better disciplined and with a plan to make the best of those advantages . . . But what plan ever lived long beyond the moment when the first spear was thrown?'

Geta grinned at him wolfishly in the half light.

'Nervous, Flavius Vespasianus? You, the steadiest of all of us?'

The older man shook his head.

'Just the musings of a man who knows his entire career turns on this day, colleague. All you're thinking about is how soon you can get your blade wet, and how much glory you can earn in a single day's fighting, whereas all I can see before me is a myriad of ways in which I can throw this one last chance to prove myself into that river, and end up with the same feeling I had the day Caligula shoved a handful of horse shit into my toga for not keeping the streets clean. Or just end up dead. And dead might well be preferable, given Rome's attitude to defeat. The prospect wouldn't bother me quite so much if it didn't also imply letting down the close friend who worked so hard to get me this position.'

The younger man laughed softly at his frown, waving a hand at the mass of Britons crowded into the land behind the river's opposite bank.

'Look at them, colleague. Every warrior in this desolate wasteland of a country, gathered from hundreds of miles around to oppose our march on their settlements. Some of those men haven't seen their own lands for months, but still they've held firm in their opposition to our advance. Their priests have told them the stories of how we treated the tribes we defeated in Gaul, how we deal with any people that resist us. They know that if they had chosen to join us of their own free will we would have spared them the horrors that follow any battle where Rome triumphs, the slaughter, the enslavements and the despoilment of their womanhood. They know that their resistance means that everything they hold dear will be torn down when they lose, and yet still they choose to fight. Gods below, Titus, they seethe with the urge to fight us! Indeed they might already have overrun us, if we hadn't advanced with such care to prevent any chance of an ambush. Their chieftains know just how bloody a straight fight would be for their people, were they to turn their warriors lose to rail at our shields while we cut them to ribbons, and so they lurk behind a river they believe we cannot cross in the teeth of their spears, offering us a battle they expect not to have to fight. Look at them. Does that really look like an army readying itself for battle?'

Both men stared across the river at the British camp, a stark contrast to the ordered precision with which the four legions and their auxiliary cohorts facing them waited in their agreed start positions, close to the river. Geta pointed at the dark mass of their enemy, his voice rich with scorn.

'They call us cowards, for not fighting man to man in their style, and yet they hide behind a narrow ditch full of water because they imagine themselves protected from our iron. Today, my friend, is the day that they will learn just how it was that we came to conquer most of the world.' He turned to Vespasianus with a hard smile. 'My father tried to stop me from joining this expedition. He asked me if Africa wasn't enough victory for me, if the capture of the chief of the Mauri hadn't already brought an adequate fresh measure of glory to our name. I just pointed to the death masks of our family's forefathers, staring down at us from the walls and daring me to give any less for my people than they did. Given the chance, I will show this ragged collection of hunters and farmers how a Roman gentleman conducts himself when the stink of blood and death is in the air.'

He nodded at the older man.

'And you, Flavius Vespasianus, I know that you will do the same. You may not come from an old established family, but there is iron in your blood nevertheless. You and your brother both serve the emperor with the same dedication as men with ten times your family's history . . .'

'Thank you, Hosidius Geta. That's high praise from a man of your exalted station.'

The young aristocrat turned to find another officer standing behind them, and he dipped his head in salute at the newcomer's rank.

'Greetings, Flavius Sabinus. Has the Legatus Augusti sent you to make sure your brother and I do our duty once battle is joined?'

Sabinus, a legatus on the general's command staff rather than a legion commander, shook his head in evident amusement.

'Far from it. The general has every confidence in both of your abilities to enact the plan we discussed. Indeed he was keen for me to remain at his side in order to be ready for transmission of the order to exploit your legions' success. I persuaded him that an engagement of the sort of ferocity we're likely to see today often places an intolerable strain on our command structure, and suggested that I should accompany your forces forward to the river bank in case either of you should by some mischance be incapacitated. After all, it only takes one well-aimed arrow to spoil a man's day in an instant.'

The legion commanders shared a swift glance, then Geta's face creased in a slow smile.

'I don't know about your brother, Flavius Sabinus, but I have no intention of being any man's pin cushion! The warrior who comes for my life will need look into my eyes as he makes the attempt!'

Both brothers smiled at the younger man with genuine fondness before Flavius Vespasianus turned back to the battlefield below them.

'My brother Sabinus has come to play the vulture, and swoop down on the feast of our success, should one of us be unlucky enough to fall in the coming battle.'

His older sibling shook his head in mock disgust.

'Your brother Sabinus has, in point of fact, come to see Hosidius Geta's German auxiliaries show us all just why it is that the legatus of the Fourteenth legion is forever singing their praises. So Geta, tell me, what is that you have in mind for your armoured savages that had you argue for them to be placed in the front line today?'

Geta nodded, looking out across the river with the hard eyes of a man who understood only too well the damage that could be done to his command were it wielded by a man without an appreciation of its strengths and weaknesses.

'A timely question. And in answering it, allow me the liberty of asking one of my own. Tell me, Flavius Sabinus, what's the greatest threat the Britons present to us today?'

The senior officer answered without hesitation.

'Their chariots, that's their greatest strength. The Britons might be one hundred and fifty thousand strong, but they're farmers and woodsmen for the most part, some brave, some not, but very few of them as well trained or conditioned as our men. Their greatest fighting capability is concentrated in each king's companion warriors, the bravest and the best men chosen to accompany their chieftain into battle. They number just a few hundred men, but they've been trained to fight from childhood, they're well-armed and superbly motivated by their priests, and they fear dishonour in the eyes of their gods far more than death itself. Combine those men with the two hundred chariots our scouts have reported and the enemy commander has the means to deliver a pair of their best warriors with each one, as fast as a galloping horse, to any point on the battlefield where they can have the optimum impact.'

Geta nodded solemnly.

'Exactly. Several hundred picked men descending on one point of the battlefield as fast as a charging cavalryman, delivered to the place where they can do the most damage almost as soon as that weakness becomes apparent. If a legion falters in crossing the river under the rain of their arrows then those warriors will pounce on us like wild animals as we try to get ashore. Who knows how many men they might kill under such a circumstance, perhaps cut down an aquilifer, or even a legatus? They could blunt or even break an attempt to get across before we could put enough men on the far bank to hold it. But if we destroy those chariots . . .'

He waited in silence while the brothers considered his words.

'But their chariot park is protected by the mass of their army. How can we hope to . . .?'

Vespasianus fell silent at the look on his colleague's face, and after a moment Geta pointed down at the Roman forces marshalling on the river's eastern bank in the dawn murk.

'Your Second Legion will be crossing that river soon enough, Flavius Vespasianus, under whatever missile attack the Britons can muster, pushing across to form a bridgehead for my Fourteenth to exploit. But if we don't do something to prevent it, then just as your leading ranks step out of the water they're very likely to find themselves face to face with a cohort strength attack from the best swordsmen they've ever faced, almost certainly before they've had the time to reform any coherent line. Unless, of course, we can destroy those men's ability to cross the ground quickly enough to be there when your boys reach the far bank. An objective in which we are assisted by the fact that they've tethered the horses a sufficient distance from the main force to prevent any harm coming to them in the night, given the number of hungry tribesmen there must be over there.'

Sabinus's eyes narrowed, and he stared down at the deploying legions and their auxiliary cohorts with fresh insight.

'You've ordered the Batavians to attack before the Second moves forward, haven't you?'

'Once there's just enough light for them to see what they're doing, yes. You are indeed about to find out just what my armoured savages are capable of . . .'

'Centurions! On me!'

With the Batavi cohorts in place as directed, drawn up in their distinctly non-standard formation in the gap between the left flank of the Ninth legion and the right flank of the Second Augusta, Gaius Julius Draco waited as his officers converged on his position behind the first row of three centuries, each one drawn up in their usual unorthodox battle formation of three ranks of eight horsemen and sixteen soldiers, with two infantrymen standing on either side of each beast. In the normal run of things he would now have been standing out in front of his men, looking for any signs of fear or weakness, and dealing with any such manifestation in his usual robust manner, but in the pre-dawn murk he had instead positioned himself in the cover of his eight-cohort-strong command, calling his officers together where they could be safe from the risk of a sharp-eyed tribesman spotting the obvious signs of something out of the ordinary. They gathered close about him, their faces fixed in the tense expressions of men who knew that they would shortly be across the river and spilling the blood of the empire's enemies.

'The Romans would usually be delivering speeches at this point, boasting of their superiority to those barbarians over there . . .' His officers grinned back at him, knowing from long experience what was coming. 'Yes, the same old Draco, eh? You all know what comes next, since it's the same thing I say before every battle. About how we don't waste any time telling each other how superior we are to those barbarians over there, because if you strip off all this iron the Romans give us to fight in, we are those barbarians over there . . .' He paused, playing a hard stare across their ranks. 'Only more dangerous. Much more dangerous. We are the Batavi!'

He allowed a long silence to play out, just as he always did, giving time for his words to sink in and letting the growing legend of their ferocity take muscular possession of each and every one of them as it always did. Knowing that his challenge to them would take the weapon that had been wrought by their Romanisation, their appetite for war made yet more deadly by the addition of the empire's lavish iron armour and weapons, and would rough-sharpen it back to the ragged edge that was what had attracted Rome to the Batavi and their client tribes in the first place.

'So why do I say the same thing once again, eh?'

'Because this will be just like every other battle we've fought for Rome? A bloody-handed slaughter?'

The speaker was a young man known as Gaius Julius Civilis to the Romans, but named Kivil within the tribe, tall, muscular and impatient in both his words and bearing, forever on the verge of fighting, or so it seemed to Draco, who viewed him with the critical eye of a man who knew he might well be looking at his successor as the tribe's military leader. Loved by his men for his pugnacity and constant urge to compete, Kivil was viewed with amused tolerance by the tribe's older officers and with wary deference by the more junior men among his peer group, who knew only too well that their apparent equality within the tribe's military tribute to Rome was a polite fiction. Kivil was a tribal prince, a man whose line would have been kings with the power of demi-gods a century before, but whose members now occupied more finely nuanced positions within the tribe. Under Roman rule the men of the last king's line were respected for their blood, and granted membership of the emperor's extended familia, and while they possessed no more official power than any other man present, now that the tribe's lands were governed by a magistrate appointed by vote, their effective control of that magistrate's appointment made them almost as good as kings. Draco cocked a wry eyebrow at the younger man, echoing the smiles of his other officers.

'I say the same thing once again, Centurion, simply because it is true. It's time for your chance to cut off your hair, if you've killed for the tribe when we've been across that river and back.'

He waited for the good-natured laughs at the younger man's expense to die away, one of Kivil's closer friends nudging the younger man with a grin, reaching out to tug his plaited mane, grown long and dyed red in the tribe's traditional mark of a man yet to spill an enemy's blood for his people.

'So the Romans have, as usual, managed to stir up the nest until every single wasp has come out to fight. See them . . .?' Draco turned to gesture to the mass of tribal warriors camped on the opposite bank, their positions mainly defined by the glowing sparks of their camp fires. 'There are enough men there to meet any attempt to cross this river and throw it back into the water broken and defeated, leaving the river bank thick with the corpses of Rome's legionaries, if the battle goes the way they expect. Except it isn't going to. Because these Britons have no idea who it is they face. They expect no more than that which they have seen from the Romans until now: ordered ranks, tactical caution and a slow, disciplined approach once the sun is high enough to light up the battlefield. They do not, my brothers, expect the Batavi at their throats like a pack of wild dogs in the half-darkness, while most of them are still thinking of their women and stroking their pricks. In time this land will tremble at the mention of our name, but for now we are nothing to them, and they do not fear us. They do not guard against us, because they do not know what we are capable of doing to them, and by the time they know that danger it will be too late.'

He looked around them.

'We attack now, as soon as you've had time to ready your men. Tell them that we will cross the river in silence. No shouting, no calling of insults to the enemy, no singing of the paean. They are not to suspect our presence on their side of the water until we're in among them. Once the first man has an enemy's blood on his face they can make all the noise they like, but until then I'll have the back off any man who disobeys this command. And

remind them that we're going across the river to do just one
thing, but do it so well that the Britons will shiver whenever
they hear the name Batavi. It might be distasteful to men like
us, but since it has to be done we'll do it the way we always do,
quickly and violently. Like warriors. And now, a prayer before
we attack.'

He beckoned to the man waiting behind him, a senior
centurion who was upstanding and erect in his bearing as he
stepped forward to address them, carrying himself with the
confidence of a warrior who understood both his place in the
tribe and his supreme ability to deliver against his responsi-
bilities. In the place of the usual centurion's crest across his
helmet a black wolf's head was tied across the iron bowl's
surface, the skin of its lips pulled back in a perpetual snarl that
exposed the long yellow teeth, the mark of the tribe's priests
who fought alongside the cohort's warriors with equal ferocity
in battle and tended to their spiritual needs in addition to their
military roles.

'As your priest my task is much the same as that of our
brother Draco. Nothing that either of us can tell you now will
make you better warriors, or more efficient in your harvest of
our unsuspecting enemy. Draco's role at this time is to assure
you that you are the finest fighters in the empire, straining at
your ropes to be released on these unsuspecting children . . .'
He waved a hand across the darkened river. 'Whereas mine is
to remind you that Our Lord Hercules is always watching us,
but above all at this time, eager for our zealous sacrifice to his
name. So when you kill, my brothers, do so with his name on
your lips, and if today is your day to die for the tribe's honour,
then die in a blaze of glory shouting his praise as you take as
many of them with you as can be reaped by a single man. If
you are to die, make your death a sacrifice to him, and send
enough of the enemy before you to earn your welcome into
his company.'

Draco nodded.

'Wise words, which are being shared with your centuries by

your priests even now. But remember, nobody here is to go looking for their glorious death. What I need most is live veteran centurions for a difficult summer of fighting, not more lines in the song of the fallen, so any man I see risking his life unnecessarily will have me to deal with after the battle if he survives.'

He waved a dismissive hand, sending them back to their centuries.

'Enough. Go and tell your men that it is time to be Batavi once again.'

'They're on the move.'

Vespasianus stared down into the gloom, barely able to make out the men of the Batavi cohorts as they advanced out of the long line of legion and auxiliary forces that had formed a wall of iron along the length of the Medui's twisting course across the battlefield. Staring across the river he strained his ears for any cries of alarm from the men who must surely be watching the river, but the only sound that he could hear was the bellowing of centurions and their optios along the line as they chivvied their men into battle order.

'How is it that they're not seen?'

Geta smiled, his teeth a bright line in the near darkness.

'Simple. The Britons do not expect an attack, and therefore they do not look for one. The fires which have kept them warm and on which they plan to cook their breakfast serve only to destroy their ability to see in the darkness. And now, colleague, watch the impossible.'

The Germans' first cohort had reached the river's eastern bank, and without any apparent pause had advanced into the water with their apparent determination unhindered by the fact that it was reportedly too deep for a man's feet to touch the bottom at that point, especially with low tide still an hour away. Vespasianus shook his head in amazement.

'They're swimming? In armour? Gods below, I heard the stories but I wasn't sure I could believe them . . .'

'Until now?' Geta grinned at the brothers. 'Believe. But that's only half of what they can do . . . . '

Swimming alongside the leading horse, the mount of the decurion who commanded his first century's squadron of twenty-six horsemen, Draco looked back at the dimly-illuminated scene on the river bank behind them, nodding to himself at the speed with which each succeeding wave of men was quickly and silently entering the water, two fully armed and armoured soldiers alongside each horse, each man using one hand to grip onto its saddle and the other to hold his spear and shield underneath him for the slight buoyancy they afforded, kicking with his legs to swim alongside the beast while the rider used its bridle to keep himself afloat. Both men and horses swam in silence, the only noise the beasts' heavy breathing as they worked to swim with the weight of three armed men to support, filling him with the same fierce pride he felt every time the tribe practiced the manoeuvre, or employed it to cross an unfordable river and turn an enemy's flank with their deadly, unexpected presence. The far bank loomed out of the murk, and the horse beside him lurched as its hoofs touched the bottom, dragging him forward as its feet gripped the river mud. Feeling his boots sinking into the soft surface he pumped his legs furiously to keep pace with the beast, its rider now wading alongside his mount's head as it forged forward, restraining its eagerness to be out of the water.

Releasing his hold on the saddle he waved a hand forward at his decurion and optio.

'Two hundred paces up the slope and hold. Form ranks for the advance and then wait for me.'

Both men nodded, vanishing into the gloom while Draco turned back to the river, waiting as the rest of the first three centuries followed the leading horses, their spacing so close that all of the seventy-odd beasts were past him in barely twenty panting breaths, as his body recovered from the exertions of swimming under the dead weight of so much iron and sodden wool. The cohort's remaining three centuries were hard on their heels, Kivil nodding his respect as he passed Draco at the head of his men with a look of determination that made his face almost comically grim, the cohort's rear rank passing him with the front rank men of the second cohort close up behind them. Their senior centurion waded ashore, water pouring from his soaked clothing, saluting as he panted for breath, and Draco returned the gesture as he turned away, having passed responsibility for the river's bank to the man whose soldiers were now pouring ashore. Hurrying up the slope he found the front rank of his own cohort formed and ready to move, a compact mass of muscle and bone with the soldiers standing alongside the horses, any uncertainty they might once have felt at the beasts' looming physical presence long since trained out of them, just as the animals were equally well-habituated to the presence of armoured men on either flank.

'Any sign of life out there?'

His optio's response was no louder than a whisper.

'It's all quiet. Want some scouts out while we form up?'

'Yes. But quietly.'

He turned back to the river and walked down the slope past the waiting cohorts, heartened to see that his command's incessant stream of men and beasts was almost invisible despite the slowly lightening shade of grey in the sky above them. Hurrying up the slope they packed in close behind the leading cohorts, men squeezing water from their tunics and upending scabbards to empty them of any remaining water as they readied themselves to fight, rubbing their limbs to massage some heat back into them. The closest of them looked at Draco questioningly, eager to be on the move. He shook his head, his words loud enough to reach only a few of his men.

'Not yet. But soon enough.'

A waterlogged figure squelched up to him, and Draco saluted as he recognised the tribune who had been given permission by his legatus to accompany them across the river, in order to provide the army's commanders with an account of the raid.

'Tribune Lupercus.'

The Roman took a handful of his tunic, squeezing out the water and looked about him.

'Well now, First Spear Draco, are we ready to attack? The fact that you've allowed me across the river must mean you've got your entire command between my delicate body and the Britons.'

Draco grinned back at him, having warmed to the young Roman in the days since Legatus Geta had appointed him to accompany the powerful cohorts fielded by the Batavi and their allies. While the Roman was only attached to the tribe as an observer, with no formal command responsibility given that the Batavi provided their own officers, the man's eagerness to fight was as transparent as that of his own men, and there was little that the tribe respected more than a man born with the urge to fight.

'We're ready, Tribune. Just stay close to me and don't do anything stupid. I've no desire to win this battle and then find myself in the shit for letting a young gentleman get himself run through with a spear.'

'Or trip up and fall on his own sword?' The Roman grinned at him in the half-darkness. 'Have a little faith, Draco. My father didn't invest in ten years of tuition in the finer arts of swordsmanship to see me end up face down in the mud of a tawdry little battlefield like this. If I'm going to die for Rome I expect the time and place to be a good deal more auspicious!'

The story continues in Betrayal,
which will be published in 2017.